ENSLAVED

PRINCE OF THE DOOMED CITY:

BOOK 4

FIRE
WYRM
BOOKS

Enslaved

PRINCE OF THE DOOMED CITY:

BOOK 4

This book is dedicated with tremendous affection and gratitude to Anna... since I basically wrote it for her!

1

ICLUTCH MY SATCHEL STRAP TIGHT AS I STEP FROM THE spiral stair onto the top floor of Vespre Library. All is quiet beneath the glittering crystal dome. Overhead the gentle twinkle of twilit stars gleams through a haze of lavender-hued clouds. A peaceful aura suffuses the air.

I don't trust it for a moment.

Most of the drafting tables and desks lining the curved wall are empty. Once upon a time, this library bustled with activity as numerous intrepid librarians went about the ongoing mission of managing the vast collection of grimoires contained within this citadel. Now there is no one in sight save Mixael Silveri, the senior librarian, who sits hunchbacked over a pile of work at his desk, absorbed in what he is doing, oblivious to my presence. Andreas is down in the vaults, re-securing a spell-binding. He will be busy for some hours at least. And as for the Prince . . .

An uneasy shiver steals down my spine. I scan the open floor, which is built around the central well-like opening of the citadel tower. I could almost swear the Prince is close by, hidden in the shadows of one of those desk cubicles. Watching me. I don't have good reason for this suspicion. It's nothing more than a feeling. An instinct if you will.

I shrug, rolling first one shoulder then the other. It's been weeks now since the Prince and I have spoken more than two words to one another. I don't remember the last time we bothered to exchange a polite "good morning" or "good night." Such familiarities are no longer appropriate between antagonists such as we.

Still, I'm never quite able to shake the impression of his watchful gaze. Even at times when I know he is absent from the library, that awareness of *his* awareness is always with me. When I'm walking the stacks in search of broken-down volumes. When I'm bowed over my own desk, writing bindings for smaller grimoires. When I'm oiling old leather covers or stitching fresh spines or practicing the endless list of Noswraith names, muttering them under my breath . . . that odd, tingling sensation will creep over me. I'll turn sharply, convinced this time I'll catch a glimpse of him peering out from behind some shelf or leaning over the rail of the curved staircase.

I've not caught him yet. Not even once.

But the feeling persists nonetheless.

Thus I scan the upper floor with care, forcing my gaze to search the shadows of each and every cubicle by turn. I even crouch to look beneath the main drafting table, though I couldn't say why. It's not as though I expect to spot the Prince seated cross-legged under there, grinning up at me like some child in a game of hide-and-seek.

Straightening, I draw a long breath. I can't stand here dithering all day. The longer I do, the more suspicious I'll appear. So I adjust the strap of my satchel and stride swiftly across the floor, my pace quick and purposeful. The weight of a book bumps against my hipbone.

Something inside it . . . *stirs.*

Hastily, I press a hand against it. The Prince was very clear on my first day in Vespre: no taking books from the library premises. My stomach gives a ticklish twist. This infraction is a terrible breach of protocol, especially considering the nature of the volume I've tucked away inside my satchel. The rules of Vespre Library are in place to keep the Vespre librarians alive and in one piece. One Noswraith broken free of its written chains has the potential to cause untold damage across the realms of Eledria.

But I'm only taking one very small grimoire, containing within its pages one very small Noswraith. And I need it. I have a plan. A good plan, I think. A plan that could change the fate and future of this library, this city. This world.

Thus, though every rule-abiding instinct in me cringes, I slip out the library door, carrying my pilfered book with me. No one calls out, not Mixael, not Andreas. Not the Prince. It's too easy. Which is upsetting in and of itself. The library's defenses are badly reduced. If word were to get out, thieves from across Eledria would descend upon Vespre. All the foolish fae lords and ladies, so eager to take and tame Noswraiths for their own devious purposes. Which of course would spell certain disaster for anyone who attempted it. No one can control a Noswraith, not even those who create them. They can only be bound and rebound and then rebound again, without an end in sight.

Which is exactly why I must do what I'm doing. Because maybe there is something more that may be done. Maybe there's a way to bind the wraiths more effectively. Maybe . . . maybe . . .

But I must test my theory before I bring it either to Mixael or Andreas. Certainly before the Prince finds out.

I shut the heavy door quietly behind me, breathe a little prayer, and count to twenty. When no one comes after me, I turn on heel and hasten down the stair, my footsteps hollow and echoing, my breath too loud in my own ears. The cavernous passages all seem to echo, hollow and crypt-like. This palace used to be more densely peopled, long ago when the trolls ruled their own city. Since the coming of the fae to Vespre, most trolls keep to the lower city and leave the palace to the librarians. Only the household guard and a handful of servants stay on, but they are outcasts from troll society.

I don't meet a soul as I make my way through the passages and come at last to a certain door. There I pause and look first to the right, then the left. There's no one around. Drawing a deep breath, I open the door and step inside.

"Watch out!"

I freeze in place, heart jumping. My half-upraised arm is wrapped in a tangle of fraying thread. More thread winds around my head and presses against my legs, a spiderweb's snarl. I peer through the dense strands, trying to make sense of the room before me. There are some old, abandoned pieces of furniture, a few troll-style decorations, outcroppings of crystal and interesting rock formations. It may have once been a luxurious salon for some troll princess. Now it's just another cavernous, unused space.

Well, not so unused anymore. In fact, it's the perfect place for little Sis to practice stringing up her *gubdagogs*.

On the far side of the room, the troll girl perches on the shoulders of her brother, Calx, who in turn sits on the shoulders of their middle brother, Har. Supporting the three of them is stout Dig, the eldest. He struggles to find his footing under their combined weight, and the two smaller boys sway and tip so wildly, I'm sure the whole tower of ungainly troll youngsters will come toppling down. But Sis stands on her tiptoes at the peak, light as thistledown, and her nimble fingers secure a thread to a crag in the upper wall.

Across the room, Lir holds some sort of counterweight in place. It was she who called out the warning. "Best step back and come along the wall, Mistress," she tells me now. Sis barks a command, and Lir lifts her counterweight a bit higher before shooting me an aggrieved expression. "It's all likely to come undone if you breathe on it wrong!"

I take in Sis's work. To my untrained eye, the whole thing looks like a chaotic cobweb. But when I cross my eyes and unfocus my gaze, I half-fancy I'm starting to comprehend the chaos that is a *gubdagog*. Not enough to understand *how* it works; just enough to grasp a sense of this troll form of story-capturing, so different from our human method of letters and written words. I can't help but admire it.

Taking Lir's advice, I sidle around the edge of the room, keeping close to the wall, ducking to avoid threads and suspended pieces of detritus. Sis babbles in trollish, and all three of her brothers gesture emphatically. Though I don't understand the words, the children and I have learned to communicate well enough over the last few months, and I get the gist.

Setting aside my satchel, I reach out to help Lir with the rope she's holding to keep the counterweight in place. It's much heavier than I expected, and I doubt my paltry efforts are much help to Lir, whose strength far surpasses mine. "How's it coming along?" I ask through gritted teeth.

Lir rolls her pale eyes. "If you ask me, it's a mess! Will you look at this nonsense?" She waves a hand, and the counterweight bobbles, ready to yank me off my feet. Sis barks a protest, and Lir quickly pulls it back into place. "I've never seen a child more determined," she continues with a sigh. "Though whether or not it will actually work . . ."

I look around at the snarl, idly wondering what story Sis is trying to tell. Perhaps I wouldn't understand if it was explained to me. Perhaps one must be a troll to comprehend. But there's power here. I'm sure of it.

Sis secures her thread and signals for Lir to let go. Lir releases her grip. The counterweight shifts up, and something in the center of the tangle falls. I catch my breath, momentarily believing the whole thing will come crashing down on our heads. Instead, there's a sense of settling, as though some sort of balance has at last been achieved.

I angle my head for a better look at the object hanging in the middle of the *gubdagog*. It looks like an old picture frame, approximately ten-by-ten inches square. Stolen from the old portrait gallery in the south wing of the palace, I imagine. The original canvas has been cut out, leaving little scraps still attached to the frame. Whose portrait did the child desecrate in the name of her art?

Too late for such questions now. I take in the rest of the debris Sis has gathered from across the palace with such care. Broken stone and trash, along with personal items stolen from various members of the household. A guardsman's boot hangs from one delicate string close by, twisting gently in the midair.

I shake my head. I'm probably mad for even attempting this, but . . . An image passes across my mind's eye: a humanoid face with a distended, snapping jaw, all tangled up in a vast *gubdagog*. It shouldn't be possible. Yet I'd seen it with my own eyes. I'd felt the potency of the magic at work, magic so unlike any I'd ever before encountered.

I must bring Sis to the low priestess. She must be trained and taught to hone this skill of hers. Umog Grush agreed to meet her, to speak with her, and to decide whether she would take her on as a pupil. Perhaps if I bring a sample of Sis's work, I might be able to sway the old priestess's decision in our favor.

"Well, Sis?" I say as the girl bellycrawls underneath her creation toward me. "Is it done?"

The child pops upright in front of me, grinning broadly. Today she has conceded to wear clothing and is clad in a little slip of a gown over a pair of comically voluminous pantaloons. While not, perhaps, the most fashionable combination, Sis nonetheless contrives to look ethereally beautiful, with her delicate features, large eyes, and moon-white skin and hair. Perhaps my wild child is beginning to gentle.

The thought no sooner crosses my mind than she springs to her feet and barks a stream of harsh trollish at her brothers, all three of whom freeze in place across the room. Their awkward, stone-hided bodies are not built for nimbly slipping under and around *gubdagog* threads like their sister. They blink uncertainly, their gazes flicking from Sis to me.

"Sis, they can't stay there while we test your work," I tell the girl sternly. "It isn't safe." I motion for the boys to do as I did and sidle along the wall. Sis sighs petulantly, then dives through the snarl to fix a thread Har's elbow pulled from place. She pouts and sulks, but eventually her brothers make it to the door, and the *gubdagog* doesn't seem unduly disturbed. Not that I could tell a difference, to be honest. "You two had best leave as well," I say to Lir and Sis.

Lir's eyes widen as I pull the slim volume from my satchel. "Is it a bad one?" she asks, meaning, of course, the monster contained within these pages.

The answer to her question is, of course, *yes*. They're all bad ones. Every last one of these horrors wrought from ink and paper and twisted minds. But I offer an encouraging smile. "Quite small, I assure you. Nothing to worry about."

She doesn't believe me. I can't blame her. Chewing her lip, Lir ushers Sis to the open door where the three boys wait. Then she looks back with a sort of desperate urgency and says, "Mistress, are you sure about this? Really, truly sure?"

I'm not. Purposefully unleashing a Noswraith goes against all the rules of Vespre Library. I don't know what penalty I'll face if my actions are discovered. Neither can I predict what damage this little nightmare might cause should it escape. But I've come this far. And it's not just Sis's future at stake. It's all of us, this whole blasted, doomed city.

"It'll be fine, Lir," I say with another too-bright smile. "Go on now. Take the children."

Sis utters another stream of protests, ending with an emphatic, "*Gubdagog* is *mine!*" In the end Dig gathers her up in his strong arms and carries her kicking and screaming from the room while Har and Calx follow, trying to soothe her in their deep, growling voices. Lir casts me a final, worried look, her pretty brows puckered tight.

Then she shuts the door behind her. Leaving me alone with the *gubdagog*. And the Noswraith.

I look at the book in my hand. To call it a grimoire is an insult to grimoires. It's just a floppy bit of leather with onion-skin pages on the very brink of disintegration. The Noswraith inside would scarcely need to flex its being to shatter the binding spell completely. It must be a very lazy nightmare indeed not to have done so by now. Why anyone would try to contain even a minor wraith in such a flimsy volume, I cannot guess.

I rest the book in my left palm and carefully open the cover. The handwriting scrawled across the first page is hurried and blotchy. Not a hand I recognize; some librarian from before my time wrote this. The story itself is quite short, though I immediately recognize the simmering force of life in the words. While this Noswraith isn't particularly powerful, it was strong enough to manifest, which is saying something.

I turn the pages quickly to the end of the spell where the wraith's name is written in bold, capital letters to secure the binding: BHELUPHNU. A shudder creeps down the back of my neck. Andreas told me something about this one during our drills. It was created by one of the former Vespre librarians. Fonroy, I believe his name was. He'd been a struggling playwright for many years, but never wrote anything of note until at last, in a fit of despair—and most likely influenced by strong substances—he produced this little one-man sketch. It tells the grim tale of a man whose great-grandmother's dying wish is for him to take care of her beloved pet. Only the pet, as it turns out, plays host to a demon. A voracious demon, who proceeds to terrorize the man, ultimately driving him mad.

The sketch was a hit . . . and the power of Fonroy's written words spawned magic in the minds of his audience. Enough magic that Bheluphnu sprang into existence here in Eledria and proceeded to work his small terrors on the inhabitants. The Prince hunted him down at last and caught him in a binding spell. For the crime of inadvertently practicing forbidden magic Fonroy was sentenced to life serving in Vespre Library.

He was killed by an altogether different Noswraith long before I arrived. The eventual fate of all librarians in Doomed City.

Hastily, I shake that thought away. Before I can talk myself out of what I'm about to do, I turn the book to its first page again and deliberately rip it straight down the middle.

The spell breaks.

The chamber darkens.

My gaze darts this way and that, searching among the tangled threads highlighted strangely by the small moonfire wall sconces. All is still and quiet save for my own too-loud breathing. I inhale deeply three times, holding each breath for as long as possible before exhaling—

Prrrrlt.

My heart jumps to my throat. Turning sharply, I duck my head to peer beneath a particularly dense snarl of threads. There. There it is, on the far side of the room. Seated just beneath one of the sconces. Pale moonfire light gleams on its fur. A large, fluffy black cat.

It blinks enormous green eyes at me.

My heart drops back to my chest, thudding painfully against my breastbone. It doesn't matter that Bheluphnu is small and inconsequential. Now that I see it, I'm all too aware that it is still a *Noswraith*. Panic thrills in my veins, but I keep every motion purposeful and slow as I slip the broken grimoire back into my satchel. My fingers find the feathery quill of my pen. I draw it out, slowly, slowly.

The cat continues to stare at me through half-closed eyes. The tip of its tail twitches.

I swallow hard. Then easing into a crouch, I hold out one hand. "Kitty-kitty," I call softly, rubbing my fingers together.

The cat's eyes widen. If looks could kill, I'd drop dead on the spot.

I bite my lip, adjusting my grip on my pen. I want to pull out the empty book I brought with me and scrawl a hasty binding. I want to wrap this creature in layers of enchantment, trap him with my words, but . . . The threads of the *gubdagog* closest to me vibrate softly. There's power here. It's strange and foreign, and I don't understand it. But I've got to give this a chance to work.

Bheluphnu's gaze fixes on my quill. He watches it like a true cat might watch a toy dangled by a child. I chew the inside of my cheek. Then, uncertain what else to try, I stretch out the quill and trail it along the floor: *flip-flip-flip-flip*.

The cat's gaze sharpens. The next moment, he drops into a crouch, haunches wriggling. His pupils dilate until the green irises all but disappear. I have just enough time to regret my decision before he springs.

With a yelp of terror, I drop the quill and start to my feet. My movements are too erratic. I step back into a swath of *gubdagog* threads, which immediately wrap around my arm. For a moment, the magic flares, compromised by my clumsiness. I freeze. The vibrating threads settle back into place, humming softly. Only then do I turn, looking down to where I'd dropped my quill.

Bheluphnu sits just where I'd crouched a moment before. He's got my quill in his mouth. As though he knows exactly what it is: a tool for his binding. He tips his head slightly to one side and begins to purr.

I've forgotten how to breathe. Every instinct tells me to run while I still can. When I take a step back, my arm pulls on the *gubdagog* threads. I cannot risk yanking the whole thing down, so I freeze again. With painstaking care, I twist my arm, trying to pull it free.

The cat drops my quill. Then he stands. Takes a step toward me. I retreat, tugging at my captured arm. The cat's mouth drops open. He utters a long, low yeowl, and his mouth keeps opening and opening, wider and wider and wider, revealing a massive red maw with five rows of razor teeth and a long, purple tongue.

That awful sound reverberates in the threads of the *gubdagog*, which sing and hum in horrible, discordant response.

With a cry, I throw myself to the ground and scoot underneath the lowest threads, feet kicking, frantic to get away. I crawl to the center of the room and that empty frame. The cat's voice rings in my ears, and the threads are alive with sparking magic.

Then suddenly, all is silent. Not a sound, not a hum. Not so much as a purr. Nothing but my own rasping breaths. Twisting in place, I look back the way I came. The cat isn't there. Did he leave? Did he escape the room? Is he even now slipping through the shadows of the palace, stalking unsuspecting members of the household?

The children!

I sit up, catching a face-full of threads. Above me, the frame sways dangerously on its delicate suspension. I pull away, desperate not to bring the whole thing down, twist my torso to the left.

The Noswraith is right beside me.

I stare into Bheluphnu's green eyes. His wicked cat's mouth curves in a smile. Then his jaw drops open once more. That long, purple tongue waggles out at me, and his howling voice rips through my ears.

I scream.

Reach out.

Catch the picture frame.

With a single tug, I bring it swinging down, drawing threads of *gubdagog* with it. The cat lets out a single, confused, *Meeerow?*

Then the frame scoops the Noswraith up.

I hardly know how to explain it. One moment, the wraith is beside me, its hideous mouth open to swallow me whole. The next, the *gubdagog* around me hums a strangely *contented* vibration. Not a sound, not something I can hear. A feeling, pulsing against my skin, my mind. The frame, balanced by counterweights, settles back into position in the center of the tangle, swaying gently. Though I cannot see it, though I cannot perceive it with any human sense, I know it contains Bheluphnu.

With a ragged sigh, I drop onto my elbows, head hanging heavily from my shoulders. I can't do anything but breathe. I might have stayed in this same position for hours were it not for the sound of the chamber door opening. "Not yet, Lir!" I blurt. I don't want either Lir or the children to come stumbling in, not until I'm certain the Noswraith is safely bound.

But it isn't Lir who stands silhouetted in the open doorway. No, for this figure wears a long, sweeping coat with bright silver buttons, and a billowy linen shirt, unbuttoned halfway down a tanned and muscular chest.

"Well, Darling," the Prince says, surveying the mess before him, "yet again I find you in a . . . shall we say a *compromising* position?"

2

I SCRAMBLE TO MY FEET, TANGLING MY SKIRTS AND arms in *gubdagog* threads in the process. Hastily I pull myself free, careful not to bring the frame and its captive crashing to the floor. With a deep, steadying breath and a hasty swipe to smooth hair back from my face, I turn again to meet the Prince's stare.

He looks at me. Long and slow. Then with equal leisure he turns his gaze to survey the mess in the room, his expression one of mild interest. At last his attention fixes on the frame, half-hidden behind me. His eyes narrow. "Dare I ask what in the worlds is going on in here?"

"I can explain." The words burst from my lips in a frightened bleat.

"I should hope so." The Prince blinks, his expression so like the cat's it makes my blood run cold. "Though how you will manage it, I am agog to learn."

I open my mouth, close it again. It takes a few tries before I finally manage, "It's . . . it's a *gubdagog.*"

"I can see that." One eyebrow slides up his perfect brow. "As you might recall, I have ruled this island for the better part of four hundred centuries. In that time, I've seen my fair share of *gubdagogs.*"

"But have you seen what they *are?*"

At this, he frowns. "What they are? Troll art, I suppose you could say. Festival decorations. Probably sacred to their god in some way. Not particularly pleasing, but to each his own."

I shake my head. Nervous excitement churns in my gut. I'd wanted more time, but this is it. This is my chance to prove what I set out to prove. "They're not art, they're . . . they're *stories.*"

The Prince's brow puckers. He doesn't bother to speak but simply turns and looks around the room again. His gaze comes to rest on the guard's shoe wrapped up in threads like a fly snared in spider silk, suspended a foot or so above the floor. It turns slowly in place. "I don't think I'm following you, Darling."

I turn from him and grip the empty frame. It's supported by three large, complicated knots. Other loose threads hang with broken bits of canvas fabric in the empty air between the gold filigree framework. It looks like junk. But when I turn the frame toward me . . . a flashing image crosses my mind of a black cat, snarling, lunging at me with claws and teeth.

I gasp and nearly drop the frame. Instead I shake my head and look again. It's empty save for those dangling threads. But it worked. It served to trap the Noswraith as effectively as any written spell. Possibly better.

"Come see." I turn to the Prince. "And try not to bring it all crashing down, will you?"

He casts me an irritable look, but by virtue of his fae grace manages to duck and weave his way through Sis's handiwork without looking completely awkward in the process. Soon he stands beside me. "Fine then," he mutters, "show me what's the bother."

Then he looks at the frame. His face goes very still. A few moments more and a muscle in his jaw ticks. He sees it. I know he does. Finally, he lets out a breath and whispers, "Impossible!"

I step back—ducking to avoid three large broken stones which clack together gently—making room as the Prince circles the frame, studying it with care. At one point, he pokes the dangling threads in the center, and I could swear Bheluphnu lashes out at him with curved claws. The Prince retracts his hand, but not in a sharp, reflexive action. He's very calm, poised. At last, he tips his head back, surveying the rest of the tangle attached to the walls and ceiling, filling most of the room. His eyes glitter in the moonfire.

I can't help watching him. It's all too easy to let my gaze linger on the finer points of his features—the sharpness of his jaw and cheekbones, the brightness of his eye, the sardonic set of his brow. His full, dangerously tilted lips. Strange . . . I'd not realized until this moment how much I've missed seeing his face. Rather more than I like to admit.

Granted, it's just because he's so beautiful. One would miss seeing the sunset if one hadn't for several days running, wouldn't one? It doesn't have to *mean* anything. The Prince and I are enemies. We can't help it. I killed his mother. He bought my Obligation. I saved his life, indebting him to me. We've both obliged each other to do things the other wouldn't wish to do. What's more, I fully intend to oblige him again. Just as soon as opportunity arises.

Only two more days until . . . until . . .

The Prince turns abruptly, catching my gaze. "Did you let Bheluphnu out on purpose?

I swallow. Then nod.

His face darkens. He takes a step toward me. Suddenly he seems much taller, broader, and more menacing than he had a moment ago. "That was reckless. Has your time in Vespre not yet taught you to treat Noswraiths with more care, respect, and fear than this?"

I steel my spine. "Would you have let me release him if I'd asked?"

"Absolutely not." His violet eyes snap like sparks. "I wouldn't risk letting even a minor wraith like Bheluphnu savage the dreams of Vespre's citizens."

Of course not. Because he is, despite all his brashness and sarcasm and vanity, a careful, conscientious ruler. While I may not like to acknowledge his virtues, even I cannot deny them completely.

But he doesn't know everything. In his care for the library and his concern for the cityfolk of Vespre, he's failed to look at possibilities beyond his immediate scope. As a result, the city survives but only under threat of constant peril. It could be better. We could be better. I'm sure of it.

I lower my lashes, take a moment to compose myself. I've practiced this conversation numerous times in my head. Only I'd always imagined I would have secured the low priestess's support and blessing before I brought my proposal to the Prince. "I . . . I believe the *gubdagogs* might be the key to saving Vespre."

"What? *This?*" He once more inspects the tangled mess surrounding us. He shakes his head. "It's impressive work, I'll grant you. I've never seen anything of Eledrian make that could hold a Noswraith even temporarily. There's magic here. Unique magic, clever even." His gaze swivels to meet mine. "But it won't last. It can't. Here." With that he reaches out, takes hold of my wrist, and pulls my hand close to the dangling threads hanging inside the frame. "Feel that. The enchantment is already beginning to fray."

I swallow hard, determined not to be so very aware of the burn where his skin touches mine. Instead, I concentrate on the humming magic of the *gubdagog,* feel the Noswraith pushing against its bonds. For now the spell of tangled thread restrains it. But the Prince is right. It cannot last.

I shake my hand free of his grasp and take a backward step.

"This is the work of a mere child. Sis's work." My voice is a little tight. I put my hands behind my back, rubbing my still-hot wrist, and clear my throat. "In fact, this is the second time she has successfully managed to catch and hold a Noswraith in one of her *gubdagogs*."

The Prince's brows lift. "Really?" I can't tell if he's interested or incredulous. Possibly both.

I hurry on, describing the squat, fat, hairy Noswraith which had infiltrated my room. How I'd chased it with quill and book. How it had slipped under the children's bedroom door only to become ensnared in Sis's creation. "I transferred it into a grimoire, of course, and Mixael secured the binding. But the knot was strong enough to catch and hold it until I could get it properly bound."

He runs a finger along his upper lip thoughtfully. "It's certainly an intriguing story," he says, turning to eye the frame and its captive once more. "Perhaps you're right. Perhaps there might be some use for trapping small wraiths such as these. But I still can't—"

"I saw a *gubdagog* holding the Striker."

My words ring sharp, hovering there in the Prince's abrupt silence. He stares at me, as though he does not comprehend. Then he tips his head a little to one side. "The Striker has been missing for over a year. All attempts to track it down have utterly failed."

"It's in the temple," I reply. "In the hall of the low priestess. I've seen it."

The Prince listens then as I describe my visit to Umog Grush and the *gubdagogs* I'd glimpsed in the darkness, illuminated by the light of the crystal on the end of her staff. As I speak, his expression darkens until he's positively glowering. "How many times have you ventured to the low temple on your own?" he demands at length.

"Never," I respond truthfully enough. "I brought Khas and Lir."

His lip curls, his gritted teeth flashing. "It's dangerous. Lower Vespre is no place for a human. You should have asked me to accompany you."

"You wouldn't have come. You wouldn't have seen the use."

"That's true enough. I certainly don't see how any benefit you hope to achieve could possibly be worth the risk to your very life."

I refuse to waver under the intensity of his gaze. "That's only because you don't value my children. But I do. They are my responsibility, and I will do all I can for them."

"You have a dangerous habit of assuming responsibilities no one else would put upon you."

"If that's the cost of caring for Dig, Har, Calx, and Sis, so be it."

He draws a long breath through flared nostrils. Then, with a quick backward step, he puts some distance between us and crosses his arms, looking down his nose at me. "So what do you intend to do exactly?"

It's not a lot, but it feels like he's relenting. "I intend to go back to the low priestess," I say, excitement tinging my voice. "I hope she will agree to train Sis and possibly Lir as well, since Lir has been helping Sis and has picked up some knack for it.

In fact, I would like to see a whole host of troll *gubdagog*-ists weaving tangles and hanging them around the palace and the library to catch escaping Noswraiths." His expression is still hard, so I hurry on eagerly. "You know there aren't enough human magicians left in the worlds to deal with the sheer number of Noswraiths here in Vespre. This could give those of us who remain a fighting chance!"

His eyes rove across my face. I'm not sure I like the way he studies me, reads me. "This idea has certainly captured your imagination," he says at last. "I don't remember the last time I saw you so animated."

A blush steals up my neck into my cheeks. But I won't let him have the satisfaction of seeing how he discomfits me. I hold his gaze. "Will you allow me to go to the low priestess? Will you allow me to show her this?" I wave a hand to indicate the frame in which the Noswraith is snared.

The Prince presses his lips into a line, irresistibly drawing my attention to his mouth. He is silent again. Infuriatingly so. Is he trying to make me burst with impatience?

I'm on the verge of speaking again, when he finally turns and sweeps his gaze across the *gubdagog* surrounding us once more. "It's an interesting proposal. I've never seen an alternate form of story-keeping intricate enough to hold a Noswraith. Indeed, I wouldn't have thought it possible. Certainly not from trolls." Then he shakes his head. "Regardless, you must acknowledge these story-threads are not practical for long-term storage. They take up far too much space."

I shrug. "It doesn't do away with the need for librarians. But it could provide a buffer. It could give us a chance."

His chin still lifted, he flashes me a look from beneath his lashes. "When you set your mind on something, there's no power in this or any world that can sway you, is there? For better or for worse, you are a force to be reckoned with."

Despite myself, I can't quite suppress the grin that pulls at my mouth. "And in this instance? Is this for better or for worse?"

"I have yet to decide." His lips tilt.

Then abruptly he sweeps a hand over his head and yanks the frame down from its suspending threads. I gasp as the whole *gubdagog* shudders, convinced the Noswraith will burst free. The Prince tenses as well. He holds up the frame and stares at it, silently daring the captive to try something. Magic twists and churns.

Then, as the *gubdagog* around us settles back into place, so too does the magic within the frame. Somehow—though I cannot begin to understand it—the spell has not been broken. Bheluphnu remains imprisoned.

The Prince turns that gods-blighted smile of his my way. "Shall we, Darling?"

"Shall we what?"

"You've convinced me. I think it's time that you, I, and that feral girl-child of yours paid a visit to the low priestess of Vespre."

3

THE CHILDREN HAVE FOUND A NEST OF *QUOUSN*. These creatures are somewhat like hedgehogs, only with scales rather than spines, and long spindly legs, jointed like an insect's, which they generally keep tucked close to their soft underbellies. They are quite common in Vespre and can be severely destructive due to their tendency to burrow through the soft sedimentary stone from which the city dwellings are carved.

They also apparently make for excellent bowling balls.

Calx lets out an ear-splitting whoop as his *quousn* careens down the passage and knocks into the assorted bric-a-brac they've arranged in lieu of ninepins. A crystal vase, a stone cup, a half-full bottle of spirits, and an ink stand fly every which way. Sis shrieks either in rage or adulation—it's hard to say which— and doesn't wait for her brothers to rearrange the objects before she sends her own little balled-up creature hurtling after the first. The two animals ping off each other and shoot in different directions, rolling underneath stone furniture. If they were wise, they would unfurl and run for freedom. But *quousn* are known more for durability than intelligence.

Sis raises her arms over her head as though she's scored some point. Whirling in a circle, she spies me at the end of the passage. Her smile widens, and she throws herself at me, shouting, *"Mar! Mar! Mar!"*

Instantly, the boys take up her cry. I brace myself for the oncoming assault of affection. The Prince, who stands but a pace or two behind me, utters an incredulous, "Gods spare us, the hordes are descending."

The next moment I'm overwhelmed. Calx's hard little body hits my thigh while Sis springs directly for my neck. Dig and Har crowd in close, arms outstretched, but thankfully don't knock me clean off my feet as they used to. "Settle down now, children!" I cry, struggling to make my voice heard above their din. "The Prince has come to see you. Please, show him your best behavior."

Four small troll heads and four pairs of troll eyes turn upon the Prince. He has only time enough to utter another, "Gods above!" before they swarm him. Calx uses Dig's head as a stepping stool in order to wrap his stone arms affectionately around the Prince's neck, giving a squeeze that makes his eyes bulge. "Children!" I gasp. "We don't throttle princes! That's *not* our best behavior!"

To my surprise, however, the Prince pries Calx's arms free with very little effort and holds the heavy stone boy at arm's length. Even as Sis climbs up his back and Dig and Har dance around his knees, he gives Calx a stern once-over. "I say," he declares, "this is as stout a specimen of trolldom as I've ever seen."

I'm never entirely certain how well my children understand any language but their own. Calx, however, takes the Prince's meaning at once. A huge, diamond-tooth grin breaks across his ugly face. I would swear he blushed if it were possible for a blush to show through that stony hide. The next moment, the Prince plunks him down heavily on his two flat feet, then deftly shrugs Sis from his shoulders. "*Gurat!*" he barks in a harsh trollish accent. "*Orghrumbu, borugabah. Mazogal!*"

I have no idea what he just said, but it works like an enchantment. Immediately all four children form a line from tallest to smallest, arms straight at their sides, heads up, eyes fixed on the Prince. I can only stand there, gaping at this miracle. Perhaps I should have asked his help managing my small brood a long time ago.

The Prince clasps his hands behind his back and looks down his nose at the four of them. He nods solemnly then turns his attention solely upon Sis. He speaks a stream of trollish, of which I only understand the word *gubdagog*. Sis beams at him and responds in her bright, prattling voice. The Prince nods and responds with one word: "*Oglub.*"

Sis positively simpers in response to this, shrugging her shoulders up to her ears and wriggling like a happy puppy. The

SYLVIA MERCEDES

Prince asks her another question, to which she responds with an enthusiastic, "*Korkor!*" a word I recognize as trollish for *yes*.

"What's going on?" I ask.

"Sis and I have just agreed to pay a visit to the low temple," the Prince replies.

"*Korkor!*" Sis lunges to take my hand, swinging my arm painfully back and forth. "*Korkor! Korkor!* I goes to see the *umog!* I goes to show her my *gubdagog!*"

The boys, jealous at this extra attention being paid their sister, protest that they too want to go. I hasten to assure them we will be back soon and even promise the Prince will have dinner with them later—though how I'm going to make good on that promise, I'm not entirely certain. It's been weeks since the Prince and I dined in each other's company, and certainly never with the children present. Dig and Har, however, are satisfied, and Calx is appeased with numerous kisses to the top of his craggy head. At last I peel away, Sis still hanging from my arm, and follow after the Prince.

Not long after, we leave the palace behind and find ourselves on the broad road leading down into Lower Vespre. Captain Khas acts as our escort, leading the way, tall, silent, and dangerous. In the last month, her broken arm has healed thanks to the magic lacing the air of this world. She keeps one hand gripping the hilt of her sword, and her wary gaze darts this way and that, on the lookout for potential threat.

The Prince, by contrast, strides along with an easy,

36

nonchalant gait, his long hair flowing over his shoulders, his open coat flapping behind him. As per usual, his shirt is only partially buttoned, and those few buttons seem on the verge of slipping. He has a habit of looking as though he's rushed from his chambers halfway through dressing, yet somehow always contrives to look polished and put-together. It's a dichotomy for which I have no explanation.

Sis walks between us, prattling on in trollish about I know not what. It's a long walk from the palace to the low temple, but the child is a bundle of energy and enthusiasm. Now and then, the Prince answers her in her own tongue. He grinds the words out in a harsh accent, but whatever he says seems to delight Sis. She peals with laughter in response to each growled remark.

Suddenly, she takes hold of the Prince's hand. I glance over her head in time to see the startled expression spread across his face. His brow puckers. For a moment, I think he's going to shake off her fingers. But he doesn't. He tightens his hold, looks up, catches my eye, and winks.

My whole face floods with heat. Blood pounds in my ears so that I almost don't hear him when he says, "One, two, three . . ." At the last second, I realize what he's doing. Responding to his lead, I adjust my grip, and together we swing Sis right off her feet in front of us. She lets out another bright, bell-like burst of laughter, kicking her little pantalooned legs up high.

The Prince's chuckle tickles my ear. It's so surprising, for a moment I don't recognize it. This isn't the scornful, mirthless laugh I've heard him utter more times than I like to count. It's sincere. Almost playful. The sound shoots straight to my heart and makes my stomach flip.

He goes on to swing Sis three more times, until I declare my arm is about to break off. Sis starts to whine in disappointment, then bursts into more giggles when the Prince scoops her up and settles her on his shoulders. She clasps his forehead and digs her pointy chin into the top of his skull, all while he grips her kicking ankles to hold her in place. She sticks a finger in his eye, and he howls and spins on heel, making her squeal with giddy delight. It's all so . . . I hardly know what to make of it. I never could have imagined the Prince like this, so easy, so playful.

It's difficult to remember he is my enemy.

We progress down into the low city, farther and farther from the twinkling stars in the perpetually twilit sky. The shadows deepen. There are few lamps to illuminate the dark, winding streets, so Khas holds a moonfire lantern out before us. Wherever its light falls, there's an impression of sudden emptiness. As though whatever was there a moment before ducked out of sight just before the light reached it.

Khas pauses at last and looks back at the three of us. Tense lines frame her eyes and mouth. "My Prince, if we keep going, we're going to end up cut off."

The Prince nods. Sis's hands are wrapped around his forehead, making it difficult to discern his expression. He looks calm enough, however, and says only, "If we leave now and come back later, the *Hrorark* will be waiting for us. As it is, perhaps we can get in and out before Anj has time to muster much of a force." He shrugs, shifting Sis in her seat on his shoulders. "We've come this far; may as well see it through."

We proceed more swiftly now. I resist the urge to reach out and slip my hand through the crook of the Prince's elbow. I don't want him to think I'm lacking in courage. Instead I stick as close to his side as I dare and try to keep my gaze focused on Khas. Was this a mistake, venturing to the low temple while the city is rife with unrest? Maybe so. But it's for the city's own sake we take this risk. Surely they can understand that.

I glance up at the Prince, at the firm set of his jaw. "Why do the cityfolk hate you so?" I ask, my voice scarcely more than a whisper. "Are you really so hard a ruler?"

He tips his gaze down to me, that sardonic gleam back in his eye. "Didn't you know? I'm a regular tyrant."

"Tell me the truth."

"Brrrrr, frosty, are we?" He shivers and hunches his shoulders, making Sis yelp in protest. But he continues: "It's not as though their fae overlords have been the kindest of friends over the many turns of the cycle. When I first came to Vespre, I was just one more in a long line of princes sent to master these folk. What's worse, I brought the library with me, for it had grown beyond Lodírhal's ability to safely contain in Aurelis."

I blink at this. "The Noswraiths were originally kept in the Court of Dawn?"

"Why of course." The Prince shoots me another sharp look. "No other Eledrian realm boasts such a library, built by my father to please my human mother. When the Pledge was first established, the Miphates gave up their Noswraith spellbooks to the fae, who then scrambled to find a safe place to store them. Aurelis was the only option at the time. Soon enough outbreaks began to occur. Books wore down, spells snapped, and nightmares stalked the halls of the palace. My mother and a few other human Obligates fought them back, but it was too much for them to handle.

"It was my father who landed on the brilliant idea of stashing the whole lot in Vespre, along with whatever human librarians he could find. When I came of age, he was only too glad to foist the governance of this whole blighted city on me and otherwise forget its existence."

"And your mother?" I scarcely dare ask the question. Any mention of Dasyra is enough to send a painful dart of guilt plunging straight through my heart. If it weren't for me, after all, she would still be alive.

The Prince lets out a small sigh. "She spent much of her time here, assisting with the library. She preferred her plants of course, but she was a powerful mage in her own right. And she cared about the denizens of Vespre even if my father did not."

We lapse into silence once more, hastening down the street in Khas's footsteps. Anger roils in the atmosphere, more potent by the moment. Anger from these trolls, occupied and exploited by those who never cared for them or their culture. What difference does it make to them how the Prince exhausts himself and his resources to keep their city from being overrun by nightmares? It was his own people who sent the nightmares to begin with.

A terrible weight of hopelessness settles in my chest.

Khas comes to a stop before a great, uncarved wall of rock. A jagged cave mouth opens at the base which I recognize as the entrance to the low temple. Two boulders stand on either side of the opening. At a barked greeting from Khas, they unfold into looming guards in full armor. Their gazes fix not on Khas or me, but solely on the Prince. One of them snarls, flashing a sharp, diamond-hard tooth.

The Prince slowly lifts Sis from his shoulders and sets her down on the ground before him. Suddenly I wish we'd not brought the girl with us, though she at least should be safe down here, among her own kind. The Prince keeps his hands firmly on her shoulders as he calls out in trollish: "*Grakol-dura!*"

"*Grazut orumum,*" the left-hand guard growls in response, while his fellow adjusts his stance and shifts his heavy, skull-smashing club from one fist to the other.

Khas immediately moves in front of the Prince. He in turn speaks a stream of trollish to her. She shoots him a resentful glare before stepping out of the way once more. He offers the guards a too-wide smile, then speaks a stream of words I do not understand save for the name: "*Umog Grush.*"

The guards say nothing. They merely step closer together and cross their massive clubs. An effective and impenetrable wall. The Prince quirks an eyebrow. Another stream of foreign words rumbled in that trollish accent that makes him sound truly ferocious. But his demeanor is as nonchalant as ever. He lifts a hand from Sis's shoulder to gesture vaguely in the air.

In that moment, Sis takes the opportunity to slip free of his hold. Before either of us can make a move, she darts right between the massive troll guards, ducking under their crossed clubs. They blink startled eyes, uncertain what just happened.

"Sis!" I cry and lunge several steps forward. The Prince grabs my elbow and yanks me back just as one of the trolls takes a ground-shaking step toward me. "No, wait!" I protest, twisting against the Prince's hold. "Please, that's my little girl!" I turn to the trolls, wishing I knew more of their language. "You've got to let me fetch her!"

"*Kurspari,*" the larger of the two trolls snarls, showing his teeth at me. They flash bright in the glow of Khas's lantern. "*Guthakug kuspari!*"

The Prince draws me back against his side, pinning me there with one strong arm. I want to fight him, but something in the tension of his body tells me now is the time to go still. He doesn't look at me, but speaks to the trolls, his tone sharp and biting. The trolls cast each other looks. "What's going on?" I hiss, my jaw tight.

"They don't believe the child is yours. They're inclined to keep her, to send her back to the mines and the service of the Deeper Dark."

"No!" I turn to the trolls again, angry now. "You can't just toss her away to your dark god like she doesn't matter! She is precious to me! She is . . . is . . ." I stop, feeling the futility of my human words against those hard troll ears. I shoot a desperate glance up at the Prince.

"*Ghorza borug,*" he says in a low voice for my ears only. "Try that."

"Will it work?"

"It can't hurt."

I turn to the guards again. "She is *ghorza borug,*" I say, trying to growl the words with all the deep, grinding intensity of a troll.

Once more the guards exchange glances. Their faces are blank slates to my gaze, but they lean their heads close together and confer in low rumbles.

"What did I say?" I whisper.

"It means *diamond daughter,*" the Prince responds. "But in their tongue, it carries more weight. The full meaning doesn't translate to your language." He looks down at me, meeting my gaze. "It only matters if you truly mean it."

My heart hammers in my throat. I'm very aware of the Prince's arm around me, holding me in place as though afraid I'll try to rush the guards again. He's so strong; even beneath the embroidered sleeve of his fine coat, I feel the corded power of his muscles. I wouldn't be able to break his grip if I tried. But I don't want to try. I want to lean into him, to rest in his strength. I want to let him comfort and protect me.

What foolishness is this? I shake my head, brow tightening.

43

Long ago, I learned it never pays to look to someone else for shelter. For as long as I can remember, I've had to defend myself. I'm not about to let my guard down. Not now. Not ever.

"Let go of me," I mutter. Then add a somewhat ungracious: "Please."

At once, his arm is withdrawn. A cold shiver ripples across my body where his warmth had been a moment before.

Just then, the two guards part. One of them stomps away into the darkness of the temple. The other stands firm, so immobile he might as well be a lump of solid granite. "What's happening?" I whisper.

"Unless I'm much mistaken, the one has sent the other to inquire after the low priestess's will." The Prince heaves a breath and glances around us. "Let's hope Umog Grush is in a hospitable frame of mind."

I let my gaze follow his. Many eyes surround us now, glinting and glittering in the glow of Khas's lantern. So many large, shadowy forms, all vaguely threatening. My heart jumps to my throat. Have I put us in terrible danger? For nothing?

A thud of heavy feet signals the return of the second guard. He emerges, whispers something to his fellow. Then together they face us. The guard on the left—who seems to be the superior of the two—grumbles something in trollish.

"Ah!" The Prince beams a smug smile down at me. "It seems we are to be welcomed to Grush's craggy old bosom after all. Khas!" The captain shoots him a resentful glance. "Stay here and watch our backs, will you?"

"I don't like it, Prince," Khas growls.

"I'm well aware, brave captain. But take comfort: the temple rules should prevent them from bashing our skulls in while we're on sacred ground." With this word of encouragement, he turns to me and sweeps his arm broadly. "After you, Darling."

4

THE DARK OF THE INNER TEMPLE IS EVEN HEAVIER than I remembered. The atmosphere is more oppressive as well now that I'm aware of the risk we've taken by venturing so far from the safety of the palace.

"Veer neither to the right nor the left," I whisper as we leave behind the moonfire glow. It's the instruction I was given on my last visit to the temple. I hope it holds true now.

"Damned trolls and their damned darkness," the Prince mutters behind me. Something touches my hand. Before I can react, long, strong fingers interlace with mine.

"What are you doing?" I hiss.

"I'm scared of the dark, obviously." His grip tightens. "As you've been here before, you'd best take the lead."

I ought to wrench free. But don't. I wouldn't want to end up in a tussle practically in the doorway of the sacred temple, would I? "All right," I growl, "stay close."

"Is this close enough?"

His words breathe against the shell of my ear. My breath catches. He stands much nearer than he was a moment before. Does he feel my thudding pulse through the pressure of his palm against mine? Do his enhanced fae senses detect every tiny reaction his touch inspires in me? Even now, even when I cannot see his physical beauty, the height and breadth and strength of him is almost overwhelming.

I inhale sharply and take a step back. "It's easier if you close your eyes," I say, my voice cold, emotionless. "Try not to step on my heels."

With that, I lead the way into the low temple.

The deeper we go, the more the passage seems to close in around us. I don't know if it's real or a hallucination brought on by this devastating darkness, but I could almost swear I hear the rocks grinding against one another as they slide in closer, closer, closer. Terror urges me to reach out, to feel the walls on either side, to make certain they remain in place. But the Prince holds my hand firmly in his grasp, and I'm grateful now for that anchoring touch. With my other hand knotted tight in the folds of my skirt, I stride onward without hesitation.

Abruptly the closeness around us vanishes. We stand at the brink of a huge chasm in a wide, empty space. Up ahead a gleam of silver light just illuminates the great stone throne which stands in the very center of this massive cavern.

"There's power here." The Prince's voice startles me after such a long silence. He speaks softly, but the walls catch the words in eerie echo. "Strange power. I don't . . . I don't know . . ."

"It's the *gubdagogs*," I say. They're all around us, though the light is not strong enough to reveal them. Vast, intricate, incomprehensible tangles of thread and debris, weaving and capturing old troll tales. Among other things. Somewhere out there, the Striker is wrapped in story-threads, struggling to break free. His malice blends with the pulse of troll magic, dark and eager for vengeance.

"Come," I urge, tugging the Prince's hand. He's gone still as a statue behind me. "Umog Grush is waiting."

The words have scarcely left my mouth when a bright peal of laughter echoes off the walls, making the unseen *gubdagogs* sway and ripple in response. "Sis!" I gasp and take a single lunging step.

The Prince yanks me back hard. "Watch out."

I look down. By the dim light, I faintly see the dilapidated rope bridge before me. My throat tightens with dread. "It's all right," I say, my words belied by the tremble in my voice. "I've been this way before. Come on."

The Prince utters another curse. "Sometimes, Darling, your courage looks rather too much like lunacy to the rest of us."

Ignoring him, I proceed onto the bridge, tugging him along after me. In some ways it was easier the last time I came this way.

Then I'd walked completely blind. I hadn't seen just how decrepit the rotten boards and frayed ropes were. Ignorance was bliss.

But Sis's laugh draws me on like a beacon. The nearer we come to the throne, the brighter the light glows, until I can finally discern the source: a large crystal caught at the end of a tall sapling staff. The huge hand gripping that staff is attached to a large, boulder-shaped person. The low priestess of Vespre. Light glints off flecks of mica in her hard stone hide as she turns her head and shoulders this way and that, trying to keep an eye on Sis. The girl scrambles around the throne like it's her personal playground, chattering in trollish all the while. The contrast between my pretty, delicate child and the fantastically ugly priestess is almost comical. Only no one would dare laugh in the face of Umog Grush.

Sis suddenly spies our approach along the bridge. A delighted squeal bursts from her lips, and she flings herself down from the throne, straight for me. She hits hard and wraps herself around my knees, causing me to stagger back heavily.

Strong hands grip me under the arms. "Careful, Darling," murmurs a low voice in my ear. The skin along my neck prickles.

"*Jirot*," the priestess rumbles, her voice rolling down like an avalanche from her high seat. "*Grakol-dura.*" She turns the staff in her hand, angling the light of the crystal so that it beams down on us. It's too bright, painful even. I put up a hand to shield my eyes, still leaning on the Prince's support. He doesn't seem to be in a hurry to let go of me. "*Grakol-dura, Umog,*" he calls over my head.

50

The priestess snorts. "Your accent stinks like morleth scat. You will not dishonor me by speaking the Stone Tongue in my presence."

The Prince's hands tense against my ribcage. Finally, he sets me upright, though one hand slips to rest against my waist, a subtly protective gesture. His voice has an edge when he replies, "While your speech, gentle *umog,* falls upon my ears like the soft petals of the *jiru* blossom caught in the blast of a hurricane."

I lower my hand, trying to catch a glimpse of the priestess's face. Will she take offense? The light is too bright; I can distinguish nothing.

After an agonizing pause, Grush lets out a bark of laughter. "Bravely spoken for an elfkin prince!" She tilts her staff away so that the crystal no longer shines directly in our eyes. Now it casts a glow across her throne and the stone platform at its base. Beyond the platform is nothing but plunging darkness, while overhead I can just glimpse the toothy edges of stalactites and the interweaving threads of the *gubdagogs.*

I look down into Sis's face. She's still wrapped around me, her shining eyes upturned to mine. "Are you all right?"

"*Korkor!*" she responds with another trilling laugh. "Umog and me is very good, and she has *hirala,* and she says I am a *karrhig!*"

I turn to the Prince, uncertain about that last word. "Nuisance," he replies and ruffles Sis's hair, making the soft pale strands stand upright like thistledown. "An insightful one, this low priestess."

Sis wrinkles her nose and fussily smooths her hair down before darting back along the creaking bridge. She leaps to the top of

51

Grush's high seat and perches there like a monkey, swinging one foot dangerously close to the priestess's ear.

Grush heaves a heavy sigh and lifts one block-shaped hand from the arm of her throne, beckoning. "Come," she says, her voice growling in the pit of my stomach, "approach. Long have I waited for our mighty overlord to pay his respects. Let us see how well you make up for your discourtesy."

The Prince keeps his hand at my waist as we cross the last few unsteady boards of the bridge and step onto solid stone. There I sink into a curtsy. The Prince, however, remains upright. I wish I dared grab his hand and yank him into at least a shallow bow. But then, he is the lord and master of Vespre, regardless of either his or Grush's feelings on the matter.

"Perhaps we are both rather remiss in our duties, *umog*," he declares. "After all, I do not recollect that you paid a call on the palace since my appointment to Vespre."

Grush's lip curls. "I am not beholden to elfkin invaders. You can wait another four centuries, and still I will not darken your door."

"Why not add a couple more centuries and make it a full millennium?"

I jab an elbow into his side. "We're in *her* house!" I hiss.

"Indeed, little prince," the low priestess growls, "listen to your human." She leans forward in her chair like an avalanche waiting to happen. "You are in my house. You and all your kind come sweeping into our world and think you have claim to all you see. You bring your monsters with you, invite doom upon those who asked for neither your friendship nor your animosity. But when the darkness closes in, it is you who quivers with terror. None of you know how to thrive in a troll world." She taps the end of her staff against the stone, a sharp crack that makes the *gubdagogs* overhead shiver. "You call yourself a prince. Prince of what? Soon you will be prince of nothing more than an island of stone. But make no mistake—the stone will last. While you and all your kind play at being immortal, dance beneath the light of the sun, thinking your days endless—the stone will last. And when at last you discover to your horror that your days have run out, when you fade and wither beneath your sun's harsh glow, ruing the loss of all you once knew and loved—*yet the stone will last.* It will go on lasting until the cycles of all these worlds have turned, and the gods choose to make them anew. And from what will they forge their new beginning? From the stone. Thus will trollfolk awaken, the sole people of Eledria to endure to the end and beyond."

The weight of the priestess's words crushes me. I feel my own smallness, my own inescapable futility. Desperately, I glance up at the Prince. I don't know what I expect to see in his face. Something onto which I might grasp and pull myself out from under this heaviness, perhaps. But his expression is a study. Impossible to read.

Then to my surprise, he bows. Deeply. My mouth drops open. I'm not the only one; Grush's great jaw sags, and her small eyes, mostly-hidden beneath the deep ledge of her brow, flash in the crystal light. "What is this?" she demands. "Do you mock me, elfkin?"

"No indeed, great *umog,*" he replies, still bowed so low, his long hair sweeps the ground. "You have shamed me with your words. I desire only to prove that I at least of my kind am capable of change before change is forced upon me." Only then does he lift his head, gazing up at the priestess above him. "You have spoken truly. It is my people who have brought doom to Vespre. While I have fought for many cycles to forestall that doom, I am incapable of thwarting it forever. But perhaps the very people whom my kin have cursed in our arrogance are those to whom we should have turned for aid in our hour of need."

"And you come now to seek that aid?" Grush snarls.

"Belatedly, yes."

"What makes you think I would be willing to grant it?"

"Because"—the Prince straightens at last, but keeps one hand pressed against his heart in a sign of reverence—"unless we are to join forces, it is not my kind who will suffer first but yours."

"Are you threatening me?"

"I am merely stating the sorry fact. Along with my remorse."

"Your remorse means nothing to me."

"But it means something to me. And I hope I might put that feeling to good use. To spur myself on to right actions going forward. Starting with . . . the child."

"Ah yes. The child." Grush turns her gaze to Sis, now perched on the arm of her chair, fiddling with a piece of string. I don't know where she came by it—possibly off her own somewhat threadbare garments. The hem of one pantaloon leg does look more ragged than when I first put them on her. "You've already taken other troll children," the priestess muses. "What's the difference here?"

"The difference is Clara Darlington."

A spark shoots down my spine. I can count on one hand the number of times I've heard the Prince use my name correctly. Each time he does, it's a shock. I don't quite know what to make of it.

"Clara Darlington," he continues, "and her desire to maintain the child's place in *Vagungad*. To honor her trollness, even as I myself have failed to." Only now does he turn to me, his eyes bright in the crystal-glow. Bright and strangely soft. A look I don't recall seeing before on his proud, sarcastic face. "She too has shamed me. And I am grateful for that shame."

Umog Grush shifts in her seat, her stony buttocks grinding. "This does not sound like the speech of a fae."

"True enough." The Prince shifts his gaze back to her. "But then, I am not wholly fae."

I don't know what to do. What to think. I hardly know how to breathe. I open my mouth, wishing I might speak, but no words will come.

Grush turns her staff and crystal slowly. "Your words mean nothing if they are not backed by actions. What do you propose to *do*, princeling?"

"I propose to beg your instruction," the Prince answers at once.

"My instruction in what?"

"*Gubdagogs.*"

This draws another bark of laughter from the priestess's craggy lips. "You can beg until you're blue! It'll make no difference. Neither elfkin nor humans can hope to comprehend the complexity of *gubdagogs.*"

"It is true." The Prince inclines his head in acknowledgement. "I for one certainly do not understand their workings. But she"— he points to Sis, busy weaving a little knotted tangle with her piece of thread—"seems to have the knack. Have a look at this if you will, great *umog.*"

So saying, he pulls the frame containing Bheluphnu from the inner pocket of his coat and holds it out for Grush's inspection. She accepts it, turns it around several times. Then starts when the Noswraith contained within makes a lunge for her, only just restrained by Sis's clever weaving.

"It's breaking down," she says at last, handing it back to the Prince. "Won't last the day."

"Well, it is removed from the rest of the working, is it not?" The Prince shrugs and slips the frame back into his coat. "Even you must admit it's impressive work."

"I admit nothing."

"What's more," the Prince continues, just as though he'd scored a point, "there is another member of my household who is said to have shown a knack for this. She too may be able to bridge the gap between the temple and the palace."

Grush narrows her eyes. "You speak of the *va-lak* girl, I suppose."

"Lir," the Prince replies. "Raised by two of my librarians but born pure troll blood."

"She is too far outside *Vagungad*."

"Perhaps by aiding in the salvation of her city she might find her way back into the holy cycle."

"Such a thing has never been heard of."

"Such a thing as Noswraiths had never been heard of until the human mages brought them into being and set them on the courts of Eledria. Vespre was not and is not immune to their malice. Even stone may dream, *umog*. And anything that dreams can be drawn into the darkness of the Nightmare Realm." He takes a step forward, his hands clenched into fists. "If the Noswraiths are to be stopped, everyone must band together. Trolls must learn new ways to be wholly troll, even as my kind must learn, perhaps, to be a little less . . . elfin. In the learning, we may grow into one another. Become stronger together."

Umog Grush settles back in her seat. Her gaze shifts from the Prince to Sis once more. She watches the girl's nimble fingers fly, twisting ever more complex knots into her thread before unraveling it and starting all over with a still more intricate design. After an interminable silence, the priestess nods her heavy head. "I will train the child. She has natural talent." She looks down at the Prince once more. "Send the *va-lak* girl to escort her to the temple tomorrow. I'll inspect her then. But I make no promises. If, as I suspect, her soul is too far gone from the stone to be reclaimed, I'll send her from the temple and never admit her again. If not . . ." She tucks her jutting chin into her thick neck. "As I said, I make no promises."

The Prince bows again. "What you have given is enough."

Realizing the interview is over, I hastily drop a curtsy. I've been silent through the whole of this exchange, little more than a fly on the wall. But when I sink into the pool of my skirts, the priestess shoots me a look. I cannot decide if it's overtly antagonistic or merely suspicious.

Grush turns to Sis and speaks a few words to her. The child stands, balancing on the chair arm, and in typical Sis fashion, drops a kiss on the priestess's broad brow before springing down and dancing to my side. Taking my hand, she leads the way out onto the bridge without a care for how it sways and creaks. The Prince follows just behind us.

We are nearly to the far side when the light goes out.

"GODS BLIGHT IT!" THE PRINCE HISSES. THE WHOLE bridge rattles when he jumps in his skin. The next moment, I hear the sharp snap of his fingers. "Come on, Darling, you know I can't manage without you."

I freeze, one hand gripping the frayed rope of the bridge, the other holding tight to Sis. A moment of decision hangs before me, a decision that feels far more fraught than perhaps it should. I draw a breath, blinking against the absolute darkness.

Behind me, I feel the Prince reaching out for my hand.

Slowly, I force my fingers to uncurl from around the rope. My stomach plunges as my body sways on those rotten old boards, suspended above that terrible drop. But I reach back nonetheless. Back into the shadows.

Almost at once, the Prince's fingers close around mine. A

shock of pure courage seems to ripple up my arm and burst in my chest. My heart surges, and blood pounds in my ears. It doesn't matter that we stand above a pit of black nothingness, surrounded by a dark more impenetrable than night. He's here. Just at my back. His hand clasped warmly in mine. Though deep down I know it's foolish, I'm suddenly convinced that we will solve whatever problems lie before us. We will save this city. We will stop the Noswraiths from spreading. We will fortify the library and strengthen our numbers.

And somehow, however improbable it may be, we will find a way to navigate the terrible rift between our two selves as well.

The feeling is there and gone again in a moment. I shake my head and growl, "Come on then," before starting forward, tugging him after me.

"Not so fast," the Prince protests. "I'm liable to trip, you know." His graceful fae stride belies his words, however, and he easily navigates the last few paces of the bridge. His hand affords me more support than I like to admit.

We've no sooner stepped from the bridge than Sis gives an unexpected tug, pulling free of my hold. "No, wait!" I cry and try to lunge after her.

The Prince's hand restrains me. "Not so fast, Darling. Remember, she can see well enough, but you'll run face-first into a block of stone. Slow but steady does it now."

I hate to admit he's right. I'm forced to slow my pace and creep back up the long, narrow path through the lower temple.

This time, the awful heaviness of stone doesn't oppress me as intently. I'm too eager, too hopeful. Umog Grush is willing to meet with Lir! Willing to train Sis, willing to give my mad little scheme a chance. I'd scarcely dared hope for this outcome and even now fear to believe it.

"I have to thank you, you know."

The Prince's voice brings me to a halt. His hand, so warm in mine, tightens slightly, making my breath catch. "Wh-what do you mean?"

"I should have made this visit a long time ago. I fear I have underestimated the importance of the low priestess and her seat of power." He sighs suddenly, his breath warm, prickling the skin on the back of my neck. "I suppose I thought as long as the trolls weren't actively attacking the citadel, that was peace enough."

I bite my lip. Then: "Well, you have been rather occupied."

He grunts. "You're too generous." Another slight pressure from his hand, and we start forward again, one careful step after another. "Nevertheless," he continues, "you've brought me—rather unwillingly, I'll admit—to a new understanding of the situation here in Vespre. Simply putting out fires as they spring up isn't going to stop the ultimate annihilation of this whole island. We must keep the fires from starting in the first place. While I'm not convinced these *gubdagogs* are the solution we're looking for . . ." His voice trails off for a long moment, leaving me to wonder if he'll finish. Finally, in a lower voice, as though no longer speaking to me: "At least they're something new to try."

A terrible wish comes over me. A wish to turn around, to face him. To try to see his face, impossible though I know it to be. There's something about this intimacy—his hand in mine in the dark—that fills me with an unnerving, fluttering, gut-churning sensation. Something like dread. But sweeter. More dangerous.

I push on, faster now. As though I might somehow outrace what the touch of his hand is doing to me, to my heart. Light gleams faintly in the distance. I lunge for it, resisting any effort on the Prince's part to restrain me. I ought to shake free of him, but I don't want to try. Partly because I'm afraid he won't let go; partly because I'm afraid he will.

Before we reach the temple entrance, I spy a small form standing silhouetted in the opening. "Sis!" I cry.

In that same moment, the Prince tugs me back against his chest and wraps his arm around me. My heart jolts so hard I nearly choke. "Trouble ahead." His voice is in my ear, a low rumble. "I can't have you tumbling out there."

Before I have a chance to think or even try to form a protest, he pushes me firmly behind him. When I try to press forward, his strong arm blocks my way. "But Sis!" I protest. "If there's trouble then—"

"Trust me, whatever danger awaits us is no danger to her." The Prince turns and looks back at me, his face half-illuminated by the light shining up ahead. His eyes glitter strangely. "I don't suppose I could convince you to retreat back to the priestess's hall, could I?"

I stare up at him. "Sis is out there. Whatever's happening, I won't be made to run and hide."

"Would it change your mind if I assured you there's absolutely nothing you can do to help?"

Whatever he has detected with those highly attuned fae senses of his can't be good. My mouth is dry, my throat tight. But I shake my head firmly.

His jaw tenses. "Just stay behind me then. I can handle the *Hrorark*. No need for you to make things more difficult."

The *Hrorark?* My stomach plunges as the Prince moves on up the dark passage. I'd known we were unlikely to make it all the way to the temple and back again without word reaching the zealot trolls, who wield more and more control over the hearts of Vespre's citizens. Somehow I'd managed to convince myself we could slip back to the palace before they came after us. I hear their grumbling voices as we draw nearer to the entrance. This must be what the Prince had detected, a deep, trollish chant, almost more a vibration than a sound. Now that we're nearer, I begin to discern the harsh words: "*Grakanak. Badogarag. Grakanak. Dorgarag.*" Over and over, rumbling through the walls, beneath my feet.

Sis turns, sees us approaching. For the first time that I can remember, her pretty little face is streaked in fear. "*Mar!*" she cries, her voice scarcely audible above the chant. She darts for me, ducking round the Prince to throw herself into my arms. I hold her tight, press her head against my shoulder. The Prince steps up to the opening and stops. Clinging to the shadows, I follow, unable to resist the urge to peer around him into the open space beyond the temple cave.

The Hrorark are there. Dozens of them. Hundreds, maybe. Where before had been deserted streets and seemingly empty houses are now crowds of trolls. Most of them are great stone creatures, but here and there a few pale, beautiful beings stand out. Foremost of these is an imposing figure I recognize all too well: Anj. The leader of the zealots. That man pursued me through these city streets with murderous intent once before. Now he stands at the front of the crowd, naked save for a simple sarong tied about his waist, his muscular torso shining in the light of glowing crystals held aloft by his followers. He's glorious. And terrifying. Like a king of old.

And he has a knife to Khas's throat.

The captain kneels before him. Bruised and battered, she looks as though she put up quite a fight before finally succumbing to the greater numbers of the *Hrorark*. Blue blood seeps from multiple wounds across her body, including an ugly gash in her forehead. She breathes hard, her teeth grinding audibly in the sudden silence as the zealots cease their chant.

The Prince stands in the opening of the temple cave, his imposing presence dwarfed by the sheer numbers of his enemies. I want to reach out, grab the back of his coat, and yank him into the shadows with me. Instead, I press Sis close, scarcely daring to breathe.

He glances back at me. "Last chance, Darling. Will you retreat into the temple and let me deal with these louts?"

I meet his gaze hard. "I'm not abandoning you."

At this, his mouth breaks in a devastating smile. "That might be the sweetest thing you've ever said to me."

My heart leaps to my throat. Before I can recover, he whirls on heel and steps out of the cave into the open space. The shining crystal lights gleam in his raven hair and glint off the golden stitching in his coat as he raises both arms. "How now, Anj!" he cries, his voice ringing in that terrible silence. "This is quite the little party you've gathered. All this just for me? I'm touched."

Anj's teeth flash. He grips Khas by the hair on top of her head, yanks her face up to display the bruises and gashes. "Hear me, elfkin prince," he growls. "If you don't want me to slit this traitor's throat, you will cede to the demands of the *Hrorark*."

"*Guthakug!*" Khas snarls and spits a glob of blood. "Don't listen to him, my Prince!"

But the Prince merely chuckles. The sound is bright and incongruous and somehow blood-chilling. "Don't be silly, dear Khas. You can't very well guard my walls headless, now can you? No, I think I'd best hear this fellow out. What's a little talk between friends?"

Khas struggles but freezes when Anj angles his blade under her jaw. A fresh line of blue blood wells, trickles to pool in the hollow of her throat. My stomach plunges. I lean against the wall for support.

"Go on, my friend," the Prince says, shifting his weight ever so slightly. "Tell me what I can do for you this fine day. Fancy another *soromskunar?* That was great fun last time, and I'm sure your goons are keen for a rematch."

"You will hand over the girl child." Anj juts his chin in my direction, proving that he can see me and Sis where we hide in the shadows. "She and her brothers will be returned to their people before they can be corrupted. They belong to the God of the Deeper Dark, and he will have his due."

"Oh, well, I'm afraid I can't help you there. You see, Darling here has gone and fallen in love with the little scamps. I can't bear to break her heart, you understand how it is."

A terrible growl rumbles in the pale man's chest, echoed by his followers until the whole space around us seems to reverberate with thunder. Why don't they all throw themselves at us, overwhelm the Prince, and rip Sis right out of my arms? But the Prince squares his shoulders, and an ineffable sense of pure *power* radiates from inside him. Even in great numbers, the *Hrorark* hesitate to charge him.

"The choice is yours, Prince," Anj cries in desperate defiance, his voice rising above the din. "You can please your woman or you can spare your captain's life. Which is it to be?" He begins to slide the dagger along Khas's throat.

The Prince spreads his hands. Magic gathers, glinting and sparking around his fingertips. In mere moments, he will let it go. But to do so will activate the curse on his blood. He will blast those furious, desperate trollfolk to oblivion, and in the process—

"*Stop!*"

I didn't realize I meant to speak. Not until I find myself standing at the Prince's side, gripping his arm. Right in full view of Anj and his followers. The Prince turns sharply, staring down at me. His violet eyes are bright with magic, orange sparks shimmering on the edges. "Please," I beg, my voice tight in my thickened throat. "Please, don't do this. Spare them."

"What would you have me do instead, Darling?" His voice is unexpectedly harsh. "Is it the child you want or these fellows? Or perhaps you're willing to sacrifice Khas to your tenderheartedness."

With difficulty I swallow. Then: "Give them me instead."

"What?"

I shake my head and force out my words in a tumble. "I am a librarian. That must count for something in their eyes. Tell them I'll trade myself for Sis and Khas."

He blinks twice. A third time. Then slowly, he shakes his head. The wild fierceness of his expression softens into something incredulous and . . . strangely tender. "How can you be so foolish and so brave all in the same breath?"

I open my mouth to respond, but he lifts his hand, brushes my cheek. Trails a knuckle gently down my skin. And all words are quite stolen away. Then he whirls and faces the crowd once more. "It's your lucky day, Anj, old boy. I'm prepared to bargain and bargain generously in exchange for my captain."

"I want none of your fae bargains," the troll growls. "I want only the child and her brothers. Them for her. Nothing more, nothing less."

"What if I offered you myself?"

"What?" The breath leaves my lungs in a rush. Then I lunge, grab his arm again. "No!"

But the Prince is already stepping forward, pulling himself from my grasp. He holds his hands out, showing how the magic he'd accumulated dissipates, leaving him unarmed. "Turn over my captain," he says, "and I'll give you myself to do with as you will."

Khas roars and lunges in her captor's arms. In his surprise, Anj lets her go, but she simply collapses, falling on her face, too weak from her beating to do more than mutter a feeble, "Don't do this, my Prince!"

Anj stands over her, large and threatening. His beautiful face is thrown back, the light of the glowing crystals revealing the shock in his expression followed by intense calculation. "You have to know we will kill you," he says at last.

"Of course," the Prince replies. "I figured as much. Though you'd be a fool to do so."

"A fool to kill the *guthakug* elfkin who has ruled over us from on high these last four hundred turns of the cycle?"

"Yes. Because once I am gone, the King of Aurelis will send someone new to take my place. Someone not so charming, we must assume."

"Then we will kill him too."

The Prince shrugs. "Sure. If you get the chance. But let's say that you do. Then another will be sent. And another. And another and another, and meanwhile the library up there—the very prison containing the worst horrors ever unleased upon Eledria—will fall apart. More and more, faster and faster, with no one left to stop it. Do you think just anyone has the wherewithal to keep Noswraiths in check?"

Anj hesitates. He's witnessed his fair share of Noswraith outbreaks over the cycles. He knows perfectly well he doesn't have the means to deal with them.

"If I have your ear," the Prince continues, taking another step forward, "perhaps I might tempt you with another offer. Turn Khas over. Leave little Sis in the arms of her human mother along with her three siblings. Let us proceed unharmed back to the palace." He pauses, draws a deep breath. "And I vow to turn the governing of Vespre over to trollfolk in the next ten turns of the cycle."

The whole of the city seems to fall silent. It's so still, I could well believe the denizens have turned to solid stone. Anj's eyes are wide as two moons, his face white and tense. I force myself to draw air into my lungs.

"Yes," the Prince continues, turning his head to take in the crowd. He seems to look into each one of those hard, ugly faces by turn. "You will choose your own king by whatever means you prefer. Vespre will be under troll rule once again."

"You haven't the authority," Anj says at last, his voice several degrees higher than before.

The Prince nods in concession. "This is true. But I am the only one in all of Eledria who can manage the library. This gives me sway among courts and kings. Sway I will promise to use in your favor."

Anj's teeth flash. "I'm thinking I would rather go ahead and kill you now while I have the chance."

"Go for it." The Prince spreads his arms wide, his chin lifting. "But let Khas and the others go."

Anj brandishes his blade.

"No!" I cry and take a lunging step, entirely without plan, only knowing I cannot stand by and watch whatever is about to happen. Before I can take a second step, however, a hand falls on my shoulder. A very large, stone hand, which anchors me in place. I wrench around, stare up at the formidable figure of Umog Grush.

The priestess steps out from the cave like a rolling boulder, massive, covered in lichen, but otherwise naked save for her necklace of crystals and skulls. She plants herself squarely in front of the temple and surveys the gathering from beneath the deep ledge of her brow. Her eyes spark like blood diamonds in the crystals light.

Then she looks straight at Anj. "Stand down, boy."

The pale man takes a step back before throwing back his head and declaring, "All that I do, I do in the name of the Deeper Dark!

I want only—"

"It's high time you stopped worrying about the needs of the Deeper Dark and started worrying about the needs of your fellow trollfolk." Grush's voice swallows up any further protests. She's simply too big, too old, too ugly, and terrible. Anj's followers draw back several paces. Several drop to their knees. She sweeps her gaze across them and raises her sapling staff. Its crystal flashes a sudden brilliant red.

"We are trolls," she declares. "Trolls live with the advent of coming doom looming over our heads. So we have lived since before the Sundering, back in the days of kings. So we have lived ever since the breaking of our world. The doom poised over our city of Valthurg is no new thing. Only the form which that doom takes has changed. We will survive. As we always have. But." Here she brings her staff down, cracking sharp against the ground. "But I would rather see us thrive. Let us not revert fully to the stone before our time." She points the crystal at the end of her staff straight at Anj, illuminating his white skin in harsh, crimson glow. "If you wish to become stone, Anj, you are free to go and do so, and take your friends with you. Meanwhile, the rest of us shall work toward a more prosperous future."

Anj looks as though he wants to protest. But in the face of his priestess, he dares not speak. Instead he bows his head.

Grush grunts and turns to the Prince. "Do you speak the truth, elfkin? Will you turn the rule of this city over to trolls within the next ten turns of the cycle?"

"So long as the Noswraiths are contained and my work in the library is not interfered with. Yes."

"And you have the means by which to honor this promise?"

"Not at the moment I don't."

The old priestess's lip curls. "And will you ever?"

He swallows. His complexion is paler than before, almost green around the edges. But he nods. "I can make no guarantees, great *umog*. I can only swear that I will work tirelessly to bring about the liberation of Vespre by whatever means are within my reach."

Slowly, Grush nods. "I suppose that will have to be enough. For now."

She turns then back to Anj and barks in trollish, causing him and his people to jump. They exchange wary glances before backing away. One by one, their crystals go out, and shadows obscure their great hulking forms. Soon, there is none left save for Anj himself. He remains where he stands, his gaze shifting from the priestess to the prince and back again. Finally, with a bitter curse, he turns away and melts into the darkness.

"I have told that brash young fellow," Grush says, addressing the Prince once more, "that if his people offer any further threat to you and yours for the next ten turns of the cycle, I will personally see them thrown from the *Vagungad* and made *va-lak* for the rest of their lives. That is your deadline, elfkin. Should you fail to live up to your promise, I will not interfere with Anj or his Hrorark again."

"Understood, great *umog*," the Prince replies and offers a solemn bow.

Grush snorts. Then she turns and, without a glance for either me or Sis, stumps back into her temple, vanishing back into her world of darkness and stone. I watch her go, heart in my throat. I know for a fact she saved our lives just now.

"Come, Darling!" The Prince's voice draws me spinning about in time to see him pull Khas's arm over his shoulder and assist her to her feet. "We'd best be on our way. I don't know about you, but I fancy a cup of tea after all these doings. What say you, Khas, my friend? Tea? Crumpets?"

"Guthakug jirot," Khas growls, and I don't need to know the language to hear the expletives. The Prince merely chuckles, however, and starts back up the long road to the palace. I follow at his heels, Sis still cradled close in my arms.

6

SIS IS SNORING SOFTLY BY THE TIME WE REACH THE
palace, exhausted from her adventures. Her little head
lolls on my shoulder, her soft hair tickling my nose.

My footsteps are heavy, stumbling. Carrying the child all that
long way up from the low temple is no mean feat. I'm not used
to this kind of physical effort, spending my days hunched over
a desk as I usually do. The Prince, by contrast, doesn't seem to
have broken a sweat supporting Captain Khas. Possibly because
the captain herself, despite her wounds, at least attempts to walk
on her own, whereas Sis is a dead weight in my arms.

We reach the front steps of the palace at last where Lir and the
three boys anxiously await our return. Lir spies the Prince and
Khas first and immediately shouts for guards to come lend their
assistance. Khas's loyal men hasten down the steps to take her

from the Prince, carrying her away despite her growling protests.

"Don't forget!" the Prince calls after them, pausing a moment to rest his hands on his knees. Perhaps he's more winded than I thought. "Tea and crumpets! It's the best medicine! Slathered up with extra butter, that'll do the trick."

"What happened, Mistress?" Lir asks, as she and the boys crowd in around me, and she takes Sis from my exhausted arms. The girl opens one eye to grumble a protest before tucking into the crook of Lir's neck and letting out a satisfied snore.

I try to smile. After everything that happened, I'm still not sure whether to be triumphant or terrified. "It went well. I think." My words are a little breathless. At Lir's concerned expression, I add quickly, "I'll tell you all about it. Later. I promise."

Lir nods, unsatisfied, but willing to be patient. "Give your *mar* kisses, boys," she tells the children, "and come help me put your sister to bed."

I drop to my knees, allowing myself to be comforted by the feeling of stony arms wrapped around me and stony lips pressed against my cheek. Calx demands to know whether or not the Prince will still be dining with them that night. "It might have to be tomorrow," I admit. At his crestfallen expression, I plant an extra kiss on his forehead. "Be a good boy now and help your sister. I'll be along shortly, I promise." Calx heaves a sigh but allows himself to be ushered away by his brothers.

I pull myself wearily up from my knees and begin to turn around . . . only to find my nose mere inches away from an unbuttoned linen shirt and embroidered coat lapels. I blink, step back, and turn my gaze up to the Prince's face.

"Did I understand correctly?" he says, one brow arched. "Have I a dinner engagement of which I was not aware?"

I jump back several paces and tuck a stray strand of hair behind my ear. "Prince," I gasp. Then setting my jaw: "I would have a word with you. Now. If you please."

His other eyebrow rises to match the first. "My, my. That is quite the imperious tone." He tips his head a little to one side, narrowing his eyes. "Very well. Would you join me for a stroll in the solarium?"

He's so polite. Which is not at all like him. It's strangely unsettling.

Too aware of the heat suddenly rising in my cheeks, I march up the stair and into the palace with only a curt nod for the guard standing watch at the door. I remember the way to the solarium well enough and hasten there without pause, not bothering to check if the Prince follows. I suspect I know why he suggested this particular part of the palace for our conversation. No trolls—not even the nosiest of troll maids—would venture into the solarium by choice. It is much too bright for their comfort. The Prince ensorcelled the chamber, filling it with sunlight drawn all the way from Solira. A powerful spell indeed, yet another display of his extraordinary gifts.

I don't stop until I reach the solarium door. Even there, I refuse to look back at him, but simply wait until he approaches from behind, opens the door, and motions me inside. I step through, closing my eyes against the sudden glare. Despite the discomfort, it's a pleasure to feel warm light on my skin. As I progress into the soft golden atmosphere and the verdant greenery of Queen Dasyra's garden, at least some of the tension knotting my limbs begins to relax.

The Prince walks beside me, matching his stride to mine. His hands are clasped at the small of his back, his head up, his face a mask of bland leisure. One would never know that mere hours ago he'd faced down his own death at the hands of troll insurgents.

He turns his head suddenly, catching my studying gaze. I turn away only to walk into a large fern leaf. I stop, sputter, and push it away, painfully aware of the Prince's amused silence all the while. Determined to reclaim my dignity, I shake my head, straighten my skirts, and turn at last to face him. "You must know why I wished to speak to you."

His lips quirk slightly. "I have any number of suspicions." To my utmost horror his gaze drops pointedly to my mouth. "And hopes."

I clear my throat and take a backward step, once more bumping into the enormous fern. But I will not let him befuddle me. I will not be bested. "Why did you do that?"

His eyes lift to mine once again. He puckers his brows questioningly.

"Don't play the innocent," I snap. "You offered your life. Your *life!* You know very well they would have killed you. What were you *thinking?*"

"I was thinking of Khas who, as you may recall, was in dire straits."

"Why didn't you offer me instead?"

"Why do you think?" His voice drops an octave, rumbling low in my gut. For a moment, a shadow seems to come over his face, and his eyes burn with terrible intensity.

I turn away, wrapping my arms tight around my middle, and push on down the path, through the foliage, making for the fountain in the center of this chamber. "You shouldn't be so reckless with your life. And how do you think you're going to fulfill this promise to hand the city over to the trolls? You know perfectly well Vespre won't survive without you."

"Since when do you care so deeply about Vespre?"

I stop short, shoes skidding in the gravel path. "Don't change the subject."

"Very well." He draws up beside me again, hands still clasped, and stares ahead through the greenery. The fountain is just visible now, bubbling merrily, its waters sparkling under the enchanted sunlight. "Since when did you start to think *I* cared so deeply about Vespre?"

"You've always cared. You've cared from the very start. You care so much, you were willing to bring me here, even when you never wanted to set eyes on me again. Even when you knew what I'd done."

I feel rather than see the small, bitter smile curving his lips. "I always knew I would have to fetch you eventually. I couldn't help myself."

"What?"

He turns, looks down at me. I can't bear to meet his gaze, but continue staring straight ahead, even as his eyes bore into the side of my face. "The knowledge that you were there in Aurelis—breathing the air of Eledria—was torture. During those five years you spent in Estrilde's thrall, not a day went by that I did not think of you."

My breath is tight and shallow. This is so not how I intended this conversation to go. I drop my lashes, study the toes of shoes, squeezing my arms tight as though to hold my very being together. "Stop it."

"Stop what?"

"Stop . . . confusing me. I'm . . . I'm telling you, you can't put yourself at risk like that. Not when so many people need you."

"And who needs me exactly?"

"Mixael. Andreas."

"And?"

"Khas and Lir and . . . and all the members of your household."

"*And?*"

"And the whole gods-blighted city!" I toss up my hands and storm on ahead, desperate to put some space between us. I march all the way to the fountain and lean against its basin. The water bubbles and froths, sparkling in the sunlight. "They may hate you," I continue, little caring if he can hear me over the fountain's gurgling voice. "But they need you. They simply don't realize what it is you do for them."

He approaches slowly, his pace lazy and unrushed. He perches on the edge of the basin, ankles crossed, arms over his chest. "It sounds to me, Darling, as though *you* are the one who cares so much."

I grip the lip of the basin. "I do care."

"Do you?"

The hope in his voice is like an arrow straight to my heart. Hastily I shake my head and level a stern frown his way. "About Vespre! About these people. I care about all of them and want them to be safe."

He is silent for a long moment. His eyes slowly move, taking in every detail of my face. I'm careful to betray nothing, to keep my scowl firmly in place. Finally, he *tsks* softly and shakes his head. "Tell me, does this mean you've changed your mind?"

I blink. "I . . . What do you mean?"

"Are you giving up your mad scheme to save Doctor Gale from his Obligation to my cousin? Are you going to let him lie in the bed he made for himself and commit your efforts to this city you claim to care for so deeply?"

All the sunlight in this chamber seems to filter away, leaving behind a world of sickly gray hues.

Danny.

Oscar.

Their faces swim before my mind's eye. To save the one, I must save the other. This is a fact so firmly planted in my heart, it's taken root and spread through every part of me. Sometimes over the last few weeks I've tried to ignore it, even to forget it. But always it's there, clinging to my spirit. A terrible growth, a parasite. Sucking the life from me.

You're not seeing rightly . . .

I close my eyes, grind my teeth. I feel the weight of their lives—Danny's and Oscar's both—pulling me down like two great millstones hung around my neck. But in the Prince's words, I hear possibilities. Of freedom. Of safety. Of change. I want it. I want it so badly. I long to reach out and accept everything he offers.

I press the knuckles of one hand against my forehead, suddenly woozy. If I didn't know better, I'd say it was fae glamour, working to confuse my senses. I'm not thinking clearly. Until I've had a good long rest, I'm not sure I'm capable of clear thought. "Never mind," I growl, turning away and putting my back to the Prince. "I shouldn't have said anything. This was foolish. Please, forget it."

I start to leave. But his hand on my elbow restrains me. Even that light touch sends a jolt of heat rushing through my body. He tightens his hold, draws me back to him. I ought to resist. I ought to pull away, put some distance between us.

Instead I lift my lashes, peer up into his face. His face which is suddenly so much nearer than it was before. His one hand remains firmly gripping my elbow, while the other lifts to my cheek, fingers sliding into my hair, around the back of my head.

"Clara," he breathes. Nothing more. Nothing more is needed

to make me lean toward him, lips parting. Drawn to his gravity with irresistible force.

Then abruptly he lets go. Backs away. His fingers withdraw from my hair, and he puts both hands firmly behind his back once more, his face falling into the habitual lines of a lazy smile. "If you need me," he says, "I'm easy enough to find. Unless I'm much mistaken, I'll be dining with a passel of troll children tonight. Until then."

With that and a polite tip of his head, he turns and disappears into the greenery with a swish of his long coat. And I'm left standing there, leaning back against the fountain basin, my heart pounding like a hammer against my breastbone.

THE PRINCE

S HE DOESN'T WANT ME TO DIE. THAT MUST COUNT for something I think.

I step into the quiet of my study, close the door behind me. For a moment I stand still, staring before me into that space. At the work mounding my desk. The books, scrolls, papers, quills, piled up on every conceivable surface, all awaiting my attention. But I see none of it.

Instead my mind's eye is taken up with that vision of her. Shining in the light of the solarium. Gazing up at me with those doe-brown eyes of hers. Eyes ordinarily so soft and demure, now sparking with that secret fire which blazes hot in her core.

"You can't put yourself at risk like that. Not when so many people need you."

I rest my head back against the door, breathe out through my nostrils. Am I really such a fool? Am I seeing only what I wish to see? Most likely.

But there's a chance. A chance I'm not mistaken. A chance that what I glimpsed in her eyes wasn't just a reflection of my own feelings.

Gods damn it.

I march to the desk, drag the chair back, and take a seat. I lean back, then frown at the odd lump in my pocket. Reaching into the front of my coat, I withdraw the little purloined frame with its dangling string and bits of ripped canvas. Somehow, impossibly, it still shimmers with magic—strange, inexplicable troll magic, so unlike any other in all the worlds. Deep inside, the Noswraith strains and pulls, yet the magic holds. It's held for hours now, far longer than I ever would have thought possible.

Suddenly, Bheluphnu lunges—a horror of gaping jaw and fiery cat eyes and ripping claws. Strands of magicked reality yank it back again, but only just.

With a sigh, I prop the frame, quiet once more, against a stack of papers. Rooting around in the desk, I find a blank book and open it before me. Study the empty page. That expanse upon which I once would have worked my magic with ease. And now?

A black box with an inlaid pattern of blue respenia blossoms sits within reach at the right corner of my desk. I pull it to me, open the lid. Gaze a moment at the quill resting on a bed of silk inside. Dasyra's quill, bonded to her. Still infused with her unique magic years after her death. Plucking it up, I trim the nib more out of habit than necessity and dip it in a pot of red ink.

Then, I sit, pen poised above the blank page.

My breath tightens. It's been some time since I last tried my hand at written magic. Not since that wretched Doctor Gale nearly bled me to death, purging the curse from my body. Slowly, slowly, my human blood has regenerated over the last few months, along with it my ability to use human magic. But the curse regenerated as well.

I feel it in me now, dark and insidious. Waiting for opportunity to strike. I've danced on the edge of this precipice so many times, dipping into my power even as I knew the backlash that must follow. One of these days I will push myself too far. And that will be it—the curse will burn me up from the inside out, leaving my body a hollow and steaming husk.

But surely a small binding like this can't be too much to ask?

Steeling my courage, I lower my hand, begin to scratch out a few simple words. Immediately the curse flares to life. First a burn in the back of my hand, then a streak up my arm to my shoulder. Sweat beads my brow. More pain, a flame licking across my shoulders, up my neck, the base of my skull. Like being stabbed with red-hot pokers.

"Damn it," I growl and drop the pen. Three haphazard lines and a scrawl of ink are all I have to show for my efforts. And the Noswraith remains unbound.

Biting back curses, I slam the book shut, and drop the quill back in its box. Then, grabbing the speaking tube under my desk, I yank it up to my mouth. "Silveri!"

A muffled answer from the other end: *"Sir?"*

"I require your assistance in my office. At once."

Mixael Silveri, my senior librarian, appears at my door a few minutes later. The man is harried and pale. The burden of his new role weighs heavily on his shoulders since the untimely death of his mother. "You called, Prince?" he asks.

"Here," I say without preamble and hold the frame up for his inspection. "Bind this properly for me, will you?"

His eyes widen. "What is it?" I watch in silence as he takes it in his hands, turns it around . . . and jumps six inches in the air when the Noswraith lunges at him, pulling against its bindings. "What in the nine hells?" he cries, fairly flinging the frame from him.

I catch it and spin it about one finger. "That, my dear Silveri, is a *gubdagog.*"

He shakes his head. "A *gubdagog?*"

"Yes."

"But it's so small!"

"Well, it isn't the entire *gubdagog.* The rest of the mess is strung up in the old south salon."

"But . . . but how does it . . . ?" He can't find the words to finish his question. I don't blame him. In all my years as Prince of Vespre, I'd never guessed at the true purpose of the great tangled structures, thinking them only another unfathomable troll oddity.

In quick, clipped tones, I inform him of my little jaunt into the city and the subsequent dealings with the low priestess. For the moment, I do not relate the agreement to turn the city over to trollfolk. One shock at a time is enough for the poor fellow.

Mixael takes it all in, his face pale and drawn. "Is Captain Khas all right?" he asks, his voice tense.

"She'll recover." It's no secret, the torch my senior librarian has been carrying for my captain of the guard this last century or so. "You can see her once you've secured this binding."

Mixael takes the *gubdagog*, turns it round in his hand again. "You really think there's any point in pursuing this? You think it could make a difference?"

"I do."

He looks at me. It's the same sharp, incisive stare his mother used to level on me. In that moment, there is so much of Nelle Silveri in his face, it takes me aback. "And you don't think your perspective might be unduly influenced by Miss Darlington, sir?"

Nelle would have put it far more bluntly. At least her son still feels the need for some tact while dealing with me.

"Time will tell," I answer coldly. "In the meanwhile, we shall see how long the grace of the priestess lasts and be grateful for a reprieve from Anj and all his infernal rabble-rousing. Agreed?"

Though the look in his eye tells a different story, Mixael murmurs a polite acquiescence and vacates the room, *gubdagog* in hand. He shuts the door behind him.

And I groan, sink back into my seat, and look down at my shaking hands once more. Gods on high! Who would have thought so small an amount of magic would leave me trembling and weak? I must fight it. But how? How does one fight a curse on one's very blood?

I run my trembling fingers through my hair. Then, pushing my chair back, I rise and go to the window. Gaze out on that sweeping view. This city. This Vespre. Mine for centuries, longer than I like to remember. My home and my prison. My greatest honor and greatest bane.

Will I indeed turn it over to Anj and the priestesses? Is it possible I won't spend the rest of my existence fighting a losing battle, warding off ultimate and inevitable doom?

Perhaps there is hope.

Perhaps I'm deluding myself.

But then, I never expected a storm like *her* to blow into my life, stirring up all which I had so neatly ordered. Seeing things I'd overlooked. Challenging me, testing me. Driving me stark raving mad. Ultimately forcing me to be better. Wiser. Truer.

Gods, how I'd hated her! Hated her for what she'd done with that unconscious, unchecked power of hers. Yet even in the very depths of loathing, I could never fully hide from the truth. The truth that, from the first moment I set eyes on her pale, terrified face, my soul was set ablaze. Not with hatred. No, this is a greater, far more terrible and destructive flame.

A flame that would burn down worlds for her sake.

Gritting my teeth, I turn from the window, face back into my shadowed chamber. I must be careful. I must ever be on my guard. Because it doesn't matter what I feel for her. There's no room in her heart for me. Not crammed as it is with those children, or that wretched brother, or her thrice-damnable Doctor Gale. What am I compared to any of these? Less than nothing in her estimation. While she?

She is *everything.*

CLARA

7

AS IT TURNS OUT, THE PRINCE FULFILLED MY promise and joined the children for dinner last night.

I'm told all about it the following morning when the four of them burst into my room as I'm preparing for the day. Three stone-hided bodies bounce on my bed, climb up my wardrobe, swing from my curtains, and cause all manner of mayhem amid a near-constant stream of chatter. Apparently, what had begun as dinner soon devolved into a competitive sport of who can spit the pits of the stewed peaches farthest over the balcony rail into the city below. Calx declares the Prince a champion pit-spitter, and Har and Dig both call him a "regular *jor-dor.*" I take it that's a compliment of the highest order.

Only Sis is uncharacteristically quiet while her brothers regale me with tales of the Prince's expectorating talents. When

I turn to her at last, she's sitting at my vanity, staring at her own face in the glass, her brow puckered and earnest. "What's wrong, little Sis?" I ask, coming up behind her and stroking her soft hair.

She turns pale eyes up to me. "I is go see *umog* today," she says, then purses her lips into a hard line. Finally, she adds, "I need hair up. Like *Mar*. So I focus."

She's so earnest, I have no choice but to pull out my brush and hairpins and set to work pinning her hair up into a tight bun such as I typically wear. I can't help wondering at her insistence. It's not a troll style. Is she afraid she'll be taken away from me if she becomes too trollish? Her face is difficult to read, her brow hard as stone.

Once I finish styling her hair, I drop a kiss on the top of her head and catch her eye in the glass. "You know I'm proud of you. Don't you?"

She blinks solemnly. Then she says, "*Mar?*"

"Yes?"

"I is . . . 'fraid."

I nod slowly. It's strange to see my wild imp child uneasy. Yesterday, she'd been so comfortable with the low priestess, you'd think they were old friends. Perhaps the altercation with Anj and his people left more of an impression on her young mind than I realized.

I clear my throat. Then, though I know my accent is atrocious, I say: "*Kaurga-hor, gruaka-hor.*" Those very words were spoken to me not long after I first arrived in Vespre. If I remember correctly, they mean, *"more fear, more brave."*

Sis's eyes brighten. She understands. Suddenly, she smiles, turns on the stool and wraps her little arms around me. She's much stronger than her size would suppose, and quite squeezes the breath out of me. But I squeeze her back for as long as she wishes. When she is done, she springs from the stool and tackles her nearest brother with tremendous enthusiasm. That hairstyle won't last the morning, I'm sure.

The next half-hour is the usual madness of making certain all four children have eaten, washed, and readied for their coming day. The boys are undergoing training with the house guard, and bristle in pint-sized spiked breastplates and helmets, gripping dull lances in their square fists. Once they're kissed and sent on their way, I take Sis's hand and walk her to the front doors of the palace. Lir is there, waiting for us. She is dressed in her finest, most traditional troll garb, including a belt of crystal flowers and small animal skulls. Her eyes are wide, and her hands twist nervously in the silky fabric of her skirts.

"Mistress," she says, when Sis and I emerge onto the front porch. "are you sure Umog Grush meant for *me* to escort Sis to the temple?"

I take her hand and squeeze it encouragingly. "I'm positive, Lir. Now go. Make me proud."

Her lips curve in a brief smile that doesn't quite reach her nervous eyes. Whatever outcome her meeting with the priestess brings will alter the course of her life forever.

Perhaps she will even be admitted back into the holy cycle of *Vagungad*, an outcast no more. I wish I could go with her, offer her my support. Instead I stand on the porch and watch until both she and Sis are out of sight.

They pause under the arch of the palace gate, turning back to wave. Then they're gone. I let out a long sigh. It's out of my hands now.

The bells are already tolling seven by the time I slip into the library to begin my work shift, a full hour late. My gaze flicks immediately to the main drafting table. The Prince is there, standing with his back to me. I'm certain he's aware of my entrance, but he does not turn to acknowledge me, not even to make some quip about my tardiness. I stand a moment in the open doorway, heart lodged in my throat. I can still feel the warmth and strength of his fingers gripping my elbow, twined in my hair. I can still feel the burning intensity of his gaze as he stared down into my eyes, our mouths mere inches apart . . .

I drag in a ragged breath. Then, tucking my chin, I pull the door shut behind me and hasten to my desk cubicle, glad to duck into its shelter. My corset feels tight, and my chest heaves uncomfortably, as though I've just run a sprint. Shaking my head, I press the knuckles of one fist against my forehead. This is getting out of hand. It was easier when the Prince avoided me entirely these last several weeks. Everything was easier.

Now, following the events of yesterday, my mind and heart are in such a tangle, and my body is hot and cold and trembling all at once. It takes everything I have not to leap from this chair, storm out of this cubicle, march up to the Prince and . . . and . . . What? What would I say? What is there left to say between us that hasn't been hinted at and danced around and suppressed until it's ready to burst from the pressure?

I curse softly and pull my hand away from my face. Tomorrow. Tomorrow is my day off. My first day off since my disastrous venture into Noxaur in a desperate attempt to find Lord Vokarum and persuade him to part with the Noswraith head he collected as a trophy some years ago. A wild, foolish, ridiculous plan. But it had served its purpose. It had forced the Prince to assert his Obligation over me. Which in turn reverted the power of Obligation back to my hands. And tomorrow, on my day off . . . I may do as I will, go where I choose. He cannot hold me; the laws of Obligation prevent him.

Meanwhile I may oblige him to do whatever I wish.

But what do I wish? What will I choose come tomorrow morning? Will I go home and visit my brother? It's been so long since I last set eyes on him. Who knows what terrible mess he's gotten himself into without me there to protect him. Surely that would be the right thing to do.

Or will I . . . dare I . . . ?

Shaking my head, I focus on the pile of work stacked before me. At least twelve battered spellbooks in need of resealing, their bindings on the verge of disintegration. All minor Noswraiths— I'm still not considered advanced enough in my training to tackle the more complex bindings. I pinch my lips between my teeth and reach for the top book on the stack. It's one I recognize at once: *Dulmier Fen.*

My heart skips a beat.

This was the first Noswraith I encountered following my arrival in Vespre. The Prince set me the task of copying the spell afresh in the very book I now hold in my hands. It's not a powerful wraith, yet it caught me, drew me into its spell. Nearly killed me.

Since then, I've encountered this particular wraith on one other occasion, when I ventured into the Nightmare Realm after Danny. There I'd walked with the young man at the center of this dark tale—a dead man, a ghost. Still suffering from both his death wounds and the guilt he bore with him into the afterlife.

Gently, I stroke the brittle cover. This spellbook should not have broken down so fast. No doubt my wandering within the spell had aggravated its collapse. It serves me right that I must copy it again now.

I pull out a freshly stitched grimoire with smooth blank pages, set my inkwell within easy reach, and trim the nib of my quill. All the while, my gaze flits back to the spellbook. In my mind's eye, I see again the image of that sad ghost boy. He'd craved nothing more than a kiss—a kiss from the true love he'd left behind when he marched off to war. The girl he would never see again.

But of course he and all the sad ghosts haunting that gloomy fen were nothing more than a story. Figments born from the imagination of some writer who lived and breathed in my own world. It is the author himself who truly lives on in the spirit of his creation. Who was he, I wonder? What pain could have driven him to write this tale? Did he experience war and the loss of his comrades? Did he carry the guilt of their deaths when he himself survived?

I open the compromised spellbook to the first page and begin to copy. One word at a time, as I've been trained to do. Careful not to let myself be drawn into the spell as I was the first time. But as the characters slowly flow from my pen, and the magic of the binding strengthens, my mind begins to wander. The world around me fades: my desk, my inkwell, my books. A hazy image of thick fog creeps in around the edges of my awareness.

Then I am no longer seated at my desk. Instead I'm ankle-deep in the black mire of a swamp, peering out through the eyes of a young captain. But this is not right, this is not safe. This is letting myself be drawn in by the spell. I know better.

With a wrench of will, I step back, step out of that perspective. I hold onto myself as I did the last time I entered this Nightmare, floating on the edge of the swamp, a little above the scene taking place below. Observing the world, but not part of it.

Below me the young soldier marches along with his ghostly crew. Sometimes they appear as men of flesh and blood, pale and haggard, but whole. Sometimes they are phantoms, flitting in and out of sight. Worst of all are those moments when their gory death wounds can be seen. One man's head is half blown away;

another is burned across most of his body. A gory gash gapes from the abdomen of my young captain, who struggles to push his own entrails back into place as he staggers on and on and on through the endless swamp.

One by one, the phantoms fade away, until my captain is alone. Still marching straight ahead. Aiming for a destination he will never reach.

What is his name? He never said. Perhaps he has no name. Perhaps was left nameless so as to better serve as an avatar for the author himself. I want to call out to him, to let him know I've returned. I want to tell him I've not forgotten him or the kiss we shared or the way he saved my life. I want to . . . I need to . . .

Hard fingers latch onto my shoulder.

The next moment, I'm yanked so hard, my chair tips onto its back legs. Ink splatters across the page on which I'd been working. I drop my pen and grab the edge of the desk to keep from going over entirely. All the air seems to have been knocked from my lungs.

"What are you doing?" the Prince's voice grows.

I gasp, wrenching my head around and gaping up at him. My mouth opens, closes, but no words will come. His eyes are dark, his pupils dilated so that the purple irises are scarcely visible. "Did you let yourself be drawn in on purpose?"

I want to deny it. But in the end, I can only whisper: "Yes."

He stares at me like I've suddenly grown horns or broken out in ugly purple spots. Finally, he curses followed by a disbelieving, *"Why?"*

"I wasn't in any danger."

"Not in any danger?" The Prince looks as though he wants to wring my neck. "This is a Noswraith! You are *always* in danger when dealing with Noswraiths. The moment you think you're not is the moment it's most likely to devour you."

I can't bear the look in his eyes. I turn away, stare down at the spell—both the breaking spell of the old book and the new one, half-copied in my hand. Touching the page gently, I shake my head. "He saved my life."

"What?"

The word is like a slap to the back of my head. I almost yelp at the pain of it. Instead I grit my teeth, turn in my chair, and face the Prince once more. "He saved my life. When I entered the Nightmare to rescue Danny, it was this wraith who helped us in the end. He could have let me die. The fen had me in its clutches, but he . . . it . . . they . . ."

"You're mad." The Prince stretches out one long arm, snaps both books shut before tucking them under his arm. "You're mad if you think there is anything to be found in any of these books resembling mercy. If you escaped the wraith, it wasn't because it *helped* you. It was luck. Or a blessing of the gods. Or just your own damned foolishness, too stubborn to give in."

My jaw hardens, teeth grinding. "You weren't there."

"I didn't have to be. I know Noswraiths better than any man living. They are the worst parts of their creators' souls, trapped in living form. They are without hearts, without mercy, without a shred of human feeling."

"Maybe, but . . . but . . ." I drop my gaze again, staring at the books he holds. "But their creators weren't heartless."

The Prince does not speak. A long, terrible silence stretches between us.

I swallow and continue, my words low and hard: "You said it yourself. You said my father could never have created a Noswraith, because a Noswraith can only be born from love. Bent, broken, battered, twisted into something dark and terrible. But love, nonetheless." I lift my lashes. "*We* are not heartless. We spell-makers. Perhaps we are not even beyond redemption. So is it not possible for our creations to be redeemed as well?"

For the first time that I've known him, the Prince is dumbstruck. He searches my face, looking for I know not what. At long last, he swallows hard and blinks, eyes softening somewhat. "I believe," he says slowly, "that you can rise above your creation. I believe you can be more, *are* more. But only if you combat it." He takes a step closer, bending his head so that I cannot help but meet his gaze. "I see the shadow in you. Everywhere you go, it is there with you, shrouding your soul. Tell me, Darling, and tell me truly—are you being haunted?"

I open my mouth. Close it again. Then I shake my head.

Doubt flickers in his eye. "Beware. Noswraiths are seductive. I've seen it happen time and again. I've watched creators forget the truth of the monstrosities they've created. They begin to let it in, draw it close, and then . . ." He pauses, his lips thinning momentarily. "Vervain is neither the first nor the last librarian to fall prey to her own shadow-self."

An image flashes through my mind—an image of Vervain, a former librarian of Vespre, now ensconced in a tower cell on the other side of the palace. Alone. Broken and living out a half-life existence. All the Prince's efforts to bring her mind back to sanity have failed. And the last time I visited her . . .

I draw back a step, bumping into the edge of my desk and gripping it tight with both hands. "I am not Vervain. I know what I'm doing. You don't need to worry about me."

His brow creases, some of his anger giving way to another emotion. Concern, perhaps. Or possibly sorrow. "So long as you serve in Vespre Library," he says, "you must abide by library rules. Which means no more little pleasure jaunts into the Nightmare Realm. Do I make myself clear?"

I want to protest. I want to point out that nothing Dulmier Fen has to offer compares to the nightmares I faced and vanquished these last several months. I want to argue that I'm strong enough, smart enough, clever enough, powerful enough . . . but even in my head, the words sound like pure hubris.

Instead I bite my tongue and nod.

"We can't lose you, Darling," the Prince continues. He reaches out to me, his fingers hovering in the air just above my hand as I grip the desk's edge. "I . . . I can't . . ." He stops, drops his chin, then tries again. "The library needs you well and whole.

We're understaffed as it is. The *gubdagogs* may help, but they are neither an immediate nor a final solution. So no more of this recklessness. Do I make myself clear?"

I swallow back the painful lump in my throat. "I will serve faithfully. I will fulfill my Obligation."

He nods. Turns to go, the two spellbooks still tucked under his arm. I watch him retreat, study the back of his head, the set of his shoulders.

Then a whisper hisses through my lips: "*Until tomorrow.*"

I shiver, a chill running down my spine. That voice . . . it didn't sound like mine.

Something tickles against my cheek. Like delicate threads, dangling from my eyelids. I reach up to brush them away, but there's nothing there.

With a bitter curse I turn back to my desk and the pile of work awaiting me.

"AND *UMOG* SAY I GIVE HER PAIN IN THE *RUK!* SHE say no one give her such pain in the *ruk* as me!"

Sis makes this declaration with all the bold triumph of a conqueror, brandishing her stone table knife and the cut of stewed meat skewered on its end. Seated across from her at our little family table, I shoot a glance to Lir. "*Head,* Mistress," she murmurs as she serves stew from a pot into my bowl. "Umog Grush claims the child's endless prattle gives her a headache."

"Ah!" I take a bite, chewing thoughtfully as Sis continues her account of her day in the low temple. Apparently, it was quite successful. Gone is the child's timidity of this morning. She's back to her usual, vivacious, exhausting little self, eager to tell me all she's learned. I don't understand half of what she says, but this doesn't stop her.

Amid Sis's ceaseless stream of talk, Har, Dig, and Calx are equally determined to fill me in on the events of their day. Meanwhile, I struggle to catch Lir's eye. My pretty maid is hard to read, her lovely features fixed as stone. I dare not guess how her meeting with the priestess went. Finally, as she wafts past on her way to firmly wipe Calx's gravy-stained mouth, I catch her by the wrist, draw her to me, and whisper, "What happened between you and the *umog?* Did you . . . Did she . . . ?"

Lir's gaze flits away from mine. When she looks at me again, however, there's a tentative smile pulling at her lips. "She did not send me away."

Well, that's something, I suppose. If Umog Grush had failed to see any hope for Lir, she would not have hesitated to say so. "And will you be training along with Sis?" I persist.

Lir shrugs. "I sat by and observed. When I took some thread, she did not stop me from copying the knots she demonstrated."

Warmth glows in my chest. It's a victory. I'm sure of it. Perhaps not a final victory—the priestess might very well change her mind and send Lir packing tomorrow or the next day. But in the moment at least I can't help hoping.

I'm too excited to eat more than a few mouthfuls. Instead I listen to my children as they try to outdo each other competing for my attention. When dinner is through, and they're all bathed and tucked into bed, I kiss one smooth forehead and three craggy ones, taking a moment to tell them each how proud I am of them. Sis clings to my neck a little longer than her brothers.

But she has a satisfied look on her face when she snuggles down into her pillows.

On my way out, I pause in the doorway and look back into their snug little room. A strange feeling quivers in my chest—hope and worry and happiness all in one. And foreboding. A sense that I should hold onto this moment, hold onto this sight of the four of them.

Sis pulls back a corner of her blanket, one eye blinking up at me. "Shut door, *Mar!*" she says in her imperious little voice. "Too much *hirala!*"

She means the glow from the moonfire lanterns in the passage is too bright. I nod, shoot her a hasty smile. "Good night," I murmur one last time. A chorus of sleepy grunts is all the answer I receive before I step back into the hall and pull the door shut behind me. Still I linger, my hand resting on the doorknob. It takes a wrench of willpower to turn, step across the hall, and enter my own room.

Lir is busy laying out my nightgown and turning back the bedclothes. I don't speak to her, sensing she's overwrought by the doings of the day. Instead, I take a seat at my vanity and begin to pluck pins from my hair. Lir finishes her tasks then stops in the middle of the room, hands folded neatly, to ask, "Will there be anything else, Mistress?"

"No. Thank you." She turns to go, but I spin on my stool and call after her, "Lir!" She looks back over her shoulder. Once more that strange foreboding tingles in my blood. I lick my dry lips then speak all in a rush: "You are brave and strong. Whatever happens, I know you will do great things."

Lir blinks. There's a sparkle in her eyes, like tears. She ducks her head, flushing prettily, her pale skin suffused in a delicate lavender glow. "Thank you, Mistress," she says, before ducking from the room.

Sudden silence surrounds me. After the din of dinner and bedtime, the atmosphere is cold and empty. I face my reflection in the vanity mirror once more. Now that I'm alone, the question looms large in my mind: *What will I do tomorrow?*

I rise, my hair still half-pinned up, and busy myself with changing into my nightgown, hanging up my dress, shaking out my petticoats and other little arrangements. When these are through, I return to the vanity and, without looking in the mirror, yank out the last of the pins and set to work brushing my hair. Stroke, stroke, stroke. A hundred strokes—that's what my mother taught me. Every night. It's a habit I've striven to maintain over the years, wherever life has led me. Stroke, stroke, stroke. The rhythm soothes me, lulls me into a stupor.

I will not think about tomorrow.

I will not think about what I must do.

I will not wonder what will become of my children if . . . if I never . . . if something were to happen . . .

Why do you think only of them? They are not your blood.

My heart stops. Slowly, slowly, I lower my brush to my lap. My eyes, staring into the mirror glass, flick to the darkest corner of the room reflected behind me. There's nothing there. Only shadow.

And yet the voice in my mind whispers: *Why do you forget the one who truly needs you? They have friends now. They have others who will care for them.*

He has no one.

No safe place.

No help.

No hope.

No one.

Just you.

A tickle of ice-cold breath on the back of my neck.

You're not seeing rightly.

My gaze snaps back to my reflection, staring into my own wide eyes. Something moves behind me. I dare not look at it directly, dare not see again that phantom figure in white, her long hair falling over her face like a veil. But she's there. Standing in that space of reality between the Nightmare and the waking world.

I drag a rough breath into my lungs, inhaling the scent of wisteria—my mother's perfume, sickly sweet in my nostrils. Rotten somehow. Her hands rest on my shoulders like lead weights.

Then that voice. Gentle, warm, and calming: *There, child. Let me help you.*

I close my eyes. There's a tug against my grip on the hairbrush. I resist before letting go. The next moment, the brush is running through my hair in long, slow, deliberate strokes.

You are becoming distracted, my love. You are letting your purpose be swayed.

I shake my head.

Hold still, now. Hold still and listen.

You know I want only what is best. For you. For your brother. I love you both more than anyone save your own dear father.

The brush continues to pull through my locks, the tines catching and disentangling any snarls. My scalp tingles.

But you must care for your brother, Clara. You are the eldest. And you are strong. He is such a delicate boy. But so very gifted! Just like his father.

Stroke, stroke, stroke.

It is our duty to protect such gifts. To nurture them, to shield them from the ill winds of this or any world.

Stroke, stroke, stroke.

Such beautiful minds need care. Like flowers in a garden.

You and I—we're not like them. We don't know what they endure, gifted as they are. We don't know how they struggle.

It's hard for them—the burden of genius.

But that is why we care for them. It is our great calling. Our noble responsibility.

You are just like me, Clara. You are strong enough to bear the pain. You are strong enough to weather the storm. Because you know the cause is right. A holy calling. The calling of wifehood. Of sisterhood. Of womanhood.

Stroke, stroke, stroke.

Remember, no one else can do what we do. Which means, no one else can understand. They cannot see as we see. And they will try to sway you, my love. They will try to convince you, saying their ways are better, their plans for you are right.

But you know.

In your heart you know.

You know how he loves you.

You know how you love him.

You only have each other. Just the two of you. Against all odds.

And you are the strong one. You are the one who must protect him.

Guard him. Guide him. Shield him.

Love him.

Love him.

Save him.

Save him.

I don't know when the rhythm of that voice and the rhythm of the brush became one and the same. I only know the voice is no longer in my ear, but in my head, and the brush is once more held in my own hand while I run it through my hair. The presence at my back, which had felt so real mere moments ago, is gone. I am alone in the room once more.

I continue brushing. Stroke, stroke, stroke. Even as the words echo in my mind:

Love him.

Love him.

Save him.

Save him.

I open my eyes. Stare into the glass.

But the face in the mirror has no eyes. Only blood streaking her cheeks, and black threads crisscrossed to sew shut the empty, bleeding sockets.

9

THE PALACE BELLS TOLL FOUR DOLOROUS STROKES when I wake the following morning.

It isn't really morning, of course. There's never any morning in this realm of perpetual twilight. The hours are marked by bells, and I cling to my human understanding of a twenty-four-hour cycle. Even now, when I peel my eyelids open and glance across the room to the cracked curtains, I half-expect to see some gleam of dawnlight peeking through. But it's all purple gloom and shadows. Just as it was last night.

I groan and press the heels of my hands against my eyes. They ache and sting all at once. But it's just because I've awakened so early. Surely. Sitting up, I push back my coverlet and climb from bed. It's an hour earlier than I usually rise, but why should I lie around? There is much to be done. So I rise. Dress. Pin up my hair. Pack a blank book and my magicked quill in my satchel. It all takes but a few short minutes, and then I stand before my mirror once more, gazing at my pale face by the light of a moonfire candle. My eyes are wide and ringed in purple hollows following my restless sleep. Slowly, I reach up. Touch one eyelid.

For an instant, I could swear I feel fibrous thread and criss-crossed stitching—

I pull my hand away, shake my head, and square my shoulders. Enough of this! I know what I must do. No more hesitation. No more dilly-dallying. The time has come to act. Turning on heel, I march across the room and step into the hall. There I must force myself not to linger, not to turn toward my children's door. They're still asleep. I shouldn't wake them. Besides, I will be back. Before the end of the day, surely! I'll be home in plenty of time to hear all about Sis's second round of lessons with the low priestess, for the boys to regale me with tales of their adventures as underling guards-in-training. I'll feed them, wash them, tuck them into their beds as usual. Nothing will change.

I just have to do this one thing first.

The palace feels gloomier and more cavernous than ever at this hour. Here and there I spy the flickering shadows of guardsmen on patrol. Other than that, all is still. Not peaceful, simply still. Now and then my pricking ears try to trick me into believing I hear bare footsteps following at my heels, but that's nothing more than my own grogginess playing with my mind.

I reach a certain stone door so cleverly hidden within the wall

I would have walked right by it had I not already known it was there. For a moment I stand still, forcing my lungs to draw several long breaths. Then, pulling my head a little higher, I knock.

Silence. Long, uninterrupted silence.

I continue to wait. And I don't knock again. He heard me. I know he did. Finally, a crack appears in the wall. The next moment, the door swings silently open.

My eyes widen.

I should be used to this by now. It's not as though this is the first time I've knocked at the Prince's door expecting a servant to answer only to be met with the vision of the Prince himself. Shirtless. Disheveled. Like he's just tumbled out of bed. And yet somehow more devastatingly handsome than ever. I try not to see it, try not to note the way the glow from the hall sconces highlights the chiseled muscles of his torso. Or the way his trousers, partially unfastened, hang low on his hips, revealing the seductive lines of his hipbones.

My mouth goes dry. Curse him! He's doing this on purpose. I'd be willing to bet in the time between when I knocked and the door opened, he purposefully disarrayed himself to this exact degree of careless allure, designed to get a rise out of me.

"Good morning, Darling," he purrs. Raising one arm, he leans his elbow against the doorframe. His wrist hangs loose, long tapered fingers relaxed. "Have you had a good look? Or would you like me to turn around so that you may complete your inspection?"

I jump back a hasty step. Gods spare me, how long have I stood here, gaping at him in dumbstruck silence? Clearing my throat, I harden my brow and cross my arms. "Why aren't you ready?"

He raises an eyebrow. "I suppose that depends on what you expect me to be ready for." His full lips quirk in a dangerous smile. "One might argue I'm ready for any number of things."

Heat roars up my cheeks. I can only hope it's not too obvious by moonfire light. "Don't play the fool. I expect you knew I would be coming."

At this, his smile melts away. "Perhaps I'd hoped you'd think better of it." His voice is low. Almost sad. "Are you really so determined? So set on this course of madness?"

I cannot hold his gaze. So I drop my eyes, only to now find myself staring at his hard, bare chest. That doesn't help, so I drop it further to my own feet, peeking out from beneath the hem of my skirt. "It is my free day." I sound much more petulant than I like, like a stubborn child intent upon naughtiness. I'm too committed now to stop, however. "I may choose where I go, what I do."

"Then visit your brother. Visit that gods-damned doctor sweetheart of yours. Go make their lives a little better with your smile and your listening ear, then leave them to the hells they've made for themselves."

A muscle in my jaw tightens. Deep inside my head, a soft voice whispers urgently: *You're not seeing rightly. You're not seeing rightly.*

"I know you, Darling." The Prince's voice once more. The sound of it draws my head back. My eyes lock with his. "I *know* you," he insists. All that insouciant charm is gone. The mask of his smile is melted away, leaving behind an expression of earnest entreaty. "You can choose better. You can be better. You are strong."

You are the strong one.

"Be strong for those who need you. Be strong for yourself."

You are the one who must protect him.

You are the one who must save him.

You are the only one who can.

Love him.

Love him.

Save him—

"Enough!" The word bursts from my lips in a cry, echoing against the stone walls. I press my hands to my ears as though I can squeeze that voice and all other voices out of my head. Then, pulling myself straight once more, I face the Prince. "You will help me."

A veil of ice falls across his features. Even his eyes seem to dim.

I swallow hard, forcing down the lump in my throat. Then, dropping my gaze to the ground once more: "I *oblige* you to help me. To accompany me to the seat of Lord Vokarum. To help me to fulfill my part of whatever bargain I must make. To see this through to the end, until the bloodgem necklace of Idreloth is in my hand, and I can set Danny free." My eyelids feel like heavy weights. With an effort I raise them, force myself to meet the Prince's stare. "I call upon your Obligation, Prince of Vespre."

Darkness gathers across his brow. Even the violet of his eyes seems to have deepened to black. His lips curl into what at first looks like a snarl. Just at the last, however, he grins mirthlessly and offers a little bow. "At your command, Mistress," he says with a flourish of one hand. Then he turns abruptly and steps back into his room.

"Where are you going?"

His voice emerges from the depths of the chamber: "I thought I would dress for our little adventure." He appears in the doorway again, leaning out. A lock of raven hair falls across his shoulder. "But if my mistress commands I go traipsing off into the unknown with her half-naked, then—"

"No." I wrap my arms around my middle and put my back firmly to him. "Please. Dress. But be swift about it."

"Your wish is my command."

10

THE CARRIAGE RIDE OUT FROM VESPRE IS A SILENT affair. The Prince wraps himself in his long coat, turns up the collar, and pretends to sleep. His pronounced snores aren't terribly convincing. Is he mocking me? Intentionally trying to annoy me out of my determination?

I'm not so easily swayed.

Ignoring him, I turn my attention out the window and watch the approaching horizon of Noxaur. A shudder runs through me, body and soul. The last time I set foot on that shore, I nearly died a dozen times—by fire, water, tooth, and claw. The only reason I'm alive today is because I dared do the unthinkable. I summoned Emma. My Noswraith. My secret weapon and my great sin.

How much blood did I spill that night? With one simple act, one flick of the pen, how many lives did I bring to a gruesome end? The men and women who died were monsters bent on tearing me apart. Nevertheless, the weight of their stolen lives threatens to crush me.

Not their lives alone either. There's also Nelle. And Dasyra.

I steal a glimpse at the Prince again, his face covered by his hood, his legs crossed, his feet propped on the carriage seat beside me. Somehow, I know he's watching me. Or at least, *aware* of me. It's that same prickling sense I've had so many times in the last month. But it's probably just my imagination.

Suddenly exhausted, I settle back in the carriage seat, rest my head in my palm, and let my eyes shut. Perhaps I nod off, for it seems like no more than a moment later when the carriage jostles, touching down on the pier. I start and grab the edge of my seat for support. The Prince, however, merely lets out a snort and otherwise doesn't stir, not even when the coachmen bellows, "Ho!" and the morleth lurch to a stop.

A troll footman climbs down from the back of the carriage. His shifting weight causes the whole contraption to groan on its springs. He comes around and opens the door, offering a block-like hand to assist me out. I bite my lip. Then, leaning forward, I grip the Prince's shoulder and give it a shake. He opens one eye, blinking blearily. Maybe he truly was asleep after all. For a moment, he looks remarkably young. Vulnerable. It's so unexpected, my heart gives a strange twist at the sight.

I quickly withdraw my hand. "We're here."

He curses and unfolds himself from his cloak. In an instant, all that vulnerability vanishes from his face. Grunting and shaking his bleary head, he swings an arm to indicate the door. "After you." His tone is not terribly gracious.

Gathering my dignity and the folds of my skirt, I climb out from the carriage, grateful for the footman's hand. It's gloomier here than I remember from previous visits. A fine mist obscures all but the nearest lanterns lining the long pier. I can scarcely discern the rocky shore at all. I shiver, pulling my cloak a little closer. Vivid memory of the first time I stood here, on this very pier, before this very carriage, creeps over me. How frightened I'd been then, on my way to the unknown and terrifying Doomed City. Now I'd give just about anything to climb back into that carriage and order the driver to carry me back across the water, back to the familiarity of the haunted library and the streets full of antagonistic zealot trolls. Vespre is where my children are. Vespre is where Lir is, and Mixael, and Khas, and . . . and . . .

I huff out a little breath. It curls in the air before my lips. Time to pull myself together. The Prince climbs down from the carriage behind me. I don't give him so much as a look. Instead, I turn to the driver. "Please, await our return. I don't expect to be long."

The driver's craggy brow puckers under his incongruous top hat. He casts the Prince a glance. The Prince shrugs and says only, "Do as the lady bids." His voice seems to ripple down the back of my neck.

Shivering, still refusing to look his way, I hasten down the pier. Mist parts before me, almost too eagerly. Like the whole of

Noxaur is ready to draw me in before swallowing me whole. But I hear the Prince's footsteps *thunk* against the wooden planks at my back and take heart. His Obligation will keep him near. I needn't face this peril alone.

I reach the end of the pier and step down among the rocks along the shore. The ground is so uneven, and the mist makes it more difficult to navigate than usual. Watching eyes peer out at me from crevices and hidey-holes, but any time I turn to look directly, they're gone. If I didn't know any better, I'd think the beach was deserted. But I've lived in Eledria long enough to know that wherever you go, whatever you do, danger—whether or great or small—always lurks just around the next corner.

I take a step onto what I think is a rock. It lurches abruptly underfoot. A yelp bursts from my lips, and I stagger, stumble . . . only to land with my back against a broad chest. Strong hands close around my upper arms. My nostrils fill with a heady perfume, that mix of leather and ink and exotic spices I know so well.

"Careful, Darling," the Prince murmurs in my ear. "Best not to step on a *cratumal*. They'll bite your ankles."

I watch wide-eyed as webbed feet stick out from under a craggy domed shell. The creature is as big as a giant tortoise but with long, strangely humanoid limbs and a head full of shaggy hair. It turns slowly, slowly. Hair parts to reveal a positively ancient face. At first glance, one might think it's a very old man. A second glance, however, and it's impossible to look past that massive, rock-hard jaw. If it did indeed catch one of my ankles, it would snap my foot right off.

The creature blinks, it's old eyes dull, disinterested. Then, still with painful slowness, it turns away and ponderously moves off through the rocks. Soon mist closes around it, concealing it from view. And I remain where I am, pressed against the Prince's chest. His cloak is partially wrapped around me, and it's nice here, in the circle of his arms. Warm and safe and secure.

I grit my teeth and push away. Without a word or a look back at him, I continue across the beach, avoiding the larger rocks, stumbling on ragged stones. I'm cold but . . . but I shake that feeling away and concentrate on climbing to higher ground above the beach. When I finally achieve the top of the sand bank, a night-bound landscape beneath a starry, moonless sky spreads before me.

The Prince steps onto the rise beside me, standing with his hands clasped at the small of his back. He's silent at first. Then: "Now what?"

I wet my cold, chapped lips. "Do you know the way to Lord Vokarum's house?"

Another silence. He's fighting the Obligation, trying not to answer. But he must help me see this quest through to the end. Which means he cannot refuse to answer a pertinent question. Finally, he grunts in grudging affirmation.

I grip the strap of my satchel. "Lead on then."

He flashes me a look. For a moment I fear he will try to talk me out of it. To my intense relief, however, he simply sets out into the forbidding landscape, tossing over his shoulder as he goes, "Stay away from the *virrora* trees. They'll eat you alive if you let them get close."

I glance warily at the dark trees dotting the countryside at intervals. Their twisted branches and enormous, waxy-looking leaves give off a faintly menacing air. I shudder and stick close to the Prince's heels as he leads me under the star-strewn sky. Somehow, by some fae magic or sorcery, he finds a road that was invisible before. A road I'd certainly not seen the last time I ventured this way. The starlight is brighter now. Or perhaps my eyes have simply adjusted. There isn't much to be seen in any case. Just the road leading across the open land. Occasionally, a small scurrying form shuffles across our path. Otherwise, we might be the only two living souls in this whole dark, lonely world.

I'm not sure how many miles we cover before I become aware of the shadow-figures. One moment I think we're alone; the next, we're surrounded. I turn this way and that, never quite able to catch a full sight. A glimpse of horns, a glance of ugly masks. A gleam of weapons. They march in silent formation on either flank, just on the edge of my peripheral vision.

The Wild Hunt has come for us.

My heartrate quickens. I pick up my pace, hurrying to match the Prince's long stride. "Do you see—"

"Yes."

"How long have they been there?"

"Since the beach." He looks down at me. "Why? Have you had

enough of this little adventure already?"

I shoot him a quick glare. Then, swallowing hard, I quicken my pace, progressing a few strides ahead of him. Movement lunges at my left. Immediately, the Prince springs forward, wraps an arm around me, and pulls me to him. "Don't be foolish, Darling," he growls close to my ear. "Stay close. These people have not forgotten what you brought to their shore a month ago. They will kill you in a heartbeat if they see an opening."

My blood thrills in my veins. I feel the perilousness of our position, yes. But suddenly, I am also aware of the Prince's power in a way I had not before noticed. His very presence is enough to keep at bay these terrible fae. For the time being at least.

"Very well, Prince," I say stiffly and shrug his arm off. "I understand. Now, if you will be so good as to restrain from manhandling me."

A bitter chuckle rumbles in his throat. We continue, keeping pace with one another. The deeper we progress into the Realm of Night, the more the hunters come out from the shadows. Soon they walk openly on either side of us, their eyes gleaming through the holes of their hideous masks, a grim escort. What would they do if we changed our minds and turned back? Something tells me I don't want to try it.

We come at last to the lip of a deep, craggy valley full of black forest. Five tall towers emerge from the center of this forest, all twisted and black, like claws trying to tear free from the soil. The impression is so strong, I blink several times before I realize that

I'm looking on the turrets of a castle.

"Skullkreg." The Prince stops to take in the view. "A charming spot, perfect getaway if you're inclined for a little blood-letting, skull-crushing, and skin-flaying now and again." He tips his head and flashes me a droll smile. "Shall we knock and see if the family's home for tea?"

All around us, the masked Wild Hunt shifts eagerly. Waiting for us to turn back, waiting for us to make a break for it. "Yes," I answer, hoping my voice matches his light and breezy tone. "Let's."

The Prince offers his elbow. Fingers trembling, I take it, and he guides me down the path into the valley. All too soon we are under the forest canopy. At least the trees here seem to be ordinary pines, not the predatory *virrora*. They crowd close, however, their branches densely intertwined, blocking the stars from view. The dark is so deep, I can scarcely see my hand before my face.

"Steady on," the Prince says through the side of his mouth. "I won't let you trip."

I have no choice but to trust him. All around us foliage rustles and cracks. It's the Wild Hunt. I know how silently they can move when they wish; we only hear them now because they want us to. They want us to know how near they are. Now and then a finger or the tip of a claw brushes my arm or my cheek. Each time I flinch and press into the Prince's side. "Courage, Darling," he whispers. "Keep your head up."

Despite his words, I find myself reaching for my satchel, tempted almost to the point of breaking to grab my book and quill. To draw upon the power I know is mine—power enough to decimate these foes. Perhaps the Wild Hunt senses the threat, for they retreat suddenly, and the forest goes still.

We pass in silence the rest of the way to the gates of Skullkreg. Great, black, and twisted, as though the metal has been tortured into shape. Worse still, they stand wide open. Ready for us. Eager.

The Prince comes to a halt. "We're expected it would seem."

I nod. It's not a comforting thought. We've come this far, however. Squaring my shoulders but keeping a firm grip on the Prince's arm, I march on. We've scarcely passed under the archway and into the courtyard beyond when the gate clangs shut behind us. I whip my head around, heart pounding. The Wild Hunt is there, just on the far side of the bars. They stare at us through the dark holes of their masks. Hungry demons gazing out from the edge of hell.

I suck in a breath and face forward quickly. If it wasn't too late before, it certainly is now. We are here. In Vokarum's stronghold. I must face the horned lord, come what may.

The front entrance of the castle is carved like a dragon's head, complete with stone fangs and red torches set into two alcove-eyes. An effective display; not one I care to see much closer. Someone stands in the open door, waiting. A woman, clad in a revealing crimson gown. A metal torc set with gemstones graces her slender throat. Above this, her face is pale as a block of ice. Her hair, which might once have been golden, is white and limp, without luster. As we draw near, she gazes at us from eyes which seem to have dulled from blue to lifeless gray.

"Welcome, Librarian of Vespre," she says, without so much as a glance for the Prince. She bows her head, long hair sweeping over her shoulders. "Lord Vokarum bids you join him for dinner."

11

JOIN HIM *FOR* DINNER OR *AS* DINNER?" THE PRINCE takes hold of my elbow as though afraid I'll dart through that door without a second thought. His fingers pinch, but I don't try to wriggle free. "I'd just like to clarify, if it's all the same with you."

The woman turns her shadowed eyes slightly to take him in. She blinks once. Then without a word she whirls in a waft of red fabric and disappears into the keep. We are clearly intended to follow.

"Come on." I pull against the Prince's hold.

"That hungry, are you?" The Prince tuts, allowing himself to be led forward. "If you'll take my advice—not that I expect you would—I'd avoid drinking anything offered within these walls."

I cast him a short glance. "What about the food?"

"Oh, I shouldn't think that'll be an issue."

His tone doesn't inspire confidence. Nevertheless, we follow the crimson-gowned woman and leave the chilly courtyard behind. Stepping through that door feels unsettlingly like slipping down a living throat. I could almost swear a blast of warm air like an exhale wafts through my cloak. But it's probably just my imagination.

All is lit within by red torches. These don't illuminate so much as emphasize the shadows surrounding us. It's stiflingly hot, despite the lofty ceiling supported by tall, twisted pillars. Ahead of us, the lady in red moves with an uncanny, floating gait, her garments billowing gently behind her. Her back is very straight, her head high. Now and then, movement stirs in the darker corners, sudden, half-lunging shapes. To these she motions sharply with one hand, sending whatever they are cowering back. By the time the Prince and I draw near those same shadows are deceptively empty. I take care not to set foot within their reach, regardless.

We follow the woman all the way to the entrance of a grand hall. This is even loftier than the arched passage we just traversed with more of those twisted pillars supporting a ceiling so high it's lost to view. What I can see are the four giant chandeliers which seem to be made entirely from skulls, both animal and . . . *not* animal. I shudder and look away quickly. At the end of the hall, surrounded by brasiers of shimmering coals, stands a chair—not quite a throne, but enough to give the effect—covered in animal hides and antlers. The heads of the animals are still affixed to their pelts, eyes wide, mouths open, tongues lolling.

Upon this ghastly seat lounges Lord Vokarum himself.

I recognize him at once, even without the hideous hunting mask. The bones of his forehead bulge to support the weight of massive antlers, each point red and dripping with blood. Beneath this crown is a face as handsome as it is cruel, all hard lines and sharp angles. He wears nothing save a black cloth slung low from his hips and draped casually across his loins. His muscular legs spread wide, and his bare feet boast talons rather than toenails. His is a deadly form of a beauty, a beauty that will go for the throat without provocation.

The lady in red wafts between the braziers and drops into a deep crouch before her lord, bowing her head so that her white braids sweep the floor. "The Librarian of Vespre," she says, once more ignoring the Prince's presence entirely.

Vokarum doesn't bother to acknowledge her. His gaze is fixed upon me. I've never felt more like a mouse daring to crawl under the cat's nose. I would not be at all surprised if he suddenly sprang from his seat and lunged. Nevertheless, I proceed until I stand no more than five paces from his chair. Directly overhead, one of those hideous skull chandeliers creaks ominously on its chain. I fight the urge to curtsy—no, to throw myself on my face at the feet of this mighty lord. But no, the urge is brought on by the glamour emanating from the horned lord. I grit my teeth, resisting.

Vokarum leans forward, his magic intensifying. In response, I pull my satchel from under my cloak. It's a simple gesture, but when I meet his gaze, the dark lord's eyes glitter beneath that broad browbone. He settles back in his seat, and the glamour dissipates, leaving me a little dizzy but clear-headed. I let out a slow breath. It seems I've won our first little skirmish. But the battle isn't over yet.

"Well, Librarian," Vokarum says at last, drumming long claws on the severed head and pelt of a wild boar which makes up one arm of his hideous throne. "You have a lot of *dakath* showing your face here."

I don't need to know the word to hear the foulness in his tone. Any response I offer will sound defensive. So I hold my tongue.

Vokarum's gaze flicks beyond my head for an instant before returning to me. "I see you've brought your pet princeling along. Did you think he would intimidate me?"

Behind me, the Prince snorts. "She doesn't appear to need any help on that score."

At this Vokarum rises from his seat, one hand gripping the hilt of a great, notched sword hung without a scabbard from his belt. "And what's to stop me even now from setting my people on you? They're eager for another hunt. This time, they'll rip you limb from—"

He stops. For while the words tumbled furiously from his mouth, I opened my satchel, snatched out both book and quill, and flipped the cover open. Now I stand with quill poised above the page, staring up into his terrifying face. He remembers; I see it in his eye. He remembers all too well who was ripped limb-from-limb the last time we met. His teeth flash again in a hard grimace under the light of his gruesome chandeliers.

Then, with a sigh, he lets go of his weapon and settles heavily back into his chair. He assumes an easy air, resting on one elbow as he gestures with the opposite hand. "Tell me, Librarian, did my lady wife invite you to dine?"

His wife? If I remember the Prince's story correctly, Vokarum took many women as his brides. Following each wedding night, he subsequently convinced them to kill themselves for love of him. From this dark sorcery, he created the bloodgem necklace which is even now my goal. I steal a glance at the woman in red. She has moved to stand silently in the shadow of Vokarum's seat. Her eyes are downcast, her hands folded in her long sleeves. Somehow, she escaped the fate of the previous wives. Not a mercy, I'd wager.

Vokarum awaits my answer. I nod, once. Satisfied, he barks, "Wife!" and snaps his fingers. The woman in red steps forward, head still inclined. "Is the meal ready?"

"It is, my love," she replies in a voice of stone.

"Excellent." The horned lord rises and motions with one arm in a sweeping, magnanimous gesture. "Come! I bid you join me at my table. There we shall drink and feast and soon become fast friends. No more limb-ripping, agreed?"

He doesn't wait for an answer, but strides across the hall to where a long table covered in a fine white cloth stands before a roaring firepit. I don't like the look of it. I like it still less the nearer we draw. A stink of blood fills my nostrils. The meal, arrayed across many platters, looks to be made up entirely of great hunks of uncooked meat sitting in pools of blood.

Three tall men wait on the far side of the table, standing beside their chairs. The first one is handsome and golden and beautiful, the middle one broad and muscular and brutish. The third is ugly as sin, with ragged black hair, a sallow complexion, and a twisted face and body which he's not bothered to disguise with glamours. All three of them fasten their eyes on me with predatory interest.

The woman in red steps to the head of the table, but Vokarum barks a harsh word at her. Immediately she steps aside, moving to a place lower down. Her husband pulls back the head chair and motions for me to take it. "Our honored guest," he says through smiling, bloody teeth.

I stop in my tracks. Cold thrills in my veins. The Prince, however, steps in close behind me, bending his lips to my ear. "Don't falter now, Darling. You're doing well. If you keep on like this, we might even get out of here alive, which is more than can be said for most of Vokarum's guests."

I shudder. Then, still holding both book and quill where Vokarum can see them, I allow the horned lord to push in my seat for me. "These are my sons," he says, indicating the three fae men. "Vaelza, Kosbar, and Golvuth." Each man bows when his name is spoken, then takes a seat. The youngest and most beautiful sits just to my left and gives me an admiring once-over. His father reaches out and hits him up the back of his head. "None of that now, lad!" He growls and turns to me once more. "You met them last month, of course, but were not properly introduced. Their sister, Asresith, is no longer with us." He inclines his head, his breath hot against my cheek. "She met her end during your last visit. We picked her up in pieces."

These words are accompanied by a dark chuckle. Before I can decide whether he's joking, Vokarum takes the seat at my right and proceeds to pour black liquid into the skull-shaped vessel before me. On second glance, I'm not certain if it is skull-shaped or truly a skull. My stomach knots.

The Prince, meanwhile, moves to stand behind the youngest son's chair. He clears his throat, drawing the fae man's gaze to him, then tilts his head and tips one eyebrow meaningfully. The fae begins to clench his fist then seems to think better of it. With one last glance at me, he rises and, without a word, moves down to the far end of the table near the woman in red. The Prince takes the empty seat, pours himself a skull-full of black liquid, and raises it to Vokarum. "To your health," he says, and downs the drink in a single draught. I can almost hear the silent addition of: *May it deteriorate rapidly.*

Another growling chuckle in his throat, Vokarum addresses me once more. "Pray, Librarian, set aside your weapons while we break bread together."

I hold tight to both book and quill, not at all inclined to slip them back into their satchel. Vokarum's eyes flash; for a moment,

I fear he will press the issue. Instead he reaches down the table and carves a great hunk of dripping red meat from the . . . I won't call it a *roast,* for I'm not convinced that slab of carcass saw more than a flicker of flame before it was served onto that silver platter. Vokarum plunks a large serving onto a plate and sets it before me. "Help yourself," he says, all hospitable grace and ease.

The Prince takes a loud sip from his skull cup, catching my eye over the brim. He needn't worry; I wouldn't dare touch a bite.

Vokarum serves up his own plate and begins eating with savage enthusiasm, tearing into the meat with his sharp teeth and spattering blood across the fine white cloth. I try not to speculate as to what that beast was before it found its way onto the horned lord's table. Something—or *someone*—he and his sons hunted, no doubt. Just as they'd hunted me.

"So," Vokarum says at last around a large mouthful, "you've come to claim your prize, have you? We expected you much sooner."

"I was . . ." I stop and swallow several times, for my throat has gone dry. "I was much occupied the last month." I flick a glance at the Prince. He leans back in his seat, swirling his drink idly. No help to be had from that quarter. I forge on, forcing myself to meet Vokarum's hooded gaze. "But I am here now."

"So I see." Vokarum cracks a bone and chews it soundly, grinding it with his back teeth. "And what exactly do you expect as your reward, hmm?"

"What do you mean to offer?"

He narrows his eyes at me. Then, he waves a bloody hand to

the far end of the table where his wife sits, carving neat little bites of her meal with a pair of delicate silver utensils. "You can have that throat-jewelry of hers. It's an heirloom of her house, the Torc of Neremyn. Said to have been blessed by a demi-goddess. My wife claims it protects against dark magic or some such nonsense."

The woman freezes, one bite of meat partway to her mouth. Then she goes on eating just as though she has not heard. "No," I reply hastily, shocked at how casually the horned lord would give away his wife's possessions. "It is a fine piece, I'm sure. But it's not what I'm looking for."

Vokarum grunts and leans back in his chair. He draws a hunting knife from the sheath strapped to his muscular calf and begins to pick his teeth. After a moment's contemplation he casually points the blade at the beautiful young man seated at the far end of the table. "How about him? You can have him for a husband."

The young man sits up straighter and tosses me a seductive smile. Was it me, or did the Prince just growl into his cup? "No," I say at once. "That won't do."

"Him, then?" Vokarum points at his next son, the broad brutish one. He's in the middle of tearing into a hunk of meat, but pauses, droplets of blood caught in his beard, to cast me a disinterested look, eyebrows raised. When I shake my head, Vokarum curses. "Fine then! You drive a hard bargain, Librarian, but have it your way. Take that one instead." He points to his eldest, the ugly, twisted creature. "You won't get a better offer.

He's not much to look at, I'll grant you, but he stands to inherit all this should he ever manage to slay me."

The eldest son turns a stare of such intense hatred my way, it freezes my blood. Red light flickers in the depths of his small, mad eyes. I have no trouble believing he's made any number of attempts on his father's life over the cycles. But he lifts his chin, curls his lip, and speaks in a low, insidious hiss, "If my beloved father so wishes it of me, I will take the Librarian to wife."

I've scarcely opened my mouth to protest before the Prince leans forward and pounds a fist on the table, rattling cutlery. "Stop trying to bargain to your own advantage, Vokarum. She's not going to take one of your gods-blighted sons, thus bringing all that mortal magic she possesses into the keeping of the Skullkreg family. She's here to benefit from her win. So offer her something of value."

"Fine," Vokarum sighs. "I promised a shower of jewels, and that offer is still good. Name your preference. Emeralds? Rubies? Diamonds?"

A momentary flash of temptation passes through me. After all, while these jewels mean nothing to this powerful fae lord, they could buy a lot of comfort back in my own world. They'd set Oscar up for life.

I bite my lip. The truth is, Oscar doesn't need jewels and wealth to throw away in pursuit of his addictions. He needs someone to care for him. To watch over him until I can return and take over the duty. I must not be swayed from my purpose.

Besides, fae gems tend to lose their luster the moment they hit mortal air.

"I want no such cheap trinkets," I declare in a bold voice. "I want a true trophy."

Vokarum's bony brow lowers.

"I beat your game," I continue, choosing my words with care, "by summoning a Noswraith. It seems to me my prize must be worthy of a Noswraith. Do you have anything of that nature?"

The horned lord is silent. He rubs one long finger across his upper lip. "I do," he says at last. "I do indeed possess such a trophy." With that, he rises and steps to a tapestry hung across the nearest wall. It's a magnificent thing, nearly ten feet square, and embroidered in terrible images of monsters and madness. A single sweep of his arm, and the whole thing comes rippling down, landing in a pool of fabric at his feet.

And there, set in an alcove in the wall—fixed in place by a metal spike, blinking as though startled from sleep—is the severed head of Idreloth.

Her skin is a ghastly shade of green, like a corpse long ago drained of life. But the eyes are alight with a yellow glow, full of malice in their depths. They flicker back and forth from behind the long sweep of her dark lashes. Her features are exquisite, or would be, were they not fixed in a terrible death leer. Her hair is long and matted with blood. More blood drips from the gory wound of her neck. Drips and drips, but never spills from the alcove, for she is more dream than reality.

She stares out at us, her gaze somewhat foggy at first. It sharpens, however, as it settles on Vokarum. Her sagging jaw twists into a smile. More blood, thick and black, oozes between her teeth and dribbles down her chin.

"Time to wake, my sweet," Vokarum says, pinching the apparition's cheek. "We have visitors." She twists on her spike, her bloodstained teeth snapping at his fingers, but he's much too fast for her. He turns to me, shaking his massive antlers sadly. "My plan should have worked, you know. I spent nearly a hundred turns of the cycle plotting, planning, and preparing. I sought out the greatest minds of Eledria, captured, tortured, and stole the secrets of any number of mortal mages. I even journeyed into the Desolation of Gorre, seeking aid for the spell I would conjure." He turns a grim look upon his captive. "It should have worked save for one small error on my part."

"Do tell," the Prince says. He reclines easily in his chair, but I can't help noticing the tension simmering from his core. The sight of that monstrosity—one of *his* monstrosities, taken from his own household against his will—must be galling him.

Vokarum heaves a great sigh. "I chose the wrong head." He strokes Idreloth's matted hair, runs a knuckle along the line of her cheek. "I didn't think it would make a difference. But this pretty lady boasts eight heads. I should have made certain I slipped my bloodgem around the prime head, for that one controls all others unless I am much mistaken. Too late did I realize my error."

He takes her chin between his fingers, digging his talons into her putrid flesh. Then, to my horror, he bends down and kisses her. Kisses her right on her bloody lips, a long, slow, lazy sort of kiss. Almost sensual. He does it so casually, one cannot help suspecting he's done it many times before. When he withdraws, Idreloth flutters her eyelashes up at him. But there's murder in her gaze.

My stomach turns over. I'm glad I've eaten and drunk nothing, otherwise I would vomit right there at the table. As it is, I can only stare in horror, wishing I could somehow unsee that dreadful sight. The Prince surreptitiously touches my hand. I start, turn to him. He holds my gaze, his expression unreadable. I feel as though he's a lifeline, the only bit of sanity I can hold onto.

"Ah well," Vokarum sighs at last. "What could have been, eh?" He returns to the table, leaving the tapestry on the floor and Idreloth's head still in open view. He stabs a fresh cut of meat and takes a bite. "You're not the first person to come around asking about my little beauty," he says, speaking around his mouthful. "Your cousin"—with a nod to the Prince—"was here a moon or so back. She'd heard the story of how I won this prize off you and was eager for details."

The Prince, who has maintained a mostly neutral expression all this time, smiles sourly and takes another sip from his skull. Is he surprised? Of course, it makes sense that Estrilde was here. She named the bloodgem as the price for Danny's freedom. Obviously she wants to take it for her own. But why? Does the Prince know or suspect her motives?

These questions don't matter just now, however. Whatever

155

Estrilde's plots or plans, I need only concern myself with Danny. I must rescue my friend, keep my head down, and leave the Lords and Ladies to their machinations.

"It is an impressive trophy, Lord Vokarum," I say, hoping he cannot hear the quaver in my voice. "A worthy prize. Indeed I will accept it as fitting reward for besting your Wild Hunt."

A stunned silence hangs over the table. The horned lord's sons have all frozen mid-bite. Even the lady in red lifts her gaze to stare down the table at me. I could almost swear I heard the chandelier skulls draw breath in shock. Idreloth on her spike swivels her dreadful eyes to study me closely.

Then Vokarum tosses back his antlered head and lets out a resounding bark. The burst of sound startles everyone at the table save perhaps the Prince. He continues to lounge and swirl his drink as casually as ever, even as the three sons grip their carving knives. I make a half-move to brandish my quill, but Vokarum merely waggles the tip of his hunting knife idly in my direction. "Your victory, Librarian, was impressively won. Even so, it was not worth such a prize. I gave a great deal to gain that pretty head. I will not give it up save for something of equal value."

My heart thunders in the cavern of my breast. "Very well, Lord Vokarum." With great purpose, I place my book on the table before me and fold my hands atop it. The horned lord's eyes flash dangerously. I hear his breath catch. "Tell me what you would have in exchange. I will bargain with you."

At this, the Prince sputters into his wine and sets the skull cup down so hard it nearly shatters. I refuse to look at him, holding Vokarum's gaze. "That is my desired prize," I continue, my voice firmer now than when I'd begun, "that you should make a bargain with me and swear to uphold your end when I have accomplished mine."

Vokarum's eyes narrow slowly, his expression a mask of malice. "There is but one bargain I would deem worthy in exchange," he says at last. "And you could never fulfill it."

"Name it."

He leans back in his chair. He's so feral and terrible. Nonetheless, glamour ripples out from him. How many women fell under the spell of his allure? Fell for him, married him, and died willingly for his sake? Like all fae, he is far more dangerous to love than to hate.

"I will bargain for my one true desire," he says. "The sole wish of my heart: a kiss. From the only woman I ever loved." I glance at the wife. But this only sets Vokarum laughing dangerously once more. "Not her!" he cries. "No, the only woman I ever loved was Seraphine of Ulakrana."

I blink. "Ulakrana? But . . . but that's the Realm Under Wave!"

"Aye." Vokarum nods, his eyes sparking with deep fire. "The kingdom of the merfolk. And Seraphine, bless her black heart, is their queen. I courted her, you know," he says, addressing himself to the Prince now, who looks on silently, his face a study. "I set sail on the Hinter Sea, seeking her who was said to be fairest in all Eledria. She lured me with her siren song; I harpooned her, and she retaliated by wrecking my ship. Ah! What a wild and terrifying courtship it was! But in the end, she abandoned me. Left me brokenhearted without so much as a kiss to remember her by." Shaking his head, he turns to me again, pointing one long finger in my face. "Get me that kiss, Librarian, and I will give you Idreloth's head."

My lips are dry, my mouth like a desert. I've heard enough stories about Ulakrana and its deadly inhabitants to know I would prefer never to see it. I feel the Prince's eyes on me, can almost hear his silent urging: *Don't be foolish, Darling. You've taken this far enough. It's time to put this lunacy aside and go home.*

But another pair of eyes watches me as well. Idreloth. In her alcove. On her spike. Her gaze is fixed like a serpent's. I dare a swift glance her way and catch a brief expression of ravenous *hope*. It's gone in a blink, replaced by a blank, horrible, slack-jawed visage of death. But I know what I saw. Idreloth wants to be made whole again.

Which means . . . which means she might be convinced to part with the bloodgem necklace in exchange for that head.

I can do this. I'm sure I can.

"Very well, Lord Vokarum." I rise and hold out my hand. "You shall have your kiss."

The horned lord's heavy brow lifts in surprise. Then he too rises, dwarfing me in size. His massive, clawed hand engulfs my fingers, sealing our agreement. "It's a bargain," he says.

12

THE PRINCE AND I CROSS UNMOLESTED OVER THE
night-bound landscape of Noxaur. I'd thought I would
feel better once we left Skullkreg behind. Instead, I find
the wide openness of the terrain unsettling. There's nowhere to
hide after all if the Wild Hunt were to set upon us suddenly. But
the hunters never show themselves, and by the time I see the
ocean again—and the silhouette of the Between Gate, arched
against the stars—I begin to breathe easier.

The Prince walks beside me, uncharacteristically silent. He's
not spoken a word since I struck my bargain with Vokarum. I cast
him uncertain glances, but he keeps his eyes to the front, never
once looking my way. I cannot read his expression by starlight.
Not that it matters; I can safely assume he's angry. As usual.

We are just nearing the edge of the cliff above the rocky shoreline when he speaks at last. "Well, Darling, it looks as though we'll be back by teatime. Do you fancy egg-and-cress sandwiches? Or perhaps a hearty game pie and a handful of strawberry tarts. My chef isn't terribly adept at such trifles; his great troll-hands weren't made for the forming of delicate pastries. But he's been practicing, bless him."

I blink, startled. "What . . . what are you talking about?"

"Tea, of course," he replies. "You know, that mid-afternoon interlude your kind is so fond of? I find most human habits dubious at best, but the teatime tradition is one for which you have my hearty approval. And, as I was saying, we should be home in time for a soothing cuppa before I must return to my work in the library. You, of course, may spend the rest of your day as you wish."

"We are not returning to Vespre." I shake my head fiercely. "Not yet."

"Of course we are. Where else would we go?"

"To Ulakrana." The words emerge from my throat high and tight. I bite my lip then try again more calmly. "I'm going to fulfill my bargain with Lord Vokarum. I'm going to get Idreloth's head."

The Prince looks down at me. Though his lips curl in an indulgent smile, his eyes spark with something sharper. "Brave words as usual, Darling. But as it is absolutely and without question impossible for you to accomplish your side of the bargain, we may as well call it a day."

I draw back from him, feet slipping in the loose soil at the top of the cliffs. "I'm going to Ulakrana," I repeat. "I will find the merqueen, and—"

"And what? Convince her to kiss an old would-be lover she tried several times to murder and left washed up on some desolate shore an age ago?" The Prince laughs, a dry, mirthless sound. "I don't know what tales you've heard about Seraphine, Darling, but let me assure you: they are none of them exaggerated."

I have heard the stories. One couldn't live in this world long without picking up rumors and whispers about the dreadful siren queen. How she uses her seductive voice to entice men and women alike to hurl themselves from the decks of their ships then tears the beating hearts from their chests and devours them. Or, if the mood takes her, she will claim a man as her lover, by whom she'll birth one of her host of ferocious daughters. The men never survive the mating; their bloated bodies wash up to shore weeks or months later. She's violent, solitary, and more inhuman—so to speak—than the most vicious fae ever to terrorize the courts of Eledria.

"I can tell you now," the Prince says with emphasis, "she will not be giving away any kisses on request."

The sea breeze whips through my hair, stings my lips with salt. I shiver and pull my cloak a little tighter. "Then I will bargain with her."

The Prince crosses his arms. "How many layers deep into bargains do you plan to bury yourself?"

I turn away, cast my gaze out across the ocean. The Hinter Sea, that great expanse of unknowable vastness that both connects and separates the many realms and worlds of Eledria. Mariners must be brave indeed to travel those waves. An unwary sailor might find himself pulled adrift from reality itself, doomed to sail on forever into oblivion.

A shudder runs down my spine. I do not relish the idea of a journey to the Realm Under Wave.

The Prince takes a step toward me. Wind pulls at his coat, billowing it behind him like wings. For a moment, I think he will reach out, take my hand. But he doesn't. He merely looks at me, his eyes hard and all-too knowing. "It's worse than you think. Seraphine has not been seen in the Upper Lands since the signing of the Pledge. She refused to condone a peace agreement with humans, whom she hates above all other beings. In a fit of rage, she retreated to her realm and established barriers which none may breach, not with the greatest magic."

There's something in his voice . . . some hesitation or . . . fear. I study his face, my eyes narrowing. "You know a way. Through the barriers." He blinks. Then abruptly pivots away from me, avoiding my gaze. I take a step nearer, pressing my point. "You know how to reach Ulakrana and the merqueen's court. You know how it can be done."

I'm right. I can see it in the tight line of his jaw, in the tension of his throat muscles. "It doesn't matter," he growls.

"It does!" Excitement and terror grip my heart. I have to keep myself from shouting. "If you know a way, you must tell me."

"It would require far more than you should be willing to give."

"I'll give what I need to. Just tell me."

"You would have to drown."

An icy chill washes over me, like a wave of death itself. I draw back a step, as though the Prince has just threatened to do the deed himself.

He turns to look at me at last, his eyes bright under the stars. "When she left, Seraphine declared the only humans who would enter her city from that day forward would be drowned humans. She has held true to her word ever since." He shakes his head then, his brow creasing with some expression I cannot name. "So you see, Darling? It's hopeless. You must give this up now."

"There's a way." I see the truth in his eyes. He wouldn't look so afraid if it were as impossible as he's trying to make it out to be. "You know a way to drown and not . . . not die."

He turns on heel and strides away from me, making for the nearest path down to the beach. For a moment, I cannot summon my voice. Then I cry out, *"Stop!"*

The force of Obligation ripples out from me and halts him in his tracks. I watch his shoulders stiffen, his hands clench into fists.

"You are obliged to work with me until my quest is complete." With slow, deliberate steps, I cover the space between us until I stand but a few paces behind him. "If you know how I may do this—how I may reach the merqueen—you must tell me."

Slowly, slowly, he turns his head, looking at me over his

shoulder. His violet eyes gleam in the starlight, sharp with dread. "There is a way, but . . ."

"But what?"

"It will involve another bargain."

I swallow. "With someone worse than Vokarum?"

"Infinitely so."

"Who is it?"

The Prince curses and runs his fingers through his hair. He's fighting the compulsion of Obligation, trying to find some way around it. In the end, however, he has no choice but to answer. "It's not a guarantee," he growls, turning to face me once more. "Not by a long shot. But if anyone can give you the means to drown yourself without dying, it's the crones."

"The who?"

"The crones. The Blessed Beldames. The Daughters of Bhorriel. Have you not heard of them?"

"No."

He raises an eyebrow. "Lucky you."

"Who is Bhorriel?" Just the sound of that name fills me with dread. Like an instinct born into my blood, unlearned but always known.

"Depends on who you ask." The Prince's teeth flash in a grimace. "Most would say she's a demon, but there are some— including the crones themselves—who worship her still. They call her the Goddess of Blood and Bargains."

"I've never heard of her."

"Of course not. All written record of Bhorriel was destroyed ages ago. Around that same time, her worshippers were hunted down and . . . let's just say they met bloody ends befitting the goddess they served. No one mourned them. But the crones survived as such creatures so often do. Slipping through cracks between worlds, hiding like rats in the walls. So they continue to practice their ancient arts. Anyone needing an impossible bargain or dark curse—anyone willing to pay the price, that is— goes to the crones for aid. The bloodgem necklace you now seek is their handiwork."

I frown. "I thought the bloodgem was Vokarum's doing."

"His doing, yes. Not his magic. He does not possess the power to construct such a spell, merely the will to activate it. He must have made a terrible bargain with the crones to receive the gem itself, which he then filled with the blood of his dead wives."

"Do all bargains with the crones involve blood?

"Yes."

"Have . . ." I'm not sure I want the answer to my next question. "Have *you* ever bargained with them?"

He hesitates, draws a long breath. Then: "Once."

"Did you regret it?"

A bitter smile. "Not at first."

He's hiding something from me. I can't begin to guess what. Some guilt, some shame. Some secret.

But it's not my business to pry his secrets from his lips. "Is there any other way we might reach the siren queen's palace?" I ask, trying not to hope.

The Prince shakes his head. "It will take powerful magic indeed to drown and not die. Death-defying magic. Such magic cannot be bought or sold without an exchange of blood. You will end up giving more than you wish. It might not seem too bad at first . . . but that's what comes of bartering with the crones."

I turn away from him, look out across the ocean view once more. The waves undulate darkly beneath the glittering stars, but my mind's eye rests upon a different view. A not-too-distant memory: the image of Danny grappling in a pit. My gentle, nurturing, kindhearted friend, forced to such brutality by the will of his cruel mistress. And when I close my eyes, another image takes his place: Oscar. My brother. Wasted and wan. Alone, abandoned. Forgotten by all who once called him friend.

How can I not fight for them? No one else will.

"I understand," I say so quietly I doubt the Prince can hear me.

He is silent for a moment. Then, his voice heavy with resignation, he says, "If you make this bargain, you will regret it."

"When you made your own blood bargain . . . do you believe you made the wrong choice?"

"No." His answer is quick, almost harsh. "I made the only choice."

I nod slowly. "This is the only choice for me. I must do this. And I must bear whatever cost may come." I lift my gaze to his face, seeing all the protests he even now fights to restrain. Setting my chin, I speak with resolve: "Take me to the crones, Prince."

13

T HE BETWEEN GATE ISN'T FAR. IT STANDS ON A promontory above the beach, an arch leading seemingly from nowhere to nowhere. But it has the potential to lead *anywhere*. Or at least anywhere marked on the dial.

Back in Aurelis, guardians stand at each of the many gates surrounding the palace, ready to turn the massive stone dials for travelers. Here, the Prince must turn it himself. I watch with interest as he slowly rolls the heavy stone, curious to know which of the marks around its circumference will indicate the portal to our destination. I recognize the mark for Aurelis itself—a sun climbing up from behind two hills, representing the Court of Dawn. Lunulyr is marked by a moon, Solaris by a blazing sun. Even Ulakrana has a mark of three concentric lines, like ripping waves.

But the mark the Prince turns to now is not so distinct. In fact it looks as though someone took a chisel and merely pounded the stone, leaving a jagged crack. "What is that?" I ask as the dial settles into place with that mark at its peak.

"It denotes the *gorre-satra*," the Prince replies. "Also known as the Desolation of Gorre. It is a realm of Wild Magic, too close to the *quinsatra* for safety. Pure magic seeps through unchecked, permeating the land, the flora, the fauna. Nothing sane dwells there—only monsters. And the crones, of course."

The air under the arch shimmers, the veils between realities thinning in preparation for our crossing. My stomach knots. It's never a pleasant experience, traveling across worlds in the blink of an eye. It's hard enough when I know where I'm going. This is much worse.

The Prince's face is grim as he dusts off his palms and faces the arch. "I'll go first," he says without a glance toward me. "I don't know what to expect on the far side. It's been a while since I set foot in Gorre. Never thought I would again." He stops, his jaw working. He wants to say something more, but ultimately thinks better of it and finishes only with, "Don't dawdle. And when you're through, be prepared to move."

I nod, though he's not looking at me. The next moment, he steps through the arch, looking for all the world as though he's about to stride off the edge of the cliff and plummet into the waves below. Instead, he flickers out of this reality and is gone.

Drawing a long breath, I wait for a count of five. Then follow.

Instantly, I regret it. That horrible sensation of delicate knives cutting away the upper layers of my skin—of my existence—comes over me. My soul cries out in protest. It's worse than ever, for this time I must travel further, deeper, requiring more layers to be sliced away. I would scream, only I have no mouth with which to scream.

Then suddenly I'm rolling, tumbling. My body—I have a body once more—careens uncontrollably, battered from every direction at once. My senses whirl, confused and clouded with pain and fear. When I come to a halt, I lie flat on my back, staring up at a sky twisted and riven with magic. Raw, red, tormented magic.

"Up, Darling!"

I blink. The Prince's face materializes seemingly out of thin air above me. He grabs my hands and hauls me to my feet. I gasp, stumble, nearly fall, and find my nose squashed flat against a broad chest. I lean into him, feel his beating heart and the warmth of his skin beneath my cheek. It steadies me. I would like to stand there a little while, maybe longer, as the rest of my body and awareness readjusts to physical existence.

Instead, the Prince pushes me back to arm's length. "Are you all here?" he demands. "Every limb accounted for?"

I nod. Though, now he's asking, I'm not entirely certain it's true.

Before I have a chance to make certain, the Prince presses me against his side, one strong hand warm at my waist. Then we're staggering forward. He urges me along with both the pressure of his arm and his low, urgent voice, forcing me to keep pace with him. My dazed eyes struggle to make sense of the world around me. I catch flashing glimpses of that tortured sky overhead. The landscape is cast in reddish glare, stark, scarred, and forsaken. Every now and then something green appears, but when I turn for a better look, it fades away like an illusion, replaced by more of this grim, blighted reality.

Worse than the land itself, however, are the creatures. So many of them, creeping, crawling, and slinking on their bellies all around us. They are either unaware of or entirely disinterested in the Prince and me, which is a relief. At first glance they look like the kind of beasts you'd expect to spy while strolling through the countryside: squirrels with bushy tails, rabbits, songbirds, hedgehogs, even a gleaming garden snake. But a second glance swiftly reveals the wrongness. The squirrels are fanged and bulbous monsters with awful, fleshy tails and scabby hides. The rabbits boast huge lantern eyes that glow an eerie green. Everything is twisted and unnatural. My stomach knots with hatred at the sight of them.

"It's the air," the Prince says in answer to a question I've not found the breath to ask. "Anything that lives so close to the *quinsatra* ends up warped sooner or later."

I get the impression the Prince is putting off glamours to deflect attention away from us as we hasten across the diseased landscape. "How long?" I ask when I can finally manage to put words together.

"Not very. Look!"

He points. I peer through the glare and strange, hazy atmosphere and see a house standing on tall stilts. Or not stilts but . . . legs. Giant, scale-covered legs. Even as I watch, one lifts and scratches idly at the other, shifting the house, which balances precariously on a crumbling foundation. For a moment the whole structure looks likely to fall. But the leg settles back down again, and the house remains in place.

I skid to a stop. I know that sight: I had a book of fairy tales growing up, and one of the stories told of a witch who lived in a house on chicken legs. Old Granny Greasespoon or something like that. It was not a favorite tale; Oscar always made me skip over it when I read to him at night.

I'd never in a million years believed I would see it in the flesh.

"Come, Darling," the Prince says, ushering my reluctant feet back into motion. He presses me closer to his side. "You wanted to make this little jaunt, remember?"

I do remember. Vaguely. Though in this moment, I'd like to go back and give that former version of myself a sound slap across the face.

The chicken-leg house stands in what at first glance looks like a kitchen garden. The nearer we come, however, the more unnatural the herbs and plants appear. Some of them drip ooze from their petals. Others stalk and eat their fellow plants, razor-sharp petals like teeth munching noisily. A narrow path leads through the various planters, and the Prince guides us onto it, weaving carefully around the more dangerous-looking shrubs.

Just as we draw near to the house, a clawed hand bursts from the nearest planter and makes a grab for my ankle. The Prince swings me to his other side and grinds the heel of his boot into that hand, which shrivels up and pulls back down into the dirt.

"Charming," the Prince says, and looks down at me with a smile. "Shall we see if the lady of the house is home?"

I want to tell him he's won. I want to beg him to take me home to Vespre. I want to give it all up—the bargains, the bloodgem, all of it.

Instead I nod.

The next moment, he's leading me up the front steps. They sway like the deck of a ship on a stormy sea as the legs on which the house stands shift their weight from one foot to the other. Somehow we make it to the porch, and the Prince knocks a brisk *rat-a-tat-tat* on the sagging door. It swings open to reveal . . . nothing. Not dark, not shadow. Just emptiness.

"After you," the Prince says.

I'd prefer it if he led the way. But that would mean leaving me alone in this terrible world. Not a pleasant prospect.

I grip my satchel strap, pull my head high. "Right," I breathe. And step through the door—

—into a bright, well-lit room, tastefully arranged with old fashioned but respectable furnishings.

The shock of familiarity nearly stops my heart. I'd know this room anywhere: Danny and Kitty Gale's front parlor in their house on Elmythe Lane. I remember when their mother purchased that set of needlepoint chairs positioned near the fire, and when Kitty crocheted the large doily adorning the tea table. That tea set too—I've sipped from those shepherd-and-his-lady patterned cups more times than I can count. It's all exactly as I remember it, down to the smallest detail.

I haven't moved a step when the Prince appears behind me, running into my heels. "Oof. Have a care, Darling," he says, catching hold of my shoulders and just preventing both of us from taking a tumble. Then he too takes a look around the space. His eyebrow quirks. "Quaint."

"How did we come here?" I gasp, finding breath at last.

"Do you know this place?"

"Yes, it's—"

Before I have a chance to finish, the door across the room— the door which I know leads directly down a narrow passage to the kitchen at the back of the house—opens, and an ancient, squat, hunchbacked woman in a lace cap appears carrying a plate of sandwiches. At first glance I cannot tell if she is human or fae. She certainly doesn't look fae, but something about her doesn't feel human either.

She spots us and gives a little start of surprise followed by a sweet smile. Wrinkles around an empty eye socket crinkle. "Welcome, dearies," she says, and waddles into the room, setting her sandwiches down beside the tea set on Kitty's doily. Then she looks around the space, her expression puckered with disdain. "Tacky," she tuts. "That wallpaper—harps, cherubs, *and* songbirds? Pick a theme, why don't you?"

She turns her single eye on the two of us. Her face creases into another smile. It goes on creasing, and the smile goes on growing, until I'm faced with far more teeth than I would have thought could fit into such a small face. Definitely not a human smile. "Well now," she says, "aren't you a pretty pair! Wait, wait . . . my sisters will want to see this too."

She hastens to the mantel where a porcelain matchbox in the shape of a rose sits as it has for as long as I can remember. When she pops the lid, however, her fat, bristling fingers don't find matches, but instead a large, many-faceted crystal which could not possibly have fit into such a container. She puts her back to us, hunches over. A grunt followed by an unsettling *squish* and *pop*.

Then she pivots on heel, facing us once more. The crystal is rammed into her empty socket. "That's better!" she declares. An eyelid appears as though from nowhere to fall across the crystal then up again. Taking me in, the old woman's expression falls. She shakes her head and tuts again. "Disappointing. So much potential, but it holds itself back. And what is that foul thing clinging to its soul?"

She takes a step nearer, shoving her long nose much too close to my face for comfort. The crystal moves in its socket as she inspects me, and my own multiplied reflection gyrates before my eyes, making my head spin. It's a relief when she steps back, her lip curled in disgust. "Miphates magic," she growls. "Written spells, ink and paper and wickedness. Nasty stuff." Then she turns to the Prince. Her thin lips twist into a smirk of satisfaction. "Now that's better! That curse you carry, boy, it's a fine piece of spellwork. One of mine, is it?"

"Beldame." The Prince offers a stiff bow. "Indeed yes, I do believe the curse on my blood was crafted by you. Or one of your sisters."

"My sisters? Pah!" She turns and spits right on Kitty's pretty floral rug. "My sisters could only dream of such craft! I remember when the bargainer came asking about that one—a curse that would target only the human blood in the half-fae victim. An intriguing and difficult bit of working, let me tell you. Mind, I had no idea upon whom my client intended to use it. No hard feelings, I trust?"

"None at all, Beldame," the Prince replies with a gracious inclination of his head.

The old woman looks him over once more, her satisfied smile only growing. "I see it's come quite close to killing you several times now. One more good burst, and you'll be done for." At this, she chuckles gleefully before waddling to the table and taking her place in Kitty's chair. "How do you take your tea, my dears? Let me guess." She flicks her gaze up to the Prince. "Black as sin. And you"—her smile slips into a sneer as she turns to me—"milky with five sugars."

She doesn't wait for our responses but proceeds according to her own wishes. The cup she hands me is filled almost to the brim with milk. An undissolved lump of sugar bobs at the surface like a belly-up fish. I quickly set it aside and murmur a polite refusal when the sandwiches are offered my way. This is the second time I've sat down to a meal without being allowed to eat. I should have stopped for breakfast before setting out this morning.

A flash of movement draws my gaze to the window. For an instant, I could swear it was the roiling sky of the Wild Magic Realm. When I blink, however, the view resolves into the familiar townhouses of Elmythe Lane. A hansom cab goes rolling by, the horse's hooves clopping brightly on the cobbled street.

Shuddering, I turn back to the crone, who slurps her own tea noisily. She wrinkles her nose and glares down into the cup. "Ugh. Humans drink the foulest stuff. Wouldn't you agree, Handsome?" she adds with a terrifying flutter of eyelashes the Prince's way.

He smiles and takes a sip from his own cup.

It's time I took what command I can of the situation. "Beldame," I say in what I hope is a respectful tone, "I have come to bargain."

"Naturally, dear." The old woman sends me another look of extreme dislike. "No one comes calling to enjoy my company now do they?" She sets her cup down so hard, I'm sure the saucer cracked. "Very well, as you are obviously disinclined to exchange civilities, what is it you require?"

"I need a way to travel to Ulakrana and return safely again."

"Ah!" The crone nods, understanding gleaming in her one

good eye. "So you must drown and not die. That is tricky indeed."

My stomach knots. "But it is possible?"

"Of course. Nothing is impossible. Just expensive."

"How expensive are we talking?" the Prince demands.

The crone smiles but continues to look at me. "I will require three drops of your blood. With that, I can keep you alive post-drowning for a time. Whether you survive the journey or the return . . . well, that will be up to you."

I glance at the Prince. He shakes his head. "Three drops is too high a price."

"I'm not bargaining with you, boy."

"You're not bargaining at all. You're thieving." He sets his cup aside and stands. "Well, Darling, it's time to go."

Ignoring him, I lean forward in my chair, meeting the crone's sharp gaze. "What's the catch?"

She blinks innocently. "Whatever do you mean?"

"There's more to it than you're saying. What happens when I give you my blood?"

At this, the crone smiles another of those too-many-teeth smiles. It keeps stretching far beyond the lines of her withered little face. *"Pain,"* she says, crooning the word softly. "You will suffer such *pain*. Not in the bloodletting—that is a mere prick. But later. Three days hence and for three days after. Pain beyond imagining. One day for each drop of blood."

I draw back, heart pounding. At first, I cannot find words. Then: "Will I survive it?"

"Of course. It's not a good bargain otherwise."

"And what do you get out of it? Out of my pain?"

"Why, I will harvest it. That pain is mine for the taking."

"And it will begin three days from now?"

"Yes."

"And last for three days after?"

"Yes."

I could do it. I could finish my quest in time, see Danny freed and sent safely home. Surely this was manageable.

I become aware of the Prince's stare. I cast him a wary glance. His complexion is pale, his expression almost desperate. "Darling, you can't be serious."

But I stand. Fists clenched, I face the crone. "How will you harvest my pain?"

"Through your blood, of course." She tilts her head to one side. "Do you need every gory detail? The secrets of Bhorriel's Daughters spelled out for you in childish terms?" She holds out one gnarled, claw-like hand. "Or will you make the bargain, little human?"

The Prince curses and moves as though to grab me. But he's bargained with the crones himself, has he not? Even he must see the value of their power when necessity drives. Sometimes bold moves are necessary for bold outcomes.

With a quick step forward, I take the crone's hand. Her grip is much stronger than I anticipated, hard enough to crack my bones. I scarcely have time to gasp before she flips my palm over and, with three quick jabs, pierces my thumb, index, and middle fingers with an iron pin. I yelp. Blood wells, and the crone, using a lace-trimmed handkerchief, dabs all three wounds in quick succession, staining the lace with three bright crimson spots.

When she lets go, I hastily clench my fist. But when I dare uncurl my fingers and look, the wounds are already gone. Thumb and both fingers still throb, but not a single drop more spills.

The crone cackles happily to herself as she folds the handkerchief and stuffs it into the front of her bodice. "Very well, child. Let us give you a way to drown without dying. Will you step into my garden with me?"

14

IT'S JARRING TO LEAVE BEHIND THE FAMILIAR COMFORT of Danny and Kitty's parlor for the horror of the Wild Magic Realm. I feel the edges of my sanity threatening to fray and am grateful when the Prince takes hold of my elbow. Without his steadying grasp, I'm not sure I would have made it down the porch steps without toppling.

The crone makes her way into her garden, moving with surprising nimbleness for a woman of her apparent age. Several of the more poisonous-looking plants snap at her, and one bristles and growls at her passing. She doesn't react so far as I can tell. Nevertheless, they seem to retreat into themselves, drawing back into their beds and planters as the Prince and I pass by.

We come to a stagnant pond in the middle of the garden.

Green, pus-like foam covers most of the surface, giving off an awful reek. Undeterred, the crone wades right in up to her waist. I stop short, watching with wide, horrified eyes. She doesn't mean for us to follow, does she? I gag, covering my mouth and nose with my hand. I'm not sure I could brave it.

The crone proceeds to the center of the pond where she reaches down deep, her arm scrabbling about a little. "Ah!" she says at last and gives a mighty tug. There's a moment of resistance; then up comes a large orange flower trailing slimy-looking leaves and a thick stem. Turning back to us, she waves the hideous thing over her head, then wades back to shore. "This is what you need, dearie," she says. Green foam clings to her skirts as she emerges, dropping in awful *blops* on the ground around her. What passes for grass in this world steams and withers away at contact. She holds out the flower to me.

I stare. "What do I do with it, exactly?"

"Oh, it's quite simple." The witch grabs the awful green stem and holds it up to her mouth. "You take this between your teeth. Then these"—she opens the awful petals to reveal two long stamen at the flower's center—"go up your nostrils. It won't stop the water from filling your lungs, but it will keep you alive."

"For how long?"

"Three hours." She smiles that toothy smile of hers. "One hour for each drop of blood."

Will it be enough? Enough to take me to Ulakrana and back again? It will have to be. I reach out and, shuddering, let the witch plop the awful thing in my hand. It feels fleshy and alive, more like a slug than a flower.

The Prince observes all this in silence. I can almost feel his astonishment, like a vibration from his soul. Up until this moment, he didn't truly believe I would go through with it. Suddenly he shakes himself and says harshly, "How much for a second, Beldame?"

"A second what?" she inquires, all blinking innocence.

He waves a hand. "A second one of those."

I turn to him sharply. "You're not coming with me! It's much too dangerous. I'll go alone and—"

"Please, Darling, don't arouse my ire with such painful absurdity." The Prince fixes his gaze on the crone. "How much?"

She gives him a long, slow, contemplative look. Then, to my surprise, she reaches into the front of her bodice and pulls out a second flower. As though she'd expected him to ask and prepared accordingly. This flower is pink rather than orange and somewhat crumpled, but she offers it to him. "No charge, pretty thing. It looks to me as though you've not got long before your own pain will begin in earnest. Then my sisters and I will harvest. Take this as a little pick-me-up. To keep you going until then."

I gape from the crone to the flower to the Prince. I don't understand what's happening. Did he also bargain away future pain in exchange for the curse he purchased? His cheeks are drained of their usual golden color, his expression hard as stone. I cannot read him.

He accepts the flower without a word and tucks it into the inside pocket of his coat. Then, turning to me, he says in his usual careless tone: "Shall we?"

There's a ramshackle gate arch on the other side of the crone's property with a small dial indicating a handful of destinations, including Vespre. The Prince, however, turns the dial to the mark of three concentric waves—the way to Ulakrana.

"Wait!" I gasp and grip his sleeve. "Will it drop us in the ocean? Underwater? Do we need to . . . to . . ." I hold up the awful flower. It drips thick ooze over my hand. The last thing I want to do is attach it to my face. But I'd also rather not try to figure it out while submerged.

"Not to worry," the Prince says, his tone cold rather than reassuring. "It will lead us to the shore nearest Seraphine's kingdom. We'll emerge on dry land."

"But where exactly?"

"I'm not certain." He casts me a short look. "But I have a good guess. Are you ready?"

The crone stands on her front porch, watching us go. The giant chicken legs under her house shift uneasily back and forth, causing the whole structure to sway, but she sways along with it like a captain on the deck of her ship. Her glinting crystal eye catches the red glare of the riven sky, making it look as though a burning coal blazes in the socket.

I shudder and turn away. I don't relish the idea of passing through the gate into yet another unknown world; but the sooner we leave this world behind, the better. "I'm ready," I say.

The air beneath the crumbling arch shimmers. The Prince motions for me to go ahead. I offer up a swift prayer to any gods who might care, then duck my head and hasten through. Before I lose my nerve.

To my surprise, the journey out from the Wild Magic Realm is much less painful than the journey in. It's still an awful, fingernail-scraping feeling all over my body with a few sharp jolts in the extremities. But I never fully lose the sense of my own physical self, and the whole experience is over in a flash. Before I'm quite ready for it, I'm staggering along a rocky landscape on a high cliff above the sea. This cliff is much higher than those lining the shores of Noxaur, a true, breathtaking height. Sheer rock walls drop a hundred feet into white foam and jagged, teeth-like boulders. I let out a little yelp, my voice stolen by a sharp ocean wind, and leap back.

The Prince appears before I've managed to draw a complete breath. No staggering or arm-wheeling for him. He strides through the tear in realities as though stepping through the door of his own house. His hair is caught by the breeze, black locks wafting, and his coat billows behind him. I wonder that he doesn't curse at the cold, unbuttoned as he is, all that skin exposed to the elements. But as always, it doesn't seem to affect him.

"Ah!" he says, and strides right up to the edge of that cliff, gazing up and down and along the jagged shoreline. He shades his eyes, then points to a promontory not far from our current position. There the crumbled ruins of a tower cling to the rocks in defiance of both time and the elements. "It is as I thought: Roseward."

I give him a curious look, shaking my head.

"The Isle of Roseward," he goes on. "It's untethered to reality and floats adrift in the Hinter Sea. Those few brave mariners who have survived the sirens often claim to have spied this island while on their travels. I rather expected this is where we would end up."

"Have you been here before?"

"Yes. Long ago."

I bite my wind-chapped lips and gaze out on the seemingly endless ocean before us. "And Ulakrana?"

He points. "About fifty miles to sea. That way."

"Fifty miles?" My knees threaten to buckle. It's only with an effort of will that I manage to stay upright. "I couldn't possibly swim that far! Even with this flower to keep me alive, how will I make it there and back in three hours?"

"You won't be swimming." Without offering an explanation, the Prince puts his fingers to his mouth and utters a piercing whistle. I watch him, baffled. Nothing happens for several moments, yet he remains standing there above the perilous drop, poised and expectant.

Then I hear it: a cry. Like a song, perhaps. Or a warble. I don't have a word that can quite describe the sound that carries on the breeze and draws my head whipping around to gaze back across the barren isle. White wings fill my vision, enormous and feathered and shining with their own gentle light. Then a being as large as a draft horse swoops overhead, trailing a long, sinuous tail behind it.

It's a wyvern. Like the one Nelle kept as a pet, but more graceful, the lines of its body so elegantly crafted, one might expect it to keep company with angels. It carves a smooth turn in the sky. The Prince backs up, making space, and the creature alights on its two great haunches where he had stood a moment before. "There you are, my old friend!" he declares, and reaches out to take the magnificent being's long, feathered head in his hands. He draws it to him, and the two touch foreheads. Both of them close their eyes and stand there for a moment.

I stare. Utterly flabbergasted. I've never seen a creature so beautiful, so graceful in every line and proportion. More astonishing still, it's made up entirely of magic. *Written* magic unless I'm much mistaken. Which means it's human magic. Living human magic.

"Is it a Noswraith?" The words blurt from my lips before I can stop them, drawing both the Prince's and the wyvern's gaze to me.

The Prince raises an eyebrow. "Does it look like a Noswraith?"

It doesn't. Not in the least. "But it's . . . The magic . . ."

"It's a daydream. Nothing but a daydream, written into

existence by the old Miphates methods." He strokes the wyvern's arched neck while it nuzzles the top of his head, mussing his hair. "Nelle is the one who taught me how to do it. Long ago when I first visited Roseward. I'd hoped I could convince it to stay with me, just as her little beast preferred to be with her. But daydreams are free beings with minds of their own. This one likes to spend most of its time here, in the place of its origin. We see one another but rarely when the isle happens to drift near Vespre."

He gazes up at the wyvern—his own creation—with an expression I don't remember seeing on his face before. For a moment, I glimpse the little boy he might once have been. It's nearly impossible to think of the fae as ever having been children. But the Prince isn't really fae, not fully fae. While he is centuries old, he is still young for one of his kind.

And suddenly he looks lonely.

Gathering my courage, I step a little closer. The wyvern turns to look at me, its large, solemn eyes blinking slowly. Then, as though coming to a decision, it stretches out its long neck and offers its nose for my tentative hand. I stroke the feathers along its muzzle, so wondrously soft and silky to the touch. "How did you come to be here?" I ask, flicking a glance up at the Prince. "How did you meet Nelle?"

"That's a bit of a story. One we haven't time for now. It involves kidnappings and rescues and vendettas and betrayals. The long and short of it is, Nelle and her husband, Soran Silveri, broke a spell which had kept me imprisoned as a child, saving me from my captor. They gave me shelter when I was vulnerable. Later on, when they needed shelter in turn, I brought them to Vespre."

I'd always known the Prince cared deeply for Nelle; I'd not realized he'd known her since childhood. There's so much about him I don't know, so much I've been afraid to ask or discover. Somehow, it's easier to let myself think of him as some sort of rogue, as casually cruel, cold, and calculating as any of the fae I've met since coming to this world. But he's not. And seeing him here with his wyvern, it's impossible to maintain the illusion. His is a heart capable of beautiful dreams and equally beautiful creations. Too bad he's trapped in this role his father fashioned for him. Were he given the space, the freedom, what wonders might he work?

The wind whistles up the cliff, biting at my face and hands. I shiver and wrap my cloak more tightly around me. The Prince notices. "You're cold now," he says, turning from the wyvern, "but you're about to be much colder when we enter the merqueen's realm. While the crone's flower will spare you from drowning, we need to make certain you don't freeze to death instead."

"How?" I ask, my teeth starting to chatter.

He studies me a moment, his brow stern. "I can work a glamour of warmth strong enough to deceive both mind and body. It should work—though once you're in the water, it will begin to break down. I cannot guarantee it will last the full three hours. But it's the best I can offer."

I nod. "Very well. Let's get on with it, shall we?" He moves toward me, reaching out. Startled, I draw back a step. "What are you doing?"

"You'll have to remove your cloak," he says. "You won't be wearing it underwater. Nor your outer dress, your shoes, your stockings. We need to get this spell as close to your skin as possible. If you want to be safe, I suggest you strip down to your small clothes."

Suddenly, all the chill is gone from my body. Blood like lava roars in my veins, pounds in my ears. I take care to let no trace of this heat show in my expression, however. I merely nod and say through a tightly-held breath, "Whatever is necessary."

I don't wait for him to reach for me again. Instead I unfasten the clasp of my cloak and let it drop to the ground. The cold wind blasts through my skirts and pulls at my hair, shivering me to my bones. But I won't let him see me hesitate. My fingers numb and fumbling, I begin to untie the front laces of my vest. A knot sticks, and I struggle to get it loose.

"May I?"

The Prince is very near, his breath hot against my forehead. I glance up at him, but it's almost too much. Hastily I look down, firm my jaw. And nod. Once. His fingers are long, elegant, and strong. They work the laces nimbly, as though he has ample practice undoing women's vests for them. Hastily, I push that thought down into the darkest recesses of my mind. Instead I focus on the hollow of his throat, so near my line of vision. Focus on the way the muscles in his throat contract as he swallows.

Then the laces are loose. He steps back. With a quick inhalation of breath, I slide the vest from my shoulders and drop it to join the cloak. After that, I undo the buttons of my blouse, first at the wrist, then starting at my neck. The Prince turns away for this, stepping once more to the wyvern. It burbles prettily at him, ruffling its neck feathers. He rests a hand on its shoulder, and they gaze out across the ocean together, offering me that little bit of privacy.

I remove my blouse then unfasten the waistband of my skirt and let it fall away from my body. The corset is next. I almost need to ask the Prince for assistance, but part of me would rather die. I manage it on my own in the end. Finally, I yank off my boots, my stockings and garters, and soon find myself standing in nothing but my chemise and small clothes. Trembling, vulnerable. And so very cold.

Not quite knowing what to say, I clear my throat. The Prince turns, takes in the sight of me. His brow tightens. "It's too much," he says. "The spell won't function as well if you're wearing that."

I look down at my chemise. It feels paper thin and exposed, but it's still better than the practically nothing I'd be left wearing without it. "It will have to do," I say, pleased when my voice doesn't quaver.

The Prince's mouth presses into a thin line. Then, leaving the wyvern, he approaches me again, standing in such a way as to block the wind. He looks oddly pale. The lines of his jaw and brow are harder than usual. He opens his mouth, closes it again. "I will have to touch you," he says at last. "To make the glamour adhere."

My heart pounds in my throat. I fear it might choke me. I don't dare try to speak again, so I drop my gaze and hold my arms out stiffly to each side, silent indication for him to get on with things.

He claps his hands together and begins to rub them fast. As he rubs, a glow forms between his palms, intensifying by the moment. I feel the warmth of it, lovely against my skin. "Hold still now," he says.

He first touches the top of my head. His hand is large enough to cover it completely, his fingers pressing into my skull. The warmth of his glamour pours out of his touch and creeps through my hair, down to my scalp. Then he begins to circle, both hands working now. One he slides down the back of my head, the other over my face. I close my eyes as the glamour spreads across my skin, my cheeks. He does the sides of my head, over my ears, surrounding me in a warm aura of light.

He moves to my neck next. And I lose all sense of anything else. Only the sensation of his touch—of his fingers, sliding down my throat, slowly, carefully, meticulous as he works his magic. The warmth spreads across my skin, but a hotter, more dangerous warmth floods my blood, my being. The rest of the world falls away, the ocean, the wind, these stark, bare cliffs. There's only room in my existence for him. For his hands, his touch. For his eyes, fixed upon me as he goes about his work.

He progresses down to my shoulders. When he comes to the sleeves of the chemise, he grimaces.

"What is it?" I ask, breathlessly.

He lifts his gaze to mine. "I told you. The cloth interferes with the magic. It will hold, but not as well and not as long."

I blink once. Then: "Keep going."

A little growl rumbles in his throat. But his hands move again, sliding down my arms, raising gooseflesh. His fingers run along mine, twining briefly, like a dance of just our hands. It's more than magic that sparks along my skin, sending thrilling bursts straight to my heart.

Then he draws both hands back up to my shoulders, rests them against my collarbone. I catch my breath as he works his way down. His motions are quick and efficient, but I cannot deny the shivering quake in my gut as his palms glide over my breasts, down my abdomen, coming to rest on my hipbones. He moves to stand behind me and trails magic up my spine, slowly, slowly.

When at last he kneels to finish his work—to draw the glamour over my hips and down each leg in turn—it's all I can do not to scream for him to stop. Or worse still, not to grip him by the hair, yank his face up to mine, and . . . and . . . what? What would I do? What would I dare dream of doing? I don't know. Because I won't let myself finish that thought. I stand like a block of ice, both hands clenched into fists. And I lock down any wild thoughts, any foolish impulses. Any dangerous sensations I have no business thinking, feeling, or experiencing.

He finishes spreading glamour over every inch of me, ending with the soles of my feet. Then he rises, a black lock of hair falling across his forehead, his mouth hanging open. Breath comes in rough gusts through his lips, as though he's just endured some terrible exertion. His face lined and stern, he roughly pushes the hair back into place and turns away from me, staring out at the ocean. Even above the rush of the wind, I hear him heave a terrible sigh.

"What's wrong?" I ask, my voice struggling through my tightened throat. "Did it not work?"

"It worked." He doesn't look back at me. Another long breath, then he turns and strides to the wyvern. "If you're determined to go through with this madness, we should set out at once. We'll fly over Ulakrana, dive in above Seraphine's city, and make our way down from there. It's going to be dark. And cold. Even with the glamour, it might be too much for you." He half-turns his head, not quite looking back at me. "Are you ready?"

I nod. His glamour has cocooned me in warmth, but my body shivers nonetheless. I wrap my arms around myself, holding tight. "Yes," I say. "Let's go."

15

WIND WHIPS AGAINST MY FACE, HURLING STINGING droplets of rain at every exposed inch of skin. Thanks to the Prince's spell, I scarcely feel it. It's as though it's happening to someone else, some other Clara in a different reality.

In truth, I'm not sure the spell is altogether necessary. Not at the moment at least. Not with the Prince seated so close behind me on the back of the wyvern, his legs framing my body, one arm wrapped firmly around my middle. My back rests flush against his broad chest, and I am painfully aware of how his unbuttoned shirt hangs open, as per usual. What is not usual is the single layer of linen between me and his bare skin. It doesn't feel like much.

Heat unrelated to any fae glamour or spell pools in my gut.

I close my eyes. Gods on high, I must stay focused on the mission at hand! My life in recent history has been fraught with danger, but this? This might be the deadliest risk I've yet taken. Not just the dive, the swim, the drowning . . . but Seraphine herself. If I should make it to her palace alive, will she meet with me? Will she take a bargain or even permit me to live? I must be quick-witted and careful. And not let myself be distracted by the feeling of a large, strong hand pressed flat against my stomach, or the thumb resting just under the curve of my breast.

The Prince removed his coat before we set off but retained both his shirt and trousers. He wears a warming glamour as well, though he claims his fae blood should be sufficient protection in the depths. I'm not in the least disappointed that he felt no need to strip off a few more layers. It makes no difference to me. None at all.

The wyvern glides smoothly despite the wind and rain. Condensation beads and rolls off its pristine feathers. It's such a beautiful being, this daydream of the Prince's. I'd not thought him capable of inventing such loveliness. I suppose not all of us are born with darkness in our souls. Some have more to offer the world than monsters.

My brow darkens. I stare ahead over the wyvern's arched neck, watching the far horizon, which never seems to draw any nearer. The Hinter Sea is so vast. Some say it's endless. I'm not sure how either the Prince or his wyvern are navigating, but suddenly, sooner than I expect, the wyvern banks and begins a stomach-lurching descent. A little scream bursts from my lips.

The Prince's arm tightens. "Don't worry, Darling," he murmurs into my ear. "I've got you."

Oh gods! The things that voice of his does to me! My limbs go all weak and trembly, until I could almost melt into him. I tighten my grip on the wyvern's feathers, force myself not to lean back into those strong arms, not to turn my face toward his, not to press my lips—

No! What is this stupidity? Even if I wanted to kiss anyone, now is not the time, not fifty feet above freezing ocean water, descending in a terrifying spiral. And I don't want to kiss anyone. Certainly not him. I want to save Danny. I want to save Oscar. I want to accomplish this mission and get on with my life.

But why can I not get over the awareness of his lips hovering so close to my ear? The rhythm of his breathing, the expanding and contracting of his chest? I close my eyes again, unable to bear the sight of that spinning ocean below. But this makes it worse. Any slight movement of his is so exaggerated. The way he shifts in his seat, the way he adjusts his hand. The way he tips his head so that his nose just grazes my ear. Everything, every fractional movement sets off small thrills throughout my body.

"Here we are," he says.

I gasp, my eyes flying open once more. The wyvern has settled into a holding pattern, gliding some twelve feet above the choppy waves. I look around. This stretch of ocean looks no different from the rest. "Are you sure this is it?" I ask.

"Quite." The Prince reaches into the front of his shirt and withdraws the two flowers he'd hidden there for safekeeping. "It's time to use these. Remember what you were told. It won't stop water from filling your lungs, it will simply prevent it from killing you for three hours. It's up to us to return to land and empty your lungs before the magic fades."

My heart careens against my breastbone. Now that I'm here, I'm not sure I have the courage to go through with this. But as the wyvern continues its gliding circle, I accept the orange flower and hold it up to my face. It's slimy, disgusting.

The Prince follows the crone's directions first, biting the long stem and holding the two yellow stamens up to his nostrils. He breathes in sharply, and the stamens disappear. He squeezes his eyes tight, grimaces, then relaxes. The flower clings to his face like a parasite. It's awful, and even when he signals that everything is well, I must force myself not to tear it off him. "It's not too bad," he says, talking around the stem, his voice a bit nasal. "A little strange, but . . ."

Instead of finishing that thought, he stands. Right there, on the wyvern's back, as we dip closer to the water. "Come, Darling," he says, holding out his arms to steady himself. "Let's get this over with, shall we?" Without ceremony, he leaps. His lean, athletic body forms a perfect swan-dive, entering the water without a splash. The wyvern keeps on gliding, and I twist in place, straining to look back, to see if he surfaces again, perhaps to signal to me one last time. He does not. I look at the hideous flower. A shudder rushes through my body followed by a little whimper. But I can't very well leave the Prince down there in the ocean alone, can I?

Holding the flower up to my face, I wince as the little stamens tickle my lip. Then, with a deep inhale, I draw them up into my nose. They creep much higher than I expected. It feels wrong. I want to scream and fling the blighted thing into the sea. I'm still able to breathe, but it's difficult. How is this going to help me underwater? I suppose I must simply trust in the crone's magic, trust she wasn't lying to me. The fae cannot lie, after all. Then again, I'm not altogether certain she *is* fae.

Before I can twist myself into knots of second-guessing, I stick the stem in my mouth, gag at the awful flavor, and pull one leg over the wyvern's neck. Now I sit with both feet dangling over the water. Hoping the wyvern's slow circle has brought us back within range of the Prince, I count to three and . . . push away.

The fall is greater than I anticipated. Perhaps it's just a trick of my perceptions, but it feels as though I plummet for a small eternity, my chemise flapping up to my waist, my bare legs kicking beneath me. Suddenly, water closes in overhead. Part of me knows the icy impact should shock me to the bones. But the Prince's magic holds. Though cold surrounds me, it can't quite reach me. If anything, I'm warmer now than I was while flying, comfortable and safe in this enveloping glamour. What's more, there's light. My whole body is coated in a golden sheen which illuminates the water for a few feet around me. But this only shows me how alone I am. No sign of the Prince anywhere. No sign of anything—just darkness.

My body jolts. On instinct, I start to pull for the surface. I can't bear to be down here in this murky world under wave by myself. My lungs are already beginning to burn, and I can't . . . I won't . . .

A hand grips my arm.

My heart lurches with terror, images of merfolk and monsters filling my head. But when I whip about, it's the Prince who shimmers before my vision, illuminated by glamour glow. His eyes stare at me above the petals of his flower. He shakes his head and signs that I should breathe. But I can't. I can't! If I breathe, I will draw water into my lungs. And I'll drown. But I have to drown, right? That's part of the deal. I cannot enter Seraphine's kingdom otherwise.

My lungs are burning, and the dark ocean surrounds me, and panic thrills in my blood. It's one thing for a crone to tell you her magic flower will keep you from dying; it's another thing entirely to believe it.

A sudden gleam sparks in the Prince's eye. *Hope.* He thinks I'm going to give up. He thinks I'm going to turn around, defeated at last. He thinks this is it, the end of my quest.

I will not give him that satisfaction.

I draw a breath.

Water pours into my mouth, around the flower stem. It chokes down my throat, into my lungs. My body jerks, jolts. It hurts more than I expected. It hurts to watch the last of my air bubbles speed to the surface. It hurts to let the water in, to feel it filling my lungs, my chest. It hurts, it hurts, it hurts, and I . . .

The Prince pulls me to him. He holds me against his chest as terror and panic and pain rush through me in waves. I can do nothing but cling to him, cling to his strength. I close my eyes, trying to concentrate on the feeling of his arms around me, of glamour protecting me. Slowly, I draw another breath. Of water. The flower stamens in my nostrils tickle but remain in place. I breathe liquid into my lungs, breathe it out again, and the stamens filter each breath.

I've done it. I've drowned but not died.

The Prince, sensing the calm come over me, pushes me back to arm's length and looks me in the eye. I nod. I cannot smile for fear of losing the flower stem gripped in my teeth, but I try to make my brow relax, to let him know I'm all right. He holds up three fingers. *Three hours,* he's reminding me. Which means we'd better get swimming.

I look down between my bare feet, down into the dark beneath us. I hope the Prince is right and Ulakrana is truly down there. Some part of me had believed I would see it as soon as I was underwater. But there's nothing. Only darkness so big, so consuming. Like the very maw of madness itself, waiting to swallow me whole.

I draw a long, watery breath through my nostrils, through the filtering stamens. Then, angling my body, I begin to swim down, pulling myself with my arms, kicking with my legs. I'm not much of a swimmer. Oscar and I used to play in the lake at the country house our family visited each summer when there was money for such luxury. But that was nothing like this.

The Prince, however, takes my hand. Nimble and strong, he pulls me along after him, as though he goes deep diving every day of his life. I try to mimic what I see him doing with his arms and get along a little better than before. As we progress, the pressure on my bones increases, but the Prince's glamour seems to offer some protection on that score as well.

All is strangely quiet and very dark. The little light from the sky overhead fades the deeper we go. Soon we are in complete darkness save for the glamour magic. A flash of silvery fin catches the tail of my eye. I stop, maneuvering my arms and legs to stay in place. I'm disoriented, unable to tell up from down anymore. I don't even know if we're swimming in the right direction.

Another flash of fin, just within reach of the glamour light. My water-filled lungs tighten. The Prince squeezes my hand, and I turn to look at him. He nods, his expression . . . encouraging? It's difficult to say through the half-mask of that flower. He juts his chin, indicating that we should continue. I allow him to pull me a little deeper.

Then, like enormous rippling curtains, the darkness below us parts. Light fills my view, sudden and blinding, pure white. I put up an arm to shield my vision. It's several long heartbeats before I dare peer out again.

Six women appear before us. Two of them carry strange globes that dangle from the end of long poles like lures. Bobbing gently in the currents, they cast pulsing glows of white light, shimmering across the iridescent hides of the giant seahorses they ride. The women themselves are half naked save for the blue, green, and purple scales they wear across their breasts and down their arms like armor. Their bare flesh is a silvery green, and gills flutter from their necks, and fins flare from the sides of their faces. Their long hair is caught in intricate braids, adorned with shells and bits of bone and teeth. The most terrible thing about them, however, is their eyes. They are large and very white, with pinpoint pupils at their centers. They fix upon the Prince and me, the intensity of their stares enough to congeal living blood.

The foremost of their number rides a seahorse so brilliantly red, it almost looks as though it's on fire. Its rider is more formidable than the rest. She wears a spined headdress that frames her beautiful, battle-scarred face. She studies us, her gaze both aggressive and bemused, as though she cannot believe we have purposefully ventured this far down into her world.

Then she opens her mouth and begins to sing. Her voice ripples through the water, tickles my ear. I remember when Oscar and I would play in the lake, we would take turns trying to make sounds underwater, trying to guess what the other had said. It was always so distorted, impossible to understand. This is different. This sound, this song, was meant to be heard underwater. The distortion is part of the melody, a strange, beautiful, haunting melody, unlike anything I've ever before heard. It's deep, wild. Alluring.

Her mouth opens wider, revealing sharp fangs. I see them without fear. Her song is too lovely to feel anything but a need to draw closer to her. When she stretches out her hand, I move to take it, ready to let her guide me down to darker depths, down to some secret lair where I will drown in the delights she offers.

A sharp tug on my arm. I start and turn to the Prince, the song-spell broken. He pulls me closer to him, puts himself between me and the merfolk as though somehow his physical body can block out their enchantments. Then, to my horror, he takes the stem from his mouth and speaks. His voice is distorted, but by some magic I can just discern the words: "I am Castien Lodírith, Prince of Vespre, son of King Lodírhal of Aurelis. My companion is a mortal mage of the first order. She has traveled far to confer with Queen Seraphine."

The foremost merwoman flashes her teeth, visibly annoyed at having her song interrupted. She begins to brandish the trident in her hand, but one of the others urges her seahorse up close and seems to say something. The first one snarls again and shakes her head, but the second persists in whatever argument she is making. All this while, I feel the seconds slipping away, feel the deep, impenetrable cold of the water all around me, ready to press through the glamour.

Finally, the leader utters a strange, ululating bark and makes a sharp motion with her trident. At once, two of the riders urge their mounts up to me and the Prince. One holds out her hand to me. I turn frightened eyes to the Prince, who has popped the stem of his flower back into his mouth. He nods, indicating that I should go. I don't like to be parted from him, but there doesn't seem to be any choice.

Summoning all my courage, I place my hand in the merwoman's. Her grip is strong as she yanks me through the water and behind her onto her seahorse's back. I wrap my arms around her muscular, sensual, scale-covered body and my legs around the barrel of the seahorse. I've ridden very little in my life, certainly never astride a steed like this. A little desperate, I turn to catch a glimpse of the Prince mounted behind another of the merwomen. I have just time enough to think how positively dwarfed he looks in comparison to her broad, muscular frame.

Then we're off. Streaking through the water at tremendous speed. Now and then by the gleam of the merfolk's pale lamps, I glimpse strange bodies of movement—schools of fish darting by in glittering formations, or larger, slower beings, shy of the light, keeping just out of view. Once I swear I saw a shark, all cold dead eyes and savage teeth. But the merwomen ride on without pause, carrying us deeper and deeper. The pressure down here would surely crush me were it not for the Prince's spell. I can only pray we reach the palace soon.

We come to a gorge at the ocean floor, alight with more of the globe lanterns like the merwomen carry. These seem to mark a passage through a bewildering labyrinth of stone. The merwomen drive their mounts into the gorge, following those lights. Here and there, I glimpse what look like giant eels darting in and out of crevices. One of these shoots out suddenly, snapping at a seahorse. Its rider, however, deftly flips her trident about and spears the eel through the eye. A ripple, almost like a shriek, bursts from the eel as it retreats into its den.

I scarcely have time to process what I've seen before we've left it far behind. I close my eyes, unable to bear much more of this, and press my face into the scaly shoulder of the merwoman. We ride for what feels like hours but may have been mere minutes. I don't look up again until a sudden intense glow of light presses against my eyelids. It's so unexpected, I cannot resist looking up just as we emerge from the gorge into a world of color.

A vast city stands before us, a dizzying array of towers and tiers through which submarine traffic moves in dizzying patterns. All is illuminated by hundreds of giant globes, the size of hot air balloons, hovering above the city at various intervals. I cannot tell if these are animal, vegetable, or pure magic. It doesn't matter—they cast rippling, rainbow-hued brilliance across the twisted spires and graceful arches, making the city shine like a dream come true.

I'd had no idea it would be so beautiful. No idea how, despite the terror of this descent and the darkness and the cold through which we traveled, my heart would leap with pure joy at the sight. No wonder the ancient tales told of men and women willing to risk their lives just for a glimpse of Ulakrana. Now I've seen it, and I would not alter any one of the decisions that led me step by step to this place.

I turn my head, trying to catch sight of the Prince, to gauge his reaction. Is he glad now too? Will the sheer beauty of the view be enough to earn his forgiveness? His face is suffused in the overhead glow but turned so that I can only see the line of his cheek and jaw. I lift a hand, thinking to wave down his attention.

But then our escort sets off again faster than before. I'm obliged to catch hold of the merwoman rider and channel all my concentration on clinging in place. The path to the city leads along the edge of a great trench. An endless abyss yawns below me in which marine creatures with trailing tentacles reflect the light from the city globes, dancing and undulating like living nebulas of the deep. It's so strange, so far beyond my limited scope of experience, I can't decide if it's wonderful or horrible. Maybe both.

We ride into the city, weaving in and out of the sea traffic, which follows no laws I can comprehend. It doesn't take long before we catch the attention of its denizens. Merwomen—but no men, at least none that I see—crowd the windows of their twisted, tower dwellings, staring at us as we pass. It's probably been centuries since any of these folk saw a living human. I cannot read their cold, fixed stares well enough to guess if they hate me for defying their queen's laws or if they are merely curious.

The palace rises from the center of the city—a vast structure situated directly beneath the largest of the glowing orbs. Its towers, turrets, and high, dizzying arches have been overlayed with the most beautiful abalone shell, swirling with color that plays tricks on my eyes and makes the whole structure seem to wave and dance. Our escorts drive their mounts to a great platform before a large, round door. There they come to a stop. The woman with whom I ride points imperiously for me to dismount. I let go and swim away from her and the seahorse. To my great relief, the Prince hastens to join me. I resist the urge to reach out and take his hand.

The leader of the party looks down at us, her face inscrutable. She speaks a single word in a language I do not understand, and the door behind us opens. The Prince catches my eye. I follow his lead, swimming awkwardly through the door into the chamber beyond, leaving our escort behind. The Prince pulls the door shut behind us, then beckons me to swim with him to the center of the tall chamber. There are no windows, so none of the brilliant light from the globe makes its way in to illuminate the space. I can see only by the light of the Prince's glamour-glow.

Suddenly, there's a rushing around me. I nearly scream, but the Prince grabs my hands. Slowly, we begin to sink. Before I know it, my feet are planted on the floor of the chamber, and the water is only up to our chins, then our shoulders, our chests, our waists. I should be glad; instead, panic surges in my veins.

"Easy now, Darling," the Prince says around the stem in his mouth. "Queen Seraphine keeps certain chambers of her palace prepared for receiving guests from the surface worlds. But you've taken a lot of water into your lungs, and you still need the flower to filter it."

I wish I could tear the flower from my face, and cough up all the water even now sloshing in my chest. It feels strange to stand here, still drowning, kept alive by magic while surrounded by breathable air. I move the stem around in my mouth experimentally.

The door opens. I let out a cry of surprise as a wave of foam spills in, unfurling almost like a carpet. Then a magnificent woman appears, splashing water in her wake.

So I have my first look at Queen Seraphine of Ulakrana.

16

SHE IS TALLER THAN ANY WOMAN I'VE EVER MET, seven feet high at least. Her limbs are muscular, perfectly formed, her skin a shining silver which glints with flecks of diamond in the glamour glow. Her black hair sweeps back from a face framed by delicate fins that shimmer purple and silver when she flares them. She wears a massive crown of shells and strung pearls, and corresponding jewelry drapes her shoulders, breasts, and loins. Otherwise, she is naked. Magnificent and merciless, heartbreaking and glorious.

Two tall guards walk at her heels. I recognize them as the two lead riders of our escort party. They stand at attention, weapons in hand and faces ferocious, as their queen gives us a long, slow inspection. Her gaze lingers on me, eyes unreadable from behind half-closed lids and green eyelashes. I feel small, foolish, standing here barefoot in my chemise. Despite the serenity of the queen's countenance, a shiver travels down my spine.

At last, however, she turns to the Prince and offers a smile. The fins around her face flutter delicately. "Castien," she says with perfect clarity in the common Eledrian tongue. "My dear and beloved friend of yore, why have you broken the sacred laws of peace between our kingdoms?"

My stomach plummets. I'd not expected a warm greeting by any means. But there's something terrifying about this smooth salutation followed by so cold an accusation.

The Prince, however, offers a gracious bow. "Great queen," he says around the stem of his flower, "I honor both your laws and your peace. I would never do anything to put either at risk."

She raises one webbed hand, pointing a finger straight at me. "And yet a human stands before me. Here, in my own realm. Somehow you have brought it through every ward I erected to prevent such an invasion." She nods to the first of the siren escorts standing behind her. "My daughter Sereia thinks I should have you spit upon her trident and fed to the sharks for your insolence." She tips her head to the second escort. "My daughter Starreth thinks we should first learn how you broke through our wards *and then* feed you to the sharks. I am as yet undecided."

I glance at the Prince over the petals of my flower mask. His expression is as nonchalant as ever, his smile downright flirtatious. "But dearest queen," he says, "I have broken none of your laws nor any of your wards. You declared that only a drowned human may enter your realm, is that not so?"

"Quite," the queen replies, the word sharp as a knife.

"And you will find, should you wish to inspect further, that my companion here—a mortal mage of the first order I might add—is in fact drowned. No air fills her lungs, only the water of your own fair realm."

Seraphine's eyes widen, long lashes wafting independently from one another like delicate tentacles. Her pale gaze fastens on me once more. Suddenly, she moves toward me. I back up several paces before forcing myself to stand firm and meet her gaze. The merqueen places a hand against my heart. The spread of her palm and fingers is so wide, she covers the whole of my chest. I can all too easily imagine how simple it must be for her to rip out the hearts of the sailors she lures into her depths. My own heart leaps painfully. I am aware of the Prince moving to stand behind me, aware of his hand just touching my elbow. But I cannot tear my gaze away from the queen.

Finally, with a flash of teeth, she steps back, blinking in mute surprise. With a toss of her head, she snarls, "Yet again, your reputation for cunning holds true. A drowned human, alive and standing before me! Clever." One of her daughters growls and takes a menacing step. The queen raises a hand, stopping her in her tracks, and tips her head. "Very well, beloved Prince, cherished friend. You have found your loophole. Now tell me why. Why have you brought it here? We have no further business, you and I. The debt I once owed I have long since paid."

This is news to me. I'd not known the Prince and the merqueen had any past dealings. Is this the true reason we were not killed on the spot when found infiltrating the boundaries of Seraphine's realm? I glance at him, trying to discern some sense of their story in his face. He merely waves a hand in my direction and takes a step back. "I am here but to make introductions. It is my companion who seeks a word with your gracious majesty, who has braved the perils of your realm to come before you." He glances sharply at me. I can almost hear him say: *You're on your own. Good luck!*

I grimace. But I have little choice now other than to meet the queen's gaze. She stares down at me from her tremendous height, pale eyes like two lanterns in the dark chamber. I've been stared at by my share of fae women—Estrilde and Ilusine both spring to mind—but their gazes are more disdainful. They find humans so far beneath them, scarcely sentient beings, worth about as much as a well-bred dog or a valuable horse. Seraphine's instead looks at me as though I am some sort of disgusting pest, crept in through the crevices and befouling her home. The hatred in her gaze is like daggers of ice.

I shiver. I haven't planned for what I should say. All my focus was simply on getting to Ulakrana. Now I'm here, standing before the queen, and I cannot very well just ask for a kiss. Can I?

"Speak, human," the queen says at last. "Speak, for I find my patience swiftly running out."

The stem of the flower tickles against the back of my throat as I swallow. There's nothing for it, though; I've come this far. Pushing the stem as far to one side as I can, I speak awkwardly around it: "I have come from Skullkreg, your majesty. From the house of Lord Vokarum. He, who has not forgotten the great love he bears for you, O glorious queen." I glance at the Prince. He raises an eyebrow at me, but offers nothing else. Drawing a breath through the tickling stamens in my nostrils, I take the plunge. "He has charged me to grant him his greatest desire: a single kiss from your lips." Seraphine's cheek fins flare. Hastily, I add: "I am come to bargain with you. To offer my services as mage to accomplish whatever task you name in exchange for said kiss."

The queen is silent. Her cheek fins continue to flutter for some moments before settling back against the sides of her face. Finally in a voice as deep as the ocean trenches: "I find human dishonesty distasteful."

My heart tightens in my water-logged chest. "Your majesty, what I tell you is true!"

"It is not." Seraphine lifts her chin. "You have not come on behalf of Vokarum. Anyone can see you are not one of his beguiled brides; you would not risk your own life for his sake. You want something. Something for yourself. Something you are willing to die for." She crosses her arms, the jewels and pearls draped across her body glinting in the light of my glamour. "If you would ask the Queen of the Deep for a boon, you must speak only truthful words."

My mouth is dry. I can almost feel the stem withering against my tongue. How many minutes remain to the three hours of life it grants me? It's all slipping away so fast.

"Vokarum possesses something I need," I say, my voice thin, desperate. "Something I must have in order to save a good man from slavery. But he will only part with this treasure in exchange for what he desires most in this world—your kiss, great queen." I fight the urge to clasp my hands, to sink to my knees and plead. Something tells me this would not go over well with the merqueen. "Thus I have come to bargain with you. Thus I have come to offer you my service. Name your price, and if it is within my power, I shall fulfill it."

Two translucent eyelids flick sideways across Seraphine's cold eyes. When they part, the fixed intensity of her stare has not abated. She is so cold, so otherworldly. So utterly without mercy or concern. My story holds no interest for her, and my powers, such as they are, must seem pathetic to her eye. Hopelessness wells inside me, threatening to choke me. Or is the water in my lungs, beginning to increase in pressure as the flower fails?

Then, to my surprise, the queen says, "You bargained with Vokarum to give him his heart's desire. Will you make such a bargain with me?"

The Prince curses softly. I feel his gaze on the side of my face, but refuse to look at him. "Yes, great queen. Your heart's desire."

The queen maintains that cold, silent stare for what feels like an age. The precious seconds of my life count down, pounding a pulse in my temples. Does she plan to keep me here, waiting on her word, until the magic wears off? Has she realized how little time I have left? Is this how she means to kill me? Panic coils in my gut, spreads through my veins. I'm just about to make a break, run for the door, and try for a desperate swim to the surface, when Seraphine turns abruptly. "Come!" she calls back over her shoulder and strides from the chamber.

The Prince is at my elbow in an instant. "Now you've done it!" he hisses. "Just when I think you can't get in any deeper."

I don't have the strength to speak, so I ignore him and hasten after the queen. I expect to plunge back into sea water, but instead, wherever Seraphine walks, the waters part and drain away before her, rushing and foamy at her feet. The Prince and I splash in her wake through dripping halls. All is echoing and damp, and the smell of salt permeates even through the stamens in my nostrils. The floors are rough; they were never intended to be walked upon. Everything is built and shaped to accommodate swimmers. I would guess they are emptied now only out of courtesy to the Prince, for Seraphine certainly wouldn't concern herself with my comfort. There are no windows, but globe lights—miniatures of the great globes illuminating the city— hang at intervals from the ceiling. Sea creatures for which I have no names cling to the water-carved stones. Decorative shells create elaborate murals, so intricate it would take an age to fully understand them.

But there is no time to stop or admire anything. The queen

leads us swiftly on, her long strides forcing me to trot to keep up. At last we come to a door which opens into a large round chamber beneath a domed ceiling. This is the first chamber which feels properly dry—as though it's never been filled with water unlike the other flushed-out passages. I stop in the doorway, gaping around me. The dome overhead and the encircling walls are all clear as glass, affording a view of the brilliant lights and the city and the ocean life swimming by. It's breathtaking and terrifying. What material are these walls made of that they can withstand the pressure of these depths?

The center of the room is dominated by a giant, open shell, the bottom portion of which is piled high with silken cushions. A figure lies there. A human. A living, breathing human. He's a young man, Oscar's age or a little younger. Painfully beautiful with the kind of heart-wrenching, fragile beauty that would inspire poets and songwriters alike. His dark hair is brushed back from a pale brow, his delicate features sunken into his lovely face. Merwomen surround him, soothing his fevered skin with cloths, holding his hands, massaging his feet. He pays them no attention, but lies perfectly still with his eyes closed.

The queen utters a soft, burbling, songlike sound. No words that I can discern, merely a delicate note. The merwomen around the bed hastily move away, retreating to the edges of the room and bowing their heads. The young man turns his face slightly and with an effort manages to open one eye. His iris is blue and perfectly human, not at all like the fixed stares of the merfolk.

"Mother," he says and raises a limp hand, which she hastily moves to take. Only then do I notice the webbing between his fingers, the delicate gills behind his ears, small compared to the other merfolk. But it's enough to reveal his true heritage: he is half-mer.

My mouth nearly falls open. I clamp my teeth tight around the flower stem but cannot stop staring. It is well known that the merqueen has peopled her entire city with her many hundreds of daughters and their daughters. I didn't think it possible for her to bear a son. There's no denying the evidence of my own eyes, however—the way Seraphine sits and holds his hand so gently, the way her hard, cruel face seems to soften with tenderness as she gazes upon him.

"Is it the rot?" the Prince's voice speaks suddenly from behind me. I start and look back at him, surprised to see true compassion in his gaze.

Seraphine lifts her face slowly, fins fluttering. "Yes," she sings. The single word carries the weight of an entire tragic aria.

At my inquiring look, the Prince inclines his head and whispers, "It's a mer sickness, not incurable among their kind. But should a human catch it, it attacks the vital organs, rotting them from the inside out." He shakes his head. "A terrible way to die."

The queen lets out a low moan. "I have birthed two thousand and seventeen daughters," she says, stroking the young man's face and gills, "but only one son. His father was the great adventurer, Ormetrius."

"Indeed?" The Prince sounds surprise. "He was thought to

have been lost at sea."

The queen smiles sadly. "Lost at sea, lost in love. A beautiful memory. A memory which lives on in his son and heir."

I scarcely believe my own ears. "The Lay of Ormetrius the Mariner," written originally in Old Araneli is a well-known feature of any classical education. I myself have read a recent translation. It was terribly dry, with pockets of excitement, but the character of Ormetrius is deeply ingrained in contemporary conscious, a literary icon. I'd never considered the possibility that he might have been *real*.

I study the half-mer young man. He must be much older than I'd initially thought if he's the adventurer's son. Then again, the air of Eledria could keep him alive and youthful for many hundreds, even thousands of years. But apparently it isn't enough to save him from this sickness.

"Is there a cure?" My voice is a whisper, but it seems to echo in that chamber.

"No," Seraphine replies. "The poison is setting in fast. Soon it will reach his heart, and he will be lost to me. Just like his father. Just like all my many loves."

She sounds so stricken—it's too easy to forget she steals and drowns all those so-called loves of hers. But then, it is her nature. One cannot blame a shark for being coldhearted and ravenous, can one?

The queen turns her predatory eyes on me then. "I would give *anything* to save my son."

Realization comes over me like a wave. What she's asking. What she needs. A cure for an incurable sickness. An impossible miracle.

"I'll do it." The words fall from my lips before I've quite resolved to speak them. They seem to echo in that large chamber, underscored by the Prince's bitter, "Gods blight, I knew you'd say that!" I ignore him and continue determinedly. "I will find a cure for the rot. I will save your son. And when I do, you owe me a kiss to be given to Lord Vokarum of Skullkreg." I step across to that bed and hold out my hand. "Do we have a bargain?"

Seraphine looks at my hand as though I've just offered her a lump of horse scat. Then she lifts her gaze to mine. "If you find a way to save my son, I will grant Vokarum his kiss." She smiles, and a barbed tongue flicks between her teeth. "I'll even make sure he *enjoys* it."

With that she grips my hand in hers, sealing her promise.

17

THE PRINCE IS SILENT AS SERAPHINE'S TWO TERRIFYING daughters escort us from the dying boy's room back to the dripping chamber we first entered. When we are ushered into the echoing space, he proceeds ahead of me and stands with his arms crossed, not looking back.

I look over my shoulder just as the door shuts. It echoes terribly, and a thrill of panic coils in my gut. The next moment, water begins to rush into the chamber. Even though I knew it would happen, I let out a yelp and turn in place. Instinct tells me I'm in danger, even though my lungs are already sloshing with salt water, and the flower continues to do its filtering work. I close my eyes as the water rushes up to my ankles, my knees. It's cold—which I shouldn't be able to notice. The Prince's glamour should prevent me from feeling it.

Is his magic wearing down?

I turn to the Prince. He still stands with his back to me, braced as the chamber continues to fill up around us. "Prince!" I gasp, while I can still get the words out. He hears me above the rushing water and turns. I hold up my hands, but there's nothing to see. "The glamour!" I manage.

Then water sweeps over my head, and I'm obliged to bite down hard on the flower stem. The Prince ducks under and gets a good look at me. Now that I'm submerged, his glamour should surround me in a golden aura. Instead there is nothing but a pale white glow which flickers faintly. His eyes widen. He grabs me by the wrist and places one palm against my chest, right between my breasts. I can feel him trying to augment the spell. But salt compromises fae magic; not to the same degree as iron, but enough to interfere with his working.

He lifts his gaze from his hand to my eyes. It's difficult to read his expression behind the masking flower. But I don't like what I see.

He jerks his head sharply and swims for the door. It opens at our approach, and we emerge from the palace into the waiting circle of seahorse riders, including Sereia and Starreth. The Prince pulls the stem from his mouth and speaks, his voice a blur of noise in my ears. The merwomen exchange looks.

The next thing I know, one of them has pulled me behind her on her mount and urged it out into the highways and byways of the city. I don't bother looking back to see if the Prince is close behind. Now that his glamour is fading, the water rushing past my face stings my eyes, and I'm obliged to keep them shut, buried between the merwoman's shoulder blades. With every passing moment, the cold and pressure intensify. There is no time anymore. Only cold. Only the vastness of this ocean around me, ready to claim me as it has so many of my kind. My mind slows, too sluggish even for fear.

I'm scarcely aware when the rider pulls her mount to a halt and unceremoniously pushes me off, leaving me floating and alone. The next moment, strong hands grip my arms, pull me close. I'm able to open my eyes just enough to see the Prince staring down at me. He turns and shouts through the water back at the cluster of riders, some angry demand. But they, wavery phantoms to my vision, merely turn and vanish back into the ocean depths without response.

The Prince puts his flower stem back into his mouth and swims for the surface, dragging me as dead weight behind him. His strength is tremendous, equaled only by his will. I try to lend some help, to kick my feet, to move my arms. But my efforts are useless. And that cold, that terrible cold, freezes straight through to my bones. When I open my eyes, the light surrounding me is little more than a thin sheen clinging to patches of my body.

Suddenly a glow from above. I tip my head back, peel my eyes open. There. Sunlight—rippling through the waves overhead. My heart leaps. To my surprise, I still have some small spark of life inside me that yet longs to survive. The last of my strength surges. I kick upward, pulled along in the Prince's grip.

Then we break the surface of the ocean. The Prince spits out his flower and coughs up a terrible gush of water. The next moment, he shouts, "Here! Here, down here!" It sounds as though he's speaking through many layers of reality as I drift away, away, away . . .

Impressions. Feelings. They flit across my awareness, there and gone again. Waves slapping in my face. Wings sweeping overhead. Cold air freezing my already frozen skin. Strong arms wrap around me and a voice whispers: "Hold on, hold on. Hold on, Darling."

I close my eyes again, let myself sink. Sink as fast as stone, down, down, down into darkness deeper even than the ocean. There I see flashes of strange, nebula-like creatures, even greater and more brilliant than those I'd glimpsed in the trench. I drift among them, wafted by their trailing tentacles and rippling fins, bathing in their strange light. It's beautiful down here in these depths. I could stay here . . . I could stay . . . I could . . .

"Darling! Breathe! Breathe, gods damn it!"

Pain jolting through my body, pressure on my chest. My eyes flare wide. I stare up into a darkly silhouetted face framed by a too-bright, cloud-churning sky. My lungs heave; water gushes forth. Some power outside my body rolls me onto my side until I cough up every salty mouthful. Then, with a horrible ripping sensation, I drag air into my lungs.

"That's good. That's better." The Prince's voice beats like a drum against my senses. I cling to that sound with all the strength remaining to my spirit. His arms are around me, pulling me close to him, his hands massaging my skin. "Gods damn me for a fool," he snarls. "I should never have let you make that swim."

I rest my head against his shoulder. Darkness and warmth reach out to envelop me. I drift into them, even as the Prince roars, "No, stay with me! Don't go away. I need you with me. I need you here. I need you. I need you, do you hear me?"

When I come to again, I'm lying on the ground once more. I blink, just able to discern the hazy image of the Prince crouched over me. A lazy, far-off awareness notices that he isn't wet through like I am—his own spell must have worked better than mine. I drift out again only to come back to the sound of ripping fabric. "I'm sorry," the Prince's voice growls, a low rumble in my gut. "You'll have to forgo your modesty this once."

He claps his hands together, rubs them fast. The next moment, both his palms press against my flesh. Warmth cuts through my frozen core all the way to the solid block of ice encasing my heart. The ice cracks. My heart, which had slowed to almost nothing, begins to beat a little faster. It hurts. Oh, how it hurts! A moan trembles on my lips.

He grimaces. His hands move, smoothing up to my throat then down across my bare shoulders and arms before returning to my chest once more. Never once does he take them from my skin but pours his fae magic straight through his palms into my body. I feel it spreading, warmth and life and pain. Down my sternum, across my breasts to my stomach, my hips, my legs, my feet, back up to my head and neck once more. He grips my hands in his, massaging the icicles that are my fingers then returns to my heart. Always back to my heart.

Slowly, slowly, my awareness rises to the surface. I moan again. And suddenly I feel something more than the warmth of returning life. A spark. A streak of electricity which dances across my flesh. It shocks me to full wakefulness at last. I stare up at the Prince's face, hovering just over mine. He's intent upon his work, his brow sterner than I've ever seen it. And that single, blighted lock of hair falls across his forehead.

I try to move my hand. Nothing happens. I close my eyes, draw a breath. Try again. This time, my body obeys me. I lift my arm, stretch out my hand. Tuck that strand of hair behind his ear.

His gaze flashes to mine. "Clara!" he gasps.

Then he's cupping my cheeks, touching my neck, smoothing damp hair back from my face. His jaw moves as he struggles to draw breath, to form words. "Clara! Are you there? Are you with me?" His palms slide down my neck back to my heart again, pressing more of his magicked heat into me. "If you can hear me, blink," he says, staring into my eyes with terrible urgency.

I let my eyelids drop. Then, realize that isn't enough to constitute a blink, I force them back up again.

"Gods be praised!" He strokes my cheek gently, almost reverently. Is that sea water on his cheek? It must be, for the droplet that falls upon my lips tastes of salt. His eyes glisten, possibly from the exertion of his magic. "Don't try to speak," he says when he sees my mouth starting to move. "It's best if you lie still, let me do what I must."

I would nod, but it's too difficult. Instead I simply close my eyes, lean into the sensation of his touch. I won't think about how humiliating this will all seem later on. I let myself experience it fully: the warmth, the magic, the heat. The delicacy of his fingers, the strength of his palms. His hands are trembling now where before they had been steady and firm. I wonder why but haven't the strength to ask.

In the end, darkness rises to claim me once more. This time, it is merely the darkness of sleep, not oblivion. I let myself sink into it, even as the Prince draws me into his arms, presses me to his chest. "Sleep now, Clara," he whispers into my hair. "I've got you. I've got you, and I won't let you go."

Then in a low, ferocious growl: "I swear by the seven gods, I won't let her go."

THE PRINCE

I HOLD HER CLOSE, PRESSED AGAINST MY BREAST. HER body is so small and frail, a precious vessel formed of clay, too fragile for the battering shocks of this world. Yet it contains the spirit of a warrior. There's life in her yet. Faint, but clinging with all that ferocious tenacity I've come both to dread and admire in her.

And I, meanwhile, feel my very heart being ripped in two.

I've got to get her out of this cold. The magic I've worked into her body is but a fae glamour. It will not serve to warm her, not truly. Not enough to revive her frozen blood. She needs a real fire, real heat.

I cast about desperately. Icy rain has soaked her discarded garments, but my own thick coat is dry enough. I wrap it around her naked flesh. She almost disappears inside of it. That I don't like. I prefer to feel her against me, to know she is yet living.

Gathering her in my arms, I stand and peer through the rain. The lighthouse. It isn't far. And it's the only possible shelter anywhere on the whole damned island.

"To me!" I bark, and the wyvern immediately crawls close and bows its head. I climb onto its back, careful not to jostle the girl unnecessarily. "Go," I command.

The wyvern springs to the air and glides along the shoreline and cliffs until it reaches the lighthouse. There it circles once, twice, before alighting gracefully on the rain-soaked ground. I slip from its back, adjusting my hold so that her head lolls from my shoulder. It falls back, her hair hanging over my arm, her white neck exposed. Silvery droplets of rain bead her skin, run between her breasts, pool in the hollow of her throat. I want to stare at her, to memorize the lines of her face and form. To know every part of her and, in the knowing, to bind her to me.

Growling fiercely, I stagger forward. The door at the base of the lighthouse tower is locked fast, just as I had left it the last time I was here. How many centuries ago was that now? I hardly care to remember. With a single kick, I burst through and step into the small dark space. A relieved smile breaks across my face. I can sense it—the enchantment in the air. Which means . . . yes! There is still fuel for the fire, still supplies in the sparse cupboards. Nothing grand, nothing luxurious. But enough perhaps to serve my immediate needs.

I lay her down before the hearth, still wrapped in my coat. My hands shake more than I like as I set about getting a fire going. A simple spell could spark it to life—but any fae blaze I might make would not provide what she needs. No, I would have to use human magic to generate true, healing warmth, and that I dare not use. Not now, not with my senses addled. I'm too likely to overreach, to cause myself lasting harm. She needs me well and whole. To help her. To save her.

So I gather flint from the box on the mantel. It takes a few tries, but the spark takes at last. Flames creep through the tinder and up dry old logs on the grate. I feed them, coax them. Only when I am certain the blaze is true do I turn to gather musty fur rugs and blankets from an alcove in the corner. These I mound close to the hearth.

Then I turn to her again. Lift her gently onto this makeshift bed. Is she still breathing? In the few minutes since I dared release my hold on her, did her soul slip away? No—I hear her delicate inhale and exhale. Faint but true. Her skin is like ice though. Wrapped in my coat, she cannot receive the full benefit of the flames.

Delicately, as though handling a porcelain doll, I ease her out of the heavy garment until she rests naked in my arms once more. Then, not stopping to think about what I do, not stopping to doubt or to question, I strip off my own damp shirt. Pull her against me. Rest her head against my shoulder, her back against my chest. Wrap my arms around her. Holding her, rocking her, as the fire grows and crackles on the grate. If I could, I would let all the warmth and life in me flow into her. As it is, I give all I can; no magic, no glamours. Just my own body heat and my urgent, defiant will.

Flickering orange light illuminates her too-pale complexion, plays across her pinched features, her frozen lips. Her brow puckers. She rolls her head to one side, nuzzling against my neck. My heart twists. Is she aware of me? Does she know where she is and who holds her?

A low moan escapes her lips. The sound cuts me to the quick.

"Live, Darling," I breathe and press my lips to the top of her head. "Live. Live to despise me. Live to torment me. Live to drive me to the very brink of madness and beyond. But live, damn you. For if you do not . . ."

I cannot finish. The words are like bitter barbs, tearing my throat. To speak more will be to cut myself, to choke, to bleed.

Instead I sit there before that blaze, rocking her gently. Holding her body even as I wish I could hold her spirit. Hold it and claim it and make it safe with me. But she feels like little more than a daydream, insubstantial, ready to fade and flit away. Lost forever in the great nothing of the Hinter.

CLARA

18

I WAKE TO THE SOUND OF A CRACKLING FIRE.

At first I don't move. It's pleasant to lie there, listening to that comforting crackle, luxuriating in the heat against my skin. I feel warm again; I wasn't sure that would ever happen. I'm wrapped in thick, soft fabric which slides sensually against my bare skin, but my feet are sticking out and rest on coarser cloth. Scents of wool and damp wood and old stone fill my nostrils.

Slowly, I open my eyes. A fireplace. I'm lying on a hearth close to a roaring blaze in an old stone fireplace. I don't recognize this place. It isn't home. It isn't Vespre. It certainly isn't Aurelis.

Something shifts behind me. I swivel my gaze to a mound of white feathers which I seem to be propped up against. With a little hiccup of my heart, I catch my breath. The Prince's wyvern.

Its delicate head rests on the end of its tail, which is curled around me, keeping me close to its warm body. It's like cuddling up to a living eiderdown mattress.

I'm very comfortable. So comfortable, in fact, I'd prefer not to move. If I move, I'll also start to think, and that's the last thing I need. Best not to remember anything about the last couple of hours. Particularly those most recent hazy, heat-filled memories . . .

Aching in places I never thought could ache, I lean back against the wyvern. It purrs companionably. And why not? I suppose a dreamed-up wyvern might as well purr. I pull whatever it is I'm wearing up closer to my chin. No, not a blanket—the Prince's coat. Closing my eyes, I draw it to my nose and breathe in the scent of him. The scent of ink and leather which never fails to comfort.

Then I frown. Cautiously, I open the front of the coat and peer down. Gods on high! I'm wearing nothing but a delicate pair of lacy drawers, still damp and clinging. My chemise is long gone. A faint memory of it being ripped off my body scratches at the back of my brain.

Firmly shaking that thought away, I turn to the fire. Damp garments and my satchel hang on the backs of chairs, arranged close to the blaze, slowly dripping. My skirt, petticoats, blouse. All discarded and left in the rain on the clifftops of that floating isle. Did the wyvern fly us back to the same isle when it scooped us from the ocean? If so, this must be the ramshackle lighthouse, for there was no other building to be seen. It had looked ready to fall into the sea at the first high wind. Hopefully it will hold on at least until my clothes have finished drying.

A noisy clatter brings me bolting upright. The wyvern flicks the tip of its tail but goes on snoozing, even as I cautiously peer over its back. A figure moves in the shadows just beyond the firelight. The Prince. Lithe and graceful as ever, he turns, takes a step toward me and into the hearth glow, which shines on his open shirt and bare chest.

His eyes meet mine. He stops in his tracks.

It's suddenly impossible to think of anything else but the sensation of his hands on my body. Life-giving hands, pushing warmth back into my frozen core. The memory sends heat roaring through my veins. I shift, pulling his coat a little tighter around my shoulders. But I can't just sit here, staring at him, letting this silence between us build.

"Prince," I murmur with a little nod. My throat is raw and scratchy.

"Darling," he responds in a clipped, businesslike tone. It doesn't sound anything like the raw, impassioned voice I'd heard just before drifting out of consciousness. But then, maybe I'd dreamt that. A hallucination brought on by near-death. Yes, I'm sure that's all it was.

The Prince comes around the wyvern's snout and crouches in front of me. To my surprise, he offers a small, steaming cup of herbal tea. "Here," he says. "May as well warm your insides too."

I reach out to accept the cup. It's too hot, but the Prince

angles it so that I may grasp the handle, no doubt burning his own fingertips in the process. "Thank you."

He doesn't answer. Instead, he deftly reaches out and pulls his coat shut a little tighter at my throat. A flush of heat rises in my cheeks. Before I can react, he stands and backs away without looking at me. "How are you feeling?" he tosses over his shoulder in that easy, indifferent tone I know so well.

I stare down at the contents of the cup. Little flecks of tea leaves float along the surface. "Sore," I answer at last.

He grunts. He stands at an angle to me, hands in his trouser pockets. The fire highlights the sharp planes of his face and gleams in his hair. "The pressure," he says. "It's bad for your body. You'll be aching for a few days at least, though I did what I could to ease it out of you."

I nod. Take a sip of tea. Then: "How long was I unconscious?"

"A few hours." He glances sidelong at me then. "Roseward Isle is not attached to any one of Eledria's realms, but floats untethered through the Hinter. It's not safe to stay here for long. We may rest tonight, then I hope you will be enough recovered for the journey back."

"Back where?"

"To Vespre, or course."

A different heat rises in me this time. Not the pleasant bubbling warmth of earlier. No, this is anger. Searing, raw. How can he possibly think I would give up now? After everything we've been through! Sure, the merqueen has made an impossible request. But why should that stop me? I've faced impossible odds before and will no doubt face them again.

Besides, I have an idea. The barest inkling of an idea, not worth speaking out loud yet, but . . .

I take another sip of my tea. It's bitter but comforting and soothes that first flare of feeling. When I'm certain my voice won't betray me, I flick a short glance up to the Prince. "I'm hungry."

He smirks. "Didn't think to pack any provisions in that satchel of yours, did you?"

"I did not expect this adventure to take so long."

To his credit, the Prince doesn't jump at the opportunity to mock me for my lack of foresight. He merely sighs and shakes his head slowly, his mouth quirked in a half-smile. "There should be food in the ruins of the great house on the other side of the island. Long ago, when Roseward was a prison, there was an enchantment in place to keep food fresh and replenishing. The worker of that enchantment is now dead, but it may not have faded entirely yet. It will take some time for me to walk there, but in the meanwhile . . ." He reaches out to touch my garments and frowns. "Don't put these on before they're completely dry. I won't have you undoing all my hard work bringing you back from the brink."

I stare down into my teacup again. "Shouldn't you take the wyvern? It'll make your journey swifter."

"No. Keep the beast close to you. Roseward was abandoned long ago, but that doesn't mean new beings and beasts haven't made their way to these shores. I won't leave you alone." Turning abruptly, he strides across the shadowy chamber to a low door set in the crumbling wall.

A surge of panic stirs in my gut. "Wait!" I cry and stand, stepping around the sleeping form of the wyvern. Too late do I remember that I'm wearing nothing but his coat. It's long, sweeping down well past my knees, but doesn't cover my bare feet and ankles. I pull it tightly around me, biting my lip as the Prince turns to look back at me. "I . . . um. Won't you need this? It's still raining outside."

His gaze flicks down the length of me. For a moment, I can't help feeling all over again the warmth of his hands pressed against my body, urging magic into my skin. Heat prickles in my gut, swirls through my limbs until I'm almost dizzy with it. Hastily I brace myself, refusing to duck my head, to turn away from him.

The Prince's eyes slowly return to meet mine. "Keep it. You have more need of it than I at the moment. I'll return soon."

He hesitates. I wait, heart in my throat. Then, with a shake of his head, he turns for the door, opens it. I expect him to be gone the next moment. Instead he pauses, one hand gripping the doorframe. His jaw works, as though he's fighting some inner battle.

At last he looks up again, catching my eye. "You fought valiantly," he says. "While I may not understand your hellbent need to liberate Doctor Gale, I cannot fault your courage. There's not one woman in a thousand who would have been brave enough to venture into the Deep Realm. You're a mad fool. The maddest fool I've ever met." He stops. For a moment the tension in his forehead relaxes, and he gazes at me like I'm . . . like I'm some sort of incredible mystery. A wonder. A dream.

Then he's gone. Stepped out into the pouring rain, the door shut firmly behind him.

THE WYVERN'S GENTLE PURRING COMBINED WITH the flickering comfort of the fire soon lulls me. I set aside my tea half-finished, put my head down, and drift off into a half-waking dream. Though I remain aware of the stone walls around me, of the rain pounding against the door, the rise and fall of the wyvern's side as it breathes . . .

I also see myself walking through the gates of Vespre Palace, side-by-side with the Prince. Twilight stars gleam overhead as though welcoming me home. A shout from above, and I look up to see the children waving at me from a high window. Sis gives a wild yell and begins to climb right out onto the sill, heedless of the danger, while her three brothers scramble to pull her back inside.

A laugh bubbles up from deep inside me. Soon I'll be home.

Home. Soon I'll be seated on the floor of my own room, the children crowded around me, telling me in excruciating detail about every moment of their day, while Lir fusses and feeds me supper, and the Prince . . . the Prince . . .

He'll be there too, of course. He'll pull up a comfortable chair, lounging like a cat, watching me through half-lidded eyes. And he'll smile. Because he'll know I've finally allowed myself to have the one thing I've truly needed all these long weary years: rest.

Selfish.

I wince. The image in my mind fades. I'm back on the hard floor of the abandoned lighthouse. The wyvern has gone. I don't know where. Though I don't open my eyes, I can tell the fire has died down. There's no light shining through my eyelids. Coldness and damp and darkness surround me. I squeeze my eyes tighter, trying to reclaim that dream. But I can't.

Because I'm not alone. Not anymore.

A figure crouches in the darkest corner of the room. I see her with my eyes shut. Huddled and small, dark hair covering her face. Her bent back is to me, and she rocks slowly back and forth. As she rocks, her voice echoes hollowly against the stone walls:

I never gave up.

Not even in the darkest hours.

I always believed there was a way to save him.

I never, ever, ever gave up.

I wasn't selfish.

Selfish . . .

. . . selfish . . .

She turns her head, peering over her hunched shoulder. Black hair parts, revealing one sewn-up eye socket. Her lips curl back in a snarling hiss.

Selfish.

With a lurch, I open my eyes and push up onto my elbows. My heart throbs. Was I asleep? I'd thought I only dozed, but apparently I'd drifted off. The wyvern's warmth is no longer at my back, but a snuffling snort draws my gaze across the room where I spy its white, graceful form with its snout down an old barrel. Searching for a snack, no doubt.

A shiver runs up my spine. I cast a quick glance to the darkest corner of the room. Still half-expecting to see the huddled, hunched-over form. There's nothing, of course. Nothing but shadows.

Sitting upright, I pull the Prince's coat closer around me. The wyvern, catching the movement from the tail of its eye, lifts its head from the barrel, a wrinkled apple caught between its teeth. It flares the feathers around its delicate face in greeting. "Hullo," I say, my voice a bit scratchy. "I . . . I hope you slept well?"

It blinks large, soft eyes. Then with a flick of its head, it tosses the apple into the air and swallows it in one big gulp. The next moment, it roots around in the barrel once more, oblivious to my presence.

There's no sign of the Prince. At least it seems to have stopped raining. Glints of pale sunlight squeeze through the cracks in the door and the shuttered windows. Hopefully he won't be soaked through when he returns, especially as he was obliged to leave me his coat.

Grimacing, I turn to inspect my clothes, arranged on the backs of several wooden chairs near the fire. One stocking is partially singed, and my blouse, vest, and skirt are all still too damp for comfort. The thinner petticoats and chemise, however, are dry enough.

I inspect the chemise, running it through my fingers. It's ripped right down the center. I let out a slow, careful breath, trying to ignore the tightness in my chest at the sight—this all-too real vision of my own peril and the Prince's desperate attempt to save me. I won't think about the vulnerability, the exposure. The sheer embarrassment of it all! If I can put such thoughts out of my mind entirely and never think of them at all, so much the better.

Never to recall the heat of his touch . . .

Of magic flowing across my skin . . .

Of fire scorching through my veins, burning like a furnace in my core . . .

Hastily, I shrug out of the Prince's coat and pull the chemise on, tugging the torn front together as best I can. The petticoats and corset go on next. At least they keep the chemise in place. I'm not exactly modest, but I'm no longer naked, and that must count for something. I hang the coat on a peg by the fire before setting to work on my hair. It's a mass of snarls, thick with salt, and not a single hairpin left to keep it in place. I comb it with my fingers, detangling as best I can.

I'm in the midst of working through a particularly stubborn knot when the wyvern lets out a little burble. Its head pops up, eyes turned to the door. I just have time to realize it must have heard something when the door opens.

I gasp. Hair slips from my fingers, tumbles about my shoulders just as the Prince ducks under the lintel and steps into the lighthouse.

He stops.

His gaze fixes on me, kneeling at the hearth.

Clad in my undergarments, my hair in utter disarray.

I cannot breathe. I cannot do anything but sit there, staring at him. A cry of surprise freezes in my throat. He still wears that same thin shirt, all undone and wet, clinging to his shoulders and chest. He's slicked his damp hair back from his face, which only emphasizes his strong bone-structure and the intensity of his violet eyes. He looks like something out of a romantic ballad, a wild-hearted lover with untamed passions, the kind who strides across moors in billowing capes and tall boots. The kind I've read about in far too many romances secreted up to my room and pored over by candlelight.

Only he's not some fantasy, some indulgence. He's real. Beautiful and terrible and real.

His lips part. His throat constricts. For a moment, I think he's going to speak. What will he say? What will he do? What do I *want* him to say or do? A thread of tension tightens between us until I can scarcely breathe.

Then the wyvern bleats cheerfully. The tension snaps. I let out a huff of air even as the wyvern glides over to the Prince, its large white body obscuring him from my sight. Hastily, I scramble to my feet and try to order my hair, fingers shaking, heart pounding.

The Prince pushes the wyvern's head aside and gives me a wry look. "What must a man do to keep you from catching your death of cold?" He jerks a thumb at his coat. "Put that thing on, won't you? I'll not have you undoing all the hard work I've put in keeping you alive."

I swipe the coat down from its peg and pull it on like armor. Then, taking care to don my most demure, meaningless smile, I turn to him once more. "Were you able to find anything? In the ruins, I mean."

The Prince pushes the wyvern's eager muzzle away from the packet he carries under his arm. He places it on the old, dusty table and proceeds to unwrap a loaf of crusty bread and a bottle of some strong drink. "The provision spells have broken down a great deal since the death of the spell-caster. But the bread is still good. And old Lunulyrian *qeise* only improves with age." He steps to a ramshackle cupboard, digs around inside, then returns to the table, plunking down a chipped glass. Using his teeth, he unstoppers the bottle, pours himself a measure of the drink, and swirls the glass before taking a sip. He hisses sharply and makes a face before declaring, "That's good." A short glance my way. "Eat, Darling. You must be starving."

As though he knows I wouldn't dare approach so long as he stands near, he saunters away from the table. By some unspoken agreement, we keep a good five feet between us at all times. It's like there's a magical barrier which neither of us dares cross.

Leaving the immediate warmth of the fire, I cross to the table and tear off a portion of the loaf. It's surprisingly soft and sweet, not what one would expect to find in long-abandoned ruins. This is powerful magic indeed. I eat several bites, discovering as I go just how ravenous I am. "Who was it who made this?" I ask after I've devoured half the loaf. "Do you know who left the spell on the island?"

"My mother."

I stop mid-chew. My stomach drops, churns. With an effort, I force the mouthful down my throat. The Prince stands with his back to me, silhouetted by the fire. His stance is wide, his silence forbidding. Like he's suddenly turned himself into an impenetrable wall. I draw a long breath, allowing my gaze to linger. He's so . . . so *impossible* sometimes. These last few days, our dynamic has shifted. Though we've been at odds, he's never shut me out. It's too easy to forget how he was when first we met: all that ice overlaying a simmering hot rage. It's too easy to forget how he hates me.

I bite my lip. He doesn't hate me. He forgave me. For what I did. He forgave me, and I believed him. At the time. But now? Staring at that broad back, trapped in this silence, I wonder if he's changed his mind. I can't blame him if so. I've not forgiven myself. I'm not sure I ever will.

I turn the bread over in my hands, still hungry, but unable to make myself eat another bite. "What was her name?" I ask softly, my voice a mere whisper of sound.

The Prince turns his head, not quite looking back at me. "Who?"

"Your mother."

"You know her name." He snorts and faces the fire again, swirling the drink in its glass.

I shake my head, though he cannot see me. "Dasyra is a fae name. But your mother was human. I suppose her true name was kept secret for her protection. She would have been vulnerable, a human queen in a fae court."

Another long silence. Then finally: "The Pledge was not yet signed when Lodírhal took her as his bride. Eledria was even more dangerous for humans then than it is now. So yes; they kept her true name secret, known only to her husband. And me." He looks into his glass before taking another swig. Only then does he say in a low voice: "Margareth. Margareth Rochefort."

I draw a slow breath. Somehow it feels right that I should know. It's not as though she can be hurt by my knowledge anymore. And this way perhaps I might come to grips with the person she was and the life she lived before I came along with my untrained pen and my careless magic.

"And Castien?" I continue after a moment. His body tenses. The sound of his name on my lips is a shock, for I have always taken such care to refer to him only by his title. I hurry on: "It is a mortal name too, is it not?"

"Ah!" He's still for several breaths. Then he turns and faces me, wearing a smile that doesn't quite meet his eyes. "You're full of questions suddenly. One must wonder why."

I drop my gaze, studying the bread still in my hands. Though several possible excuses race across my brain, none of them sound convincing. In the end I mutter, "Never mind," set the bread down, and move to the assortment of garments hanging before the fire. I touch the blouse, hoping to find it dry enough to wear. It's still quite damp.

The Prince watches me silently. I feel his gaze on the side of my face. When I dare glance up, there's an odd expression in his eyes. Something like . . . *hunger*. He blinks, and it's gone. Gone so completely, replaced by his usual blasé disinterest. He takes another gulp from his cup, finishing off the drink. Then, setting the glass down on the ramshackle mantel, he swipes the blouse from my hands. "Here, let me have that." He pulls it through his fist, and the fabric begins to glow. It's not unlike the magic he used on me before our venture to Ulakrana.

"Are you glamouring it?" I ask.

"If I did that, when the glamour faded, you'd find yourself walking about in damp garments once more. No, this is a drying spell."

I frown. "Does it require human magic?"

"A bit."

I snatch the blouse back and retreat three paces. "No!" Our eyes meet. Firelight flickers in the depths of his eyes, highlighting his surprise. I shake my head fiercely. "Don't do that! Don't use your human blood and . . . and . . . Do you remember what the crone said?"

"I remember." His voice is a deep rumble.

I keep going, unable to stop myself now. "She said one more surge of human magic would *kill* you!" I wring the blouse in both hands as though I could wring his neck. "Why would you risk it? For something so . . . so stupid?"

His mouth quirks. "Darling, I assure you a simple drying spell isn't going to herald my sorry end. Have a little faith in me."

I turn away. "It's not worth it." Hands shaking, I drape the blouse back over the chair. His gaze is still fixed on me. I wish he would look away. I wish he wouldn't stare so. Like he's seeing straight into my heart and understanding the tangle of my feelings better than I do. Scowling, I catch his eye. "What?"

He leans one elbow against the mantel, all relaxed grace, a stark contrast to the upright tension of mere moments ago. That half-smile still tips his lips, faintly mocking.

Then abruptly: "She named me after her brother."

I blink, momentarily not following this shift in the conversation. He continues regardless, leaving me to catch up. "Apparently they were quite close. This was before she met my father, of course. Before their Fatebond sprang into being. My uncle was not pleased when Lodírhal stole her away. Mother claimed he got used to the idea eventually and made her swear she would name her firstborn in his honor. Lodírhal was against it. But it wasn't often he could gainsay my mother anything she wished."

I study his profile thoughtfully. Sometimes it's easy to dismiss these people of whom he speaks as mere figures in a story unrelated to mine. But they are his family. His history. Which means they matter. To me. Possibly more than they should.

"Do you have a fae name as well?" I ask after a little silence.

"I do." He casts me a sidelong glance. "These days known only to my father. But one day, I'll offer that name as a gift to she who will be my wife. If she accepts me, she will speak it back. And I will come to her from anywhere in all the worlds."

Again that traitorous flush of heat envelops me. Gods above, why am I reacting like this? It's not as though I wasn't aware of this practice among the fae. Of keeping hidden names known only to parents and spouses. Of course, when the Prince finally takes a bride, she will receive that secret. It's a well-known tradition.

Suddenly the room around me feels small. Small and close and much too warm. I'm probably just too close to the fire. I should back away. Yet, I cannot seem to move. I can only stand there, looking at him. Watching the way he studies my face.

Watching how his gaze travels slowly across my features, finally dropping to rest on my lips. Now my eyes are on his lips as well, and though I don't remember moving, the distance between us has somehow shrunk. Did he advance toward me? Or did he draw me to him with that irresistible gravity of his? It doesn't matter. Nothing matters anymore. Just the nearness of him.

The wyvern lets out a honking bray.

Startled, I leap back, shocked to find how few inches remained between us. I grip the back of a chair and turn away, even as a curse hisses between the Prince's teeth. He pivots, strides across the room to where the wyvern noses at the door. "There, fool beast, is this what you need?" he growls and flings the door wide.

The wyvern slips out, all sinuous grace. Golden light streams through the opening, edging the Prince's silhouette in a gentle glow. "Ah!" he says, his voice bright and a little too loud. "Now here's a happy chance. It would seem Roseward has carried us into the Dawn Realm. Aurelis should be a short flight away, and we can use the gates there to return to Vespre. Just as soon as you're dressed, Darling," he tosses back over his shoulder, "we'll be on our way. There's no knowing how far or fast this island will drift."

With that, he steps through the door and pulls it shut behind him, leaving me alone in the damp darkness of the lighthouse, beside the crackling fire.

20

MY BLOUSE IS STILL FAINTLY DAMP AS I BUTTON the wrists and collar. I don't care. Nor do I mind the lingering dampness in my skirt or vest. My cloak, at least, is dry enough. I don it last of all, pulling the hood up to cover my wild hair. Then, satchel strap slung across my shoulder, I step out from the lighthouse into the dawnlight.

The Prince stands on the edge of the cliff, his arms crossed, his stance wide. Wind tosses his hair, but somehow never snarls it, blast him. He watches the wyvern as it performs dizzying aerobatics above the ocean waves. It swoops low and snatches a large flapping fish in its great hind talons. This it carries to a lower portion of cliff, where it proceeds to swallow its catch whole.

Shivering, I tuck my arms inside my cloak and draw as near

to the cliff's edge as I dare, standing on the Prince's right. "Ah, Darling," he says, his voice brisk as the sea breeze. "I see you're clothed at last. Excellent." He juts his chin to indicate the wyvern. "We shall be off as soon as the beast has finished its breakfast. There's no rushing a wyvern at its meal."

I nod and turn my gaze out across the sweeping view. The horizon of the Dawn Realm outlines the lower sky. Through a haze of pink clouds, the magnificent towers of Aurelis City are just coming into view. For some reason I cannot explain, the sight fills me with foreboding.

I pull my cloak a little tighter and shoot a sidelong glance at the Prince. His brow is unexpectedly stern. "What's wrong?" I ask quietly, half-afraid of being heard.

Immediately his face melts into a brilliant, devil-may-care smile which he trains upon me at full intensity. "Whatever gave you the impression anything was wrong?"

I won't let him put me off so easily. "Your face. You looked a million miles away just now."

"Oh, not so far, I'm sure." Then for a moment he drops the wryness, the sarcasm. Instead he heaves a heavy sigh. "I had not thought to return to Aurelis until . . . well, until the funeral. In fact, I wasn't entirely certain I'd return even then. The funerals of kings are so often accompanied by coronations, you see."

I shouldn't pry. I should bite my tongue, leave him to his thoughts, put some distance between us.

Instead, I find myself asking, "Was your relationship with

your father always so difficult?"

The Prince catches my eye, one eyebrow lifted. "I suppose you'd know a thing or two about difficult fathers."

I shrug and offer a half-smile.

"My earliest memories of my father are . . . different." The Prince's jaw tenses as he lifts his eyes to the horizon once more. "I remember him as loving. Devoted, even. In fact, unless recollection deceives me, I had quite a happy childhood. But then, you know, there was the kidnapping. That certainly put a damper on things. An old enemy of my father's, a Noxaurian lord by the name of Kyriakos, stole me away and imprisoned me for a handful of centuries. Not that I was aware of it. I was imprisoned in my child's body, suspended in time."

He speaks with such careless ease. But the horror is there underscoring each word. I'd not known he'd endured such hardship, such cruelty in his early life. But then, there's so much about him I do not know, so much that goes against the assumptions I made early on in our acquaintance.

"It was Nelle and her husband who saved me," the Prince continues. "Inadvertently, perhaps, but I was no less grateful. I returned to my parents soon after. Lodírhal, realizing what had happened, set out at once to kill Kyriakos only to discover him already slain and his stronghold torn apart." He tips his head my way. "That was thanks to Soran Silveri's Noswraith, I understand. Not a pretty end, even for a monster like Kyriakos.

"My father was never the same afterwards. And once the spell was broken, I grew swiftly to adulthood. We rarely saw eye-to-eye on . . . anything, if I'm honest. Mother acted as a go-between, but Lodírhal and I were both relieved when I left for Vespre. The appointment made sense, occupied both my time and talents, and gave us some much-needed space. Initially, it wasn't meant to be a permanent assignment.

"Then the queen died. And my father blamed me for her death."

"What?" The word bursts from my lips in a short cry. "He blamed *you?* But you didn't . . . you weren't . . ."

The Prince looks at me sadly. "Such an impassioned defense, Darling! Don't forget, it was *my* job to contain and control the Noswraiths. I didn't reach Aurelis fast enough. The only mortal mage on hand with power enough to stand against a wraith of that magnitude was the queen. Even she couldn't beat it in the end. By the time I arrived, it was already too late."

Sickness knots my gut. I can't speak. I can scarcely breathe. We are silent for a time, lost in our own dark thoughts. Shame, blame, anger, sorrow. A whole storm of emotion swirling around us, interchangeable and intermingling.

"Not long after that," the Prince continues at length, "the curse latched hold of my blood. Someone . . ." He pauses, then repeats with rancor, "*Someone* saw opportunity. A chance to drive the wedge more deeply between the king and his son." He shakes his head. "Lodírhal never had to say anything. I knew the minute the curse took hold that I could never be his heir. Not I. Not the cursed, half-blood son . . . the very man he blamed for the death of his Fatebound wife and his own ultimate demise."

Two tears slip through my lashes and streak down my cheeks. I wish . . . I wish many things. I wish I could find that one, simple word that might dispel this storm and bring us both to safe harbor. Does such a word exist? Maybe not. Maybe there's nothing I can say.

Instead I reach out and take his hand.

A shock of lightning shoots up his arm. He turns, stares down at me. It takes all my courage to lift my gaze to his. But once I do, I'm trapped there. Transfixed by his eyes, so wide, so full of pain, so full of . . . something else. Something deeper than pain. Something wild and dangerous and sweet.

"Clara," he breathes.

My lips, chapped by the cold breeze, part. I let out a short breath. Then with more daring than I knew I possessed I whisper: "Castien."

A brash burst of trumpet song erupts in the sky above us. I start, whirl, and gape up at the sudden oncoming rush of great winged creatures, swooping down upon Roseward Isle. The glare from the dawning sunlight glints off golden armor, and I'm obliged to shade my eyes before I can finally discern who and what they are. Soldiers from Aurelis, mounted on winged horses. And Lord Ivor Illithor riding at the front.

"Gods damn and blast it!" the Prince snarls. "What is he doing here?"

He is magnificent. Like a manifestation of legend. His golden hair is braided back from his forehead, and he wears a circlet across his brow, marking him as the king's heir. His armor is brightly polished, and his steed is stormy gray dappled with blue, a living storm cloud of a beast.

My stomach plunges. I pull my hand from the Prince's just as Ivor's mount descends, landing between the lighthouse and the cliff's edge. Four more riders join him, pulling their horses up short behind his.

"Welcome, Ivor, old chap!" The Prince raises a hand in greeting. "Fancy meeting you here. Come to save the day, have you?"

Ivor's cold gaze passes right over the Prince to settle on me. His eyes sharpen, the expression powerful enough to send a dizzying rush through my body. I take a step back, heartrate quickening. But I don't want him to see me shrink. I don't want him knowing what effect he still has on me, no matter the time or distance between us.

So I stand my ground and lift my chin a fraction. He says nothing at first, merely tips his head slightly before returning his attention to the Prince. "Rumor reached Aurelis that the Haunted Isle had once more drifted near our coast. We set out immediately to make certain no danger threatens our people. Only to find you here. Far from Vespre." His eyes narrow slightly. "What are you doing here, Prince?"

"We're having a picnic. What else would we be doing?"

"A picnic."

"As you see."

"On the Haunted Isle."

"May I remind Your Heroicness that Roseward hasn't been haunted these last three centuries? It's quite a pleasant little getaway. Indeed, allow me to recommend it to you and my fair cousin as a honeymoon destination. The air positively *reeks* of romance."

Lip curled in a disdainful sneer, Ivor turns to me once more. "Are you well, Miss Darlington?"

"Oh, I . . ." Warmth floods my cheeks. Hastily, I offer what I hope passes for a demure smile. "Quite well. Thank you, my lord."

"Is your master treating you . . . appropriately?"

A dangerous growl rumbles in the Prince's chest.

"I am perfectly well," I reply, my voice a little higher than before. "We are . . . We were merely stopping here a moment on our way . . . elsewhere. In fact, we were just preparing to leave when you arrived."

Ivor inclines his head. "Do you require a lift?"

Before I can respond, the Prince slips a hand around my waist and pulls me to his side. "We have our own accommodations, thank you. In fact, we were just on our way to Aurelis to access the nearest Between Gate. If it's all the same with Your Mightiness, of course."

Ivor's face is stone. After a long, slow stare, he says only, "We will provide you with an escort and see you speedily on your way." Then he holds out a hand and looks directly at me. "You may ride with me, Miss Darlington."

The Prince laughs outright, interrupting any reply I might

have made. "And bruise herself on that bony beast of yours? Not likely. I am perfectly capable of comfortably conveying my own Obligate hither and thither."

With that, he whistles sharply. The wyvern, happily preening its wings post-breakfast, pricks its feathery head. Then, launching from the cliffside, it glides smoothly over to us, causing the winged horses to stamp and snort beneath their uneasy riders. But the wyvern simply flattens itself on its belly before the Prince, who catches me up and swings me onto the beast's feathered back. I just have time to gasp a breath and grip a handful of white feathers before the Prince settles into place behind me, wraps his arm around me, and pulls me back against his chest.

I dare a glance at Ivor. The man looks ready to decapitate someone.

"Shall we then?" the Prince purrs. "I don't know about the rest of you, but I'm eager for all the comforting sights of sweet home."

Ivor's lips thin. For a moment, I fear he will speak. No, worse than that, I fear he will demand some form of mortal combat here and now. Instead he yanks his mount's head about, raises an arm high, and shouts a command. The next moment, all five riders are in flight, their beasts leaping from the cliff's edge.

"Hold on, Darling," the Prince murmurs in my ear a moment before he urges the wyvern into motion. I have the awful sensation of my innards going weightless as the beast leaps out into open air. Then its wings catch the updraft, and we circle into the sky, our faces aimed at last for Aurelis.

Soon Roseward Isle is lost in the fog behind us as it continues its lonely journey across the Hinter Sea.

21

THE RUSH OF WIND IN OUR FACES MAKES TALKING difficult. I am grateful for this small blessing. As we glide through the air above the ocean, my mind is in far too much turmoil to bear conversation.

Something has changed between the Prince and me. This journey has brought us together in ways I'm not sure either of us is prepared for. Is it irrevocable? When we return to Vespre, will we fall back into the same mildly antagonistic dynamic we've known up to this point? It doesn't seem possible. But I don't know what can or should happen next. What I want to happen next.

I tuck deeper into my cloak. Trying to ignore the pressure of the Prince's arm wrapped around me, the awareness of his chin resting close to my shoulder, I focus on the horizon ahead of us. My stomach knots. The Prince believes we are bound for home. He doesn't know I've not given up on my quest. Not yet. I have an idea. A mad, possibly forlorn hope of an idea. Perhaps I shouldn't even try it. But if I don't . . .

Selfish.

The word echoes in the deepest recesses of my mind. I can't give up. Not on Danny. Not on Oscar. Perhaps I will fail. But if I do, I will fail knowing I did everything, *everything* I could.

But how will the Prince react when he realizes?

All too soon, flanked by Ivor and his mounted warriors, we're across the water and approaching the magnificent towers of Aurelis. I've never seen the center of Lodírhal's kingdom from this angle before. Somehow it's even more magnificent, a massive palace-city boasting hundreds of shining turrets which catch the dawnlight and shine like gold. Numerous gardens of lush green and glittering waterfalls cascading from one level to the next make the whole structure feel as though it sprang naturally into existence, grown rather than built. I've become so used to the stone and gloom of Vespre, the sight is quite overwhelming.

"We'll head for the gate as soon as we've landed," the Prince speaks suddenly close to my ear. "Lyklor will be glad to see us. If all goes well, we'll be back in Vespre by dinner."

I chew my lip. Then, shouting a little to be heard above the wind: "Since we're here, I should like to pay a visit to Thaddeus Creakle."

His arm tenses. "And by that you mean you truly intend to visit Doctor Gale, I take it."

"No!" I shake my head vigorously. "No, it's just the last time I was here, I didn't get a chance to see Mister Creakle. He was always kind to me and helped me so much when I first came here. I . . . I feel I would be remiss not to pay him a call." The lies fall so easily from my lips. Or not lies exactly. Half-truths. But close enough I taste their bitterness.

The Prince growls softly. "We've been away from the library more than a full day now. We need to get back. Who knows what's happened while we're away?"

The truth of his statement makes my shoulders knot. I close my eyes and swallow hard. "You should go." The words come hard, but I force them out. "You go back, and I will join you soon. I promise."

The Prince doesn't reply. The next moment, Ivor gives a shout, motioning with one arm. His riders begin their descent, and the wyvern falls in behind them. We circle down to a garden lawn on the east side of the palace where, even from this distance, I spy the magnificent figure of Estrilde waiting to greet her betrothed. My skin crawls. I wish I dared beg the Prince to turn the wyvern's head around and fly us far from here.

Too late now. The wyvern lands with a rustle of wings, settling heavily on its haunches, and nervously tosses its feathered head. The Prince murmurs soothingly, reaching around me to stroke the beast's neck. Then he slides to the ground and turns to assist me. His strong hands on my waist lift me easily from the wyvern's back. He swings me around like we're performing some sort of dance before setting me lightly on my feet.

A flush stains my cheeks. I back away quickly, putting a little space between us. Only then do I glance over at Estrilde. My former mistress. Danny's enslaver. Who even now grips Ivor by the back of his head and yanks him down into a passionate, possessive kiss. Ivor submits to her embrace but pulls back a little sooner than his lady might like, straightening his shoulders before he turns . . .

And looks straight at me.

I drop my gaze to the ground, flushing harder than ever.

"Castien!" The princess's musical voice trills brightly in the air. "Dear cousin, have you thought better of my invitation and come to celebrate with us?"

"Celebrate what, fair Estrilde?" the Prince replies, smooth as butter. "Is there something worth celebrating of which I am unaware?"

Estrilde's face goes fixed and hard around her smile. "Spring Summit Night is upon us. All Eledria will be here to toast my forthcoming union to Lodírhal's heir. So yes, indeed—there is much worth celebrating."

The Prince offers a gracious bow. "If my beloved cousin says so, who am I to disbelieve her?"

"Ilusine will be there," the Princess continues, her expression morphing into one of loving concern. "I understand the two of you had some sort of quarrel. Again. The ball will be an excellent opportunity to set all to rights. Everyone knows the two of you were made for one another."

A stone drops in my gut. I suddenly find it difficult to breathe. The Prince doesn't look my way, but Ivor's gaze is hard on me, noting every little fluctuation of face and feature. I wish he wouldn't look at me like that. Not with his bride right there, clinging to his arm. Gods on high, how has my life become so complicated?

"Be sure to wish Ilusine my best." The Prince's voice breaks through the dull thudding in my ears. The next moment his arm is around my waist, pulling me to him. "Unfortunately, the grimoires aren't going to mind themselves, now are they? So unless you want a host of Noswraiths attending your little dance, I'll be on my way."

"If you're sure you won't change your mind," Estrilde purrs, her grip on Ivor's arm tightening. "The invitation stands." With that, she turns her betrothed firmly around with her and sets off through the garden, her gossamer gown of sunrise pink wafting behind her. "My love!" she says, loud enough to be certain we both can hear it. "Now that you've seen to our city's safety, do come amuse me, will you?"

Ivor allows himself to be led away. Likewise, I find my elbow gripped and my feet pivoted the opposite direction, guided by the Prince's firm hand. The wyvern folds up its wings and falls into pace behind us. I cast a last, tentative glance back over my shoulder, peering around its feathered body and—

"Don't look back!" the Prince snaps.

I swing my face forward again. Too late. I'd already caught Ivor's gaze, also turned for a last glimpse of me. My face heats. I blink hard, trying to steady my senses.

The Prince curses. "I don't understand what's wrong with you ladies, always falling for that bastard's glamours. What do any of you see in him exactly?"

"Oh, I don't know." I toss my head, determined not to reveal any embarrassment. "His godlike beauty might have something to do with it."

"Godlike? Is that what you call it?" The Prince grimaces. "The man's pretty enough, I'll grant you. But have you seen him dance? He's got the grace of a gargoyle. Absolutely no sense of rhythm."

"There's more to a man than his dancing ability, you know."

"I beg to disagree. You can always judge a man by his dancing. If he moves with grace and confidence upon the dance floor, it speaks to his character. If he's a clodhopping lumpkin, you know he's got a black heart to match."

"Or perhaps it simply means he's devoted his energies to more important things."

"And what, pray tell, is more important than dancing?"

"Chivalry. Devotion to duty." I shrug. The argument sounds lame even in my own ears. But I'm committed now, so I add, "Honorable exploits."

The Prince snorts. "Oh, Ivor has exploits enough to his name. But if you think that man has devoted his energies—as you so eloquently put it—to anything more noble than base brutality, you're much mistaken."

Brutality? I frown. Of course Ivor is a warrior, but he's always seemed so gentlemanly, so dignified. Yes, I've glimpsed flares of passion in his eyes, heard it in his voice, but never anything I would describe as brutal.

I glance back again just as we're reaching the end of the garden. "Eyes forward, Darling!" the Prince snarls. Once more too late. Because Ivor too has paused under an arch and turned back. Which means he's caught me looking at him. Twice.

Even from this distance, I see his mouth twitch in an almost-smile.

"Gods damn it, why are you encouraging him?" the Prince growls, yanking me after him through the garden door. The wyvern makes itself small and slinks after us into the palace halls. Household members walking by stop to give us odd looks, shocked at the sight of the feathery beast waddling in our wake.

"I'm not encouraging him," I protest, conscious of how my voice echoes in these vaulted halls.

"You most certainly are. And believe me, Ivor doesn't need encouragement. He's more than happy to make an ass of himself all on his own."

"Now you sound jealous."

"Jealous?" The Prince halts abruptly, pulling me to a stop. I turn and meet his stormy gaze without flinching. "What makes you think I would be jealous of a cretin like Ivor Illithor?"

My throat tightens. What am I supposed to say? I hadn't

intended anything particular by the remark, but now it's struck home, and I . . . I don't know what I'm supposed to do. The Prince stares down at me so intently. He's not about to let me walk on without saying something.

I clear my voice and shrug one shoulder. "Because the king chose him over you."

His brow darkens. He leans in closer. "And you think that matters to me?"

"Of course it matters." I refuse to let my gaze waver. "How could it not? Lodírhal is *your* father. You are his only son and should be his heir. Ivor has taken everything from you."

"Ivor has taken nothing from me I care about." He draws closer still, until the hall, the arches, the windows, the walls around me are lost, and my world is made up of nothing but those eyes of his. Dark fire sparks in their depths. "Not yet at least."

This is dangerous. There isn't enough space between us, and yet . . . and yet last those few inches feel like an eternal gulf. What would it take to finally cross that gulf? Does either of us have the courage? We keep dancing on the brink, and yet every time the moment comes . . .

I close my eyes. In that one simple act, the power of his gaze is shattered. Wrenching away, I continue down that hall, not even seeing where I go, trusting my feet not to carry me into a wall. "Tell yourself whatever you need to." My voice is light and thin. "It's not my business."

"Oh, isn't it?" The harshness of his tone brings me up short.

I stand, fists clenched, but don't look back at him. "You make everyone's business yours. Just not mine. Why is that do you think?"

"I don't know what you're talking about."

"No? Then why else are we going to the library even now to look up some miraculous cure for Queen Seraphine's ailing son?"

My mouth drops open. But I cannot speak. Neither a lie nor an explanation will form on my lips.

The Prince steps to my side, looking down at me. "I know what you're doing, Darling. Thaddeus Creakle is a good soul, but I know he's not the reason for this little detour. Besides, I can't imagine you letting the matter go so easily. No, no, for once you've set your mind to something, you'll see it through to the bitter end."

I let out a short breath. Then, clenching my teeth hard, I gather handfuls of my skirt and stride on swiftly, leaving the Prince to follow in my wake. Or not. Just as he chooses.

I don't care.

22

GOLDEN LIGHT FILLS EACH PASSAGE AS I HURRY on my way. Every surface gleams, illuminated in that dawnlight aura which I used to take for granted before I was forced to pack my things and leave for the Doomed City. It's so beautiful, so airy, enough to brighten even the most shadow-haunted heart.

Yet I find Aurelis has lost much of its former appeal. As I cross paths with the palace denizens—some familiar faces, some strangers, all coldly disinterested in me—longing grows in my heart for Vespre and the people I left there. For the children and Lir, Mixael, and Andreas. Even stern Khas and her stony guards, some of whom I now know by name. All those faces who, mere months ago, were frightening strangers to me. Now the mere thought of them fills me with homesickness.

But no! This can't be homesickness for Vespre is not my home. It never will be. Home is with Oscar. Always with Oscar.

I won't forget. And I won't be foiled.

The Prince and his wyvern follow some distance behind me. I feel him there, though I refuse to look back again. Why doesn't he just give up and leave like he should? Take the chance I've given him, escape his Obligation, and return to his city? I wish he would. I wish he would abandon me, leave me to manage on my own. Because that's what I always do. I manage. No help. No support. Just me against the worlds.

It will happen eventually of course. He'll tire of me, tire of trying to talk sense into me. Tire of trying to make me see things his way. Then he'll drop me at last. And it will be such a relief when it finally happens. The suspense of waiting for the inevitable is much worse than the reality will be. Sure, it will hurt like the nine hells when he finally gives up. But I've been hurt before. I'll push through.

What I cannot bear is this terrible, agonizing, tentative glimmer of *hope*. This frail blossom struggling to bloom in my heart. This wish, this gossamer dream that maybe, *maybe,* he will be different. Maybe he won't give up on me. Maybe he'll stick with me through all the madness I'm putting myself through. Maybe he'll even find the secret words to convince me to let go. To leave all this behind . . .

Gritting my teeth, I hurry on, determined to outpace both

him and my own traitorous thoughts. At last I turn a corner and approach the library doors. Beautiful, golden, shining Aurelis Library, with its pristine shelves made of interlaced white branches, and its tall windows through which more golden light pours. And all those books. Lovely, leather-bound volumes of parchment and ink, none of which contain living nightmares eager to eat you the moment you crack their covers. For the first time since landing in the City of Dawn, the tightness in my chest relaxes just a little. A long sigh escapes my lips.

The familiar slumped figure of George Nobblin sits behind the reception desk. He looks up lazily when I enter. "Hullo, Mister Nobblin," I say approaching the desk and smiling politely. He blinks, no spark of recognition in his eyes. He's been serving out an Obligation for many long years now. The time in Eledria has dulled him; though I suspect he never was a sharp fellow to begin with. "Is Mister Creakle about?" I continue. "I'd very much like to speak with him."

Nobblin glances behind me. I feel the Prince standing there, though no doubt it's the wyvern that causes the junior librarian's brow to pucker. He flicks his gaze back to me. "Mister Creakle is working in the back rooms today."

"Thank you."

I take several steps in that direction, when a sharp snap of fingers and an arresting, "Hold on!" stop me in my tracks. I look back questioningly into George Nobblin's scowling face. "I'll need to see your library pass."

"I don't have one. I'm a librarian."

"No, you're not."

"I am. Mister Nobblin, it's me. Clara Darlington. I worked here with you for five years."

Nobblin reaches into an alcove under the desk and removes a hefty ledger. With quick, practiced efficiency, he pages to the long list of librarian names: all those human Obligates who have served in Aurelis since the time of its founding. Then he turns the book around, pushes it across the desktop, one bony finger pointing to a particular name. My own. With a line scratched diagonally through it.

"Yes, well." I push the book back. "You can still clearly see that is my name."

"What I can clearly see," Nobblin replies in his most acidic tones, "is that while you may have *once* worked here, you no longer do. Therefore, according to the rules of the library, you require a library pass to enter."

It's one of the hard-as-stone rules, written by Queen Dasyra herself. The fae are sticklers for laws, and the mere act of writing it down has served as effective protection for the library and its bounty of invaluable texts and manuscripts for generations. I, however, am not fae. Written law cannot prevent me from entering. Time to change tack.

I tip my head, letting my loose hair fall across my shoulder. Granted, it's bushy with sea-salt and not exactly the glossy mane one would prefer under these circumstances. But it's all

I've got. "Come, Mister Nobblin," I say with what I hope counts as a bewitching smile. "Surely you will allow for extenuating circumstances. I'm only here a short while, and I daresay Mister Creakle would be ever so disappointed not to see me."

"I wouldn't know." Nobblin's tone suggests I think rather too highly of myself. "What I know is that a library pass is required to enter through these doors. Any attempt to thwart library rules, and I shall be forced to summon the king's guard." He slams the ledger shut and tucks it back into place under the desk. "If you would like to fill out the proper forms, I can begin the process of validation."

"How long will that take?"

"Three days."

"*Three days?* Mister Nobblin, please—"

"I have a pass."

Protests die in my throat as the Prince strides up to the desk, leans on one elbow, produces a small, yellowed card from I don't even know where on his person, and places it under George Nobblin's nose. The words *Official Library Pass: Aurelis Library, Court of Dawn* are faded and half-smeared away, but still legible along with the scrawl of the Prince's own signature.

Nobblin's mouth creases. I'm not sure it's a smile, but I don't know what else to call it. "Enjoy your time in Aurelis Library. Please, do not hesitate to ask one of the librarians for assistance." He waves a welcoming hand.

The Prince smirks and pushes upright from the desk. "All

right, Darling, moment of truth. What is the name of the volume you require?"

Part of me wants to persist in the little fiction that I'm here to visit my old mentor. But what's the use? "*Zaleria Zintoris*," I say softly, lowering my lashes so I need not meet his smug gaze. "*The Book of Stars*. It's found among Lunulyrian songs and legends. Second floor. The author is Hycis Larune."

"Indeed?" The Prince snorts. "Will there be anything else?"

"That will be all. For now." I bite my lip then add, "Thank you."

He gives me a long, searching look. No doubt trying to discern how a book of songs can possibly connect to Seraphine's son and the rot he suffers. Let him wonder. I never said my idea was complete. I'd like a chance to refine it before I share. "As it pleases you, Mistress," the Prince says, offering a sarcastic bow before turning to enter.

Nobblin, however, puts up a staying hand. "No animals in the library."

"Ah, quite right." The Prince turns to the wyvern, which stands just outside the doorway. He snaps his fingers. The wyvern ruffles its feathers and makes an irritable mewling noise. He snaps again, and it heaves a long-suffering sigh. Then it folds its wings tight to its body and . . . keeps on folding. I hardly know how to explain it, the sight is so strange. But when the wyvern is through, there's no sign of the white-feathered beast. Instead a single piece of folded parchment lies on the ground.

The Prince swipes it up and tucks it carefully into the inner pocket of his coat. Then he turns to Nobblin, whose face mirrors mine—slack-jawed and blinking in surprise. "If I may?"

Nobblin nods and motions with a limp hand. The Prince casts me a smug smile. "Shut your mouth, Darling; that's a singularly unintelligent expression. You said yourself, it's a spell." Then he saunters away into the stacks and out of view.

I remain at the entrance. Impatient. Frustrated. Twiddling my fingers, pacing to and fro. Sometimes familiar faces stroll by. They spare me little more than passing glances before hurrying on their way. Apparently, I'd made little impact on my fellow librarians over the years. And the library itself . . . though at first sight, the glorious beauty of it lifted my heart, a second and third glance leaves me cold inside. I simply don't belong here anymore.

But where do I belong? Among the monsters and nightmares of Vespre? Perhaps. And perhaps in the darkest, truest parts of my soul, I've always known it to be true.

I don't like this. I don't like these slow moments, alone with my thoughts and feelings. Better to stay in motion, better to be always in action. Better not to allow myself time for doubt. Because now I can't help but wonder—

"Clara?"

I whirl on heel. A figure clad in footman's livery stands in the passage just outside the library entrance. "Danny!"

He's a far cry from the bruised and battered, half-naked man I'd seen last time I visited. His hair is combed back from his forehead, emphasizing his sunken eyes, his hollow cheeks. He's still handsome, of course; Estrilde would hardly have him in her personal service were he not. She'd send him back to the fighting pits and never think of him again.

"Clara, what are you doing here?" Danny grips the door frame with one hand, his knuckles tense and white. He's fighting the pull of Obligation. No doubt he's on some errand for his mistress, and the longer he delays fulfilling it, the more pain he will suffer. A vein stands out on his brow.

Hastily I jump to his side and take his arm. "Come, let's walk together," I say, smiling a little desperately. "Where are you going?"

He takes a step, and immediately his face relaxes. "The Princess requires a specific berry, the juice of which supposedly augments the glamour on her lips. I am to fetch it from the south garden. Everything is in uproar. Preparations for the ball, you know."

He sounds so exhausted, it makes my heart ache. "But you're no longer . . . She's not making you . . ." I can't quite bear to say it. Instead, I point at the floor, indicating the dark underbelly of the city where I'd last seen him.

Danny shakes his head and offers a weary laugh, though his eyes are haunted. "The crowds grew bored with me. For the time being. The Princess may well change her mind, but . . ." He drags his feet, walking as slowly as he dares without activating the Obligation. I remember all too well how delicate a balance that can be. "It's good to see you, Clara."

A trace of his old smile colors his voice, but when I look at him, I can discern no glimmer of it in his face. "It's good to see you too, Danny." I wish I knew what else to say. "Have you . . . have you found your feet then? Made any friends?"

"Hardly." He laughs bitterly. "In some ways it was better Under. At least the brawls kept me active, kept my blood pumping, kept my rage burning. Now it's all the same. Hour upon hour of *standing* with nothing to occupy my mind. Knowing the Princess may summon me at any moment. Knowing as well she probably won't." He pinches the bridge of his nose, grimacing. "When I think about the children back at Westbend Hospital . . ."

I drop my chin. Any feeble words of comfort I might speak die before they reach my tongue.

"I had a free day, you know," he continues after a short silence. "I'd intended to use it to try again. To find the bloodgem necklace for Estrilde, to break your Obligation and mine. In the end . . ." He sighs and passes a hand down his weary face. "In the end, I simply went back to see Kitty."

He goes on then to tell me what it was like, visiting his sister after a month-long disappearance. How frantic she was, almost hysterical. How when he explained the situation to her, she called him mad and tried to summon a doctor. "Things are not well for her," Danny admits. "She has some inheritance from our parents, but without me there to support her . . ." He shakes his head heavily. "She'll have to take a job. Become a companion to our great-aunt Gerthsted."

"Kitty hates old Lady Gerthsted."

"Everybody does. But Kitty's a brave soul. She'll get by."

The pain and regret in his voice could break my heart. This is everything I'd feared would happen, everything I'd warned him about, all come to pass.

"Did you see Oscar?" I ask quietly.

"Oscar?" Danny blinks down at me. "No, I've not been to see him since . . . since . . ."

He can't say it. But we both know. He's not seen Oscar since my brother pounded him in the face for kissing me against my will. Not a moment either of us wishes to remember. Oscar had seen the act as far more threatening than it was and reacted impulsively.

"Oscar is . . . very protective," I offer lamely.

A shadow falls across Danny's face. "I could never hurt you, Clara. Oscar should know that. After all these years, he should know that at least."

I hold my tongue. Like I always do. It sticks to the roof of my mouth, but I hold it. And only when I'm sure I have it under control, do I say, "Oscar needs help."

Danny lets out a sharp breath. "Oscar needs to learn to stand on his own two feet."

"Don't say that!" I shake my head, gripping his hands. "You know how hard everything is for him! Please, Danny, you mustn't give up on him. We have to help him, we have to—"

"I know what I have to do." Danny looks down at me, his eyes deeply shadowed. "I am going to get that bloodgem necklace. I'm going to save us both, I swear it." He curses then, his face lined with pain. "I must go. Estrilde won't wait much longer. Clara, please, trust me. I'm going to figure this out. Somehow." He touches my cheek with one hand. For a moment, his expression melts into a phantom image of the boy I once knew and loved. "I'm glad to have seen you again. You give me hope."

With that he turns and hastens on his way. This time, I do not follow him. I can only stand there, watching him go. Blood throbs in my ears. All this time, I've been telling myself that saving Danny would somehow be saving Oscar too. But what if I'm wrong? What if Danny intends to leave Oscar to rot?

What if all this is for nothing?

I bow my head, press my fist against my forehead. Their faces swim before my mind's eye—Danny and Oscar and Kitty. All those poor children at Westbend Charity Hospital. Even the tortured face of Seraphine's son. I can almost hear them begging, pleading for me to do something, anything.

And always, always in the back of my head, that dark, whisper:

Love him.

Love him.

Save him . . .

"Darling?"

I suck in a sharp breath and whirl about. The Prince approaches, stepping through patches of golden light which fall through the windows. The sight of him sends my heart lurching to my throat. "Why did you wander off?" he asks even as he pulls a slim book from under his arm and offers it to me.

I take the volume in both hands, press it to my heart. "I . . . saw someone I knew." He gives me a look, but I ignore him, turn away sharply, and lay the book across my arm. The *Zaleria Zintoris*. Opening the soft leather cover, I flip through pages. All those old Lunulyrian songs, captured in written form by a mortal mage who traveled to their world long ages ago. The songs are not written in the tongue of the Lunulyrians, as there are no known characters that might capture those sounds. But it has been translated both into Old Araneli—which I don't speak—and Serythian, my own language. Hycis Larune was a human mage from Seryth, after all. A convenient turn of events.

"I am struggling and failing to comprehend what mad little scheme your mad little brain has concocted," the Prince says, arms crossed, face peevish. "Anytime you care to share, Darling, I'm agog to hear it."

I lick my lips, turning page after page. Finally, I come upon the song I'm looking for: "Crown of the Volodaris." Turning the book around, I hold it up for the Prince's inspection. "Here. This is what I need."

He looks. Raises an eyebrow. Lifts his gaze to mine. "Because . . . ?"

"Because I'm going to Illithorin's Waste."

The Prince could not look more shocked if I had suddenly slapped him. "The waste? The Burned Realm? The High King's Ruin?" His other eyebrow rises to match the first. "Are you insane?"

I might be. Illithorin's Waste is one of the more infamous landmarks in all Eledria, the site of the last great war between dragons and the fae. Neither side won, and the land that was once the center of a unified Eledria, the seat of the High King's power, was decimated.

"Why would you want to go there?" the Prince persists. "There's nothing. Nothing but empty, endless desert as far as the eye can see. Pockets of poisonous fumes still linger in the deeper recesses. Whole cities were burned and then buried, lost forever."

"I know." I pull the book back, pressing it to my chest once more. "But I also know the legend—the tale of the High King, and the gift the gods bestowed upon him. The Water of Life."

The Prince scoffs. "You can't be serious."

"It is real, isn't it?" I persist. "Others have seen it. Others have found it. Even after the great war."

"Sure. Plenty of adventurers have set out in search of the High King's gift. Some have returned to tell the tale. Two even claimed to have drunk from the fountain."

"Did they?"

He shrugs. "Perhaps they did, perhaps they didn't. As far as I know, both are still alive and kicking about Eledria somewhere. That may or may not be testimony to the mystical waters and their powers; the fae are a long-lived bunch as general rule. But, Darling, do be serious." He reaches out as though to take the book from me. I turn quickly, avoiding his hand. "You're not about to make your way across that wasteland."

"I am."

"How?"

I press the book to my chest and meet his eyes defiantly. "I'll navigate by the stars."

He blinks. "By the stars?"

"Yes."

"Have you forgotten where Illithorin's Waste is located?"

"No."

"In Solira. The Realm of Sunlight. There are no stars. In fact, that part of the sky won't see nightfall for nearly one hundred turns of the cycle. You'll have a long wait."

"I have a plan."

"Do you now?"

"I do."

"Well in that case." He throws up his hands. "I take it all back. If you have a *plan,* then of course! Of course, we should set out at once! What's one more suicidal quest after all? But I warn you." He points a finger in my face. "Even if you somehow manage to navigate by stars where there are no stars, then what? You know the fountain will be guarded."

"Yes, of course. I've heard tell of the guardian of the Water of Life." I shrug. "But that's all right. If it were easy, everyone would go drink their fill every day, and the waters would soon lose their powers. It has to be difficult or it wouldn't matter. That's just the way stories are."

He eyes me narrowly. "All right, I'll bite. Tell me what this great plan of yours is."

"That is none of your concern, Prince. I ask only that you

escort me to the gate that will lead me nearest to Illithorin's Waste. From there . . ." I hesitate, swallow. "From there you may do as you like. I won't Oblige you to go any further with me."

He gives me a withering look. "Oh, no. No, no, no, Darling, I'm afraid it doesn't work like that. You can't drag me this deep into your madness then expect to cut me lose. No, I'm afraid you're stuck with me a little longer." With that he snatches the book from my hands, turns it over, and shakes his head, baffled. With a defeated sigh, he shrugs and hands it back to me. "Shall we be off then? I can't wait to get lost and perish in a burning desert under a blistering hot sun. Sounds like a grand old time to me."

Though I try my hardest to stop it, I cannot help the smile that breaks across my face.

23

APPARENTLY, THERE ARE NO GATES LEADING TO Illithorin's Waste. The region is utterly condemned. Some say it's damned by the gods themselves. No one dares dwell within a hundred miles of its cursed borders.

So when Lyklor has spun his dial, and the Prince and I have both stepped through the shimmering air of the Between Gate and felt our essences thinned and stretched across the veils of reality before snapping back into physical shape, we find ourselves deposited in the middle of a verdant forest full of chirping birds and slithering sounds in the underbrush.

I pick myself up and dust off my cloak and gown, both of which are suddenly much too hot and heavy for this atmosphere. The Prince, who arrived moments ahead of me, has already stripped off his coat and slung it over his shoulder. "Best leave that," he says, indicating my cloak. "We can fetch it on the way back."

I fumble with the clasp and let the wool fabric drop in a pile at my feet. I hesitate then, tempted to do the same with my outer vest. I glance up at the Prince, who catches my eye just for a moment before turning a disinterested gaze away into the lush greenery around us.

Biting my lip, I grab my satchel strap. Sweat-dampened hair already sticks to my forehead. I push it back with one hand. "How swiftly can your wyvern carry us to the borders?"

The Prince fishes in his coat pocket for the parchment spell still tucked in there. "I'd say about three hours. But we must find a clear space from which it can takeoff first. Best foot forward, Darling!"

With that, he strides off. I have no choice but to hasten after him.

Many eyes watch us as we progress—strange Eledrian beings, denizens of this fae forest. Birds sing in sweet harmony, their voices faintly threatening. Once I glimpse a creature that seems to be made up entirely of moss and bark, like an old, half-rotten log suddenly turned animate. It watches us through the empty hollows which serve as eyes before lumbering on its own way. A delicate horned fox races across our path, and somewhere in the distance, I swear I hear the lonely cry of the wanderloo. Though I know innumerable dangers surround us at any given moment, it is very beautiful, almost peaceful, though my blouse is soon sticking to my back in sweat-damped patches underneath my vest.

At last we find a clearing large enough for the wyvern to

stretch its wings. The Prince unfolds the parchment and lays it down on the ground. The next moment, the feathered beast sits upright, shaking its head, ruffling its feathers. It twists its elegant neck back and chews the feathers at the base of its tail, growling irritably, but when the Prince approaches, it gives him an affectionate nuzzle.

"Come on then." The Prince turns to me and holds out a hand. "We've a long flight ahead of us."

I hesitate. But only for a moment. Then I accept his hand, refusing to acknowledge the sparkling tingle of his touch. Nor will I admit to the flutter in my belly when he grips my waist and lifts me onto the wyvern's back. Gods spare me, I should be used to these little moments of contact by now! But every time we touch is like the very first time.

And when he mounts the wyvern and settles behind me on its back—when he puts his arm around me and holds me close, murmuring, "Hold on, Darling," in my ear—it's enough to undo me entirely.

I don't have time to catch my breath before the wyvern spreads its wings. The muscles of its powerful haunches coil, and it springs into the air. I close my eyes, glad for the Prince's support as we pull up and above the canopy of trees into the sky above. There the beast catches an updraft and soars in a wide circle. At some gentle guidance from the Prince, it turns its head south. Soon it falls into a steady rhythm of pulse and soar, pulse and soar. Wind whistles through our hair and garments, cooling and drying the accumulated sweat.

After a while I dare to open my eyes and look down on the treetops, the hills, the valleys far below. It's such a beautiful world. I've read accounts of Solira's beauty before, of course, this Realm of Sunlight. I've heard tales of its mighty queen and her incomparable daughters—one of whom I've met. Ilusine. Winged and golden-skinned and gorgeous beyond all reason.

"Everyone knows you two were made for one another."

Estrilde's voice purrs in my memory. It's the truth, of course. No one who saw Ilusine and the Prince together could doubt their rightness for each other. But it's not the whole story. The Prince turned her away. He doesn't love her. He can't, because . . . because he loves . . .

"There." The Prince's voice breaks through my reverie. He points, and I raise my gaze to peer over the wyvern's feathered crest. There on the far horizon. Blankness. All the green and lush landscape around us simply vanishes into heat-seared haze.

"Illithorin's Waste," I whisper. The wind steals my voice, carrying it away.

"They say the High King's Palace was so mighty, so majestic, it could be seen from every realm of Eledria without the aid of magic." There's unexpected sorrow in the Prince's voice. "They say when it went up in flames, it burned for a century. A warning to every living fae. To those who dared overindulge in the gift of the gods, who sought to make themselves like the gods in immortality."

He falls silent once more as the wyvern carries us over the

lonely miles. The distance to the waste slowly shrinks. Sometimes I close my eyes, unable to bear the unfathomable vastness of it. Sometimes I look down, watch the trees and rivers go by below. Sometimes however, I dare look up and see that tragic scar upon the world. In my mind's eye, images of dragons and fire and destruction perform their inevitable dance of annihilation. A war ordained by the gods themselves.

The nearer we come, the more I find myself reluctant to enter that realm. Even the prospect of diving into Seraphine's kingdom did not fill me with such dread. I could turn back. But I've gone beyond doubting now. Determination burns in my veins. I set my face to that horizon, blinking into the wind, and no longer let myself look away.

Finally we come to the edge of the waste, a stark line where the greenery suddenly gives away to nothing but rolling, endless sand. The wyvern goes into a gentle holding pattern, growling softly, unwilling to enter. I see at once how dangerous it must be. Once we go beyond sight of the green land, we risk becoming lost in that vastness. How many others have ventured in, lured by the promise of healing and life the fountain offers, only to perish in that heat, their bones long since buried and forgotten?

"All right," the Prince says, his mouth close to my ear. "This is your moment, Darling. Reveal this daring plan of yours, will you?"

I swallow painfully, my throat dry. Then I say, "Fly on."

"Fly on? Into that? With no map, no stars, no charts. No supplies. Perhaps you *want* us to die."

I smile then. Because I know. This plan of mine will work. I don't know how I know, but . . . it will. It will.

"Do you trust me?" I say.

"Trust you?" The Prince snorts. "To be mad and reckless, absolutely."

"Then fly on."

The wyvern makes another wide circle. Rather to my surprise, the Prince takes a handful of feathers and tugs, bringing the beast's head swinging to face the wasteland. The wyvern utters a burble of protest, but at the Prince's insistence pulses its wings once, twice, three times. Then we're over the border, leaving the green world behind as we plunge into the desert's clutches. "I hope you know what you're doing," the Prince mutters.

I don't bother to answer. Instead I pull my satchel in front of me, reach inside, and grab the slim copy of *Zaleria Zintoris*. The wind is rough, pulling at the pages, but I press it open and page through until I come to the set of verses I need. I begin to read out loud:

> *"Tho' laurels and coronets may fall*
> *To Time's unyielding hand*
> *And fade to ruin beyond recall,*
> *Will no degradation mar this,*
> *Shining bright o'er sea and land,*
> *The Crown of Volodaris."*

Though the translation into Serythian loses some of the

might and power of the old Lunulyrian song, I feel the ancient glory suffusing the words, captured by Mage Larune's pen and magic. And I have magic of my own—magic which I have practiced before without knowing what I did. Magic which now and then Estrilde would unleash from her clutches so that I might entertain her guests, bringing to life songs and poems as I read out loud. Letting the words enter my heart and soul then emerge from my lips with stunning power.

This is the glory of mortal magic, more profound than any glamour. For as I read, as I draw upon that magic which has been inside me all along—that magic which the Prince freed when he bought my Obligation from Estrilde—the old song of stars and constellations comes alive around us. I feel it happening, though I dare not lift my eyes from the pages before me. I continue reading verse after verse of that ancient song once sung in foreign tongues in honor of stars and constellations, beings of glory and beauty more ancient even than the fae themselves. I feel the awe of those ancient singers, feel the wonder of the mortal mage who first heard them sing and sought to capture some small essence of their song so that others may know it too. Their wonder, her words, my voice, combined.

And when I come to the end of the final verse, I lift my head to see it. Night sky. Surrounding us. Brought to vivid life. By me. By my magic.

"Gods above and deep below!" the Prince breathes. The arm wrapped around me has gone slack. When I twist to get a better look at him, I find his jaw open, his eyes wide in absolute shock.

"It's not real," I whisper, half-afraid of breaking the spell. "You can feel the sun still, can't you?"

The Prince shakes his head. Finally, he lowers his gaze, meets my eyes. His expression is one of rapt wonder. At first I think it's for the magic. But then . . . then I wonder if it's just . . . *for me.*

"You are so much more than I ever suspected." He breathes the words like a prayer. "You magnificent thing!"

I stare into his eyes. For a moment, I forget the magic I've just worked. I forget my mad plan, the many layers of bargains I've ensnared myself in. Forget Danny and Oscar and everything. There's just him. Here with me. Looking at me like that. Like I am the very miracle he's been searching for all his life. Looking at me like—

The wyvern dips. I gasp, grip a handful of feathers, and face forward once more. My heart races, and I'm once again painfully aware of the Prince's arm around me, of his chin hovering just over my shoulder, of his lips so near my ear. But now I also see how thin the starry sky surrounding us is, how quickly the magic will fade.

"There!" I cry, pointing a little to our left where the Crown Constellation burns brighter than all other stars in the sky. "The centermost star is Volodar. It was said long ago that the High King was crowned in stars, and the jewel of his crown could guide all weary travelers to his seat. Unless I'm much mistaken, if we follow that star, it will take us to Volodaris."

"You're not mistaken," the Prince admits even as he turns the wyvern toward that guiding point in the sky. "Your mad little scheme has a spark of brilliance to it after all."

It's strange to travel under nightfall while still feeling the heat of the sun burning on the back of my neck. Every now and then I read several verses of the song just to keep the spell alive. I haven't the strength for a full reading. But it's enough.

So we soar over a featureless landscape of rolling dunes, deeper and deeper into the wasteland, following an illusion. I can't help thinking of the stories I've read of adventurers lost in deserts, pursuing mirages until they finally met their bitter ends. Best not to dwell on such tales; it might hurt the magic.

Eventually—whether hours or years or millennia later—two tall spires appear on the horizon like teeth emerging from the sand to tear at the sky. "There!" I cry, the first I've spoken in an age. My throat is parched and dry, and my voice cracks so that I hardly recognize it. "What are they?"

"They," the Prince answers softly, "are Iardi and Luthana, the twin towers of Volodaris, the highest points of the High King's city." A shudder runs through his body, and he adds in a lower voice, "I did not think to see them again."

Again? I turn slightly, trying to catch a glimpse of his face by the false starlight. He has been here before? Was he one of the adventurers to seek the Water of Life? Why did he not tell me? I hold my tongue, uncertain I should give voice to the questions suddenly brimming.

To my surprise, however, the Prince volunteers: "It was when my mother died."

My heart jumps to my throat and sticks there. I wait, both afraid he'll say more and afraid he won't.

"She didn't die immediately," he continues at last. "She clung to life for some days following her encounter with the Eyeless Woman. My father, more desperate than I've ever seen him, conceived a mad scheme to save her. The turn of the cycles was right, and stars appeared in the heavens above Solira. He took this as an omen from the gods, and we set out together, determined to fetch the Water of Life and save her.

"But we were not prepared for the guardian of the fountain.

"We followed the Volodar, just as others have done before us and others will in times to come. By luck or grace, we made our way to these very towers and found entrance into the palace itself. We descended through the cavernous halls, scorched and yet still beautiful. Remnants of the glory of ages past.

"In the center of Volodaris lies the fountain and its ever-present guardian. She is Oasuroa, last of the Dragons of Othorion. She and her brothers and sisters were sent by the gods to take back the fountain and its waters. The others all perished in the war that followed, but Oasuroa—she whom the elfkin named Bringer of Death—remains. Ordained with holy purpose, she guards the waters of the sacred fountain, ensuring none but those of purest heart should benefit from its blessing.

"Now my father believed even Oasuroa would be convinced by

the purity of his motives. No man ever loved a woman as Lodírhal loved Dasyra. So when he stood before the terrible beast and begged leave to take but a mouthful of water home to his dying wife, he did not doubt what the dragon's answer would be.

"But Oasuroa looked at him long and hard with her one good eye. For a great while she studied him without speaking. At last, however, she declared my father's motives impure. As a Fatebound, he would die himself at the loss of his wife. The dragon declared that Lodírhal was as much motivated by survival as by love."

The Prince falls silent again for some while as we draw nearer and nearer to those two great towers. Finally, wondering if he'll even hear me over the whistling wind, I ask, "And you?"

"Oasuroa turned to me next." His voice is rough with shame, with sorrow. "But she asserted I did not seek my mother's health so much as I sought to redeem myself in my father's eyes."

I can offer no answer, no comfort. Nothing I can say will ease his pain, will make him feel any less of a failure.

"Lodírhal would have fought the beast," the Prince continues, speaking into my silence. "He would have let himself be burnt to a cinder attempting to reach the fountain. But I wrestled him down, pulled him out of there alive. I could not have done so were it not for the weakening in his flesh caused by his bond to my mother. He did not thank me for it. I believe he would have preferred to die down there, never forced to face a world without Dasyra in it."

The wyvern circles the towers now, searching for a place to land. They are even more impressive up close than they had seemed from afar, so dazzling and tall under the magicked starlight. We land at last, and the wyvern stomps its feet and holds out its wings, giving us space to dismount. The Prince helps me down, and we stand together, staring up at the tower. My magicked sky is fading now; sunlight gleams on those sand-blasted stones, glaringly bright. There are inlaid precious gems and carvings etched into every square inch, thick with dirt but still visible, still beautiful. I cannot imagine how magnificent the original palace must have been back in its glory days.

"How are we to get in?" I wonder.

The Prince grunts and approaches the tower, circling around its base. I follow, not liking to be left alone, and the wyvern grunts and trails behind us. We've nearly circled the whole structure when we come upon a door partially buried. It's cracked open. "This is how Lodírhal and I got in five years ago," the Prince says, digging some of the soft sand away from the opening. With a little effort, he pries the door open a few more inches. "There's magic preventing the sand from getting into the palace itself. An old spell—whether fae or dragon, I cannot guess."

I peer through. It's dark inside. Pitch dark. I draw a steadying breath.

"Here, this will help." The Prince passes his hands over one another then claps. When he pulls them apart again, a little sphere of light glows between his palms. He hands it to me. It's cool to the touch but burns brighter than a candle. "Find a lantern to carry it in as soon as you can," he warns. "Fae enchantment won't last long in your human hand."

I look up sharply from the little glamour light. "Aren't you coming with me?"

To my horror, he shakes his head. "Oasuroa cast me out. I am forbidden by the gods themselves from approaching the sacred waters again. I cannot go with you, Darling."

My breath catches. Slowly, I turn from him to that dark doorway. How small and frail the light he's given me seems in the face of that blackness. Blood throbs in my ears. I only faintly register the instructions the Prince is giving me, directions through the palace, how to reach the fountain, how not to get lost in the enormous, twisting passages. When he's done, I'm still standing there, still staring into those shadows, into that dark. Wondering how in the worlds I've come to be here.

"You don't have to do this, you know," the Prince says softly behind me. "We can turn back. It's not too late."

But I scarcely hear him. For in that darkness, deep down, a subtle voice hisses: *Selfish*.

"Wait for me, Prince," I say, squaring my shoulders. "I shall return soon." Then, holding the enchanted light up high, I enter the palace of High King Illithorin.

24

IT'S A LONG DESCENT DOWN THE TOWER STAIR. ROUND and round, down and down, until my head is dizzy and my knees are wobbly and weak. Still I keep going, cradling the Prince's light in the palm of my hand.

I can't see much by that gentle glow. Here and there mere impressions of ancient, ornate architecture reveal themselves. A great deal of gold, delicate filigrees and moldings, melted by dragon flame, blackened by dragon smoke. But it's enough to provide a glimpse into an age long ago, grander and more glorious by far than Aurelis or any of the other fae courts.

There's a sense of slow *crushing*. The weight of time and sand pressing in on all the spells which keep this place standing. One day, possibly soon, that magic will give out. Then the palace will be drowned in this desert, lost forever along with its precious fountain. I simply have to trust that day is not today.

At last I step from the tower stair out into an enormous, vaulted space of which I can see very little. Here and there a hiss of falling sand tickles my ears. I shudder, thinking of the chinks and crevices in the enchantment holding this place together. Best to keep moving. Best to complete my business and get out of here as soon as possible. I don't let myself consider whether my motives are pure enough to satisfy a dragon. That's a problem for future me.

"Find the story," the Prince had said when telling me how to make my way. *"It's depicted on the walls. Follow it, and it will lead you to the fountain."*

I shuffle across the floor to the far wall, holding up my light. But whatever images may once have graced this space were long ago melted in that crucible of dragon flame. Still, something must have survived, or the Prince would not have given such instruction. I continue, crossing the great space to another wall, then another. The glamour light flickers, threatening to go out. My heart jumps. The idea of being stuck down here in total darkness . . . no. No, I simply cannot have it.

The Prince had said to find a lantern, which must mean there are lanterns to be had. A hasty search produce a dented, dingy old globe of some metal tracery shaped like a sun. When I put the light inside, immediately the metal transforms into gold, creating the illusion that I carry a small sun before me. The

Prince's little spell is certainly happy contained in that globe. Its light brightens tenfold. As a result, I'm able to get a better sense of my shadowy surroundings.

And there—there, on the far wall at the very end of this enormous corridor, a massive mural gleams. Though my legs are exhausted from the stair, a sudden surge of eagerness sets me running. The nearer I draw to the mural, the larger, more overwhelming it seems. It's five times the size of even the tallest fae man and rendered in elaborate mosaic work with a million multi-colored stones. Fire-proof stones, apparently. Though dragon smoke has dimmed their hues, the images remain clear, almost lifelike. I wonder who did this work? The elfkin themselves are not creators. Perhaps it's dwarven make. Or even human.

The mural itself depicts a story with which I am unfamiliar, legends of some ancient hero—Illithorin himself, unless I miss my guess. It extends down the wall, turns a corner, and continues from there. I follow it as the Prince instructed, holding up my globe and studying the images, trying to make sense of the tale. It seems Illithorin performed a series of heroic acts in the name of the gods—tremendous feats of strength, brilliant maneuvers of strategy and cunning, all while wooing any number of exotic beauties from across the worlds. I've never encountered any of these stories, not in all my years working in Aurelis library. I have to wonder how true they are, if at all. Most likely Illithorin himself invented them as a means of securing his reign over a united Eledria.

There must be some kernel of truth, however. For the gods did in fact bestow a great gift upon the High King. I see it portrayed in detail on the largest, grandest wall of all—the moment when all seven gods reached down from heaven to establish their holy fountain. From that day forth, the fae were blessed with extraordinarily long life. So long, we humans tend to think of them as immortal.

I linger longer than I should at this final image, drinking in the details of the story. It's incredible. When I turn to look back along the huge passage I've just followed, at the panels of legend and myth depicted here, a deep longing opens inside of me. If only I might return here someday. Not in pursuit of some mystical waters, some forbidden blessing from the gods. No, simply to come with book and paper, to write down the story as I am able to understand it. To give it a chance to live again in the minds and hearts of readers.

Tears prick my eyes, spill over onto my cheeks. This is the kind of work I was born for. Not creating monsters. These gifts of mine were intended for greater purpose. Searching out and rediscovering old stories. Capturing them with ink and paper, bringing them back to life in exciting ways. Restoring the glory that once was lost, making it new.

But what's the use of such dreams? I step back from the wall, dropping my gaze to my feet. It's nothing but a fantasy. That sort of life could never be mine. It's not a life I could share with Oscar, therefore . . .

I dash tears from my face and lift my gaze to that image on

the wall once more. This time, rather than seeing the story portrayed, I look for the door the Prince told me was hidden within the image and spy it just where the crowned image of Illithorin stands with his arms outspread. A massive door, so big I fear I won't be able to budge it. But when I put my hands to it and push, it swings open.

Thus I have my first view of the mythic Water of Life.

At first glance, my mind tries to tell me that one of the gods is here, come down from the high heavens into this realm under sand. But no, it is no living god. Instead it is a vast statue of white stone depicting a god-like being. Whether man or woman, I cannot tell; it hardly seems to matter, not for someone so far beyond such limitations. In one upraised hand, it holds a massive ewer from which spills a stream of light. Or water. Or both—I'm truly uncertain which. All I know is that it spills from the ewer into a broad circular pool lined in shimmering gold. The water brims over the edge of the pool and cascades down at least fifty gold steps into a second gold-lined pool, this one larger than the first. It stretches two hundred feet long and fifty feet wide, filling up the space. The light and the gold combine to generate a holy aura, driving back the shadows of that echoing chamber. It's wonderful, beautiful, and somehow terrible all at once. I long to leap forward, to plunge headfirst into that lower pool, but simultaneously shrink away, condemned by my own unworthiness. It's all I can do to muster the courage for a single step into that chamber.

That's when I hear the unsettling sound of deep, deep *breathing*.

I stop. My hand trembles, making the globe lantern waver. It's far too small a light against the deeper shadows of that chamber. Especially not when there's a dragon somewhere inside. A real, fire-breathing, scale-armored dragon. Somehow, up until this very moment, I'd blocked that idea from my mind. All my concentration was simply on making it this far. Now, it seems rather a pertinent consideration.

I gulp, the muscles in my throat tight. That unsettling sound and sensation of hissing sand falling from overhead creates a gentle susurration. With an effort, I find my voice. "Are you there, Guardian?" I call out softly.

"*Yes.*"

The next moment an unseen slithering mass smacks against my legs, knocking me clean off my feet. I'm not hurt. A little bruised maybe. But I lie as though paralyzed, unable to find the courage to pull myself together, to rise. My heart stops beating for what feels like an age, before leaping to my throat and pounding hard enough to choke me.

Something moves through the shadows just to my right. My gaze latches onto it, follows it. Follows those long, sinuous coils curving round and up and up until finally a hulking image of scales and wings and claws and teeth seems to manifest out of nowhere right before my eyes.

"Oasuroa," I gasp. "Bringer of Death."

"So you know who I am, do you?" One great, fiery eye blinks

down at me. The slitted pupil dilates, focusing with far too much interest. "Very good." The voice is hot as steam, underscored by the hiss of falling sand all around. "It's always nice to have a little recognition from one's snack."

The dragon takes an earth-shaking step forward, crawling into the light from the fountain. It gleams against her crimson scales, her fire-blackened teeth, her enormous, cruel claws. She arches her neck, and a magnificent orange crest unfurls atop her head, making her seem even more impossibly large and dreadful. "Come, little mouse," she says, smoke coiling from her flared nostrils. "You know my name; tell me yours in turn. I prefer to know the proper names of my meals, especially as they are so few and far between these days."

My blood seems to have turned to water. But she can't just *eat* me. Can she? No, surely not. She's meant to judge my heart. She's trying to intimidate me, that's all. Trying to test my courage, my resolve. I must show her what I am made of.

With more difficulty than I like to admit, I pull myself to my feet. I can scarcely believe I'm truly standing before that dreadful, beautiful being. I've read a fair share of stories featuring dragons in my day. Never did I dream I would one day take part in such a tale.

"Glorious Guardian," I begin tremulously. It's a good start. Oasuroa flutters her crest, a pleased rumble in her chest. So the stories I read were true: dragons do love flattery. "Glorious Guardian," I say again, "my name is Clara Darlington. I have traveled from afar to seek your—"

I break off as the dragon lets out a low, horrible moan. At first I don't understand what I'm hearing. My mind tells me it must be another growl, that she is even now preparing to snap me up in her terrible jaws before I can speak another word.

Instead, she turns her great head to one side, revealing her other eye. Or rather, where her other eye used to be. Now there is nothing but a ruinous wound and a bejeweled sword hilt protruding from the socket.

As though suddenly forgetting my presence, Oasuroa paws at the sword, then lifts her head and lets out another piteous moan. The next moment, she's scrambling into the pool itself, her large body mostly submerged. She half-lumbers, half-swims to the steps of the golden waterfall, which she climbs, limbs shaking, until she reaches the upper pool. There she sticks her head into the gleaming stream of water-light falling from the statue's ewer before plunging her snout into the circular pool itself. Loud slurping echoes to the highest, unseen vaults of the chamber.

I watch mutely, mouth ajar. What should I do? Should I dart forward and try to steal a few drops of the precious water while the dragon's back is turned? Would the magic of the fountain lose its blessing if taken in such a way? I reach into my satchel for the small waterskin tucked inside.

Before I can make another move, however, the dragon lifts her head, lets out a huge, blustering sigh, and turns, muzzle-dripping, to glare down at me from her one good eye. "Don't even think about it, little mortal," she growls. "Seriously, did you think you could pull one over on the last of the Ageless Othorion? Before the gods thought to form your kind from primordial ooze, I was already older than your tiny mind can fathom. So"—she slumps back down the steps, splashes through the lower pool, and, with a groan, heaves herself onto the cracked tile floor— "let's have no more of this foolishness. Tell me why you think you're pure enough to gain the gods' blessed gift, and I'll tell you why you're wrong. Then we'll make with the snacking, shall we?"

This last threat is spoken without any real menace, for the dragon's head is slumped between her forefeet. She closes her one good eye, breathing laboriously.

I chew my lips. Then taking a single step toward her I say quietly, "What happened to you?" Hastily I add: "Great and Glorious One."

Oasuroa's nostrils flare, issuing a billow of thick black smoke. "What happened to me?" Her eye opens, a thin yellow slit. "That damned, fire-roasted Illithorin happened to me, that's what. After his people had slain all mine, and mine had slain all his, and there were just the two of us left, I burnt him to a crisp, right in his armor. I thought he was done for, but when I drew near to make certain of it, he lifted one blackened arm and plunged this hideous stinger of his straight into my eye. With his last, rattling breath, he gasped out a death-curse: the most powerful curse there is. *'Let this blade be an unending torment!'* he declared. *'Never shall it be removed, not while my blood still runs blue in the lands of Eledria and beyond.'* With that, he went and died before I could force him to take it back again."

She rubs forlornly at her face with one huge, claw-tipped hand. No matter how she paws at the sword, it will not budge. Instead, a trickle of fresh lava-hot blood oozes down her cheek like flaming tears. She shakes her heavy head and utters a mighty sob. "Every so often, I drink of the fountain for relief. But it never lasts. Illithorin over-indulged on the gods' gift, resulting in powers unmatched among his kindred. His curse is as strong today as it was when first he uttered it. Damn him to the deepest of the nine hells! May all my brothers and sisters find him there and give him another good roasting!"

With that, she looks at me. Expectantly. As though I'm meant to offer some comment.

I clear my throat and say the first thing that comes to mind: "You seem to have suffered a vast deal, Splendid One."

"I have, yes. Thank you for noticing." To my relief, Oasuroa closes her eye again and rolls her head to one side. Her lips curl back from her sword-sharp teeth in a grimace. "No one ever seems to care about *my* pain, do they? All the tiny people. All those elfkins and menlings and *adventurers*"—this last spoken with venom. "Creeping insects! Consumed by their insignificant problems, here today, gone tomorrow, while I remain suffering the endless pain of a martyr, over and over, without reprieve. And all they can say is, 'Well, it's just a dragon, isn't it?'" She opens her eye and fixes a hard glare on me. "Dragons feel pain the same as anyone! More so, I daresay. The greater the being, the greater the agony, would you not agree, little snack?"

It's hard even to entertain the idea of contradicting someone who refers to you in such terms. I nod at once, taking care my face expresses nothing but utmost sympathy. "You carry a mighty burden, O Mighty One."

"I do." Another heaving sigh. "And all in silence, long-suffering to the end. Ever devoted to my great duty."

"You are an inspiration."

"An inspiration? I like that." She tips her big head, crest fluttering faintly despite her pain. "Thank you for understanding. It's nice when you insects have something like common decency about you." Then, with a roll of her one eye, she slumps her head back down on her crossed forepaws. "I suppose you want to ask for a sip of the waters now, don't you?"

"Oh, I . . . well . . ."

"No point denying it. You're polite enough, I'll grant you, but politeness will only carry so far. Besides, I grow bored with you." She yawns hugely, displaying many rows of teeth, a long, purple tongue, and a glow of flame in the back of her throat. It's like peering into hell's own furnace. When she's through, she smacks her lips a few times, licks her snout, and blinks at me again. "Let's get on with business then. Tell me, why do you deserve to taste of the gods' blessing? Is your heart pure of motive and intent?"

"Yes," I answer at once. Perhaps conviction will go some way toward convincing the great beast. "I do not come seeking the waters for myself but for a boy. A young man, the merqueen's son, who suffers from a rot for which there is no cure. I would bring the Water of Life to him so that he may—"

The dragon growls something which, despite the depth and reverberation of her voice, sounds an awful lot like, *"Hogwash"* to me. She flutters her crest again, this time with irritation. "Listen to the snackling! Going on about some boy whose name she doesn't even know!" She fixes her terrible one-eyed stare on me again. Fire dances in the depths of her pupil. "Tell me why you've really come, or I'll put an end to this interview here and now."

My lungs constrict so tight with terror, I fear I won't be able to find the words. At last I manage to stammer, "My . . . my friend is . . . he's been enslaved . . ." Then I stop. Because this isn't about Danny. It never was, not really. "My brother," I whisper. The words come out in a whisper, almost lost in the murmur of falling sand and the gurgle of the fountain waters. "My brother . . . he needs help."

The dragon narrows her eye. "He's sick?"

"Yes. But not with a sickness these waters can cure."

"Curious." The dragon pushes up onto her haunches, sitting tall and upright before me. "Explain yourself."

So I do. In stumbling words, I tell her how I intend to save Oscar. How I found myself on this mad quest, journeying across Eledria, making bargain after bargain. "And so I came here," I finish at last. "The Water of Life is the only chance Seraphine's son has, as there is no cure for his rot. If I can save him, then the rest should come together and then . . . and then . . ."

"And then you'll be right back where you started."

"What?"

Oasuroa chuckles. It's such a terrifying, cacophonous sound, it makes me leap back several paces, hands over my head in defense. She neither notices nor cares. "Did you never stop to think, little snackling?" she continues, shaking her head with something between bemusement and weariness. "All this just to land you back in the same place you were at the start of your journey. Striving always to help a brother who cannot be bothered to help himself. Running a race that never ends for which there can be no winner. And why? Why do you do this?"

The moment of truth. The moment that will decide my fate.

"Because I love him," I whisper, lowering my lashes and staring down at the floor. "Because that's what you do for the people you love. You fight for them. Even when they haven't the strength to fight for themselves. Especially then. Because they're your family. Because, in the end, they're all you have."

"Ah!" The dragon lifts one gnarled hand, pointing a claw at me. It gleams in the air, mere inches from my chest. It's so razor sharp, it would take but a single quick flick for her to rip my heart out, skewered on the tip of that nail. "There's the ugly truth at last."

"There's nothing ugly about love." I tear my gaze from that claw and look up into Oasuroa's curse-ravaged face. "My love for Oscar is the purest—"

"One more word, little snack, and I'll eat you where you stand." The dragon shakes her head. The tattered wings at her back open wide, stretch, and close once more. "I can stomach no more of these lies."

I hesitate. But some compulsion drives me to say, "I speak only truth, O Great One."

She snorts, emitting a spurt of red fire and a coil of inky smoke. "Oh, I'm sure you think so. But as you must have learned by now, a perceived truth is often not the same as truth itself. In fact, it may be the very worst of lies. And no matter how firmly believed,"—she leans in closer, her lip curling to reveal a flash of teeth—"you cannot slip such lies under a dragon's nose. I'll sniff out the falsehood every time. The truth is, little snackling, you don't really love your brother. Not the way you think you do. What you love is the *idea*. Of saving him, of controlling him. Of forcing him into the health and happiness you have decided he needs. And in so doing, of proving to everyone around you how you were strong enough, smart enough, caring enough, loving enough. Where others failed, you succeeded. Indeed, you're very much like every other human I've ever encountered. Obsessed with power and position. With dominance."

Her words fall upon me like a stream of sand, soft and gentle at first, but soon heavy, suffocating. I struggle to breathe, struggle to think. Struggle merely to stand there before that monstrosity. That ancient, angry, wounded, fire-breathing being of terrible power, who stares down at me with her one eye burning straight to my core.

She can't be right. She can't be.

"I . . . I love him," I whisper.

"Maybe you do. Maybe you don't." Oasuroa shrugs. "But you certainly don't love him enough. And you're not taking a drop of the fountain. Not so long as I am living. Now"—she leans forward, snaking her enormous head toward me, breathing her hot breath into my face until beads of sweat line my brow—"are you going to fight me? I fancy a little brawl before supper. You did bring weapons, did you not?"

Mutely I shake my head. My body is too numb even to feel proper terror.

"Ah, well," Oasuroa sighs. "I have no appetite for devouring weakling prey. If you can't bring yourself to give me battle, be on your way. I feel a headache coming on." She claws at her face again, whimpering sadly.

I turn to leave. My limbs are like wooden posts, answering vaguely to the input from my brain, but only just. Staggering a little, I make my way to the door, even as the sounds of flowing water, falling sand, and my own roaring blood throb together in painful harmony inside my head. Is this it then? Have I failed? Will Seraphine's son die? Will Danny continue to serve out his Obligation? Will Oscar . . . *Oscar* . . .

I whirl on heel, face back into the big chamber. "I will bargain!"

The dragon is already slinking away into the shadows but stops. Turning her heavy head to look back over one wing, she eyes me suspiciously. "What did you say?"

"I will bargain," I repeat. "Tell me what you want in

exchange for one sip of the Water of Life. If it is within my power, I will do it."

She flashes her teeth. "There is no bargain that would induce me to break my solemn oath of protec—"

"What if I break your curse?"

Oasuroa goes very still.

"You said Illithorin's curse passed to his kin to carry and sustain, am I right?" I persist. "What if I find whoever holds the curse and convince them to let it go? To let your torment end? Would that be worth a *small* infraction against your gods?"

She's thinking. She's actually thinking it through, weighing the pros and cons of such a sin. I wait in a hush of silent expectation. Part of me thinks she'll flame, burn me alive for my insolence. But she doesn't. And as the moments flit by, I begin to hope she won't.

"You won't manage it," she says at last.

"But I might."

"It's impossible. All Illithorin's children were either dead or lost by the war's end."

"Whatever is lost may be found."

"You won't manage it," she growls again, as though trying to convince herself. As though the wild hope I've just offered is too sweet, too desirable, she must talk herself out of it. "You cannot hope to find the High King's heir."

"I'm a librarian," I reply with a half-smile. "I'm good at this kind of thing."

With a last flare of her crest, the dragon lifts her head and lets a small burst of flame erupt from her throat. Then: "Very well! Very well, little snackling! You break this curse and rid me of this damn-roasted sword, and I will give you what you ask: a single sip of the waters. Which you must not take for yourself, mind."

"Done!" I cry. Striding forward, I hold out my hand. "We have a bargain, Oasuroa."

She stares down at me, puzzled and perhaps a little disgusted. Slowly, she extends one forearm and places the tip of a giant claw in my grasp. "We have a bargain," she agrees.

25

SUNLIGHT GLEAMS THROUGH THE UPPER DOOR OF the tower as I climb back up the long, winding stair. My magic has worn off by now, and the stars have faded away entirely. Hopefully I won't have any trouble summoning them back again for our return journey.

My legs are weak, my body almost fainting with exhaustion when I finally emerge from the tower and step blinking and bleary into the glare of the Soliran sky. The Prince, standing watchful close by, leaps forward with a cry of, "Darling!" and catches me just as I crumple to the ground. He crouches and holds me close, rocking me gently. "Are you all right?" he asks, brushing hair back from my forehead and peering into my face. "That damnable dragon didn't hurt you, did she?"

I cannot speak until he's fetched one of our waterskins and poured most of its contents down my throat. I gulp it gratefully and use the splashes to wash my dusty face and hands. All this while, the Prince never takes his hands off me, constantly touching my back, my shoulder, my head, my face, as though to reassure himself that I'm truly here. The wyvern paces, fluttering its wings and trilling nervously, whether from concern for me or in response to its creator's tension, I cannot say.

At last, I lean back against the tower wall. Even on the shaded side, the stones are hot. I let my chin sink to my breast and release a long breath. "I didn't get it. The Water of Life."

"Well, no." The Prince takes a seat beside me, legs bent and elbows resting on his knees. "I could have told you that would happen. I'm just glad you didn't end up cooked alive. Oasuroa is not always so gracious to her visitors, as I know from personal experience." He runs a hand down his face. Then, to my great surprise, he smiles and lets out a little huffing laugh. "I suppose that's it then. Never would have thought this little quest of yours would take us so far. I'll admit, I'm impressed by your persistence. But I'm glad to make an end of it at last."

I bow my head. I'm almost too ashamed to utter my next words. They slip out in a whisper: "I made a bargain."

The Prince's keen ears prick. The smile vanishes from his face. "Tell me I heard that wrong."

I close my eyes. "I made a bargain. With the dragon. I vowed to find the High King's ancestors and beg them to release the death-curse he placed upon her."

The Prince listens in mute dismay as I tell my tale. Neither question nor comment passes his lips. Only when I'm through, and the silence between us has lingered far longer than I like, does he curse softly and run both hands through his hair. "By this time, nothing you say or do should shock me. Yet somehow you always manage to exceed even my expectations." He tips his face back, staring up at the distant sky. "Gods, Darling! You *bargained*. With a *dragon*. But of course you did! Because you are you, and your tenacity knows no bounds. I've truly never met your equal for courage or sheer stubbornness."

Despite the heat and the sweat rolling down my spine, I shiver. "Maybe you've just never cared about something so deeply." I wrap my arms around myself. "Maybe you've never loved someone so much you'd be willing to give up everything for their sake."

I feel how sharply he turns to me, though I don't have the courage to meet his gaze. We're sitting so close, our shoulders almost touching. The heat of his body is warmer even than the sunbaked stones at my back.

"You're wrong, Darling," he says softly.

My breath hitches. The muscles in my shoulders tense.

"You're wrong," he repeats, in a voice as deep and dark as the night. "To really love someone is to be willing to give them up. To know they are free to make their own choices, for better or for worse. To allow them that freedom. To let go . . . even if it means watching them fall."

I grind my teeth, tucking my chin in even tighter, allowing my hair to fall along the side of my face. "That doesn't sound very loving to me."

"Then perhaps you are the one who doesn't understand love."

I turn my head slowly, letting my hair part so that I can peer at him sidelong. "And you?" I ask softly. "Is this how you love, Prince? Will you always let go?"

His eyes burn into mine, twin violet flames. They drop to focus on my lips before traveling with slow reluctance back up again. There's pain in his gaze, and when he draws breath, it shudders through his lips. "I don't know if I can." His voice is a low growl, rumbling in my gut. "Not when every selfish urge tells me to hold on fast."

I tip my head. "You admit you are selfish then."

His hands, resting on his knees, clench into fists, knuckles white. "I am." He turns and stares out across the endless expanse of blighted desert. "I am the most selfish man I know."

I look at him. Study him. Take in every detail of his features, so beautiful even when knotted with tension. His words reverberate through my soul like the pulse of my own heart.

Suddenly, I cannot resist. Not one moment more. I lean forward, catch him by the face, and press my lips against his cheek. For a moment, I simply rest there. Holding him. Feeling his skin so hot against mine. It isn't much. Such a small point of contact. But after dancing on the edge of the vast gulf between us for so long . . . it feels like *everything*.

He sits frozen in that simple embrace. Then he lets out a ragged breath, pulls away, turns to me, catches my shoulders. My head whirls, and my body flares with heat that has nothing to do with the desert surrounding us. I can see nothing but him, feel nothing but his fingers digging into my flesh. In his eyes I see my own desperation reflected back. My own longing and need. I can hardly tell where I end and he begins.

The whole of my existence centers on this one fixed point in time. This one moment, this one chance.

Then he shakes his head. The pain, the longing, everything I thought I was reading in his face vanishes. "Don't go all soft and soppy on me, Darling," he says, smiling one of his awful, beautiful, heartbreaking, devastating smiles. "You're the one with the mighty quest to complete, remember?"

With that he rises. As he does so, that gulf rips open between us once more. It's an almost physical pain, like having my chest cleaved in two. I can only stare stupidly at the hand he extends to me.

"Come," he says, his voice distant through the drumming in my ears. "It's time we left this gods-blighted desert behind us. I'm sure you have a scheme in mind for curse-breaking. You can tell me all about it on the flight back to the gate."

I try to breathe. My lungs tighten around a sob I cannot, *will not* utter. With excruciating pain, I pull air into my chest cavity, hold it. Let it out in a faint shudder.

Then I place my hand in his. By the time he's pulled me to my feet, my face is a mask. Calm, collected, faintly smiling. Revealing nothing of the turmoil inside.

THE PRINCE

SHE STRUGGLES TO BRING BACK THE STARS.

I watch her in silence as she stands with her back to me, murmuring out the words she read before with such passion. All that power, all that magic which had risen up from the depths of her being and poured out from her lips in such a spectacular display seems to have shriveled up. The most she can conjure is a faint, watery impression which fades moments after appearing.

"I'm sorry," she says at last, slamming the book shut and turning to me. Her face is as serene as ever, an unreadable mask save for a telltale shimmer in her eyes. Even that vanishes when she blinks, leaving me to wonder if I imagined it. "I . . . I think I'm too tired at the moment for magic."

"Never mind, Darling," I reply and pat the wyvern's arched neck. "This fellow knows the way well enough. Having flown it once, he won't forget anytime soon." It's true, for the wyvern has learned over the centuries of its existence to find its way unerringly to and from the floating isle. Its instincts are well honed, and will be able to discern meaning from the terrain which to our eyes remains as featureless as the open sea.

She nods and tucks the book of songs back into her satchel, lashes lowered, gently fanning her cheeks. She does not look up, not even when I reach out, place my hands around her waist, prepared to assist her up onto the wyvern's back.

I freeze. Just for a moment, a mere instant of breath. But in that fraction of time and space, a whole lifetime's worth of longing threatens to overwhelm me. I want to kiss her. I burn to feel her lips on mine. To draw her to me, press her to my breast, to take everything I've been hungering for all these long, sorry months, all these damnable years, since the first moment I set eyes on her terrified face.

But I can't. I won't.

Her gesture—impulsive and sweet as it was—doesn't mean she feels what I feel. For me, the searing heat of her lips against my cheek was like the sudden explosion of the worlds into being. For her? It was what it was. A kiss. A token of gratitude. Possibly even some affection or regard.

But if I dare take it to mean more than it was, if I dare wrest from her more than she intended to give . . . Gods! I couldn't live with myself.

So I lift her onto the wyvern's back and swing up easily behind her. But here is more excruciating torture, this feeling of her body nestled between my legs. And when I snake an arm around her abdomen to steady her, when I draw her back against my chest, bracing her as the wyvern spreads its wings and takes flight . . . ah! It is bliss. Or as close to bliss as a worthless blackguard such as I could ever aspire to.

Surely this quest of hers must end soon. She may not yet be ready to acknowledge it, but there is no continuing from here. The dragon's bargain is impossible, her hope of fulfilling it utterly forlorn. No, it must end. Then we will return to Vespre. All will go back to the way it should be. And not a moment too soon; the last few days of proximity have proven a terrible test on my resolve, my patience, my self-control.

Once we're home, that tension must ease. She will ignore me with that same frosty frigidity I've come to know and loathe so well. Or she will train that agonizingly meaningless smile of hers my way. Never once knowing how I live for it. How my very existence depends on each look, each glance she offers. How I crave such graces as I crave food, light, air, and water.

The wyvern circles higher and higher above the forlorn towers of Volodaris. The air is thinner, and the little figure in my arms begins to shiver, her teeth to chatter. I wish now I'd not made her leave her cloak behind. Pulling her a little closer, I draw upon my magic, wrapping it around her like a blanket. But she tenses so hard, I give up and loosen my hold once more.

To my great relief, the wyvern chooses a direction and begins to fly. It seems like forever, but eventually a faint line of green appears on the horizon. There's still a world out there beyond this wasteland. A world that must be faced, a reality that must be met with fortitude.

But for now, as the wyvern's wings fall into a steady rhythm, I allow myself the luxury of simply being. Here. With her. Of feeling her small and trembling in my arms. Every now and then, a splash of water tickles my cheek. Does she weep? Has her exhaustion driven her to such extremes? She must be devastated, after all her striving, for her quest to meet such a barrier. If only I could comfort her; if only I were the kind of man she would turn to for comfort. Then I would make her tremble indeed. Tremble and quake and cry out in ecstasy, all her hopes and sorrows, all her fears and losses forgotten in a moment of pure bliss.

A dream. A fantasy.

Perhaps she does not hate me anymore, though the gods know I've given her little reason not to. Perhaps we have even formed an uneasy sort of alliance, found a footing of mutual respect.

But if she knew who I really am—if she knew what I've done and what I've kept from her all this time—her hatred would be unending.

CLARA

26

THE WYVERN'S WINGS BEAT A STEADY RHYTHM, speeding us on our way.

As we go, my heart slowly settles to a more regular rhythm. After all, it wasn't so very terrible, was it? Maybe I'd let myself believe something I shouldn't. Maybe I'd misunderstood what he was saying. Let myself fall into a little dream of make-believe, imagining something between us that was never there. But it's not as though I'd bared my whole heart and soul to the Prince!

It was a kiss. A simple peck on the cheek. Nothing more. What did it matter in the long run? If he can shrug it off so easily, why can't I?

And I will. I swear by all the seven gods, I will.

But for the moment a few stupid tears slip through my lashes, trail along my cheeks, and flit away into the empty sky. I can only hope none of them betray me by splashing on the Prince. The last thing I need is for him to know I'm weeping like some soppy maiden from a ballad.

It isn't until we've crossed the boundaries of the desert and begun the long flight back to the Between Gate that the Prince breaks the awful silence between us. "So you have a plan for searching out High King Illithorin's heirs, do you?" he says in that easy, uncaring tone that's like a knife to my heart.

I nod. I do have an idea. A very simple idea. But just then, I don't have the strength to voice it.

The Prince, to his credit, doesn't push me. He grunts and allows silence to fall once more. So the hours slip by with agonizing slowness, punctuated only by the beat of the wyvern's wings. At last, the Prince spies the gate below us. We descend in a slow, lazy spiral, landing in the same clearing as before. It feels like a hundred years have passed since we set out from this place. I slip from the wyvern's back, refusing the Prince's offered hand for assistance. He doesn't look at me but pats the wyvern's neck then marches into the forest, leading the way to the gate. I follow, trying not to look at him, trying not to read something, some meaning, some hint as to his feelings in the set of his shoulders and the back of his head.

How could I have been so mistaken? How could I have misread everything that took place between us?

I really thought he would kiss me. I really thought . . .

We come to the crumbling old gate. The Prince circles it to find a decrepit dial with only a few faint marks still visible on its face. "Where to?" he asks, casting me a brief, idle glance.

I draw a breath. The word *Vespre* is there on my lips. Suddenly I want to let all this come to an end. This journey has only led me deeper and deeper into these layers of bargains, each more impossible than the last. I want to return to everyday life, to fall back into the old patterns of avoiding the Prince and him avoiding me. To let that distance between us go back to what it was even just a few days ago.

To forget any of this ever happened.

Instead, I answer crisply: "To Aurelis."

A muscle in his jaw ticks. His gaze flickers as he draws a long breath through his nostrils. Then, without a word, he turns the dial. The air beneath the gate art shimmers.

I walk straight through without another word and emerge on the other side into the gentle golden light of dawn.

Thaddeus Creakle is at the front desk when I step back through the doors of Aurelis Library. He looks up idly from behind his square spectacle frames only for his face to wrinkle in a delighted smile. "Miss Darlington! You have returned!" He closes the ledger before him and comes around the desk, holding out his hands to me.

George Nobblin, loading a trolley nearby, shoots an unpleasant look my way. I ignore him and clasp Thaddeus's hands warmly. "Mister Creakle, I'm so happy to see you. I hope you are well?"

"Ah, as well as can be expected." The old man shrugs then takes a proper look at me, his expression melting into one of baffled concern. "You seem to have been . . . busy."

It's the nicest possible way to reference the absolute disaster of my appearance. I'm covered in dirt, my hair thick with salt and all fly-away about my face. I've never looked such a mess in all my life. "Busy." I nod, smiling wanly. "Yes indeed, Mister Creakle. I have."

Then the old librarian's gaze shifts from me to the Prince, who stands leaning against the doorway. "Your Highness," he says, dropping my hands and offering a stiff bow. "It is an honor as always. May I be of service?"

"That depends. Can you talk my Obligate out of this next fool's scheme of hers?"

Is it my imagination, or is the Prince avoiding my gaze? I steel my spine, determined not to indulge in such thoughts. "Never mind him, Mister Creakle," I say brightly. "I do have a rather urgent question for you however."

"Oh?" Thaddeus's brow puckers. "Is it about that young man, that new Obligate from a month ago? Let me see, what was his name—"

"No, no, this isn't about Daniel Gale. I am searching for information on the great houses of Eledria. Specifically genealogies." I hesitate before adding, "More specifically, the genealogy of the High King, Illithorin."

"Are you now?" Thaddeus's brow puckers still more with bafflement. "Whatever for?"

"Please, sir; it is terribly important."

He scratches one ear thoughtfully. "Well, Miss Darlington, if you say so. Queen Dasyra did make it a practice to record the histories of the great families. The fae as a rule don't care for such things, and the king told her she was wasting her time. The queen, however, insisted that even the long-lived fae must take care to preserve knowledge of their own histories. And that, she claimed, started with remembering where one came from." Thaddeus tips his head, eyeing me from beneath his bushy brows. "She was an astute one. A true librarian to the core."

My heart beats a strange rhythm. Up until this moment, I'd suspected my little plan rather too simple to bear fruit. Now possibilities beckon. "Where are the genealogies kept, Mister Creakle?"

Nobblin is visibly displeased at the senior librarian's willingness to admit me without a proper library card. Thaddeus, however, waves away any protest without a second thought and bids me follow him. The Prince saunters along at our heels, keeping his distance but never quite letting me out of his sight. Thaddeus leads us up a flight of stairs and on to a back room tucked away from the main stacks. There behind closed doors are shelf upon shelf of records. They're old and dusty, and the air is heavy with the weight of bygone days.

"It's all here," Thaddeus says, indicating the books with a sweep of his arm. "Do you think you can manage on your own? I hate to leave Mister Nobblin alone at the front desk."

I hasten to reassure the senior librarian and wave him on his way. Then, as the Prince takes up another languid, lounging position against this doorpost, I set to work.

The sheer number of volumes is intimidating. Dasyra organized them according to court and region, but I can find no trace of Illithorin's family among the Soliran high families. I go through each surname with care, searching for clues. After all, the fae never write out their names, so Dasyra's spellings are approximations. It's quite possible the true lineage of the High King has been mixed into other families over time. The only saving grace of the whole endeavor is the longevity of the fae themselves. Were these human family lines, it would take me years to get through them. As it is, I'm able to parse through most of the Solian records within an hour or two.

The Prince stands by observing throughout. Never once does he offer his assistance. Several times I consider Obliging him to sit down, pick up a volume, and do his part. But I'm not sure I have the stomach for it. I'm not sure I want to speak to him at all. Ever again.

Finally, with a growling huff, I toss aside the last volume of Soliran high fae. Nothing. Not a single name struck me as even a possibility. But then, who's to say Illithorin's surviving family would have settled in Solira? Perhaps following the war and the disintegration of the united Eledria they chose to remove themselves further. They may have even changed their name, depending on how public feeling ran at the time toward the king who had brought such destruction down upon the worlds.

Sighing heavily, I pick up a volume from the Aurelian section. Though I will read through all of them, I start with the names beginning with *I*, just in case something stands out to me. After a quick skim and skip over the first several, I come to the bottom of a page near the middle of the book.

There, in Thaddeus Creakle's own hand, written in fresh ink, is this notation:

And in the fifteenth centennial cycle of the Fourth Age, Lord Ivor of the House of Illithor was named Heir of Aurelis by will of King Lodírhal the Magnificent. He is bound to wed Princess Estrilde Lodírith, thereby securing the line of succession for the king's own blood, for the stability of the nation and the health and happiness of its people henceforth.

I sit there, cross-legged in the middle of that room, surrounded by piles of books and papers. Staring. At that name. That name which should have jumped out at me from the very beginning.

Illithor. Ivor *Illithor.*

It is the work of a few page-turns to find the chronology of Ivor's family: *Ivor, son of Ilbryn, son of Inarie, daughter of Iluathin, daughter of Ilythyrra, last surviving daughter and heir to all that remains of Illithorin the Glorious, High King of Eledria in the Second Age, founder of his line.*

The text goes on to offer a brief account of Illithorin's rise and fall, listing the names of his children and grandchildren, most of whom did not survive the war and the scourge of dragon flame. Only the youngest daughter, Ilythyrra, who was but an infant at the time, was spirited away by a courageous battle-maiden-turned-nursemaid. Thus the line of Illithor was spared from total destruction.

But the kings and queens of Eledria, now liberated from subjugation to their high king, were in no mood to see his blood rule over them again. They would have hunted down and killed Ilythyrra, infant though she was. So her nursemaid carried her into the human world where they lived in a quiet way throughout her days. Those days were long indeed, for she had drunk from the Water of Life in her infancy and retained its blessing, even in the magic-starved air of that world. She passed that blessing down to her children so that, mixed with human blood though they were, they lived far longer than others of their kind.

It was Ilythyrra's great-grandson, Ilbryn, who finally returned to Eledria and made a name for himself as a warrior in the Spire Wars before the time of the Pledge. He made himself indispensable to King Lodírhal and became one of his inner circle. Half-fae though he was, he took a fae wife. Who bore him a son.

And there it is, written as plain as day in the chronicler's hand: *Ivor Illithor.* Descendent of the High King.

I shake my head slowly. Ivor himself had told me some great-grandmother of his was human, which explained his ability to pick up small amounts of written-magic with time and effort. Does he not realize the true extent of his human blood? Indeed most of his line was more human than fae due to his great-great grandmother's exile. Perhaps that truth was hidden from him for his own protection. Following the Pledge, it was illegal for half-blood fae to live in Eledria for many centuries. It's quite possible Ivor knows neither the extent of the human blood he bears nor of his exalted lineage.

"You could catch pixies in that mouth of yours."

I clamp my jaw shut and turn sharply to the Prince. He still leans indolently against the doorframe. "Well?" he says, eying me through half-closed lids. "I can see you've had some sort of revelation. Out with it."

I can't find the words. Instead I hold up the book for his inspection and watch his face as he reads through the lines. His brow constricts. I see the moment when realization hits. He raises an eyebrow, turning his attention back to me. "So. Your golden hero springs from a mighty line of majestic imbeciles. Why am I not surprised?"

"It's a noble lineage. Even you must admit it."

"I must and will admit nothing of the kind. Illithorin was a blessed idiot who got greedy and ended up roasted for it. Ivor is no better than his blood, I daresay."

I snatch the book back, slam the cover, and get to my feet.

357

"I must talk to him."

"To whom? Ivor?"

"Yes! I doubt he even knows about the curse on Oasuroa. He has no reason not to let it go. If I were to ask him—"

"You think he's going to simply give up an ancient, powerful curse like that at your request?" The Prince folds his arms and sniffs. "You overestimate Ivor's generosity. Even you don't hold that kind of sway over him."

I clutch the book to my chest, dropping my lashes to avoid his gaze. "I don't know what you mean."

"Oh, don't you?"

"Besides." I shake my head and lick my lips. "It doesn't hurt to ask, does it? I'm sure he will be reasonable."

"I am sure he will be anything but." The Prince takes a step forward and swipes the book from my hands. Before I can react, he sidesteps around me to slide it back in its place on the shelf. "Regardless, you won't be able to talk to Ivor anytime soon."

"Why not?"

"Did you forget? Tonight is Spring Summit. He will be quite busy at his own betrothal ball."

I purse my lips, planting my hands on my hips. "That's all right. I'll speak to him after."

The Prince spins on heel, crosses his arms again, and leans back against the shelf. "Need I remind you that a ball of this nature is likely to go on for days? Maybe even weeks. Once my fae kindred start making merry, there's no knowing how long their revels may last."

I frown. I don't have days, certainly not weeks. Though time passes differently across the various realms of Eledria, I gather it's been nearly two days since I bargained with the crone. I only have tonight, one full day, and the next night after before that great pain she promised will begin. I need to complete my mission first.

"Very well," I say. "I shall simply have to interrupt. He will understand when I've explained matters to him."

The Prince snorts. "You really think you'll be allowed anywhere near Estrilde's festivities looking like that?" His eyes rove over my frame. The dust, dirt, and grime caking my worn dress, my hair still thick with salt from my deep-sea plunge, my skin sallow, my whole frame sagging and exhausted.

I draw myself up straight. "Very well, Prince." My voice is cold, imperious. I meet and hold his gaze, harder than I've managed since that terrible moment when I stared into his eyes, waiting for him to respond to my impulsive kiss. Waiting, waiting . . . only to be rejected. Only to have everything I thought had been building between us for days, weeks—even months—thrown back in my face and made to seem utter foolishness.

But I won't let that moment ruin everything. I won't let it leave me cowed and weeping and weak.

"You are Obligated to help me," I say, pouring all the force I possesses into the words. "What would you suggest we do?"

He draws a long breath through his nostrils, his jaw hardening.

But the longer he resists his Obligation, the harder it becomes. I know from experience. I have only to wait.

Finally, he lets out that breath. His lips pull back in a deceitfully easy smile, only just on this side of a grimace. "Well," he says, tilting his head to one side, "for starters, you're going to need a gown."

27

FOLDS OF IRIDESCENT LAVENDER SEEM TO SHIMMER with their own light, creating a sense of movement and life in the otherwise still cloth. The fabric was obviously spun from real flowers, using magic to turn silken petals into delicate filaments. Living flowers bloom across the skirt as well, and vines weave along the hem and fluttering sleeves. Adding to the overall effect, butterflies of the same hue flit around the skirts. They're so realistic, I'm almost able to ignore the glamour-light trailing in their wake.

It is by far the most incredible gown I have ever seen.

"It was my mother's," the Prince says, holding it up for my inspection. "A bit out of date for current Aurelian fashions. But pretty enough, I should think."

We stand in the dead queen's old apartments, which are kept fresh and ready as though she might any moment return to this life and require their use. The Prince always claims them during his infrequent visits to Aurelis. No one stopped us from entering this time. The Prince marched right into his mother's dressing room, rummaged through her bountiful collection of fine garments, and returned to where I waited in the main sitting room with this.

I stare at it, awed. Queen Dasyra had an affinity for plant magic, so it's no surprise she would favor gowns of living blossoms. My stomach clenches even as I fight the desire to reach out and touch the beautiful cloth. "Do you have anything else?" I ask, not meeting the Prince's gaze. "Anything not quite so . . . much?"

The Prince snorts and shoves the gown into my arms. "Into the washroom, Darling, and clean yourself up. I'll not escort you anywhere begrimed as you are. Quick now, or we'll miss all the fun."

"I thought you said the *fun* would be lasting for days?" I mutter but offer no further protest as I'm ushered to a half-open door. Though the idea of wearing Dasyra's gown makes me uncomfortable, the lure of the washroom draws me like a fly to honey.

Carrying the dress carefully in my arms so as not to let it touch my filthy self, I step into the chamber and push the door shut behind me with my heel. For a moment, I lean back against the door and simply breathe. Breathe in the humid air, the sweet smells rising from the hot-spring bath set into the floor. Breathe in the perfume of Dasyra's flowers, still living, blooming, thriving even five years after her death. I open my eyes, gaze around this space that once was hers. It's like a secret garden and hidden lagoon all in one. The in-ground bath is so natural and surrounded by so much greenery and growth, one could easily imagine stumbling upon it in the depths of some enchanted grove.

I find a safe place to lay the gown. Then, fingers trembling, I strip out of my limp and pungent garments, grateful to leave them in a pile on the floor. My first step into the steaming pool makes me hiss and catch my breath, but I adjust quickly. With a sigh, I sink deeper down, not quite willing to immerse myself—not after my recent journey to Ulakrana—but happy to let the hot water wash away my aches and pains.

Despite the natural setting, Dasyra's washroom is fully stocked with all the most luxurious essentials. I find soaps, lotions, creams, brushes, everything I could wish for to make myself fresh and neat. All the while I keep my mind focused on what comes next: on finding Ivor, on drawing him away from the ball for a few private words. Of what I'll say, how he'll react, what it will mean.

I absolutely will not think of that moment outside the tower. Of how the Prince had looked at me. As though he saw all the possibilities of the worlds in my eyes. Of how I had waited in glorious suspense, hoping, believing, longing . . .

I splash hot water in my face. Then, growling softly, I climb from the pool, wrap a towel around my body, and go in search of means to dry my hair. A little exploration reveals a Fire Bonnet: a five-petaled flower which, when coaxed to open, emits a steady, vertical, pinkish flame. Using a comb and brush, taking care not to singe any stray strands, I comb my hair until it gleams. I consider searching for pins to put it up but change my mind when I discover the gown is off-shoulder. I prefer not to display quite so much skin, but my loose hair may serve as a covering of sorts.

Once I've donned the gown and done up the row of buttons under the right arm, the butterflies dancing about the hem fly up suddenly to settle in my hair. It surprises me, but when I try to wave them off, they merely flutter and rearrange themselves into a living crown. They seem determined, so I leave them be and go in search of a mirror. I find one tucked between two silver-trunked saplings. Standing before it, I turn this way and that. I hardly recognize myself. Certainly the figure in the glass is a far cry from the salt-and-sand-caked gremlin who'd staggered through the door.

I grimace. Really, what had I been thinking, throwing myself at the Prince like that while in such a ridiculous state? No wonder he practically ran away screaming. Well, maybe not screaming. He didn't even run away. I almost wish he had . . . anything would have been better than that expression of sardonic dismissal. Like I was nothing more than an amusement, a comical little curiosity. A diversion.

I stare at myself in the glass. My expression is drawn, solemn. I know I look well. Beautiful even, in my own very human way. But I don't come anywhere near the incredible beauty of the fae. I don't belong in their world. In *his* world. I don't belong with him.

You know where you belong.

I blink. In the flash of darkness behind my eyelids, I see myself in a reflection of black glass. My eyes are sewn shut. Blood pours down my cheeks, my neck, pools in the hollow of my throat. Drips to stain the bodice of the gown.

With a gasp, I open my eyes again, staring at that lovely vision of myself in lavender, crowned in butterflies. It doesn't seem real. As though the mirror shows me nothing more than a glamour, an illusion, while the truth lurks underneath.

Sighing, I turn away. There are several doors leading to and from this chamber. Suddenly eager to be on my way, I choose the nearest one, grab the latch, push it open. A rush of cool air makes my skin prickle as I step from the humid air of the washroom. The chamber I step into isn't Dasyra's bedroom. It's a smaller, sparser space, intended for a servant no doubt. There's a small copper tub and a washstand in the middle of the chamber.

And there before me stands the Prince. Facing away from me. Unaware of my presence. He holds a pitcher of water over his head, pouring it over his upturned face. The scented stream flows through his black hair, across his golden-brown skin, his shoulders, trailing in rivulets down his muscular back and firm bare buttocks.

I stand transfixed. I cannot breathe. Cannot think.

My heart seems to have forgotten how to beat.

The Prince lowers the pitcher, shakes his head. Droplets

fly, several of them striking against my bare shoulders and the exposed skin of my bosom. Startled back to life, I catch a short, shaking breath.

He turns.

His eyes widen.

"I'm sorry!" I gasp, throwing up a hand over my eyes as I stagger back through the washroom door, slamming it behind me. Crumpling my skirts in both hands, I flee through Dasyra's greenery, take the first door I find, and stumble through it. Somehow I make my way back to the front room, escape the queen's suite, and stand in the palace hall outside.

My heart races like I've just fled the Wild Hunt.

What have I done? How could I have made such an error? I close my eyes, press both fists against my temples. Trying to force that image out of my mind. Not just the image of his body, so sculpted and glorious—every masculine contour highlighted in streams of silvery water—but the look in his eye. The shock. The heat.

The fire.

No! Stop it!

Blood pulsing, skin flaming, I pick up the hem of my skirt and flee through the palace, unconsciously pursuing the faint strains of distant music.

28

THROUGH THE TALL, ARCHED WINDOWS OF AURELIS palace, I catch glimpses of indigo sky spangled with stars. It's a strange sight here in the Dawn Realm. Ordinarily, Aurelian nightfall consists of nothing deeper than a purpling twilight which lasts a mere few hours. Spring Summit, however, brings on proper darkness, and only comes to Aurelis every dozen turns of the cycle. This is my first time observing it. It's unsettling to say the least.

To combat the dark, every corner, hall, passage, and alcove has been lit with glamour-lights—shining lanterns full of magic in every color imaginable. They give off a dancing aura and perfume the air with delicate and enticing aromas. The lights gleam off my iridescent dress, causing it to emit its own radiance, and making me all-too conspicuous. I certainly attract more than a few unpleasant glances from the various human Obligates I pass on my way.

I lower my gaze, tuck my chin, and keep on going. My frantic run from the queen's suite slows to a more sedate pace which belies the hammering of my heart. My whole body shakes from sheer *embarrassment*. That's all, though. Just embarrassment. I mean, I've glimpsed the Prince shirtless more times than I can count, but this? This was so much worse, so much more, so much . . . so . . .

No, I won't think about it. Time to wipe that image from my mind, focus on the present. On gaining access to Estrilde's ball. On finding Ivor, drawing him aside, making my request as simply and eloquently as possible. If I'm lucky—if I'm very lucky indeed—I'll be on my way back to Illithorin's Waste within the hour. Maybe I won't bring the Prince with me. Maybe I can get Ivor to send one of his men to carry me on one of those powerful winged steeds. That would be simpler, surely. No need to involve the Prince at all.

I follow the sound of music through the winding passages and come at last to a doorway opening out onto the enormous Aurelis gardens. Here, fae of all kinds from all corners of Eledria gather, glorious in their strange and beautiful raiment. Most pay me no mind. While my own gown is the equal of any of theirs, the moment they set eyes on my face, it's like I cease to exist. I'm merely human, after all. Unworthy of their notice.

I slip in behind a cluster of twittering woodnymphs—ladies of the Lildrolath Forest, I believe, judging by the color of their bark-skin and the glossy shade of their green, leafy hair. They step through the door and descend the broad stair into the twilit garden below, pausing at the base to give their names to the footman standing there. He announces them, and they progress into the tiered garden, blending in with the rest of the mighty company. From this view everything seems quite decorous. Musicians hidden in a grove of blossoms play delicate strains, and guests perform dances of grace, elegance, and refinement, gowns and capes twirling, jewels glinting.

But this is only a display. Elsewhere, the festivities will already be growing rowdier, bawdier. Before Summit Night is through, there will be orgies in secret places all over the palace where dangerous drinks are imbibed and inhibitions cast to the four winds. *Rothiliom* will burn in the eyes of the dangerous revelers. Those places I dare not venture. I'd like to think Ivor himself will not take part in those aspects of his betrothal celebration. I've never seen his eyes gleam green with the effects of *rothiliom,* though Estrilde certainly indulges in the drug more often than not.

I stand at the top of the stair, allowing other guests to flow past me and join the throng below. I must be careful. I must keep my wits about me. A human drawn into the revels of the fae makes for an easy target. Perhaps I should have waited for the Prince to finish his . . . his . . . to make himself ready and escort me.

I grip my skirts hard in both hands and hastily push that

thought down. This is my quest after all. Yes, he's been useful; I know perfectly well I would never have made it this far without him. But things are different now. He and Ivor detest one another. It's best if he stays out of my way. His presence won't make things any easier.

Straightening my shoulders and adjusting the set of my hair, I slowly descend the broad stair. Music dances and whirls in the air around me, making me a little dizzy. I take care not to move too quickly, to draw no undue attention my way. As I near the base of the stair, the footman standing at attendance, turns, inquiring, "Your name, please?"

Then he stops.

His jaw drops.

Slowly, his gaze roves from my face down to my bare shoulders, all the exposed skin of my upper body, the perfectly-fitted bodice, the bounteous folds of shimmering skirt and living blossoms. With an effort, he yanks his eyes back to my face.

"Clara!" Danny gasps.

I'm hardly less surprised. He is the last person I want to meet just now, dressed in this gown, with this particular purpose in mind. "Doctor Gale," I say quietly. "There's no need to announce me. I'm not here to—"

Before I can finish, he grabs hold of my upper arm and drags me around the curve of the banister into a shadowed place beyond the lamplight. "Danny, let go of me!" I bleat, momentarily forgetting propriety. "What are you doing?"

"What am I doing?" he hisses, yanking me close to him, his fingers digging hard into my flesh. "What are *you* doing? You cannot barge into the princess's ball uninvited!"

"I'm not uninvited." I refuse to wriggle in a vain attempt to get free, but instead glare up into his face. "Estrilde invited the Prince. I'm here as his guest."

"His *guest?*" Danny's teeth flash, his lip curled back in a snarl. "Have you taken leave of your senses? Have you no idea how dangerous this is?"

"I'm perfectly aware. Let me remind you, I've lived and served in Eledria these last five years."

Pink light from a lantern hung in a nearby fruit tree highlights the lines of his face and flickers in the depths of his eyes. Eyes which rove down to my too-exposed bosom once more. Gods! I begin to wish I'd thrown this gown back in the Prince's face and insisted on wearing my travel-stained garment.

I pull against his hold. To my relief, Danny lets go and takes a step back from me, running both hands through his hair. "Please, Clara," he says, his voice thin and a little desperate. "Just go. Get out of here. I couldn't bear it if . . . if he were . . . if something were to . . ."

"I'm not going anywhere." I smooth the front of my gown with both hands, very aware of the spot on my arm where his fingers had pinched. "I'm not here pleasure-seeking. I have a mission to accomplish, so if you wouldn't mind—"

"What mission?"

I stop and chew my lip. I'd not wanted to let him know; he won't take it well. But in the moment, I cannot think of a way to put him off.

"I'm trying to save you," I say softly, dropping my gaze to the button in the middle of his waistcoat.

"You *what?*"

"Hush!" I cast a glance around, but we don't seem to have attracted any attention to our shadowed hiding place. Nevertheless, I take a step nearer to Danny and lower my voice. "I'm trying to get the bloodgem necklace for Estrilde. But it's . . . complicated."

Danny's eyes round still more. All traces of that sweet boy I once knew seem to have fled his face entirely, leaving a severe, rather terrifying stranger in his place. "You're mad," he breathes.

"Oh, so it's mad when I attempt to fulfill Estrilde's demands, but not when you do?"

"It's *my* role." Danny shakes his head, jaw grinding. "It's *my* role to save *you.* That's how it's meant to be."

I throw up my hands. "Danny, life isn't like storybooks! You don't get to be the dashing savior while I play the swooning damsel. I learned a long time ago that no amount of swooning is going to do me or anyone I love any good." Lifting my chin, I look into his eyes, my resolve hard as stone. "I'm going to save you. Whether you like it or not."

He stares down at me. Shock, horror, shame, heartache—all these and more swirl in his eyes.

376

Then, he takes several steps back into the lantern light, lifts his head, and bellows, "Guards!"

"What are you doing?" I lunge forward, slap a hand over his mouth. He wrenches back and calls again, louder than before. "No, Danny, please!" I protest.

Too late. Two guards in golden armor appear, manifesting as though from nowhere on either side of me. "This human has tried to access Princess Estrilde's ball without an invitation," Danny says, pointing at me.

"That's not true!" The guards grasp me by the arms. I twist, trying to catch some glimpse inside their deep, dark helmets. "I'm here as a guest of Prince Castien of Vespre!"

"A likely story," the guard on my left growls as they drag me from the shadows behind the banister and fairly lift me off my feet to carry me up the stair. I twist to look back, to look down at Danny. He gazes after me, his expression tortured but firm. He means this for the best, but just now I almost hate him.

"Well, well, well, what do we have here?"

The guards stop abruptly. I stagger and would fall were it not for their grips upon me. I whip my head forward, gaping up at the figure standing three treads up, resplendent in gold-braid and jeweled cuffs and billowy white silk shirt, his black hair swept back and held in place by the band of a simple stone crown.

The Prince takes me in slowly, his gaze approving. Just as though I'm not standing with my feet almost an inch off the ground, poised between two massive and unyielding guards.

His mouth curves. "Well met, Darling," he purrs. "I must say, while I like the ensemble as a whole, I don't much care for these accessories." He waves a hand at each guard in turn.

"We caught her trying to infiltrate the princess's ball, Your Highness," the guard on my right growls.

"Gods, you make it sound so dire." The Prince widens his eyes and mimics the guard's voice: "*One tiny human girl has infiltrated the ball; sound the alarms! The whole kingdom is imperiled!* Thank heavens, my father employs men of such stalwart stuff. What would we all come to otherwise?" He holds out a hand to me. I can't very well take it, pinned in place as I am. "Let her go, gentlemen," he says. "She's my guest. And I won't have you bruising those lovely arms of hers."

The guards exchange glances over my head. I can feel their resistance; but this is the king's son, after all, miscreant though he may be. With a nod from one and a sigh from the other, they set me back on my feet and let me go.

I stagger a little and, out of necessity more than desire, reach out and catch the Prince's offered hand. He smoothly guides my arm through his elbow and tucks me close to his side. "Shall we then?" he asks and proceeds smoothly down the stair between the two guardsmen, leaving them in our wake. He continues on past Danny without so much as a glance his way. I dare shoot him a quick look from under my lashes, but cannot bear the sight of his bloodless, strained face.

Hastily I look forward, heart pounding. Painfully aware

of the Prince's proximity, and suddenly unable to ignore the reality of my last glimpse of him. Gods spare me! What am I supposed to do? Is there any way to make this right or, at the very least, less excruciating?

"Would you care to take the lead, Darling?" the Prince murmurs, dropping his lips close to my ear as we move into the crowd. "I'm happy to bring up the *rear.*"

I freeze. Fire roars up my cheeks. He knows exactly what he just said, gods blight and blast him!

The Prince chuckles and guides me deeper into the throng. We weave our way among clusters of guests who, this early in the festivities, have not yet broken from their original parties but still stick together, eyeing up their fellow guests. The Prince nods and smiles at everyone we pass just as though they're all old friends. Some call out to him in pleasant voices. Some sneer and pointedly turn away. None of them spare a glance for me, for which I am very thankful.

"Ah!" The Prince arrests a passing server, lifting two glasses from her tray. He holds them up for my inspection. "What do you think of that, Darling? Quite pretty, yes?"

In my five years in Aurelis, I've never seen the like. Rather than liquid, the glasses seem to contain dancing mist and churning foam in a variety of colors which mingle but never mix. It reminds me of the light-display in the abyss of Ulakrana, captured in miniature. "It's incredible," I admit.

When I start to reach for the glass however, the Prince turns away, *tsk*ing and shaking his head. "No, no, Darling. You may look, but no touching." He catches my eye and winks. "Now what is that quaint little human saying of yours? Oh, yes! *Bottoms up.*"

He quaffs the brew in a single gulp, even as heat roars up my neck and floods my cheeks once more. If I could strangle him then and there and get away with it, I would. Instead I spin on heel and march away without a word, determined to disappear into the crowd and never, never, never face that man again for as long as I live.

There's a hurried, "Here, take these," and a clatter of glasses behind me. The next moment, a hand catches my arm, whirling me in a flurry of glimmering skirts and pulling me a staggering step. I land against the Prince's chest . . . his bare, chest, I notice with chagrin. Yet again his shirt hangs unbuttoned beneath his fine coat. He slips his other hand around my waist and smiles down at me, that dangerous, dazzling smile that never fails to steal my breath away.

"You're not getting away that easily," he murmurs.

The next moment, he's swept me onto the garden dance floor beneath a ring of floating glamour-lights. He didn't ask. He didn't give me a chance to fight or protest. And now I am here. Dancing, with him. All around me, the Lords and Ladies of Eledria whirl in time to the romantic strains floating from an arbor where human musicians hide. I should be with the other humans—hidden from sight, ignored save for my usefulness. Not here among the majesty of the fae, shining in their glamours, radiant in their most splendid displays of wealth and near-immortal glory.

But none of that matters. Not now. Not with the Prince holding me in his arms. He guides me with gentle but irresistible purpose, whirling me into music which floods my senses, filling me up to the very deepest parts of my being. I could float away on that sound, that feeling. But his hand at my waist acts like an anchor to this world. A world made up of just the two of us. His other hand holds mine, not out and away, but pressed close to his heart.

I realize he's spoken. "I'm sorry, what did you say?" I blurt stupidly.

His smile grows, glamour-light glinting off his white teeth. "I said it was foolish of you to venture here all on your own. Don't you know how dangerous it is for humans at fae revels?"

I find my voice with an effort. "I grew tired of waiting. I feared the whole event would be over by the time you'd finally managed to button your shirt. Which, I'll note, you still haven't done."

He shrugs. "Buttons are such cumbersome things. So fiddly, and they just won't ever stay put. But seriously, Darling." He drops his chin, bringing his eyes closer to the level of mine, forcing me to meet his gaze. "You sprinted from the place so fast, leaving me quite abruptly in your *posterior* view, as it were. What's a man supposed to think?"

Another wave of heat. But this time, a little smile plucks at my lips. I drop my gaze to his collarbone. "Stop it."

"Stop what?"

"Stop playing the fool."

"Why? You know you love it."

I shake my head. "I do *not*. I'm here about a serious matter, and . . . and I must not . . ."

"Stop and enjoy the view along the way?"

I can't even begin to formulate an answer to that one. The Prince guides me through a sweeping turn then contrives to pull me closer. His hand slides up from the small of my back to the bare skin of my shoulder blades, fingers splayed and hot. "Don't worry, Darling," he whispers close to my ear. "I fully intend to take all of this very seriously indeed. *After* we dance."

We speak no more then; what words could possibly be said as that river of music catches and carries us away, like two blossoms floating on the foam? I'm lost in it, lost in him. The closeness of him, the scent of him, the warmth of him. Just *him*. How many times have I been warned? How many stories have I been told of mortal maidens swept up by handsome fae men, dancing under the starlight until they lose themselves entirely? I never knew how easy it would be. Or how happily I would go, ready and willing to be carried outside of myself, pulled into his atmosphere, burned in his heat.

I'm losing my head, losing all sense of self-preservation. Yet I don't feel unsafe. Of course that's part of the stories too, isn't it? Part of the glamour, part of the ultimate headlong flight to destruction: that belief in one's perfect safety.

But when I gaze into his eyes, so near to mine, so full of fire and that sweet, sweet music . . . I know he could never hurt me. Never.

When did we stop dancing? The other dancers continue to whirl around us, skirts and capes fluttering like wings, arms upraised and sleeves billowing. But the Prince and I stand in their center, gazing at one another. Lost in that world of our own. He looks hungry. Starving. As though he would devour me if given the chance. His hand lets go of mine. He slips it instead underneath my hair, gripping my neck, drawing me toward him.

So I wasn't mistaken after all. Everything I'd thought was happening between us . . . it was real. This is real. This place, this point in time.

His mouth opens, like he's going to kiss me, like he's going to consume me. I lean into him, as hungry as he, as desperate for that feast we've been denying ourselves for far too long.

"Clara," he breathes, his lips so near I can just about taste them. "Clara, my darling, tell me to stop."

I can't. I won't. A little whimper vibrates in my throat. I start to rise on my toes, to close the last of that agonizing space between us—

"Mind if I cut in?"

The Prince curses. The word is so foul and spoken so harshly, it makes my hair stand on end. His hand falls away from my neck, and he turns abruptly, his mouth twisted in a smile even as his eyes flash like twin blades at the looming figure of Lord Ivor.

"Absolutely!" the Prince cries, in a voice so unexpectedly

savage, I half expect the golden fae to stagger back bleeding from some wound. "By all means, insert that glorious nose of yours wheresoever it wills. Is not all this in your honor, my lord?" He sweeps a hand, taking in the dancers, the sights, the splendor of the deepening night. Then he fixes his gaze on Ivor again, his smile shrinking just a fraction. "Or should I say, my liege?"

"I am not your liege," Ivor replies coolly. "Not yet." He turns to me, and his hard expression softens. "Clara Darlington," he says. I find myself once again the subject of scrutiny as his gaze travels up and down my gown and figure. I'm beginning to wish I'd begged the Prince to find me one of Dasyra's old gardening coveralls. "You look remarkable."

"Hence your need to remark upon it," the Prince growls.

"Have you business here, Castien?" Ivor demands. He wears glamoured ram's horns this evening which sprout from his brow and coil on either side of his head, more imposing than any crown of gold and diadems. His body is clad in a green doublet, open in a deep V down the front to expose his powerful chest, and his muscular calves and thighs strain at the seams of his fitted trousers. He is so large and imposing, and other than the horns themselves, none of it feels like glamour. He is too beautiful to be anything less than perfectly real.

The Prince smiles up at him like an impudent cat grinning in the face of a bear. "Oh, don't you recall? My fair cousin invited me. And how could I bear to miss this celebration of your great love? You and Estrilde were positively made for one another. As fine a pair of vipers as ever knotted tails."

I want to smack him, to hiss at him for silence. The last thing I need is for Ivor to drive us both out of here on the ends of the guards' lances before I get to make my request.

But Ivor merely narrows his eyes. "Tread carefully, Castien," he murmurs. "You're not in your own world anymore."

"Nor yours either, I fancy," the Prince replies with a significant nod.

Both Ivor and I turn where he indicates. In that same moment a pair of trumpets sound, followed by Danny's voice crying out: "Lodírhal the Magnificent, King of Aurelis!"

An open litter of gold silk appears at the top of the stair. There the king lies propped up on numerous pillows. My stomach plunges at the sight of him. The last time I saw Lodírhal, he had been a man in his prime. A little faded perhaps, a little gaunt. Now he looks like an old man. Gray, withered, his face lined, his hands veined. Loose skin sags around his jowls, and white hair clings to a balding scalp. There are no glamours around him, for they could do him no good.

This is wrong. The fae do not age, at least, not so horrifically or so fast. The broken Fatebond has finally caught up with him. He will not last much longer.

Yet even now he has not lost his dignity. He holds his head up as high as he can, and in his eye gleams his steel-hard will. He is king, after all. Even broken beyond all hope of recovery, he is king.

Estrilde walks beside the litter, more glorious than I've ever seen her in a gown of shining sunlight, no doubt imported from Solira. She wears a coiling pair of antelope horns, burnished gold and studded with gems. The glamours surrounding her are palpable and plenteous. At the sight of her, one feels the urge to love, to worship even. I grimace, repulsed at the feeling, and draw back a step, half-hiding behind the Prince. The last thing I want is to be noticed by Estrilde.

"I must go," Ivor says, turning to look at me. "I must meet Estrilde to officially open the ball." He speaks as though the Prince isn't there, standing like a wall between us. "I'll find you later when I can, Clara Darlington. Will you save a dance for me?"

I nod, even as the Prince mutters, "Why, so you can crush her feet with those great boots of yours?"

Ivor ignores him and swiftly slips away through the crowd. I wonder if he too realizes it would be better not to draw Estrilde's attention my way. Is he putting distance between me and himself as a means of protection? My pounding heart warms a little at the thought.

"Ass," the Prince growls. His gaze follows Ivor even as the golden lord approaches the king's litter and bows deeply. He turns away, looking down at me, searching my face for . . . I'm not sure what. "You look pale, Darling," he says. "Perhaps it would be best if we sat out the next—"

"Castien! I did not think to meet you here."

A vision in glittering blue appears before us. Ilusine—golden-skinned and shining like a living sunburst, framed by her mighty golden wings. The last time I glimpsed her, she and the Prince had just parted ways with bitter words between them.

I detect no bitterness in the warm-as-summer gaze she fixes on him now, however. She takes both his hands in hers, pressing them eagerly, and plants a chaste but somehow claiming kiss upon his cheek. "I thought you meant to avoid Aurelis until . . . certain matters were settled," she says, pulling back and giving the Prince a knowing look. "Not that any would blame you."

"Ilusine." The Prince nods, and doesn't withdraw his hands from hers. "It is good to see you as always. Are you still angling for the throne you desire? Still think you have a shot with Ivor?"

"Nine hells spare me, no!" She shudders, her wings rustling prettily. "Your cousin is more than welcome to him." She tosses her head. "I always preferred a little more subtlety of mind and a little less brutality of arm. But he suits Estrilde well enough."

"She has a certain affinity for the cretin, that's true."

They seem to have forgotten me entirely. The music is playing, the dancers are beginning to move around us. And they are there, together. It is Ilusine who stands in the sphere of his world, taking up his attention. I back slowly away. It seems to me as though the Prince and Ilusine are drawn to one another even as I had believed he and I were drawn. It is just the music after all. The dangerous fae enchantment and glamour of which I've been warned more times than I care to remember.

But I know the rules. I've known them since my first arrival in Eledria. They were impressed upon me in no uncertain terms:

Never anger the fae. Never trust the fae. And never, ever, as you value your life, love the fae.

The Prince starts to turn, his gaze searching. Ilusine speaks, drawing his attention back to her. She takes his hand. Then they are dancing. Pulled away into that river of sound among the other dancers even as I slip further and further from the edge of the floor into the shadows of the garden.

"Do you see? Do you see?" a creaky voice speaks off to my right. I spy one of the woodnymphs I'd glimpsed earlier, eagerly bent to gossip in the ear of a bejeweled dwarven dame. "The king's son is dancing with the Soliran princess! And I thought they were done for good."

"Oh, that's just the way with the two of them," her companion replies with a knowing nod. "One turn of the cycle, they're not speaking. The next, they're back in each other's arms. You know they say she's his Fatebound."

"Do they?" The nymph utters with a surprised rattle of branches. "I've heard the rumors that he, like his father before him, is destined for a Fated Love. But if it were the princess, would they not have come together already?"

The dwarven dame shrugs. "The ways of the Fatebond are strange. But they are always drawn back to one another; that speaks volumes, does it not? Aye, I would not be at all surprised if the rumors proved true . . ."

By then I've backed away too far to catch any more, my stomach knotted so tight, I nearly double over with the pain of it. I stagger, stumble, make my way deeper into the shadows.

Suddenly hands grip my shoulders. "Clara, are you all right? Did you drink fae wine? Clara, answer me!"

"Danny!" I gasp, tipping my head back. I can just discern his face by the light of the nearest lantern, and it is the most welcome sight in all the worlds. "Please, take me somewhere. Away from here. Anywhere. Now."

29

DANNY LEADS ME UP THE STAIR AND INTO THE palace. I'm practically blinded by unshed tears and must trust him to guide me through the throngs of merrymakers still arriving, still pouring through the doors into the deepening Summit Night. Once inside, the air feels suffocating. I struggle to breathe, pressing a hand to my side and gasping to hold back on a sob.

Worry tainting his voice, Danny murmurs encouragements I do not fully hear as he leads me at last to a quieter portion of the palace. He opens a door, and I step inside, surprised to find myself in Estrilde's receiving room. I've rarely seen it without Estrilde herself in occupancy. It feels strangely dark and ominous. The tall windows gaze out on an unfamiliar night sky, and the air hums with faraway music.

"I'm sorry, I didn't know where else to bring you," Danny says, noting the stricken look on my face. "I'm not permitted to roam the palace at will but must return to the princess's suite if I am not on duty."

"And your duties now?" I ask, just aware enough to feel concern.

"I'm charged to serve the princess's guests this evening," Danny answers with a wry smile. "You are a guest of hers, are you not?"

I manage a shrug but cannot muster the voice to speak. Danny leads me to a chair by the wall. Not one of Estrilde's beautiful settees or lounges, merely a simple wooden, straight-back seat where her Obligates may perch, awaiting her will. I sink gratefully down, my full skirts settling like a lavender cloud around me, and lean my head against the wall. Danny hovers over me, his hands nervous as he paces. "Is it the wine?" he asks. "The music? Did you eat something?"

"The music, I think," I answer faintly, closing my eyes. The last thing I want is to try to explain to him. To tell him I'd let the magic of the night seep into my blood, filling me with enchantment. Leading me once more to believe what I know to be impossible. Urging me to trust, to cast myself out into that abyss of possibility . . . only to fall . . .

I bow my head, burying my face in my hands, squeezing my jaw tight to keep back another sob. "I'll be all right. I just need a moment, I just—"

The door opens. Danny sucks in a sharp breath. I peer through my fingers, heart lurching with terror. Moonlight gleaming through the windows reveals a tall, broad figure standing in the doorway. Clad in green. Crowned in magnificent ram's horns.

"Your mistress requires your services elsewhere, boy," Lord Ivor says, addressing Danny without looking his way. Danny begins to protest, but stops short when the golden fae adds harshly, "Go."

With a last, desperate look my way, Danny turns and marches from the room. He cannot resist the force of Obligation. Not for long. He sidles past Ivor, who steps into the room and shuts the door behind.

So I am alone with the heir to Aurelis.

He stands over me, breathing heavily. When I dare glance up, there's such a dangerous gleam in his eye, it sends a jolt of fear straight to my belly. I lower my gaze at once, knotting my hands in my lap. A dozen different words spring to my tongue—excuses, protests, trivial pleasantries. All of them die before spoken. I sit there, dumb, stupid. Frightened.

Suddenly, Ivor drops to his knees before me. His hands grip mine, and he gazes into my face, his eyes almost level with mine. I want to look away but cannot. I am mesmerized, fascinated. "Clara," he says. "I am tortured beyond all bearing."

I open my mouth. All I can utter is a breathless, "Lord Ivor, I . . . I think perhaps we should return to the dance. Princess

Estrilde will be—"

He shakes his head. Tears spark in his eyes. One even spills over, tracing a line down the hard plane of his cheek. The sight of it, of that single tear on the face of so proud and strong a warrior is more terrible than I can express. "Do you think I care about Estrilde?" he demands, his voice wrung with anguish. "Do you think I care about any of this? When I saw you on that dance floor . . . when I saw you with him . . ." He reaches up as though to cup my cheek in his great palm.

With a surge of strength, I spring to my feet and step around him, backing into the room. I've never moved so fast or so nimbly in all my life, not even when fleeing the Wild Hunt. Somehow I feel I've never been in more danger. The smell of him, the musk of him . . . it's overwhelming, intoxicating. Thrilling.

He rises, graceful in every move and gesture. Moonlight gleams off the coils of his horns, reflects deep in his eyes. "Tell me, Clara," he says, taking one step toward me then another. "Tell me what I can do to prove to you what I feel. I know my words mean nothing to you, cruel mistress that you are. So end my suffering—give me a task. Give me a burden. Beg of me a boon. If it be in my power to prove by strength of arm or force of will what a hold you have over me, I shall do it."

My heart flutters. I should run. He's not my master. My Obligation belongs to another, which means he cannot force me to stay. But do I want to run? I don't know. Everything in me seems to be of two minds, one part desperate to remain, to throw myself into his arms and seek the comfort offered there, the other . . .

I draw my shoulders back. My chest rises and falls with the quickness of my breath. Once again I wish I'd refused to wear this lovely, revealing gown. But I clench my fists, inhale deeply, and speak all in rush, "Will you lift the curse on Oasuroa?"

Ivor blinks. The agony in his face melts away into confusion. "What did you say?"

"Oasuroa. The dragon who stands guard over the Water of Life. She bears a terrible curse placed on her by your ancestor, Illithorin, the High King."

"I know about the curse." His voice is short, sharp. "It is the most powerful magic remaining to my family line and has withstood many generations. But . . . but I don't understand. How do you know about it? About the High King, the dragon, and . . . and why should you care?" He takes a step closer, dropping his voice an octave. Gone is the desperate tone of the impassioned lover. "Who told you I am Illithorin's blood?"

"No one," I answer hastily. "The information is all available in the library records. I was searching, you see, because . . . well, I made a bargain."

"A bargain? With whom?" His eyes flash. "With Castien?"

"No!" My skirts rustle as I back up two paces. "No, I've made no bargains with the Prince. I am . . . I am attempting to . . ."

How can I possibly explain? Ivor won't care about Danny. He won't care about Seraphine or her son. He certainly won't care about Oscar. No one cares. No one but me. Which is why I must do this on my own. No one is going to help me, not even the Prince save when forced by Obligation. I am all alone. As I have always been.

I raise my chin, facing Ivor, determined not to flinch. "My bargains are my own business. You asked how you might prove yourself? This is it. I need you to free the dragon from her curse. Nothing more. Nothing less."

Ivor studies me closely. Now the first flash of surprise has passed, the anger in his eye fades away, replaced by subtle cunning. Even that vanishes after a few more blinks, and something of the passionate, tormented Ivor returns, if perhaps more subdued than before. "This thing you ask is not impossible, to be sure. But difficult. I would be a fool indeed if I did not bargain with you in turn."

"What?" My stomach clenches.

He smiles, a gentle sort of smile that does not suit him at all. "Why should you be surprised? You are familiar with the ways of Eledria. It would be imprudent of me to lift a curse of such age-old power unless I made certain it was worth my while."

"And . . . what would be worth your while, my lord?"

"One thing and one thing only."

In his gaze I see something of the hunger I'd glimpsed in the Prince's eyes when we danced together. Only this hunger makes me shrink away from him, trembling. He stretches out one hand, and the expression is at once replaced by one of tender longing, forlorn and yet holding on to the barest thread of hope.

"I want you, Clara," he says. "I want your Obligation. If you convince Castien to sell it to me at last, I will lift the curse on Oasuroa."

The whole floor seems to tilt under my feet. Only the greatest will keeps me standing upright. This is too much, too much.

But then again . . . *why not?* After all what does it matter if I exchange one fae master for another?

A sudden throb in my head. I seem to hear again that wild, magic-infused music dancing in my veins. I feel the Prince's arms holding me close, see those vivid eyes of his staring down at me, drawing me toward him. Was that nothing but glamour and trickery? Perhaps. He does not want me. Of that I am certain. Otherwise, he would have kissed me when I offered myself so brazenly. He does not want me. He wants only my power, my service. Why should he have me and not Ivor? I don't want to be Ivor's Obligate, but . . . but even more, I need to escape the Prince. I need to get away from Vespre, away from his presence, his atmosphere. I need . . . I must . . .

My mouth opens. And it seems as though some other voice speaks through me, hollow and echoing: "Very well, my lord. If I can convince the Prince to sell, we have a bargain."

I stumble from Estrilde's chambers almost as breathless and

unsteady on my feet as I was when I entered. Only now I don't have Danny's supporting arm. I hasten down the passage but stop after a turn to press my back against the wall, hand against my heart, and draw several long breaths. It's painful—like my lungs have been put through a wringer. My head is light, whirling.

Love him, the voice inside me whispers. *Love him . . . save him . . .*

"Darling!"

The Prince's voice rings out like an alarm bell, echoing down the vaulting hall. I stand up straight, whirl in place, and see him striding toward me, long coat billowing in his wake. His face is lined and would look furious were it not for the fear simmering in his eyes.

"There you are!" he cries as he draws near. "I swear, I turn my back one moment, and you've wandered off into gods only know what trouble. I've been hunting everywhere for you, including the library. Where were you?"

By this time he's quite close. So close I might reach out and place my hand on his heart again, right where it had rested as we danced. My gaze fixes there, on that very spot, even as I answer coldly, "I was seeing to the mission, of course."

He growls softly. The sound rumbles in my belly, boils in my blood. "Ivor. You've spoken to him?"

I nod. "He's agreed to lift the curse on Oasuroa. For a price."

The Prince waits. But I can't say it. I open my mouth, but the words won't come.

It doesn't matter. His eyes widen. His mouth becomes an ugly, terrible leer. "Never," he snarls, and turns away from me. With quick, long strides, he marches back up the passage, as though ready to march straight out of my life.

"Wait!" I hasten after him. "You haven't heard what I have to say!"

"I don't have to. I know what he wants. I've seen the way he looks at you. Gods! I've fended off that snake's demands already, haven't I? And now you want to throw yourself into his coils!"

I stop and watch his retreating back. I won't chase him. I don't have to. "What does it matter? What does it matter if it's you or him or Estrilde? Whichever way you look at it, I'm still trapped here against my will. Still serving out my sentence, far from home, far from my family. Far from everyone I love."

He halts. For a moment, I think he won't turn around. Then he whirls on heel, facing me down the long passage between us. "And what of Sis?" he says. "What of Har and Dig and . . . and what's the last one's name again?"

"Calx," I whisper.

"Yes. Calx. What of them? You're telling me you don't love them? Or Lir?"

I lower my lashes but take care to answer in a calm, steady voice. "I care for them. Of course I do. But . . . but Oscar . . . Oscar is my whole heart. If I could, I would be with him now. And I will save him. No matter what it takes."

"And you think *this* will save him?" The Prince waves his arms in a grand sweep, as though in one gesture he can encompass Ivor and all the sundry bargains I've made over the last several days. "Stop deluding yourself! You cannot save him. How can you not see the truth? Some people cannot be saved because they do not want to be saved."

"You're wrong." Tears pour down my cheeks. Gods, I didn't even know I was crying until just now. I sniff loudly and shake my head. "You're wrong."

You're not seeing rightly.

"Oscar needs me. He needs someone to understand him. To be present with him. If I'd been there all these years, he wouldn't have sunk so low. If I'd been there . . . If you hadn't . . . if you hadn't done this to me . . ." The words stagger. With an effort, I force them out, my voice rough and breaking. "You should have just let Lodírhal kill me. Then I wouldn't have to live with the knowledge that my brother is out there, alone. Dying by slow degrees. Every good thing in his life stripped away."

Suddenly the Prince is right in front of me. How he crossed that distance so silently, so swiftly, I cannot say. But he's there, and his hand grips mine as though he would pull me back from beyond a brink. "You must stop torturing yourself over that boy. Let him go! Free him and free yourself."

I shake my head.

"I will not sell your Obligation to Ivor." His voice is thick. If I didn't know any better, I'd think he was holding back tears. "Your quest ends here."

"No," I whisper. "I have obliged you to aid me. Until I have the bloodgem necklace in my hand, you must do as I say."

Save him . . .

Save him . . .

"This is it." I pull my gaze to his face, look into his shimmering eyes. "This is what must be done."

"Darling," he breathes. "Please."

"I charge you by the Obligation which stands between us to sell my contract to Lord Ivor."

He looks as though I've driven a dagger into his gut.

I continue, relentlessly: "When you have done so, you must return to Illithorin's Waste and claim the Water of Life from Oasuroa. Take it to Queen Seraphine and see her son restored. Then she must fulfill her bargain, granting Lord Vokarum his kiss. When that is done, you must take Idreloth her head. Claim the bloodgem necklace. And bring it to me."

Part of me knows I'm insane. It's both lunacy and cruelty to place this burden on him. Part of me knows I am sick. And some very small part of me, some tiny shred of awareness, feels the weight of Noswraith hands clamped down on my shoulders, pushing, pushing, pushing.

I draw myself straighter, meet the Prince's gaze and say it once again. "By the Obligation which stands between us, I . . . I . . ."

He's resisting. I feel it already. I can see the pain in his face, the tension in his brow. "Don't do this." He grinds the words through gritted teeth. "Don't make me."

I want to relent. More than anything. I even open my mouth to take it all back, to release him, to break his Obligation to me once and for all.

Instead another voice speaks through my mouth: "I command you. Go."

The Prince draws a ragged breath, his eyes fixed, staring.

Then he pivots on heel and marches away, leaving me behind in the dark of Summit Night.

30

TO MY GREAT RELIEF, GEORGE NOBBLIN IS NOT standing guard at the library front desk. The junior librarian who lounges there, half-asleep, scarcely looks my way as she waves me through.

I offer a polite nod and step gratefully back into the familiar stacks. It's strange to see it all shrouded in night-gloom. No glamour-lights have been hung about the place, for the fae would not bring their revels here. All is quiet and still, with most human Obligates serving at the ball. I meet no one as I make my way deeper and deeper into the shadowed seclusion.

What have I done? My heart pounds so painfully, I press a hand against my chest. I feel faint, sick. And trapped. So terribly trapped. How could I have been so foolish?

But no, no. I did what I had to do. There's no other way to lift Oasuroa's curse. I'm willing to make whatever sacrifice is necessary, and . . . and . . .

Well done. Emma's voice whispers in the back of my head, soft as a half-remembered lullaby. *Well done, my love. We do what we must. Every sacrifice is worth it in the end. We must save them. We must save them—*

"Miss Darlington!"

I look up, confused. I seem to be leaning heavily against a shelf of books, my breath coming in short, painful gasps. Through the darkness and the haze, I can just discern Thaddeus Creakle's square spectacles gleaming on the end of his nose. He holds a lantern high, his eyes widening in surprise at the sight of my ball gown. "Why, Miss Darlington, this is a surprise. You do look rather well, don't you?"

It's too much.

I burst into tears. Great, fat, soppy tears, accompanied by choking sobs. Poor Thaddeus leaps back a step or two, wholly unprepared for such a deluge of emotion. But he steels himself and hastens to me, wrapping an arm around my shoulders. "There, there," he offers timidly. "You've had a turn, haven't you? Come with me, my dear. We'll find you a quiet place to rest, to recover yourself."

He keeps up this gentle crooning as he guides me to his favorite workroom in the back of the library. The sight of all those bookbinding tools, those stacked and scattered pages, and numerous leather volumes halfway through repairs, makes my heart twist with something between pain and relief. This is where I belong. Here is work which always needs doing, and these books won't try to kill me while I'm at it. Maybe it will be good. To return to Aurelis, to keep company with Thaddeus and the other librarians, to forget . . . to forget . . .

"Here, Miss Darlington." Thaddeus eases me onto the work bench then fishes into the front of his robes and produces a large handkerchief. Accepting it gratefully, I dab at my eyes and blow my nose, gasping out apologies to which he responds with a gentle, "No, no, not at all." Only when I've finally managed to calm myself and drawn a few steadying breaths, does he ask, "Is there anything I can do?"

I twist the sodden handkerchief in my fingers. "There's nothing anyone can do. I . . . I fear I've made a terrible mistake."

"Oh?" Thaddeus perches on the bench beside me and rests his hands on his knees. "Well, surely even the worst mistakes can be undone again. The first step is acknowledgement of error, and there! You've covered that already."

I sniff and dash a last stray tear from my cheek. "I don't think it's as simple as that." Seeing the concern in his wrinkled face, I hastily shake my head and force a little smile. "But in other news, I hope I'll be rejoining the library staff soon."

"Is that so?" Thaddeus smiles back and pats my hand fondly. "I must say, I would be delighted to have you back. None of these others are worth half of you, and the pixies have been causing all sorts of trouble lately. In fact, I would love to—"

"Clara!"

My blood runs cold. Still seated, I turn sharply to the half-open door, gripping my skirts. I know that voice too well to mistake it.

"Clara Darlington!"

Muttering under his breath, Thaddeus gets to his feet, steps to the chamber door, and utters a threatening librarian's, *"Hsssssst!"*

A figure in elegant livery steps into view beyond Thaddeus's stooped shoulders. Danny. Pale as the dead, his shoulders straight and firm. He bows to Thaddeus. "Your pardon, Master Librarian. Lord Ivor has summoned Clara Darlington to attend upon him at once. Have you seen her?"

My heart sinks like a stone. Immediately, the vicelike grip of Obligation takes hold. I know then that the Prince has done as I commanded. Up until this moment there was a part of me which had hoped he would resist, would find a way to break my hold over him. And I would hate him and rail at him for thwarting my plans and secretly bless him without even knowing I did so.

But no. The Obligation holds me with a force I've not felt since I was Estrilde's minion.

"Miss Darlington?" Thaddeus turns to me, his brow crinkled with concern. "Do you know what this might be about?" His voice trails off as he gets a good look at my face. "Oh," he finishes softly. "I see."

I step out from behind him. "Thank you, Mister Creakle." I offer back his handkerchief, but he shakes his head, indicating I should keep it. I smile weakly then turn to face Danny, my expression a careful blank. "Yes. I'm coming."

Danny is silent as he escorts me from the library. Once outside, he tries only once to speak, but cannot seem to find the words. He manages only a faltering, "Clara?"

I cast him a sad look. The Obligation is pulling me, leading me away from him. It hurts, and I cannot linger, so I quickly take his hand and squeeze it. "Have courage," I whisper. "It's going to be all right. You'll see."

Before he can answer, I gather up my skirts and hasten away. He does not call after me or try to follow. Perhaps his own Obligation to Estrilde prevents him from doing so. What a pretty pair we make—he enslaved to Estrilde; me to Ivor. A well-matched set, some might say. But not for much longer. The Prince must even now be well on his way to Illithorin's Waste. How he will find his way to the towers, I cannot guess. But he will. I know he will. And he'll retrieve the Water of Life, and he'll fulfill each of those mad bargains I've made. He'll be back with the bloodgem before I know it. Surely.

I remember the way to Ivor's chambers, though I've never been inside them before. Estrilde used to send me with little messages and gifts for him. That was until she began to suspect his partiality for me more than a year ago. I've not been near his apartments since. Now the pull of the Obligation urges me on. It isn't long before I'm standing in front of his door, knocking timidly.

It opens at once. One of Ivor's servants, a dwarf man with a thick black beard, greets me as though he knows who I am. "Lord Ivor awaits you in the front room, miss," he says, beckoning me. I nod and slip through the door, following the servant down a short passage. He opens another door, peeks inside, and announces, "Miss Darlington, your lordship." I draw a long breath, let it out slowly. Then, taking hold of my courage with both hands, I step through.

And find myself staring into the Prince's violet eyes.

He's here.

He's *here.*

He shouldn't be, but he's here, leaning against the arched window frame across the room, arms crossed, face masked in a nonchalant smirk.

I stop dead in my tracks. My heart seems to have stopped as well. Because he's here. I'd convinced myself he was long gone, and now . . .

"Welcome, Clara Darlington."

Ivor stands by the fire. I'd not even noticed him. With a wrench, I turn and meet the triumphant smile spread across his face. He extends a hand to me. I want to resist. But what if he gives a command, forces me to comply? With a little dip of my chin, I rest my fingertips against his. He takes hold, squeezing just hard enough to make me wince. "At last," he says, drawing me two steps nearer. "You cannot know how long I have wished to claim this fair prize."

With that, he raises my hand to his lips and kisses it. In that moment of contact, I can almost feel the wave of glamour washing over me, leaving me dizzy, almost giddy at the sight of his beauty and the smell of his musk. But somehow, through the fluttering of my heart and the warm pulse of my blood, I know it's only glamour. I want to shrink back, to yank my hand from his grasp. Instead, when he straightens and meets my eyes, I smile blandly. To my relief he relinquishes his hold on me. I put both hands behind my back and take the smallest step away.

"I must return to the ball now," he says, his voice low and urgent. "Estrilde is expecting me. I've instructed my servant"— with a nod to the dwarf still standing in the doorway—"to direct you to your room. You will be comfortable, I'm sure. And when my duties are seen to, I will find you, and we will discuss plans for your future."

"Thank you, my lord," I murmur.

Across the room, the Prince clears his throat. I don't look at him. I can't bear to. But Ivor casts him a terrible glare and growls, "Very well, Prince. Take what you must according to our agreement. Then I would urge you to return to your little troll rock with all speed."

"Not to worry, my lord," the Prince replies cooly. "I have things to do, people to see. Bargains to fulfill."

Ivor casts me one last look, pure victory glowing in his eyes, before striding from the room. The dwarf closes the door behind him, leaving me and the Prince alone in the flickering firelight.

For a long moment, we neither move nor speak. I stand with my eyes downcast. He remains leaning against the window frame, idly gazing into the night and the garden and the festivities below. Finally he pushes off, puts his hands behind his back, and saunters toward me. I watch his approach warily, watch him draw near to the fire and rest one hand on the mantel. Leaning over, he studies the flames. He might well be contemplating the merits of casting himself into them.

After a terrible eternity of silence, I open my lips. "I'm . . . sorry."

He turns slowly, one bright eye catching mine. Then, eyebrow raised, he pulls away from the mantel and is once more in restless motion, circling me like prey. Still he does not speak.

"Why are you here?" I demand at last, anger fortifying my spirit. "Why aren't you on your way?"

"Oh, believe me," he growls, "I will be gone in short order. Leaving you in the lion's den just as requested."

"Lord Ivor is an honorable man."

"Ha!"

"He's always been kind to me." I bite my lip before continuing, "Which is more than I can say for you."

"Kind? Ivor? Whatever *kindness* you think you see in him is nothing more than a ruse to get what he wants from you."

"Oh, and you're any different?"

He stops dead in front of me. His head is bent, his shoulders back, his eyes dark and hooded. For a moment, his jaw works, as though chewing on the words he will speak. Then, through gritted teeth: "I've never pretended to be kind."

It's my turn to laugh, a single bitter burst. "That's true enough. You've hated me from the day we met."

"Can't say I'm feeling a great deal of *liking* for you now."

"Excellent. Then you'll be well rid of me. One more burden you can shrug off. Like your kingdom and your crown."

"I've never cared about the kingdom or the crown."

"No?" I turn to face him fully, chin up, fists clenched. "Nor me either, I suppose. Go on, Prince. So long as we're being honest with one another, you may as well say what you mean."

His features freeze. The hot energy of his spirit seems to be coated in ice. Slowly he shakes his head. "I've long since ceased to expect honesty from you."

My nostrils quiver. "I've never lied to you."

"No. You prefer to lie to yourself."

I try to hold his gaze. But can't. The anger burning in my heart is too great. If I look at him one second longer, I will explode.

So I turn away, stare into the fire. Breathe, just breathe. And don't let the tears escape.

The Prince draws near. Too near. His hands are still behind his back, but somehow, I remember too vividly the way they'd felt against my skin. I close my eyes. But I cannot shut off my awareness of him or the way my skin trembles when he whispers, "Oh no. No, Darling, you don't get to hurl such bitter words at me if you can't take a little missile slinging in return. Perhaps neither of us has been fully honest. But I don't look at my face in the mirror and see only a mask I've convinced myself is the truth."

In the darkness behind my eyelids, I seem to see that gruesome reflection again. My own face. Covered in gore. Both eyelids sewn shut.

"Well. It's done now, isn't it?" My voice is shaky and small. "I'm back in Aurelis. Soon Danny will be home. I'll serve out my Obligation and return to my own world. You and I should rarely cross paths. Perhaps never. We can be grateful for that at least."

Silence. Then the Prince breathes out a long sigh, stirring the fine hairs of my neck. "You are such a fool," he says, his voice a deep rumble. "But I'm the worse fool, I suppose. I see what is happening, what I'm allowing you to do to me. And even now I cannot seem to stop myself."

"Stop what?" I turn to him then, eyes open, pleading. "Go on, Prince. Speak your mind."

His brow puckers. "Will you force me to answer?"

I feel then the yawning depths before me—the terrible reality of what his answer, spoken out loud, will mean. Especially now. Now when my Obligation belongs to another.

I drop my head. Shake it once. "No. Fulfill what I have commanded of you, and I will consider your Obligation ended. There need be no further ties binding us."

He takes a half-step toward me. From the tail of my eye, I see one hand start to reach out. But he stops. Slowly closes his fist. Then he turns and marches across the room to the door.

"Wait."

He pauses. When I dare turn to look after him, his head is bowed, his shoulders set as though bearing a great burden. He doesn't look back.

"What did Ivor pay for me?" The words emerge small from my lips but seem to echo in the silence of that room. "What price did you set for my service?"

"A small one." He turns his head partially so that I can just glimpse one eye. "The opportunity for a word with you in private."

My stomach knots. My Obligation might not be worth much, partially used-up as it is. But the Prince could have sold it for a great deal more. "And . . ." I stop, pinch my lips together before continuing. "Was it worth the price?"

"Hardly. My words are wasted on you."

A tear slips from my lashes, races down my cheeks. "I'm sorry you made such a poor bargain after all."

With that I turn away from the fire and march to the window. It is open to the night and looks out upon the magically illuminated gardens. A cool breeze dances across the trees and blossoms, rises to chill my bare shoulders. Down below me the fae dance and laugh. From this vantage, I spy a couple tucked away behind an arbor, locked in amorous embrace. Oblivious to the world around them, lost in a small sphere of pleasure meant only for them. I observe them from this distance, and somehow that glimpse of their delight only makes my heart harden and sink.

Behind me, the door opens. Shuts.

I let out a strangled sob and grip the windowsill, leaning heavily upon it. Another tear falls, then another. I dash at my cheeks but cannot seem to stop them. My chest burns as though my heart has been set ablaze. I can only wish this agony would end.

Suddenly, a hand slips around my waist, presses flat against my stomach. I catch a breath. A single tug, and I'm drawn back against a warm, broad chest. Breath tickles my ear, and another hand touches my jaw, gently trails down my throat.

"I will come to you." His mouth rests just against my ear, his voice low and deep: "Should you need me. For any reason. Not for Obligation, only for need."

I'm shaking, shuddering. But he holds me closer, as though he can hold me together, keep me from bursting into a million pieces.

"Call my name," he whispers. "I will come to you. From anywhere in all the worlds, I will come. Just call my name."

"Castien." My throat vibrates against his fingertips.

"No." He leans in closer, his nose against my temple. His lips just brush my skin. Not a kiss, a mere stroke of contact. "Not that."

Then he speaks a single word, softly. Breathes it into my ear.

The next moment he is gone.

31

THIS CHAMBER HAS BEEN PREPARED JUST FOR YOU, miss. You'll be comfortable here, I'm sure."

I scarcely hear a word the dwarf says. I stand in the doorway, staring into the room. My room.

It is . . . very nice. More than nice. It's the same basic size and shape as the room I'd had while in Estrilde's service, but everything is plated in gold. The bed. The wardrobe. The washstand. Gold. Even the curtains are embroidered in gold threads and the mirror frame covered in gold leaf. It looks like it's meant for a princess, not an Obligate.

I'm reluctant to enter. But what else can I do? I offer the dwarf a timid smile. "Thank you."

He touches his forehead deferentially. "If you need anything, don't hesitate to ring the bell," he says before slipping away down the passage.

I watch him go. Then I step into the room and move around it slowly, inspecting each item by turn. On the gold vanity is a set of gold combs, all with my name engraved in them. The wardrobe is packed with gowns as well—beautiful gowns, all my size.

An uneasy feeling coils in my gut. Which is silly, of course. This is not unlike my arrival in Vespre, after all. I'd been surprised then to discover the far too-nice chamber the Prince had arranged for me in advance. But somehow it had not struck me in the same way. For one thing, my name hadn't been carved into every conceivable detail. Gods spare me! It's even etched into the fancy headboard and embroidered into the bed curtains. How could Ivor have prepared all of this? Had he done it back when he first came to Vespre, seeking to purchase my Obligation? But . . . why?

I take a seat at the vanity, uneasily meeting my own gaze in the mirror. My eyes are hollow and red-rimmed, my cheeks far too pale. I need to pull myself together, face this new reality head on. It's not so bad, after all. No more Noswraiths trying to eat me at every turn. No more zealot trolls eager to bash my head in, or agonizing long hours poring over scratchy writing, my hand cramping, my back aching, my eyes blurring with fatigue. Life will be easier now.

As for Ivor? Well, according to the laws of Obligation, I cannot be obliged to . . . to . . . to engage in certain personal services at the behest of my Obliege Lord. Fae law can be dangerous and rarely benefits the humans involved. But this at least is sure.

So no. I needn't worry on that score. If indeed there were anything to worry about. Ivor is passionate, but I'm not foolish enough to think he would throw away everything he has with Estrilde for the sake of a passing fancy. Certainly not for a mere human.

But if he did . . . if he were . . . and if Estrilde found out . . . Would she risk the wrath of her betrothed and future king by outright murdering his servant?

A shudder rolls down my spine. I must be careful. Remain on my guard.

Rising, I move to the wardrobe and begin to sort through the vast array of garments there. I need to change out of this ballgown. To my dismay, however, there isn't a single practical ensemble to be had. Everything is fantastic or elaborate, all in brilliant hues and revealing cuts. These are the clothes of a fine court lady, and yet all are perfectly tailored to my size. Hands shaking, I dig deeper until I find what looks to be a nightgown. The fabric is soft, clinging, and practically translucent, but it's the best option I have for the moment.

I change into the garment, carefully putting aside Dasyra's lavender gown. The butterflies, all a little drab and limp following recent events, happily flutter away from my head and tuck themselves into the folds of fabric out of sight. Tomorrow I'll find someone to take it back to the queen's apartment. Then I need never think of it again. Nor of how it felt to be held in the Prince's arms as the music swelled around us, carrying us away in its magic—

"Where is she? Can I see her?"

A jolt shoots through my body. I whip my head around, staring at the door. That voice, muffled, but sounding from just outside. It sounded like . . . but it couldn't possibly be . . .

"Not now." A deep, growling answer. "It's not time, I tell you. Come away at once."

Ivor. I would know his rumbling tones anywhere. But the other . . .

With a sharp intake of breath, I spring forward, grab the door, and wrench it open. Peer out into the passage. It's empty. At the far end, the door leading to Ivor's personal quarters, is just swinging shut. Whoever was here a moment before has gone.

Blood pounds in my head. I can scarcely draw breath. Because that voice . . . that voice . . . I swear I know it.

I swear, it sounded just like Oscar.

THE PRINCE

T HE DRAGON SHIFTS LIKE A SERIES OF ROLLING hills, starting with the top of her head and rippling down her massive body to the end of her spiked tail. The waters of the sacred fountain slosh around her, little waves of foam and froth, shining with holy light. She lifts her heavy snout and jaw and swings them dripping to face across the hall. One bright eye gleams red as a demon's lost soul.

"Who dares approach the Water of Life?" Her voice is a warning dark as hell. "Be you pure of heart or black of intent, you cannot . . . oh, damn." With a heavy sigh, she sags back down and rests her head on the edge of the pool. "Do you know, I don't really care anymore. I've had just about all I can take of you heroes and all your comings and goings."

Then her eye narrows. She sniffs, inhaling streams of her own smoke. "Step a little closer, why don't you? There's something about your stink that smells familiar."

I stand in the doorway, gazing down upon the monster in her pool. At her command, I come forward, head high, hands outspread to show I bear no weapons. "Great Oasuroa," I say and bow. "We meet again."

"Again? Ah, yes!" With a surge of rippling muscle and scale, the dragon sits upright in her pool. Her wings rattle, her crest flares. She opens her jaw, and flames dance between her teeth. "I seem to remember banishing you from these premises. Did you think I was joking, little elfkin? Or are you of a mind to be roasted?"

I meet her gaze without flinching. "I'm not here of my own volition but out of Obligation to one I care about.

The dragon tilts her head. "If you care so much, why is it an obligation?"

"It's complicated."

"It always is with you snacklings, isn't it?" Oasuroa sighs and slumps deeper into her pool, sending a wave sloshing over the edge. It rolls across the floor to dampen the soles of my boots. Heat from her body causes the sacred waters to steam. Condensation beads my brow, and my shirt clings to my body in damp patches. "Very well," the dragon growls, "you might as well tell me as not. Who sent you?"

"The librarian. Clara Darlington."

Her crest flares again, fluttering with interest. "Indeed?"

"According to your bargain," I continue, "she has convinced Illithorin's heir to relinquish the curse under which you suffer. Thus she would claim her promised reward: a single mouthful from the Water of Life."

Oasuroa's body begins to tremble. "You're lying."

"As you have already noted, I am elfkin. We are incapable of lying."

"And what a lie that is!" The dragon rolls her one good eye. "Don't think I can't smell the human blood on you, boy. You positively reek of it. Not to mention the curse you bear. Ugh! I don't remember that being there the last time you paid me a visit. It's quite nauseating, frankly."

"Do you want that sword removed from your eye or don't you?"

She is silent, puffing smoke from her nostrils like an engine. "Very well," she says finally. "Draw near if you have such a death wish. But I give you fair warning! Should you prove false in your promises, should the sword not come free, I will eat you in a single bite and not bother roasting you beforehand. Do we understand one another?"

"Absolutely, Great Oasuroa."

So the dragon, still half-submerged, rests her head on the pool's lip. I approach, moving carefully but without hesitation. My boots splash in puddles of sacred water until I stand before her ruined eye and the sparkling jeweled hilt protruding from it. Taking hold with both hands, I send a silent prayer winging to whatever gods might care to receive it. Then I pull.

The blade slips out in a smooth easy glide. With a last flash of priceless jewels, it disintegrates to dust in my hands.

Oasuroa utters a bellow of either pain or joy, it's impossible to say which. She rears her head, rears her whole body, and roars so loud, the high domed ceiling above shakes, and streams of sand come pouring down all around us. "At last!" she cries. "At last and at last! For countless turns of the bloody cycle I've carried that curse with me, unable to escape the prick, the pain! Sometimes it drove me halfway to madness, sometimes right over the brink! And now . . . and now . . ."

Words failing, she opens her throat and emits a gout of flame, like a volcano erupting from her gut. I leap back, narrowly escaping her lashing tail, and retreat, hands up to shield my face from the heat. "Oasuroa!" I cry, helpless to make myself heard over her noise. "You must fulfill your end of the bargain!"

I'm obliged to repeat myself several times before the jubilant dragon finally ceases her uproar and turns her eye on me once more. The other eye is still ruined, gushing with a fresh surge of lava-bright blood. But she smiles a magnificent, toothy dragon-smile. "Very well, elfkin. Claim what is due your mistress. And tell her . . . tell her . . ."

Her voice trails away. Her good eye narrows. She stares at me, studying me even as I kneel to fill the small waterskin I brought along for the purpose. I secure the stopper and, as she doesn't seem to have more to add, bow once more. "I will take my leave,

Great Oasuroa."

"Yes," she replies, her voice vibrating softly. "Take your leave. And tell your lady mistress the truth."

I pause halfway to the door. Turning, I look back over my shoulder, back into that hideous, smoke-wreathed grin. "I've told her no lies."

The dragon chuckles. "How like a fae you sound! We all know a truth omitted will sting just the same as any falsehood." She lowers her head, bringing her face down to the level of mine. "I see the truth of your rotten little soul. She'll never be yours, elfkin. You've offered your heart, but even if she accepts it, she'll throw it back in your miserable face the moment she learns of your falsehood."

"I don't know what you're talking about," I answer, my jaw hard as stone.

"Oh? Another lie? How charming."

Oasuroa turns away then, dragging her great scaled body and limp wings back into the shadows behind a curtain of falling sand. Her voice echoes to the domed ceiling as she tosses it over her scaled spine: "Don't say I didn't warn you. Now be off! Before this whole place crumbles down upon your head."

Tucking the waterskin into the front of my shirt, I turn and flee that chamber, leaving the dimming light of the fountain behind forever.

business not their own."

"But are you?" I lift my head, peering up at him. "Is that what this is? Fate?"

"Yes." He pushes up onto his elbow so that he can level a look at me. "The truth is, Darling, the very moment I set eyes on your face, I knew. I knew I had met the one the gods intended to be mine. But the circumstances . . ."

He doesn't finish that thought. For which I am grateful. It would be agony to bring the death of his mother into this moment with us.

"Humans," he goes on after a moment, "have rather more leeway than the fae when it comes to the Fatebond. They generally don't turn rabid and fanatical, obsessive. And they don't fade away and die if the bond goes uncompleted. For the fae, the experience is far more *challenging*, shall we say.

"As an *ibrildian* half-breed, I hoped I might have some say in the matter. So I allowed Estrilde to take you on as her Obligate, despite knowing your powers were wasted in her service. And for five years, I thought of you. Every day. Thought of your face as I saw it first when I stormed into your father's house with murder in my heart. Those eyes—so soft, so gentle, so full of terror. Yet how they sparked with defiance as you placed yourself between me and your brother! You would defend him against any foe, no matter how terrible. You would fight me, though in every way outmatched, though I could strike you down with but a wave of my hand!

"That moment . . . that courage . . . that grim, stubborn defiance . . . it stayed with me. Haunted me. And I hated you for it! Hated you because you had pierced my heart. A wound from which I would never recover.

"Still," he sighs, "I might have let your years of Obligation slip away were it not for the death of Soran Silveri and the desperate need of a new librarian at Vespre. I cursed the gods then for placing me in that situation, railed at them. I declared that, while I might make use of your power, I would never succumb to their little games."

"So . . ." I pinch my lips together before continuing. "So you do believe this is all just the work of the gods? That you've been forced and manipulated into what you feel?"

He chuckles warmly and tips my chin, forcing me to look at him. "While it may have been the gods who forced my hand, it was you who showed me who you really are. That heart of yours, which cannot help defending the defenseless. Your courage and cleverness. The way you see the world so differently from anyone I've ever met. I plucked you from all the comforts of Aurelis and threw you into a veritable pit of darkness, only for you rise to meet the challenge head-on. Not one complaint. Only more of that willful determination to best me and survive. More than survive. I watched you take in those children, rejected by my people, betrayed by their own, and create a home for them out of nothing. From there you built a bridge between the palace and the low city where I never believed such a thing was possible, risking your own life in the process. You've worked miracles before my very eyes!"

My face roars with heat. I feel more naked now than I did when he undressed me. It's almost painful to hear such praise on his lips, knowing how unworthy I am. After everything I've put him through these last few days, how could I ever hope to deserve his love? How could I ever hope to deserve him?

"I fear perhaps the Fatebond has warped your perspective," I whisper.

You're not seeing rightly . . .

But he cups my cheek in his hand, gazing down at me with such an expression of tenderness it could break my heart. "On this at least my sight is truer than yours. If you will permit me, I'll gladly devote a lifetime to teaching you how to see yourself as I see you."

It's too much. I cannot bear that look of his. He's like the summer sun, and I have no shade in which to hide my pale naked skin. I turn away, breathing hard. "Some said you were Fatebound to Ilusine," I murmur, desperate to change the subject.

He laughs outright. "Were you jealous? I do so hope you were jealous. You're so solemn and serious and painfully difficult to read! I thought perhaps when I danced with her at Vespre on the night of *Hugag* that maybe . . . maybe . . ."

"You *wanted* to make me jealous?"

"More than anything. Jealous women are apt to act upon their passions, and I very much wanted a glimpse of your passionate side." He drops his eyes, lets them run languorously down my body pressed up tight against his. "A little more than a glimpse, perhaps."

"And jealous men are so much better controlled are they?"

"Hardly. I should have liked to kill your Doctor Gale several times over by now." His face darkens. "And I fully intend to kill Ivor."

With those words, reality crashes back down on us, an avalanche of inescapable dread. I push away from him, sit upright on the desk. Suddenly, it feels very small, very hard, very uncomfortable. "Come back to me, Darling," the Prince says gently.

But I shake my head, slip off the edge, and gather up my dress from the floor. The Prince rises, still naked and glorious. I cannot resist a lingering glance his way. "I have to go," I say, stepping into the gown. "Ivor hasn't noticed I'm gone yet and . . ." I can't bear to finish.

He understands, however. Rising, he wraps himself up in his dressing gown. "Don't forget this," he says and swipes up something from the ground before handing it to me. It's the bloodgem. Heaven spare me! I'd totally forgotten it. After all this, all the struggle and peril and pain, it seems so insignificant.

But it's not. It's Danny's freedom. And I will give it to him after all.

"Thank you," I whisper.

The Prince ties up the back laces of my gown with far more reluctance than he'd ripped them open. When they're secure once more, he sweeps my hair to one side and kisses my shoulder, holding me close against his chest. I close my eyes, allow myself to be in that space with him. Just one moment more.

"Please." I turn suddenly and wrap my arms around his neck. "Please, my Prince. Don't die."

His brow puckers. "Your Prince?"

"My Castien," I amend and pull him down into a kiss.

No sooner do our lips meet, however, than the awful constriction of Obligation tightens around my throat. I gasp and yank back, staggering at the pain. The Prince's eyes flash with understanding. "I'll kill him," he growls. "Damn the rite, I'll kill him here and now!"

"No." I press my hands against his chest. If I could, I'd force him to return to Vespre safe and sound. Gods, have I only made things worse? Have I only made him more determined to use whatever powers are at his disposal to annihilate his enemy, heedless of the consequences? "Please, Castien. Win your victory. Win your crown. Win my freedom. But do not die for it. Do not die for me. I could not bear it if you . . . if you . . ." The Obligation tugs even more sharply than before. I stagger back several paces, gripping my throat as though to loosen the invisible bond. "I must go." I turn pleading eyes up to him. "And you must let me. If you love me at all, you will let me."

He follows me to the door. I fear he'll follow me all the way to Ivor's chambers and go through with his murderous intent. At the last, however, he stops and kisses me one final time, though I wince at the pain. Then he looks into my eyes, cupping my face with his hands. "I will save you, my Darling. Whatever else happens, I promise you that."

With his words in my ear and his kiss still warm upon my lips, I slip from his chambers back out into the crowd of people waiting in the passage beyond. They part around me, their expressions confused, their eyes very large and staring.

Flushing mightily, I duck my head and hasten through their midst, the Obligation jolting me along every step of the way.

37

I VOR IS SUNK DEEP IN A CRESCENT-SHAPED BATH, surrounded by a cloud of scented steam when I step through the door into his private washroom. Estrilde perches elegantly just behind him, massaging his shoulders. Her hands knead and pull with sensual possession, running up and down his chest, his neck, his hair. She gives me a hard, distasteful look when I appear.

"I understand," she says, "that you are responsible for the state of my newest Obligate." She bares her teeth. "I like my footmen pretty. It'll take a bit of glamour work to fix him up right, and much longer for any actual healing to take place. You selfish beast."

I stare at her. I'm trembling hard, terrified to be alone with either of them. But Castien's true name burns on my tongue.

I know what will happen if I call it—and they know too. Ivor's gaze is hooded, but there's a subtle wariness to his expression. And Estrilde's bitter cruelty is too obvious a mask for her fear.

As I'm not obliged to, I make no answer, but stand with my hands neatly folded, my heart racing. I can still feel every place on my body where the Prince's hands and lips touched, and the memory makes me stronger, braver. Looking over Ivor's head, I meet Estrilde's harsh eyes, my gaze steady, unflinching.

An animal growl rumbles in the princess's throat. I could almost swear I see her hackles raise. But Ivor catches her hand, draws it to his lips, then takes one of her fingers in his mouth and sucks it. All the while his gaze is upon me.

My stomach knots. But I refuse to let even the smallest reaction reveal itself on my face.

"My love," Ivor says, his voice a low purr, "my heart, will you kindly see to it that my sword is readied? I'd prefer to spill your cousin's blood cleanly rather than be reduced to hacking him to pieces for the pleasure of the crowd."

"Of course, beloved." Estrilde nibbles his ear before catching his mouth in a long, lingering kiss. Then she rises, her steam-dampened gown clinging to her breasts and hips, and saunters across the washroom, passing me on her way to the door. As she draws near, she pauses suddenly and sniffs. Her eyes narrow. "Ugh! Just when I thought Castien couldn't stoop any lower." With a curl of her lip, she moves on, out the door, shutting it behind her.

So I am alone with Ivor once more. Standing before him as he lounges naked in his bath. I fix my stare on the wall beyond his head, a faint smile on my lips, though I know his fae senses can detect the trembling in my knees.

Ivor dandles his hand in the water, idly flicking scented bubbles. "So," he says at last, "you gave yourself to the half-breed prince, did you?"

Heat rushes from my gut to my face. But I don't have to answer. So I won't.

Ivor shakes his head, shifting in the water. "It's a shame. It will only make things harder for you when I destroy him. Oh, don't worry!" he adds, just as though I'd spoken. "You shouldn't die from it. Humans rarely respond to the mate-bond quite so extremely as do elfkin. It will hurt, though. You will suffer and cruelly." He smiles. "But I'll be here when your suffering is through. And I will forgive you."

Three days of pain . . .

My heartbeat quickens. It takes all my willpower to maintain that blank, bland expression on my face. That little half-smile that means nothing, gives nothing, allows for nothing.

Ivor rises in a rush of water and foamy suds. Naked, dripping, he steps from the bath and, with unhurried grace, retrieves a robe and drapes it over his shoulders, only lightly belting it at the waist. Every movement sends a ripple of glamour wafting over me. But his magic no longer affects me as it once did. Glamours break like waves on rocks and wash away. Perhaps my bond to the Prince protects me; or perhaps I've seen too much of Ivor's true colors to be deceived anymore.

He moves to a chair, takes a seat. "Well?" he says. "What are you waiting for? Assist me."

Obligation pulls. Though everything in me is repelled, I step behind him, drawing a steadying breath. There's a set combs on an ornate table. I pick up one and begin to run it through his hair. Such soft, silky, perfect hair. With methodic strokes, I pull free any tangles or snarls, all the while trying to imagine myself elsewhere . . . back in Castien's arms, tangled up with him on that desk . . .

Ivor growls softly. Then he catches my wrist. I stiffen. The Prince's true name springs to my lips. I could summon him, but . . . no. That would lead only to a bloodbath here and now. At least with the Rite of the Thorn there should be some rules, some decorum, some measure of protection. I hold my breath and my tongue.

Ivor is still for a long, tense moment. Waiting. He knows how near I am to calling out. But when I don't, he exhales softly. "What is it you see in him?" he asks at last, tugging me around to stand before him so that he may peer up into my face. "What makes him so much more worthy in your eyes?" I don't respond. "He was your master," he continues. "Now I am. He did not grant you your freedom, no more than any other fae lord would. He bought you and sold you, and now he has had his way with you. But in him you see your savior, and in me, your captor. Why is that?"

I shouldn't let him provoke me. I know better. But the words come anyway: "He has never enforced his will on me."

Ivor smiles. "Neither have I. You entered my bed chamber of your own free will, remember?"

A cold, slimy sensation creeps down the back of my neck. When I pull against his hold, he lets go. Shuddering, I slip behind him once more, go back to combing his hair. Ivor leans back, sighing. "You have such an idealized view of Castien. It would be sweet were it not so pathetic. If you knew what he truly is, if you knew everything he has done, you would be grateful to me for slaughtering him later today. Because make no mistake: I intend to bleed every drop of blood from his body, be it blue or red."

My hand shakes so hard I can scarcely keep my grip on the comb. Ivor turns, looks up at me. "Perhaps you won't thank me at first. But someone else will. Someone you care about."

I stare into his gold eyes, so cold and cunning. What is he saying? What does he mean?

"Yes, Clara," he continues. "Someone you care about more than anyone. More even than Castien himself. Can you not guess who I mean?"

I shake my head. Somehow, deep inside, I know what he's about to say. But in that moment, I cannot accept it, cannot fathom it. If I could, I would stop him from speaking.

"Your brother." His lips curve. "*Oscar.*"

Ice ripples through my veins, freezes me in place. *Run, run, get out of here!* Every instinct cries out for escape. But Obligation and agonized curiosity alike keep me rooted in place.

"Yes." Ivor chuckles. "I know about your brother."

"How?" The word whispers through my lips, a mere breath without sound.

"I made it a point to learn everything I could about you. I wanted to know you, to understand you. To do so meant understanding where you came from. So I used the Between Gate, traveled back to your world. There I found your brother. A wretched creature but no wonder considering the curse he carries."

"You cursed me, you witch!" Oscar's voice echoes inside my head. *"If it weren't for you . . . if you hadn't done this to me . . ."*

I shake my head, protests spilling from my tongue in a rush: "Oscar isn't cursed! He's sick. His mind isn't right, and it makes him desperate. He doesn't mean the things he says."

Ivor shakes his head slowly. "I'm sorry to tell you, Clara Darlington, but your brother is indeed most disastrously cursed. One of those nasty, ingenious, powerful curses which could only be crafted by the Blessed Beldames, the Daughters of Bhorriel. Someone must have been quite determined not to let the boy access his magic to be willing to place such a burden on him."

The whole room spins around me. The comb drops from my numb fingers, and I grip the back of Ivor's chair.

"It didn't take much to figure out who." Ivor's voice pours relentlessly into my ear. "Do you want me to tell you? Or do you want me to spell it out with your little human alphabet? Will that make it easier for you to understand?"

I wrench away, stagger blindly through the steam. *No, no, no!*

This cannot be true! But . . . but at the same time . . .

The Prince must have seen Oscar's potential. He'd just witnessed what I and my father had made, crafting the Eyeless Woman together and bringing it to life. We had both exhibited terrible power, but Oscar? Oscar was always the most gifted one. His magic, his ability, must have been tremendous. So why not block it entirely? Why not place a curse on him, keep him from ever fulfilling his promise? Protect the worlds from him and all he might create . . .

And in the process, break him into little pieces. Strip him of the one good thing in his life, the one source of beauty and relief for his tortured soul. Drive him to drink and drugs and debauchery, desperate for something to alleviate the pain.

Steam curls before my eyes, stings my nostrils. I shake my head, and my swimming gaze lands upon Ivor's cruel face. "You're deceiving me," I say. "Your words are nothing more than poisonous implications, but you will not say what you mean. Your fae blood prevents you from speaking an outright lie."

Ivor shrugs. "I thought perhaps to spare your feelings. But if you need more . . ." He leans forward, resting his elbows on his knee. When he speaks, he enunciates with perfect clarity: "It was Castien Lodírith, son of Lodírhal, Prince of Vespre, and renounced heir of Aurelis who bargained with the crones and placed a curse upon your brother, Oscar Darlington. A curse which even now poisons your brother's soul."

I can't breathe. I find and lean against the wall, determined

SYLVIA MERCEDES

not to let my legs give out.

Ivor rises and approaches through the steam, smiling like a demon infiltrating a dream. He leans over me, one hand pressed against the wall by my face. "I'll leave you now," he says. "I must make ready for the rite. You will attend Estrilde in my absence and observe all from the royal box. I hope to hear your voice in the crowd cheering me on. After all, once I've skewered Castien on the end of my blade, the curse on your brother will be broken. Then perhaps you will appreciate your gracious lord and show him the proper deference and"—his eyes run slowly down my body then back up again—"gratitude."

With those words, he leaves me. Leaves me in that hot, steaming chamber, pressed against the wall. Shaking so hard I can scarcely stand.

38

SOUNDS, COLORS, SMELLS DANCE ACROSS MY SENSES. A storm of chaos from which there can be no escape. And in the eye of that storm, my soul stands. Numb. Unfeeling. Immobile even as my body moves and breathes and acts according to natural impulses.

All Aurelis is in uproar over the rite. The betrothal ball is forgotten, and the merrymakers come together now eager for a display of violence and blood. Princess Estrilde, surrounded by her entourage of friends and admirers, preens and prattles, projecting absolute confidence in the outcome of the coming battle. She has adorned herself in crimson silk, and her nails are glamoured to be black, long, and curved like raptor talons. A crown of black antlers sprouts from her forehead, bejeweled in dangling rubies like drops of blood. She looks as though she belongs in Lord Vokarum's hall.

Obligated by my master to serve his betrothed, I stand at the back of Estrilde's party, carrying the end of her long red train. She does not look my way. I may as well not exist for all the attention she pays me. For this at least I am grateful.

We progress from the princess's chambers through the palace, making our way to the viewing box from which she and King Lodírhal will observe the rite. Fawning courtiers crowd as close as they dare, offering her their best wishes for her future husband's success and the securing of both his crown and hers. No one bothers to mention that, should the Prince and Ivor manage to kill each other, Lodírhal would be forced at last to give the throne to his niece. Such words would be tactless, inappropriate to speak in the presence of a devoted bride-to-be. But everyone is thinking it. I can see it in their wary faces.

I drop my gaze, study the black embroidery on the edge of the garment in my hands, concentrate on placing one foot after the other. A dull droning pulses in my ear. And lower still, in the depths of my mind, voices whisper ceaselessly.

Clara, Clara, my darling, I love you . . .

Three days of pain . . . then will I harvest . . .

He bargained with the crones . . . placed a curse upon your brother . . .

And deepest of all, down in the darkest pit of my mind: *You're not seeing rightly . . . you're not seeing—*

"Clara!"

Startled, I turn. Danny steps from an alcove, emerging behind Estrilde's party, avoiding his mistress's gaze. He staggers to my side, limping, struggling. Though someone has swathed him in glamours to hide his many wounds, they cannot hide the pain scoring his features.

He reaches out to take my hand, and I don't have the energy to resist, though it means I must carry Estrilde's train one-handed now. "Clara, did he hurt you?" Danny whispers, his voice strangled. "Gods on high, if he so much as touched you, I swear I'll kill him with my bare hands!"

Danny. Sweet Danny. Gentle, kind, good Danny.

Oh, what have they done to you?

"No," I whisper, shaking my head and squeezing his fingers. "I'm unhurt. I swear."

He looks at me, his desperate eyes scanning my face. He doesn't believe me. No doubt the hollows under my eyes, the pinched line of my mouth belie my words.

I turn away, unable to bear his gaze. Then, dropping his hand, I reach into the front of my bodice. I'd half-forgotten the bloodgem I'd tucked down there for safe keeping. Its evil miasma burns against my fingertips. It's a relief to draw it away from my heart. "Here," I say, pressing the stone into Danny's hand.

He looks down at it. His eyes widen. "Clara, is this—"

"Give it to Estrilde. She must break your Obligation then."

"What about you?" He lifts his gaze back to mine. "This was

meant to break your Obligation, Clara. Not mine. It was meant to save you."

"I don't care." I shake my head viciously, the words grinding between my teeth. "As long as you're home safe, Danny, I don't care about any of the rest of it."

With that, I duck my head and hasten on, leaving Danny slumped against the wall. I hope he'll do what I ask. I hope he won't try anything stupid. At least let this one small thing work out for the best—let Danny return home to his sister, let the two of them not suffer any worse for having known me.

We step through a doorway out into the open air, following lantern-lit walkways. Summit Night is still deep and dark overhead, but it's hard to discern the twinkling stars through the glamour glows all around. We approach the arena, a great open-air structure which I have only ever seen from a distance. I cannot comprehend either its size or the noise emanating from it. My senses lock down, erecting high walls, a feeble protection around my pathetic soul.

We climb a stair, Estrilde up ahead, me many paces behind, still bearing her train. The stair leads to a canopied box swathed in golden curtains and richly furnished. Servants flit about with trays of dainty fruits, skewered meats, and glasses of sparkling brews. Garlands of golden roses—*ylyndar,* the Rose of Dawn, an emblem of Aurelis—wreathe the balcony rail overlooking the arena. The whole space reeks of their perfume.

In the center of all is Lodírhal—the withered, gray king,

propped up on a pile of cushions to oversee proceedings. As though he weren't blind and insensible to the activity around him. Is he even aware of where he is or why? Does he know that in mere moments his son and chosen heir will fight to the death all for the sake of that golden crown resting crookedly on his balding head?

Estrilde drops a kiss on her uncle's hand. "Dearest uncle," she proclaims, more for the benefit of the courtiers present than the king, I suspect, "I cannot tell you how delighted I am that my beloved will have this opportunity to prove his fitness to rule before all Aurelis and Eledria. Surely even the most foolish doubters will exclaim at the wisdom of Lodírhal the Magnificent in naming Ivor Illithor his heir."

The king turns his head, blinking vaguely in Estrilde's direction. His lips move, but not a sound emerges. Estrilde takes her seat beside Lodírhal, close to the viewing rail. Her friends and companions assume places around her, all in attitudes of deference. I, along with her other attendants, move to stand by the wall.

Only now do I dare turn my gaze from the box out to the arena itself. My heart drops.

It's a vast space—far greater than I imagined. An enormous circle, ten stories high, with viewing boxes at every level situated between graceful white arches and gold columns. Spanning the vast space are bridges—ten bridges, all angled differently, overlapping one another, creating a vertical as well as horizonal space for the opponents. But they are not what sends this stone of dread dropping in my gut.

It's what's down below.

The arena has no floor. Instead, it has been built above a great mist-shrouded pit. A gash in the worlds, a plunge into some strange reality. Whatever magic is used to close it off has been unlocked, revealing those terrible depths. The mist is like a living thing, twining and churning. Here and there raw *quinsatra* light flashes in colors beyond the ordinary spectrum, and something vast and coiled undulates into view before once more retreating into that murky shroud.

I'd known the Rite of the Thorn would be bloody and brutal. I'd not expected this. Nothing like this.

I lift my gaze from that pit, taking in all the beautiful fae gathered in their boxes, eager for the entertainment to begin. Their bloodlust is palpable, a pulse in the atmosphere as terrible as the flashing lights below. These are the same folk who venture into the City Under to watch slaves and Obligates beat each other to death for their enjoyment. The only difference now is they need not hide their vile cravings from polite society. Here it is acceptable. Here that same brutal sport is sanitized in the guise of heroic prowess.

Bile burns in my chest. In all the years I've lived and served in thrall to the fae, I've never felt such a strong upsurge of disgust. I hate them. I hate them all. If I could, I would rend them apart limb by limb. I could do it to. With a flick of my pen, with a single written word, I could summon darkness, evil. I could see them all screaming, dead—

A sudden blare of trumpets. I jump in my skin, shocked from a stupor. All the world has taken on a surreal filter. Dark specks dance on the edges of my vision. This can't be real. The Prince—Castien—*my husband*—he won't die. He can't die.

But if he does then Oscar . . . Oscar . . .

You're not seeing rightly.

I press my knuckles to my temples. I want to scream, but cannot, dare not. I can only stand against that wall and watch the nightmare play out.

The trumpet fanfare finishes with a flourish, and the crowd goes wild. Overhead, the Summit Night moon shines bright, gleaming on cascades of flower petals suddenly falling from every viewing box—some gold to honor Ivor; some purple to honor the prince. There's so much more gold than purple. Most of these people expect Ivor—a warrior born, uncursed and whole—to defeat the half-human son of the king.

A fae lord rides into the arena on winged horseback, landing on the fifth bridge in the middle of the vertical space. I recognize him: Kiirion the Fair is his name. The one-time lover of Mary West, a human girl I once knew who forgot the perils of loving the fae and suffered for it. The sight of him brings her face to mind. My stomach knots. I never thought I'd find myself standing in Mary's shoes.

Kiirion dismounts and takes the center of the bridge, raising his arms and simultaneously raising a cheer from the onlookers. "Who's ready for a king-making?" he cries.

A hearty roar from the Lords and Ladies. They're ready for anything so long as they are entertained.

When at last their voices subside, Kiirion swings an arm to the right. "Behold!" he cries. "The chosen heir of our beloved King Lodírhal the Magnificent! The Golden Rose of Aurelis, your champion, your future, your liege—Lord Ivor Illithor!"

A fresh cascade of gold petals fills the air as Ivor steps into view, appearing under the arch at the far end of the fifth bridge. He strides out to the center, arms raised to receive adulation. He's breathtaking—shining with golden glamour-light from the inside out. A sword hangs from a thick belt around his waist, and armor protects one shoulder, but otherwise his torso and legs are bare, all his musculature on full display.

Gall rises in my throat. I wish I could bend over the balcony rail and be sick.

Once Ivor has reached the middle of the bridge, Lord Kiirion holds up a hand. "But!" he cries, and the crowd quiets once more waiting for what they know must come next. "Every rose has its thorn. And so I give you, the challenger—son of the king, forsworn heir of Aurelis, come to reclaim his bloodright and prove his fitness by might of battle and favor of the gods— Castien Lodírith, Prince of Vespre!"

Another roar of enthusiasm. Another cascade of flowers, purple and gold together, twirling, glittering, disappearing into the mist below. I am scarcely aware of any of it. All my attention fixes on that figure standing at the far end of the bridge. The Prince.

518

My Prince. Glamour-lights are turned his way, illuminating his proud, upright figure. He too is clad only in light armor, his body displayed for the admiring gazes of friend and foe alike. His hair is swept back and secured at the nape of his neck, a style I've never seen him wear. It emphasizes the gorgeous sharpness of his cheekbones and jaw, the vicious intensity of his eyes. If I did not already love him, I would surely fall for him beyond all recovery at this sight. As it is, I remember too well what it felt like to be held in those strong arms, to press my lips against the chiseled indentations of that chest, the hollow of that throat . . .

But he betrayed me.

He cursed my brother, my Oscar.

He withheld the truth from me even as he took me, kissed me, entered into me. Claimed me as his wife.

I realize suddenly that I've left my place at the wall, moved to the balcony rail. Gripping it hard in both hands I lean out, heedless of the fall, desperate for a better sight of this man I love and loathe and long for all in the same breath.

"Back to your place, human," Estrilde snarls behind me.

I turn. Look at her. Meet her cold, merciless eyes. I do not speak. I do not have to. I simply let her see me. The real me. Not the mousy librarian, the Obligate she once bullied and abused. No . . . I let her see instead the face of one who has killed. One who has created, summoned, and unleashed forces of darkness far beyond Estrilde's small and mean-spirited reckoning.

One who knows exactly how to do it again.

A muscle in the princess's cheek tightens. Then she lifts her chin. "Fine. Stay and watch your lover be cut down like a dog. It makes no difference to me."

Lodírhal stirs on his cushions beside her. His faded eyes flutter, open, revealing milky irises. He tries to sit forward then groans and drops back on his cushions even as concerned attendants crowd close. I have no sympathy to spare him. I turn my attention back to the bridge below.

Lord Kiirion states the rules that govern the Rite of the Thorn— no magic may be used, neither fae nor human. Not even glamours are permitted. The battle itself will end in one of two ways—either upon the sword or with one or both opponents fallen into the mist below. Should one fall, he shall be given a count of ten to reemerge. If he does not, the winner shall be proclaimed.

"Have you heard and understood?" Kiirion demands.

"Aye," Ivor responds. The Prince nods, grimly silent.

"Very well." Kiirion sweeps a hand. "Let the glamours be gone."

I watch in terrified fascination as Ivor's glamours melt away. I've always believed he didn't wear beauty augmentations, or not many. Only now do I realize how mistaken I was, how taken in by the subtle magic of which I'd been unaware. Gone is the glorious golden lord. This man's face is creased in hard, terrible lines, his body riddled with scars. He's enormous—that at least wasn't a glamour. If anything, he'd disguised himself into far more lithe and graceful lines than reality. He looks like an old, scarred bear with a broad, scowling forehead and a leering mouth and jaw.

The Prince, by contrast, is still himself. He's a little slighter and slimmer, perhaps, not the image of fae perfection his glamour projects. Still beautiful enough to stop the heart of any unwary lass.

But his face . . . his face is one I hardly recognize. It's the face of a killer. He looks at Ivor with absolute murder in his eyes.

Ivor looms over the Prince, widening his stance to seem even broader and more dreadful. His supporters shriek and fawn. If one were to judge by size alone, there wouldn't even be a contest.

Lord Kiirion looks more staggeringly beautiful than ever by contrast to the two of them, but somehow his beauty is rendered cheap. He's nervous too and hastily backs away from the competitors to climb into the saddle of his winged horse. He spurs it into flight, weaving through the bridges until he hovers above the arena in sight of all viewers.

"May the gods themselves show us favor tonight!" he cries, brandishing a small gold staff. "And may Tanatar, God of Battle and War, determine the future of all Aurelis, revealing unto us the true heir to the throne."

As the crowds' thunderous applause, squeals, and cheers erupt once more, and more purple and gold flowers fill the air, Kiirion lifts his staff high above his head. With a cry of, "Let the battle begin!" he swings it down in a single stroke.

32

SPRING SUMMIT NIGHT STRETCHES ON AND ON.
It's difficult to keep track of time. In Vespre, the palace bells tolled out each hour, and I was able to structure some sort of day-and-night facsimile for myself. Aurelis generally has some mild fluctuations from dawn-glow through to the delicate twilight which passes for night in this realm.

But during Summit Night, there's no clear way to map out the minutes or hours. All I know is my deadline is counting down, slowly but inexorably. My deadline to three days of pain.

Well, so be it. I made the bargain in good faith, didn't I? And the crone said I shouldn't die. I've endured my share of agony in this life. What's three days in the grand scheme of things? So I tell myself when I crawl out of bed after a long but restless sleep. It's still dark outside my window, but I set to work making myself ready for whatever happens next. I wash my face in the golden washbasin, dry it on a gold-threaded towel, then sit before the gold-leaf mirror and stare at my hollow face in the glass. There's no ghoulish image of sewn-up eye sockets this time. Just my own haggard, sunken-eyed reflection. These last few days have been brutal. It's no wonder I've started hearing things. Impossible things.

Things like my brother's voice sounding in the passage outside my room.

A shiver ripples down my spine. Oscar once told me he'd met someone. I'd put enough pieces together—particularly his addiction to *rothiliom*—to gather that someone was fae. But it couldn't be . . . it simply couldn't be . . .

No. I'm obviously delusional. And the uneasy sleep I'd just had tossing and turning in this sumptuous new bed hadn't helped matters. How could anyone sleep in a room like this anyway? My name surrounds me, blaring at me, as though Ivor himself is even now calling me over and over and over and over in that deep, longing-infused voice of his.

Getting dressed and arranging my hair is more complicated than it should be. I don't want to wear any of the gowns or use the ornate combs glinting with my own bejeweled name. But there's nothing else to be had. Eventually, I choose a gown of shimmering spring green trimmed with delicate gold braid. The neckline is low, curved in a sweetheart over my breasts, but at least there are sleeves. They perch right on the edge of my shoulders, ready at the least provocation to fall romantically down my upper arm. I'll take care not to make any sudden movements. The skirt, at least, is long and full, though when I take a step, a slit up the front runs all the way past my knee. Still, for the fae, it's positively demure. I don the gown, vowing to return to the queen's suite in search of my own discarded work dress at the next opportunity. For now, this will do.

Feeling a little foolish and exposed, I step from the bedchamber, relieved to leave all that gold and glitter behind me. Ivor has given me no commands, so I slip from his apartments and steal my way across the palace unimpeded. The ball is still just getting warmed up—laughter echoes down every passage, and the music waxes wilder and more wanton by the moment. Steering away from the noisier, more brightly lit halls, I make for the library. There, at least, I may find both quiet and, hopefully, employment. Anything to take me outside of my own head. Anything to stop me wondering . . . worrying . . . wishing . . .

Thaddeus is at the front desk, thank the gods. His face brightens at the sight of me but dims when he takes in my gown. "Miss Darlington," he says gravely, closing the book before him and peering at me over his square spectacles. "I heard rumor Lord Ivor purchased your Obligation."

"Indeed," I answer, painting a smooth smile on my face, "and I am eager to return to my duties here. Might I be of help in the workroom? Or I'd be happy to reorganize the chronologies. When I was sorting through the volumes the other day, I had a few ideas."

Thaddeus blinks. Then he removes his spectacles and slowly cleans them on the sleeve of his robe, taking so long over them I feel a scream building in my throat. I swallow it back and wait with every appearance of patience until he finally sets the spectacles back on his nose and looks at me again. "Has Lord Ivor himself commanded you to come here?"

"No," I admit.

"I dare not risk putting you to work until I've received instruction from my master." He tips his chin into the depths of his white beard. "I hope . . . I very much hope things will turn out well for you, Miss Darlington."

His words are sincere, but in his eyes, I see the truth: he already considers me a lost cause. He looks even more sorry for me now than he did when I first learned I was being sent to Vespre.

"Thank you, Mister Creakle," I reply, the brightness of my voice belying the tension in my gut.

Turning to make my escape, I spy a book on the return trolley, right at the top of the stack. *Zaleria Zintoris,* the Book of Stars. My heart skips a beat. Did the Prince return it? Does this mean . . . is it possible he's already been to Illithorin's Waste and fetched the elixir from the dragon? I reach out, touch the cover of the book. And suddenly, with all my heart, I wish . . . I wish . . . *Oh, I wish . . .*

Turning sharply, I stride from the library. My footsteps carry me through the palace and out to the gardens, avoiding merrymakers and all places where light and music congregate, I flee instead through shadows, ducking and weaving, heart racing as though I'm being pursued. A half-mad idea forms in my mind. Ivor has given me no command. Might I possibly pass through the Between Gate, find the Prince? Might I release him from this foolish Obligation and set him free? Apologize for my foolishness. Tell him how I hate myself for what I've done to him.

But I never come anywhere near the gate. Long before it's in sight, some invisible tether stops me so hard, I nearly choke. My hands fly to my throat even as I fall to my knees. I bow over, my bare back prickling at the cold wind like a shivering finger trailing up my spine.

And so I remain for some while. Weeping. Alone. Cursing myself for the fool I am.

It's impossible to wander anywhere in the palace without running into merrymakers. Estrilde's ball has spilled from the garden and continues to spread, until I can hardly turn a corner without coming upon a pair of fae locked in a clinch. Sometimes more than a pair—sometimes whole clusters of them, all in various states of undress, oblivious to the world beyond their small sphere. Their eyes are bright, glassy with *rothilliom,* their laughing voices slurred, their beautiful bodies contorted.

Shuddering, I hasten away, too aware how quickly the fae can turn from amorous to ravenous. One glimpse of a frightened human face would be enough to set them upon me like a pack of hounds, as dangerous as the Wild Hunt in their own way. In the end I've no choice but to return to Ivor's apartments. I'll shelter in my room for now and hope my new master will remember to give me work soon.

Ivor's chambers are eerily quiet when I slip through the side door and into the back passage leading to the servants' quarters. I don't meet anyone, which is a relief, but reach my own room, step inside, and close the door. Leaning my head back, I close my eyes, breathe out a long sigh.

"At last."

Ice lances down my spine. Whirling on heel, I face into the room.

Lord Ivor. He's there, seated on my bed. Grand and beautiful and shirtless. Nothing adorns his upper half save garlands of golden flowers. His horns are gone; instead he wears a jeweled band across his brow which does little to tame his tousled mane.

Just to see him is to feel lust burn in my veins. I want to run to him, to throw myself into his arms.

Instead I grip the doorknob at the small of my back like it's my last lifeline. "Lord Ivor," I manage, my voice thin and small. "What are you . . . ?" The words won't come. With tremendous effort, I whisper, "You will be missed. At the ball."

He rises. Light from a single candle reflects off all the gold in the room and paints his muscular frame in a burnished glow. He stalks toward me with predatory grace, but his eyes are soft, gentle. "Clara, Clara," he murmurs. "I could not slip away soon enough. What joy does a ball hold for me when I know you are here? And yet when I came, it was only to find you gone. Where were you? Why did you not wait for me?"

He's so dizzying, so dazzling. I lean back against the wall as he draws nearer and nearer still.

But this isn't right! I'm his Obligate. I find a small knot of resistance in the center of my heart and cling to it. "I require employment, my lord," I say, even as he rests one hand against the door by my head, leaning in toward me. "If I am to serve you well, I must have duties to which I may apply myself."

"Of course, of course." He winds a lock of my hair around his finger. When my breath catches, he smiles. "What sort of employment did you have in mind?"

I drop my gaze, focus on the cleft in his chin. "If it pleases you, my lord, I should like to return to my work in the library."

He frowns. "What?"

For a moment, his glamour wavers. I draw a deep breath, strength returning to my limbs and soul. I still don't dare meet his gaze, but repeat with quiet firmness, "I should like to return to my work in the library. Thaddeus Creakle could use my help. The chronologies, you see, are not well organized. And there's the extensive catalogue of legends of the First Age which was never completed, and those old manuscripts from—"

Ivor's teeth flash. He takes a step back, and again I find myself able to draw a deeper breath than before. My chest rises and falls with the effort, and I feel terribly exposed in this low-cut gown.

Ivor stares down at me, his eyes narrowed, his beautiful face lined. Then, abruptly: "Why do you resist me?"

I dare a glance up into his incredible golden eyes. "My lord?"

"Time and again I have offered myself to you. Offered everything I have, everything I am. Each time, you put me off. You dismiss me like some disfavored lackey." His fists clench, and his voice drops to a dangerous rumble. "Who do you think I am?"

My throat closes tight.

"I have fought in the deadly Behemoth Wars, slaughtered enemies ten times my size by the sheer force of my will. Singlehandedly did I win victory after victory in the name of my king. I have clawed my way up from the depths in which I was born—killed, destroyed, cursed, and maimed to get where I am. And now?" His eyes flash, shimmering with a tint of green *rothilliom* glow. "Now I stand before you, a king on the cusp of claiming his throne. And you dare defy me?"

I don't know what to do. The room is so small, and he is so large, and his swelling wrath so intense. But the Obligation holds. He cannot force me. Not in matters of my heart. Nor can he harm me, at least not overtly. Even his glamours can only push me so far.

Dropping my eyes, I offer a demure curtsy. "My lord, I am eager to be of service. Name the task you would give me, and—"

His fist smashes into the vanity mirror, shattering the glass. Then he rounds on me, his hand bleeding. Glamour swirls around it, disappearing the cuts, but the wound is still there. I can smell the blood. I stare up at him, no longer able to disguise my terror.

"Love me," he says. His words contain the full force of command. But it's a command from which the law itself protects me. I clench my teeth. "Love me," he urges, stepping closer. I press back into the door, trembling in every limb. He curses viciously and pounds his wounded fist against the door, just beside my head. I choke back a scream and turn away. "Love me, gods damn you," he growls. "I need you to love me. It's all I've ever needed from you."

I don't weep. I don't beg. I don't apologize. I scarcely breathe.

Finally, just when I'm certain I cannot bear a moment more, he snarls, "Move."

Hastily, I sidle away, making room for him to pass. He opens the door, steps out into the passage, and slams it shut behind him. It rattles in the frame, echoes inside my head, throbbing in time with the pulse of my heart.

All of Aurelis now seems more dangerous than Vespre ever did. If I could, I would stay hidden in my room for . . . well, forever, honestly. Hidden and cursing myself for my stupidity.

Gods, above! It's not as though I didn't know what Ivor wanted. Though I've tried to deny it, he's been persistent in his attentions. Somehow, I'd never truly believed it would go this far. Particularly not in the midst of his own betrothal celebration!

Granted, he and Estrilde are not Fatebound; they can and likely will do as they please, keeping lovers on the side once the initial passion of their union fades.

Estrilde would never stand for Ivor taking a human lover, however. Particularly not me.

I shudder, collapsed in a heap on the floor, arms wrapped around my abdomen. My only real hope now is that Ivor will simply lose interest. He is fae, after all. An ancient being with many lifetimes' worth of experiences. He'll forget about me soon enough. The Lords and Ladies' passions burn hot and flare out quickly. I just need to keep my head down and stay out of sight in the meanwhile. Which, granted, will be difficult now that I'm serving in his household.

My stomach lets out a cavernous growl. I press my hand against it. How long has it been since last I ate? A fleeting memory of enchanted, crusty bread flickers in my mind. It feels so very long ago.

Well, I can't stay here. I'm starving. And I can't think straight on an empty stomach. I used to have friends among the Obligates working in the palace kitchens. They'll be busy keeping up with the demands of the betrothal feast, but surely someone can be convinced to find me something safe to eat among all the dangerous fae fare.

I rise, wipe my eyes. Adjust the sleeves of my gown and straighten my hair. My hand trembles when I reach for the doorknob, but I grip it firmly, pull the door open, and step out into the passage. For a moment, I stand still, shivering. Listening. Tense. But this is foolish—it's not as though Ivor is going to jump from one of these rooms shouting, *"Boo!"*

Gripping my skirts with both hands, I creep down the servants' passage to the door at the far end. There I pause again, draw a long breath. Then open it, step out into the next room . . .

And find myself staring straight into Danny's battered, bloodied face.

THE PRINCE

I STEP TO THE LIP OF A DEEP TRENCH FILLED TO THE brim with blood. Darkness surrounds me, churning and alive. Sometimes faces appear—images of ecstasy melting into horror before vanishing. All around me, just on the edge of my awareness, the atmosphere is full of screams.

"Idreloth," I call, my voice loud and firm, echoing through the Nightmare Realm. "I have come to bargain."

On the far side of the trench, mist parts. Now at last I behold the Eight-Crowned Queen in all her glory. She is beautiful. Terrible and beautiful as only a nightmare may be. Her prime head is visible, a glorious image of savagery, with bloodstained teeth that would tear flesh from bone with ease. She sits upon a massive throne, some twenty feet high, made up from the naked bodies of men and women contorted into unnatural positions, clinging to one another. Upon this gruesome seat she lounges, one hand draped across her bare hip, the other resting under her chin.

"Welcome, my sweet, my love," she purrs in a voice of pure poison. *"It is not often that my dear ones come to me of their own accord."* The contorted bodies beneath her squirm and whimper only to be silenced by a soft hiss between her teeth. Then Idreloth stands, displaying her naked flesh, and tips her head to one side so that cascades of dark hair fall across her soft, round shoulders and ample bosom. She runs a hand down her torso, her throat vibrating with a soft moan. *"Tell me, have you come to taste of the pleasures I offer?"*

I stand like stone, unmoved by her display. Instead my gaze fixes on the glinting black jewel resting between her breasts. A powerful aura of dark magic pulses around it. The bloodgem. At last.

I hold out a box of carved ivory, small enough to fit in the palm of my hand. "I have your head, Idreloth. Here you may see the proof." With that, I hand the box over to the lowest body of the living throne. The pale, twisted creature passes it on to the next and the next, until finally it reaches the Noswraith herself. She narrows her red eyes but accepts the box and lifts the lid. Another hiss escapes through her clenched teeth. She turns the box around, revealing the two eyeballs resting inside on a bed of silk.

"Where is the rest?" she snarls and takes a step down, her foot planted on the back of a supplicant. *"Tell me!"*

"Safe in my keeping," I reply. "You will have it in exchange for that necklace you wear and for my own safe passage out of your realm."

Her eyes flash. Her teeth bare. But she peers into the box again, and an expression of exquisite longing contorts her features, somehow rendering her simultaneously more terrible and more beautiful. *"I must have my head,"* she murmurs, as though to convince herself. Then addressing me once more: *"And is this trinket all you would have, my dear? Is there not something more you would ask of me?"* Again, she runs a hand down her body, trailing between her breasts, down her hips, between her thighs. *"I smell the longing in you—the heart given but not accepted. The pain, the need. I can give you ease, sweet one. I can give you relief and release."* She smiles sweetly. *"I'm sure I can find a face more to your liking."*

With those words, her head rolls back grotesquely as though her neck has suddenly broken. When it straightens again, her features have changed—large, doe-brown eyes, a soft, full mouth, delicate cheekbones, and that determined jaw. All framed in a bounty of wavy, nut-brown hair.

My lip curls. "No fantasy you offer could hope to match the dream I cherish, however forlorn it may be. I want nothing from you save that necklace you wear." I hold out a hand. "Give it over, and I shall have my man write your head back into this spell where it belongs."

The Eight-Crowned Queen snarls. The image of that gentle face vanishes, replaced with a vicious visage. Enormous teeth bulge from her mouth, black and sharp as blades. Then, with a sigh, she yanks the necklace from her neck and tosses it in a flying arc. I catch it, clench my fist around it, and immediately turn to go.

"We'll meet again, my love!" Idreloth calls after me. *"You and I are not yet finished. Your city, your world will yet taste my delights and curse you for keeping me imprisoned so long."*

I make no response but hasten back through the churning darkness. My pace is swift but not swift enough to imply flight. I know too well how easily provoked a Noswraith may be at the prospect of fleeing prey. So I part the mist with one hand, refusing to look over my shoulder, no matter how the fine hairs on the back of my neck prickle or the flesh crawls up and down my spine.

At last I spy the open doorway through which a bookshelf-lined chamber, a pedestal, and a great grimoire are visible, along with my own physical body, bowed over the pages of that spell. Mixael Silveri and Andreas Cornil, my last two surviving librarians, stand close by. Their eyes are fixed on me, their brows tense and worried. I hasten on, step through the door . . .

. . . and open my eyes, staring down at the scrawled words of the spell before me.

"There!" I cry and stagger back from the pedestal. "There, Cornil! It is done. Now do your work—write that cursed head back into the spell where it belongs and seal that demon fast."

Andreas leaps into action, taking my place before the grimoire and writing furiously, his quill scratching out the pre-arranged words. Mixael, meanwhile, approaches me where I sag against the nearest bookshelf. "Are you well, sir?" he asks. "Did she . . . ?"

I shake my head, breathing hard. The act of entering the Nightmare required no magic—any fool, be he mage or madman, may dream. But my heart races nonetheless. "She did not touch me," I assure my senior librarian, "have no fear, Silveri. And look!" I nod to the awful, eyeless head resting on the floor beside the pedestal. As Andreas writes, it begins to fade from this reality, returning to the realm of its origin.

At last the head vanishes entirely, and Andreas slams the book shut with a triumphant, "There! 'Tis finished."

"What a relief." Mixael mops his face with a handkerchief. "It's high time that foul thing was back where it belonged. Idreloth was growing more fractious by the day, keen to enter this world and reclaim her missing piece. I'm not sure how much longer we could have held her at bay."

I nod a begrudging agreement. Though I don't like to admit it, this is one good wrought from this foolish quest to rescue that gods-damned Doctor Gale.

I touch the front of my shirt, feeling the hard lump where the bloodgem lies. My Obligation will lead me back to Aurelis soon. Back to her. How will she respond when she sees I have fulfilled her mission? How will she look at me? What will it be like, standing in her presence again, knowing I have given her my name, knowing she has not—

My breath catches.

My eyes flare wide.

"Prince?" Mixael's voice comes from a distance, through many veils of reality. I'm aware of him, aware of his words, but . . . but . . . "Prince, are you all right? Can you hear m—"

A bolt of light. Like lightning, flashing from the heavens, piercing stone walls, foundations, layers of earth. All the way down to the depths of this horrible cell, many stories beneath the surface of the world. It strikes me to the heart, bursts through my body, fills me with pain. Charges me with heat and energy and life and power such as I've never before experienced. I don't know what this is. I don't know what is happening. It's too much, too great, too overwhelming, and then—

I fall to my knees. Blinking, dazed. Staring down at my own two hands, pressed into the floor beneath me. In some other realm Mixael and Andreas are calling out to me. I cannot hear them, cannot heed them. My ears are filled with a different sound.

A voice, soft and low. Trembling with fear. Both far off and intimately near. Whispering into my heart, my soul.

One voice.

Hers.

CLARA

33

HE'S NAKED. TIED TO A CHAIR. BLEEDING FROM his nose, from cuts across his face, his torso, his arms, his legs. So much blood. So much pain. His eyes are swollen shut.

For a moment, I don't recognize him. My mind won't accept that this vision, this horror, could possibly embody the same person as my childhood friend.

Then a cry bursts from my throat. I lunge forward, falling over myself to get to him. My fingers seek and find the ties securing his arms and legs but shake too hard to be of any use. The ropes are sticky with his blood.

"Danny, Danny!" I cry, touching his face, touching his shoulders.

He groans, tries to lift his heavy head. "Clara . . ." Then one of his awful eyes opens. His vision sharpens. He jerks back in the chair, body convulsing with terror.

I whirl. Ivor stands behind me, leaning against the open doorway. There's blood smeared across his face and body, and he looks the warlord he truly is. Monstrous. Terrifying. Powerful.

I stare at him, caught in a trance of horror. Then: "You did this?"

He need not answer. The situation is plain as day.

I leap to my feet, placing myself between him and Danny, shaking my head in wild desperation. "You can't! His Obligation belongs to Estrilde! The law—"

"The law prevents her from harming her own Obligate." Ivor's voice is cool and detached, a terrible contrast to his bloodstained body. "It's not her fault if some other injury befalls him outside her knowledge." With those words, he strolls into the room, pushes past me, and stands over his prey. Danny jerks and twists in his bonds as Ivor runs a long finger under his chin, propping his face up. "I've always enjoyed the way humans scream. It's not quite like anything else in the worlds. Not a squeal, not a roar. Such a unique pitch and timbre." His eyes flash, meeting mine. "You care about this one, I understand."

"My lord, please . . ."

"You've moved heaven and earth trying to break his Obligation, to free him from my beloved Estrilde's clutches. Venturing to Illithorin's Waste, prying into my family history, bargaining to end age-old curses . . . Indeed it would seem this one at least commands some of your true feeling."

He takes hold of Danny's throat, squeezing. Danny's feet scramble. He doesn't have much strength left to resist.

"What do you want?" I cry.

Ivor smiles dangerously. "Do I not have everything I want already? A kingdom in the palm of my hand. A beautiful bride to warm my bed and increase my power across the realms? More than enough pretty playthings to keep me occupied." He leans in, licks blood off Danny's cheek. "Human blood, like human screams, has its own distinct flavor. I'd forgotten how delicious it can be."

"Leave him alone." My voice has gone cold, hard.

"Why should I?" Ivor tips Danny's head from one side to the other, as though toying with the idea of snapping his neck.

"I'll . . . I'll give you what you want."

Those predatory eyes of his flash to mine once more. "And what is it you think I want?"

"My service. I'll do . . . I'll do what you ask."

"*Anything* I ask?"

A pit opens in my soul, yawning and endless. "Anything."

"Of your own free will? You must say it. You must say it for the law to be satisfied."

"Of my own free will."

Ivor lets go. Danny gasps an agonized breath, his chest expanding. I collapse on my knees before him, cradling his face, trying to catch his eye. He shudders, groaning. His bloodied lips move. "Clara . . . Clara . . ."

Ivor growls. When I look up, he juts his chin, indicating a door across the chamber. "In there."

Danny shakes his head. "Clara, no . . ."

I stroke his cheek, wiping away the wetness of both tears and blood. My own face is wet as well; I don't know when I'd begun to weep. "It's all right, Danny," I whisper. "I said I would save you. I'll get you home to Kitty. I swear it."

Then I rise, deafening myself to Danny's continued protest of, "no, no, no!" which turns into a wordless moan. Gathering my skirts, I march across the room to the door. Take the latch in my hand. Open it. Step through.

The inner chamber is large and shrouded in gloom. Not at all like one would expect to find in Aurelis. Gold cushions and animal-skin rugs mound the enormous bed in the center of the space. A massive skylight arches overhead, revealing the dancing stars of Summit Night. Candles lit and placed on every spare surface emit a spicy, seductive scent that stings my nostrils.

Danny lets out one last guttural cry. His voice cuts off abruptly as Ivor steps into the room behind me and shuts the door.

Unhurried, the fae lord moves through the shadows until he stands before me. His gaze is lingering, lascivious. "Of your own free will." His tongue runs along the line of his teeth. Then he reaches out, grips my jaw, forces my face up. "Look at me."

The Obligation quickens. I lift my gaze to his.

"Say my name." He stares into my eyes, hypnotic and dreadful. "Say it how I want to hear it."

I swallow. My lips part.

A breath of sound eases from my throat.

A whisper, a sigh.

Ivor frowns. His grip on my chin tightens. "What did you say?"

Something jolts in my chest—a surge, a bolt of lightning shooting out from my core. I scream . . . but not from pain. No, this sensation does not hurt. It *overwhelms*. Every sense, every thought. Every memory, fear, or desire. My arms fling wide, fine hairs standing up across my body, scalp prickling, fingertips sparking. My eyes are blinded by pure, shining light which glows inside my head, bursts from inside me, and lances across the worlds, burning as it goes.

Then it passes.

The light fades.

Darkness creeps in, tunneling my vision, bringing with it an awareness of the world around me.

I blink. The figure of Ivor resolves into clarity. He stands back from me several paces, his eyes wide. I watch his expression slowly morph from shock to *terror*.

"What was that?" he demands. Then, breathing hard: "What have you done?"

I don't know. I don't know what's come over me. That blast wasn't like any power I've ever before encountered. Not fire, wind, water. Not magic. It's something much deeper than any of these, beyond even the force of the *quinsatra*.

Ivor whirls abruptly, marches across the room to a display of weaponry on the wall. He grabs a sword, yanks it free. Then once more he bears down on me, teeth flashing sharp. All other thoughts and feelings vanishing in the face of absolute panic. I back away then whirl and rush to the door, struggling to turn the knob.

Ivor grabs the back of my gown. Whirls me around, slams me against the wall. "You are *mine,*" he says, his sword gleaming in the tail of my eye. "You belong to me. Of your own free will you entered this chamber. Remember that!"

He bows his face over mine. I turn so that his lips catch my cheek. He snarls, teeth scraping against my chin. That strangling grip on my throat shifts to my jaw, turning me toward him, holding me painfully. His mouth hovers just over mine.

"You want me," he breathes. "You desire me. You long for my kiss." Glamours pour off him, rippling like waves. It's so thick, I can almost see the magic, red and raw. "Give me what I need." He leans in, closer, closer. "Give me everything."

Then his lips press hard against mine. I'm numb under the force of his glamours, stunned, immobile.

An ear-splitting crash.

A rain of shattered glass.

A cyclone of white feathers.

I scream, and Ivor pulls away just as the white wyvern crashes into the center of the gold bed. The great beast raises its head, feathers flared, and snarls. I scarcely see it, however.

My gaze fixes instead upon the Prince.

He springs from the wyvern's back, lands in a crouch. His head yanks up, eyes flashing like wildfire. Magic and power ripple in the atmosphere around him, building up in terrible pressure. He rises. His head is low, his shoulders hunched.

He speaks in a voice of absolute darkness: *"Take your filthy hands off her."*

Ivor's grip on my face tightens. He raises his sword. "I'll do what I like with my own—"

The Prince lunges. Ivor's blade whistles through the air just above his head as he ducks. Faster than thought, he grips Ivor's arm and wrenches sharply. Ivor utters a small gasp.

The next moment, the Prince has him by the belt and the hair atop his head. That strange, otherworldly power coursing through him, burning the air around him, he physically wrenches the fae lord off his feet, hurls him across the room.

Ivor crashes hard into the far wall. But he rolls, springs to his feet. Though he dropped his sword, he pulls a knife from somewhere on his person. With a feral snarl, he prepares to spring into attack. Then freezes.

The Prince stands before him, tall and terrible. His fingers move in the air even as his mouth mutters strange words. Magic drawn straight from the *quinsatra* warps and moves in the air around him, gathering thickly in his palm.

I stare, momentarily too stunned to react. Then, with a gasp I realize—he's reciting a written spell. Activating its latent power. If he hurls that blast, he will expend a huge amount of human magic and . . . and . . .

"No!" I throw myself in front of the Prince, between him and Ivor, both hands upraised. "No, don't! *Please!*"

The Prince's eyes are dark, frenzied. At first I fear he cannot see me. When at last his gaze meets mine, the expression there frightens me to the core. But I don't flinch.

Behind me, Ivor chuckles. "You see, Prince?" His voice is an ugly sneer. "She's mine. You sold her to me, and the binding cannot be undone. My Obligate will die for me."

"She'll never be yours," the Prince snarls. He begins to raise his shining hands again.

With a strangled cry, I stagger forward, grip both those hands in mine. The heat of magic burns, but I won't let go. "Please!" I cry. "Don't be stupid!" Tears pour down my cheeks, unchecked. "Don't . . . don't . . ."

He cannot speak, cannot answer. His wrath is too hot, too wild and potent. He wrenches free of me, begins to draw back one arm, prepared to hurl his blast.

"Go on!" Ivor taunts and holds his arms out wide. "Try it. See if you have the power to take me down. We all know what will happen if you do."

I grab the Prince's arm then reach up and catch his cheek, struggling to pull his face around, to force him to look at me. "It's not worth it. *I'm* not worth it. Don't throw your life away for me. Please, please! I can't . . . I can't . . ."

I'm sobbing, babbling, incoherent. The Prince is like stone and fire and impenetrable ice all at the same time. His nostrils flare. I could almost swear I see smoke curling on his breath.

Ivor laughs again. "You cannot free her, Castien. You sold her to me, and I will never let her go. She's mine. You've lost."

The Prince's teeth flash. "You cannot have her."

"And why not? You've never been able to stop me from having anything I wanted. Your crown, your kingdom, your father's regard. And now"—his smile is beautiful as the cruel winter dawn—"your *wife*."

His what?

My arms go slack. I drop my hold on the Prince, back away, mouth open. What did Ivor just say? I must have misheard. In my frenzy, in my terror. Or there's been some misunderstanding or . . . or . . .

The Prince braces again, even now prepared to send his blast hurtling across the chamber. The pent-up force inside him will rip him in two. Nothing else matters. Only him. Only saving him, preventing him from destroying himself. So I do the only thing I can think to do.

I hasten across the room and stand in front of Ivor. My back to him, my gaze on the Prince. A living shield.

The Prince's eyes fix on mine. "Stand aside."

I shake my head.

"Stand aside, Darling. Now."

I lift my chin, drag a ragged breath into my lungs. My will rises to meet his, my feeble human soul—such a straggling, pathetic thing before his mighty fae wrath. But I won't back down.

At last, he lowers his hands, hissing a curse between his teeth. For a moment he stands there, silent and still. Then he drags a terrible breath into his lungs. "Very well, Ivor," he says in a voice of stone. "You've forced my hand. If it's all or nothing you want, that's what you shall have."

Before I can think or react, he whips a knife from his belt, cuts his own hand, staining the blade with purple blood. Then he flings the knife. It whistles past my skirts, sticks to the ground just at Ivor's feet.

Ivor's gaze fixes on that quivering hilt for the space of five breaths. Then slowly he looks up. His golden complexion turns pale.

The Prince smiles. It's such a charming, deadly expression. "By the blood in my veins," he says softly. "In the name of my father and his father and his father before him, I, Castien Lodírith, Prince of Vespre, demand the Rite of the Thorn."

34

ALL THE FESTIVITIES HAVE COME TO A SCREECHING halt, the betrothal forgotten. Instead Ivor's chambers are a flurry of excitement as his attendants, Obligates, and members of his doting entourage prepare for the battle about to take place. It's like a storm has burst inside the palace. I can hear it rumbling and growling, echoing through the halls and across all Aurelis.

The Prince has come . . .

He's challenged Lord Ivor . . .

The Rite of the Thorn . . .

The battle for the crown . . .

No one takes any notice of me. As one of Ivor's Obligates, I'm put to work of course—tucked away in a corner of his chambers, stitching the hem of a fine cloak he is to wear when visiting Tanatar's Chapel to be blessed by the God of War and Battle. With every stitch, I offer up desperate prayers . . . only not for the one who will be wearing this cloak.

Danny is gone. I don't know where or how he was taken away. When I fled Ivor's bedchamber, the room beyond was empty. Is he in dreadful pain? Is someone treating his wounds? The questions ring dully in the back of my head, but I can scarcely pay them any heed.

Most of my mind is taken up with that image of the Prince. Bursting through the skylight. Hurling Ivor across the room. Drawing on his cursed magic to blast my enslaver—and himself—into oblivion.

"Your wife."

Why had Ivor said that? What could he have possibly meant?

My stitches run wild. I'm obliged to pull them out, try again, refocus my attention on that simple hem.

Nearby several Obligates whisper together in low, conspiratorial tones. "I never believed it would come to this," one of them says. "Not with the Prince crippled under that curse as he is."

"But really," says another, "it was inevitable, wasn't it? He couldn't very well stand by and let some other heir be named. He must fight for his rights as Lodírhal's son."

"The Prince never did seem to care much for Aurelis or the throne," the first voice protests. "He's too much like his mother. Too human."

"I heard it was a woman who drove him to it," a third puts in slyly.

"A woman? Estrilde?"

"No! I heard it was Ilusine. She was seen dancing with Ivor at the ball. They say the Prince went mad with jealousy."

"It must be her. Everyone knows they're Fatebound, but for some reason the Prince won't seal the match."

"Afraid to be tied down like his father, perhaps. Seeing her with Ivor may have been just the thing to push him over the edge—"

I can't take any more of this.

Rising abruptly, I drop cloak, needle, thread, and step away. No sudden jerk of pain stops me; Ivor himself did not set me the task, and I am momentarily free in my movements. So I slip from the workroom, slip from the apartment into the outer passage. Any moment I expect my Obligation to pull me up short. It never does. With each step I take, my courage rises. Soon I've gathered up my skirt and run through the palace, all the way to the queen's suite.

There's quite a crowd gathered outside the door. All the various people of the Dawn Court, eager to curry favor with the Prince. After all it's possible he could win the day and become the new king-apparent. They'd best be careful, of course—cursed as the Prince is, the odds are definitely in Ivor's favor to win. But Ivor is not without his enemies, nor the Prince without his supporters.

The sight of that crowd does nothing to raise my spirits, however. They're a flock of vultures, eager to pick at whatever bones may come their way.

Ducking, weaving, elbowing, pushing, I make my way through

the thick of them until I stand before the door. I'm small enough, insignificant enough, no one pays me any heed. Only when I reach the door itself and knock does anyone bother speaking to me: "He's not opening up. No one's been permitted inside yet, not even the priests come to help him prepare his soul."

I shiver, casting the speaker a sidelong glance. It's a tall, elfkin man, one I do not recognize. His face is not kindly exactly, but neither is it cruel. Of course, it might just be the glamours he wears, making him seem less threatening.

I don't bother to answer but face the door again. Closing my eyes, I lean my forehead against the panels. "Castien," I murmur. "Can you hear me?"

Then, low enough I'm sure no one else will hear, I breathe another name . . . a mere whisper of sound . . .

The door opens so abruptly, I stagger to catch my balance. The crowd gasps, draws back several paces. All of them stare. At the Prince.

He's shirtless. Naturally. Not just shirtless; he wears nothing but a towel wrapped low around his waist. Water drips down his neck, his torso, pools at his feet. He surveys the gathering. One sardonic brow rises slowly up his forehead. "Come to enjoy the pre-show performance?"

Before anyone dares answer, he catches my arm and draws me into the room, shutting the door firmly behind me and dropping the bolt. Only then does he turn to face me. "I knew giving you that name would cause trouble."

My face heats. I turn away, but my eyes keep bouncing back to him, drawn by that image of muscular strength and beauty. He must be wearing a glamour. Surely.

"Don't worry, Darling," he sighs, sauntering off to the washroom. "Spare me your maidenly blushes! I'll make myself decent, have no fear."

He vanishes through the doorway, leaving me alone in the room. The very room in which, months ago, I'd dragged his fainting carcass across the floor and propped him up on pillows pulled from the lounger. The space feels different now. He's had a desk brought in and placed near one great window.

Something about that desk draws me. I step closer, my curiosity idle at first. But my eyes widen as I take in the piles of papers and ink strewn there. They're spells. I pick up one, then another, then a third. Written spells—human magic. My hands begin to tremble. I want to tear these pages into pieces, fling them out the window. There's so much potential magic gathered here, just waiting to be unleashed. Human magic. The Prince's magic. Magic that, once used, would mean his death.

"You know what they say about those who snoop don't you?"

I whirl, clutching those pages to my chest, and face the Prince. He stands in the washroom doorway, clad now in a silky dressing gown. He leans one elbow on the frame as he surveys me with all the insouciant ease of a housecat. One would never guess at the violence I'd glimpsed burning in his eyes such a short while ago.

"I'm not entirely certain how the rest of the maxim goes,"

he continues, rubbing his upper lip idly. "Something about snoopers snooping out their own demise. I'm sure the original puts it far better."

"What are you doing?"

"Misremembering popular aphorisms, apparently."

I shake my head, holding up the spells. "These. What are you doing with these?"

He tips his brow at me. "What does it look like?"

"It looks like you're preparing to kill Ivor. At whatever cost to yourself."

He pushes away from the doorframe and glides into the room, hands in the pockets of his dressing gown. His hair is still damp, swept back from his forehead, but leaving wet patches across his shoulders. He's so beautiful it hurts. It hurts far more to see his face so barricaded.

He circles to the far side of the desk and stands there, eyeing me coldly. "Ivor's had it coming," he says at last. "For a long, long while."

"Oh, Prince—"

He holds up one hand. "Under the circumstances, you might as well drop the title."

I dip my chin. "I can't go around calling you by . . . by your true name. Can I?"

"Certainly not." His voice deepens by an octave. "I only gave that to you for desperate moments. Which, I might add, do *not* include dragging me from my bath so that you may intrude upon my privacy."

I let the pages drop back to the desk, staring down at them unseeing. "You shouldn't have done it." I shake my head, determined to force back prickling tears. "You shouldn't have given me that name. It . . . it wasn't meant for me."

"I am perfectly aware of the circumstances in which such names are and are not meant to be given." He pulls back his chair and drops gracefully into it. "Which of us was born and raised in Eledria, hmmm?"

I won't let him put me off. Not now. Not when there's so little time. "When did you write these?" I demand.

"These old spells you mean? I don't know. Some years ago. Back before the curse fell. They're potent though, if cast correctly."

"You can't use them."

He shrugs. "It's true, the Rite of the Thorn is traditionally fought without magic. Even glamours are forbidden within the arena. But I fully expect Ivor to make use of every trick to his advantage. I intended to be prepared."

My throat is so dry, I cannot swallow. "What will happen," I ask, my voice scratchy, "if you win the rite?"

"Then everything belonging to Ivor will become mine. Titles, inheritances. Any particularly choice knickknacks." He leans forward, resting his elbows on the desk and steepling his fingers. "And, of course, any Obligates he's collected over the years."

The front of his dressing gown parts, revealing his still damp and gleaming chest. I blink and hastily avert my gaze. "And if Ivor wins?"

"He won't."

"How can you know?"

"Because I will see to it that Ivor does not walk out of that arena alive."

I draw a shivering breath. "If you use this magic you will die."

The Prince sighs. "Yes. Most likely. There was never very much doubt on that score." He leans back, tipping the chair onto two legs. "Chin up, Darling! If Ivor and I do indeed manage to kill each other, your Obligation will be broken. You'll be free to return home. Which, by the way . . ."

Setting the chair back down with a thump, he pulls open a drawer of the desk and draws something out from inside. Rising, he comes around the desk and approaches me. My heart leaps then plunges as he takes my hand, opens it, and places something cold and hard in my palm. I look down, dumbly. Unable for some moments to grasp what it is I see.

Then I gasp. "It's the bloodgem."

The stone is black but stained red from the inside out. Filled with the blood of Vokarum's victims. The magic it exudes is the most powerful I've ever encountered, far greater than the deadliest grimoires in Vespre Library. The crone's evil magic pulses with malignance, as though it would poison any soul in the vicinity. It makes me sick just looking at it.

"How did you do it?" I look up at him, shaking my head in disbelief. "How did you manage all those tasks so quickly?"

He shrugs. "Time moves differently across the worlds. And I

474

was, shall we say, *motivated.*" He stands so close. Close enough I can just feel his breath against my forehead. His voice is deeper than it was before. Almost gentle. "You can pay the price for your Doctor Gale. Free him from his Obligation. Then the two of you may return to your world, just as you wished. Return to your world and live out your life with those you love."

I lift my gaze only to find myself locked in the mesmerizing hold of his eyes. If I didn't know better, I'd think he'd glamoured me, so intense is the draw I feel for him.

But there is no glamour here. No magic. There's just him. Him and those beautiful, deep-as-night eyes of his.

"I hope you'll think of me," he says. "Now and then. Not too often, of course. I wouldn't want the memory of my devastating good looks to mar your happiness in any way."

I close my hand around the gem, squeeze it tight. What must he have gone through to get it? All the perils of those foolish bargains I'd made, followed by a journey into the Nightmare Realm to face Idreloth herself. He shouldn't have done it. He should have found some way to resist his Obligation, to fight me, to break whatever hold I have over him. He shouldn't have risked so much. He shouldn't risk more now.

"Why?" The word trembles on my lips. "Why are you doing this?" He doesn't answer. "I won't have you die. Not for me. I can't bear it." Desperation makes me angry, frantic. "There must be a way out. Tell Ivor you retract your challenge. You've completed your Obligation to me. You can go home to Vespre, you can leave now before—"

He takes my hand. It's a simple gesture, but it stops me short. "Darling," he says softly, "you know it's far too late for any of that. Whether in life or in death, our fates are bound. Forever." He tips his head, looking at me from under his brows. "Do you understand?"

I shake my head. I don't. I won't.

"You spoke my true name. Only one woman in all the worlds may do that. For her I would give my life. I would give a thousand lives—to see you safe and whole and happy."

One day, I'll offer that name as a gift to she who will be my wife.

If she accepts me, she will speak it back.

Something in my chest burns. That same place where that jolt of power had burst from me the moment his true name crossed my lips.

"You knew what would happen," I whisper. "You knew it would come to this."

"I had an inkling, yes."

"Yet you gave me your name anyway. Why?"

He shakes his head.

"Why?" I demand more fiercely.

He looks at me. Really looks. No barricades, no masks. I see everything there in his face. Gone is the insolent charm, the uncaring ease. He is all heat and fire only just held at bay by a bare thread of will. It hurts, it physically hurts him to restrain the force of his feeling. But restrain it he does and answers only: "Does it need to be said?"

"Yes," I reply.

Then I grab him by the lapels of that dressing gown and pull his mouth down to mine.

35

I'VE THOUGHT OF THIS MOMENT SO MANY TIMES. Dreamt of it both idly and in the dead of night when the walls of my room seemed to close in around me, and my body warmed with aching need I scarcely understood.

But those thoughts, those dreams, they were private. Foolish things, intended only for me. And when I shook myself awake, when I rose from my bed and went about my day, they could be locked down inside the vaults of my brain, ignored and, to an extent, forgotten.

This—this is different. It's no dream. Nothing about this moment can be locked away or forgotten. This is a moment that changes everything. *Everything.*

He's frozen under my touch. It's like kissing a statue, so hard, so immobile are his lips. That first thrill of contact is followed quickly by a thrill of terror. Terror that yet again I've misjudged him, misjudged what I thought was happening between us. Terror that this burning need inside me is mine alone and I only imagined I saw it reflected in his eyes.

But I don't stop. I redouble my grip, slip a hand around the back of his head, and pull him against me, pressing my body into his. It doesn't matter anymore what he thinks. I'm here. All of me: heart, body, and soul. He may not take, but he cannot stop me from giving, from throwing myself into that yawning gulf between us in desperate hope that he will catch me. This is our last chance. There will be no tomorrow. There's just here and now and us.

Suddenly his resolve snaps.

He grabs my face. His hands are so large they cover both sides of my head, his strong fingers digging into my hair as he pulls me closer and opens his mouth, deepening the kiss. Now I feel it—all that heat, all that pain, all that hunger roaring up from inside him, engulfing me in the inferno. I welcome it, relish it. Let myself sink into that blaze. My body erupts in his fire.

When at last he draws back, it's only by an inch. Only enough that we can both gasp for air. He stares down at me, the violet of his eyes vanished behind dilated black pupils.

"I love you," he rasps. For a moment he looks shocked, as though he cannot believe what he just said. "I love you," he repeats, both declaration and confession. "Clara! Clara, my darling, I love you. To the very depths of my worthless heart and being. The battle is lost—the war is done. You've won. You've conquered and destroyed me. Love me or loathe me, it makes no difference now." He strokes my cheek, my neck, smooths hair from my forehead. Gazes at me as though beholding the very source of all life. "Though you cut me a thousand times, still would I come back to you. I'd crawl on my knees, pleading the grace of just one glance. I'd dare any risk, renounce any prize— crown, kingdom, my very hope of heaven—for the chance to make you mine."

Then he pulls me to him, crushes me in his arms, and kisses me. Kisses me like it's the last moment of our lives, and all the fires of endless hells are ready to consume us. I wrap my arms around his neck, bury my fingers in his hair, answering his kisses in kind, again and again and again.

Suddenly he scoops me up, hands firm about my waist, and sets me on his desk, heedless of the spells and debris scattered there. An inkstand topples; black ink stains my dress. I don't care. I don't care about anything now. Only him and his arms and his lips and his body, so warm and close and strong. The split in my skirt allows ample room for him to draw near. I wrap my legs around his waist, but it's not enough. It can't be enough. Not with him about to face death, not with me bound to a monster, not with everything between us teetering on the brink of oblivion.

Hands shaking, I yank his robe down from his shoulders. It falls, hanging from the loose belt, displaying his damp, naked torso to my hungry gaze. I rest my hand on his heart, then smooth my palm down, gliding over the chiseled muscles of his chest, his abdomen. He tries to catch me in another kiss, but I pull away, laughing, too quick for him. Instead I lean forward and press my mouth to the hollow of his throat. That first touch is trembling, tentative. The second is desperate, eager, needy. I kiss his throat, his collarbone, down to his chest. Indulging the impulse which has been brewing in my mind for far longer than I care to admit.

He groans. His fingers slip through my hair, down my neck, trailing sparks of sensation with a mere glancing touch. They play along the curve of my shoulder, toy with the gold trimming of my sleeve. Gently, he slips his finger under that trimming and draws the sleeve down, exposing my shoulder.

He stops. Steps back a pace. Gazes at the expanse of skin revealed. As though he would memorize this moment, make it last a lifetime. Then slowly, almost reverently, he traces one fingertip lightly up the smooth skin of my upper arm. Around the bone, across the curve of my shoulder. Brings it to rest at the hollow of my throat.

I shiver, my eyes half-closing, breath catching, and take hold of his hand. Raising it to my lips, I kiss his fingers—those long, elegant, strong fingers, which I have so long admired, so long yearned to feel against my skin. I lift my lashes, catch his gaze. His eyes are hot, melting my insides.

Slowly, deliberately, I press his palm to my breast, covering my beating heart.

His breath shudders, rough against my forehead. His hand trembles, but he does not pull away. He stares deep into my eyes. Studying me, reading me. Learning my every secret desire.

Finally, with agonizing slowness—as though we have all the time in the world—as though I might not be yanked out of this room any moment by my Obligation—as though he isn't planning to get himself killed in a vain attempt to save me—as though I'm not crying out with my whole body and soul for him to hurry, hurry, *hurry*—he inclines his head. Kisses my shoulder. My throat. With a moan, he ventures lower still, exploring the curve of my breast.

Sensation explodes across my skin. I'm dizzy, intoxicated. Drunk on his touch, drunk on my own desire. With each brush of his lip, each nip of his teeth, each stroke of his tongue, I grip the desk's edge for support, desperate to keep myself from tumbling. But why resist? Why not simply surrender?

"Darling," he murmurs, his breath hot and panting. "Darling Clara, I beg of you . . ."

"What?"

"Tell me you love me." His lips press against the skin above my fluttering heart then retreat. Breathing hard, my chest rising and falling, I open my eyes, look down at him. Behold that hungry flame dancing in his gaze. "I must hear you say it," he says. "If only once."

In answer I catch his face between my hands. Firmly, I draw him up. He bends me back over the desk, his fists planted on either side of me, caging me in his arms. But I do not feel trapped. Not now. Not even with the cords of Obligation entwining my very spirit. Here in this space, in this moment, possibly for the first time in my life . . . I feel free.

"I love you, Castien," I whisper, breathing the words against his open, hungry lips. Then I smile; the relief of finally speaking those words out loud makes me light up inside. I'd not even realized how long I'd been holding them in, tamping them down, forcing that light to dim. Now I feel I could blaze like a star through even the darkest night. "I love you, *Lianthorne.*"

The kiss he gives me in answer is overwhelming, all-consuming. I wrap my arms around his neck and open my mouth wider, inviting his eager tongue to tangle with mine. A growl rumbles in his throat. All that reverent gentleness gives way to primal need. Demanding and ravenous, he kisses me, touches me, his mouth, his hands everywhere, bringing me to life.

I respond in kind, yanking the belt of his robe until it falls away and the whole garment tumbles to the floor. My greedy hands smooth down his back and then lower still.

He smiles, his mouth against my neck. "I thought I said you could look but no touching."

A telltale flush somehow manages to roar up my cheeks even now. "Is that really what you want?"

"You know what I want." With another low growl, he pulls me upright, grips the back laces of my gown, rips them open. I slip from the desk and, with a little shimmy, let the whole garment drop to the floor in a pile of green beside his dressing gown.

Now I am bare before him as he is before me. He looks me up and down. Devouring me with his eyes. When at last his gaze returns to my face, he says only, "Gods, Darling!"

I don't understand it. I don't pretend to. I know I am not like the ladies of Eledria, my body sculpted to perfection with glamour and power. I am just myself—lowly and imperfect and so very human. Yet when he looks at me like that, I could believe I am a goddess. His goddess, the worthy recipient of his most ardent worship.

He lays me down upon the desk. Touching me as he touched me once before on the clifftops of Roseward. Only this time is different. This time, the heat generated from his palms isn't magic. It's him—him and the fire he calls to life inside me. His touch, his kisses incinerate all thought, all reason, all fear. There's nothing but him, but us, here in this moment that is entirely ours.

Soon I'm breathless, gasping, clinging to him. The desk beneath me feels as though it's a tiny craft tossed upon vast and stormy seas. The whole room pitches around me, sending my stomach into delightful tumbles. Oh, how does he do this? Where did he learn the secrets of my body which I myself did not know? I close my eyes, close every outer awareness, concentrating fully on those sensations he calls to life inside me.

"Please," I whimper. I don't understand this need, but some instinct tells me he and he alone can fulfill it. "Please, please, please."

But he shakes his head. "I do not want to hurt you, Darling. No matter how my body craves to take, you must first allow me to give."

I open my mouth to protest. But then his hand slips between my legs. Deft fingers dance across my center. I catch my breath. My heart throbs to a new rhythm now, one which he creates. Faster and faster and faster until . . . Oh, gods, no! Why does he stop? I let out a wordless cry, ready to scream though I hardly know why. Something has built inside me, something I do not recognize in myself. I want to beg, to plead, to demand. But I cannot form the words.

It doesn't matter. He takes me by the hands, gently pulls me up to a seated position. The whole room seems to dip and roll, so lightheaded am I under his influence. I try to catch his mouth with mine, but he won't be caught. He draws me to the edge of the desk, parts my legs. Kneels before me. "This," he says, kissing the hot skin of my knee, my inner thigh. "I've dreamt of this so many a long and lonely night. Yet every time I woke believing myself cursed never to know these delights in truth." He looks up at me, his whole heart in his eyes. "Will you grant me this indulgence?"

I don't know what he intends. But in that moment, I would give him anything. Anything.

"You may have me." I swipe that one errant lock of hair back from his forehead. A simple gesture which thrills me straight to my heart. I shake my head at the pure wonder of it, a laugh bubbling on my lips. "You may have me, Castien. However you want me."

He smiles that devastating smile of his.

Then he buries his face between my thighs.

I cry out in surprise, grasping the back of his head. A moment later, I throw my own head back, eyes closed. My whole body rocks gently, writhing to the tempo he creates in me. I begin to quiver, to shake. I don't know what's happening, don't understand this mounting force, this power which is so new and strange. A magic entirely of his creation.

"Castien!" I cry half in fear, half in frenzy. "Castien, Castien!"

My voice breaks in a deep, wordless moan as my whole body explodes with delight.

He remains a little longer where he is, teasing my pleasure to the very last. When eventually he rises and stands before me once more, I am too dazed to answer his smile. My vision is unfocused, swimming. He smooths hair back from my brow and kisses me again with his warm, swollen lips. I catch hold of him, pulling him to me. Everything else is forgotten. Our peril, the near certainty of disaster awaiting us in the next few hours. There's no room for such fears. Not here. Not now.

"I'm ready," I say, my voice breathless with want.

This time he doesn't resist. He steps between my legs, takes hold of my thighs, and eases himself into me. I catch my breath, surprised at the sharpness. He pauses, looking down. "Darling?" he asks, all concern and tenderness.

I wait, counting out several slow breaths as my body adjusts to him. When the tension relaxes, I nod.

He begins to pulse. A deep, profound rhythm of connection. I wrap my legs around him once more, press my hands against his shoulders, his back, his buttocks. Draw him in, nearer, closer. It hurts, but I want it. I want it more than I've ever wanted anything, even the gift of ecstasy he just gave me. This is more than mere bodies, mere physical sensation. This is every great and wonderful force of the universe held in this small point of time and space. As though it was always meant just for the two of us.

"You are mine." He pants the words between thrusts, his breath hot on my skin. He lifts his head, gazes into my eyes. Softly, he cups my cheek in his palm. "Whatever may come. Today, tomorrow, and eternity, you are mine. My own. My wife."

His wife.

Yes. Of course.

It was true the moment he whispered his secret name in my ear.

There is no need for a gown, a chapel, a ceremony. No need even for vows. He has already given himself to me. I'd not realized it then. But I do now. I understand too what it meant when I spoke that name for the first time. When I accepted and laid claim to the promise it bore.

He is mine; I am his. We belong to one another. No matter what may come.

Forever.

"Husband," I breathe.

He smiles, his very soul suffused in joy. Then he buries his face in my shoulder. His lips spark against my neck, my jaw, before finally finding and claiming my mouth in a beautiful, bruising kiss. All the while he pulses harder, harder. I grimace, gasp, but then . . . at last! I feel his release an instant before he cries out. I grip him hard, our bodies quaking together, and breathe out a sigh at the pure glory of our joining.

And I know in that moment—possibly for the first time in my life—I am where I truly belong.

36

I SHIFT IN HIS ARMS, KNOCKING YET ANOTHER STACK of papers from the desk. They slip and slide to the floor in a gentle susurrus, followed by the *thunk* of the last remaining inkpot.

"Perhaps," I say, my voice muffled against his shoulder, "it would have been easier if we'd, I don't know . . . *walked* the ten paces to the bedroom?"

The Prince—Castien—snorts. "Taking you across my desk has been a long-time fantasy. Taking you across my mother's bed? No. Definitely not."

I flush and flick the end of his long nose. He answers by rolling over and kissing me again, quite thoroughly. I know we need to stop with this indulgence, to face reality and the situation we find ourselves in. But reality is just too big and too terrible, and his kisses are so sweet and warm. So I let myself be lost for a little while.

When at last I pull away, rather than question him about the impending fight, I say quietly, almost shyly, "Am I really your wife?"

He looks down at me, drinking me in. Like he's lived his whole life parched only to stumble upon the Water of Life itself. "Yes," he answers with a sigh of complete satisfaction. "You are my wife. I am your husband." He chuckles then and arches a brow. "For better or for worse."

I touch his cheek gently. "You knew what would happen. When you gave me your name."

To my surprise, he shakes his head. "I hoped. It was a risk to be sure. The magic of the true name is great indeed. I knew if the bond between us were true then you would respond to it, and it should have the power to bring me to you before . . . well, before any unpleasantness took place. But if you did not feel the bond—if you did not love me as I love you—you would not have been able to speak it as you did. I would not have heard you. I would not have come."

A shadow passes over my soul. I rest my head against him once more, listening to the beat of his heart. Then, after a moment, I frown. "I heard you were destined to be Fatebound."

"Oh, yes?" There's a smile in his voice. "I'd suspected that little rumor was going about. People do so like to talk about

TIME SEEMS TO SLOW, SLOW, SLOW. ALL THE FORCE and pressure of that split second before either warrior moves concentrates into a small eternity of existence.

I stand at the balcony rail, every atom of my body taken up in that sight. In Castien. In the way his muscles coil like a tiger's as he drops into a crouch. The mounting power—not magic, but the power of his essential being—swelling inside him, ready to burst. I feel it all there, the lethal potential, the murderous intent.

My lips try to form his name.

Then with a painful snap, time jumps back into full motion. The Prince launches himself straight at Ivor even as Ivor rushes him. Steel clashes, sparks. The crowd erupts in roars of approval even as I gasp, grip the rail, my confused gaze struggling to follow the movements of either party. One instant, I'm certain Ivor's blade will cleave Castien in two. The next, he leaps nimbly out of range only to retaliate with a blow that looks likely to strike Ivor's head from his shoulders. Ivor blocks, blades shrieking against one another.

Below them the mist churns. Like a sentient being, somehow aware of their struggle. Light flashes, red, orange, and other colors for which I have no name. Those great, coiling tentacles ripple in and out of view.

A collective gasp from the onlookers. It's as though all the air has been sucked from this enormous space and held in their lungs. I cannot breathe. Something is falling, spinning, tumbling. It takes a few blinks to realize it's a sword. One of them has dropped his weapon, but as they grapple together, I cannot tell who.

With a great bellow, Ivor swings his whole body around. The Prince, caught off balance, flies wide, catches his feet, staggers, and goes over the edge of the bridge.

My heart lurches. A scream rises in my throat, but before I can utter it, he turns nimbly mid-air and lands with perfect grace on the lower bridge. He takes no more than a breath to recover before he's running, running, leaping. He grips a sword in his hand. It was Ivor who lost his weapon then. Ivor, who now seeks to maintain the high ground, springing to the next bridge above, putting a little distance between himself and the Prince as he angles for advantage.

The Prince doesn't give him a chance. He leaps from one bridge to the next, quick as a cat leaping from branch to branch. Heedless of any peril, of coils and churning magic, his focus remains fixed upon his prey. For that is what Ivor has become— majestic, massive, and terrible though he is, he cannot match the Prince's rage. Something burns in Castien, an inferno that would make even the bravest warrior blanch.

My head spins as I watch them climb, descend, leap, and duck. Now and then they come back together, exchanging blows. Castien has the advantage so long as he retains his sword, but it also slows him down. He jumps up once swinging, but Ivor ducks and lands a terrible blow to his midsection. I gasp as though receiving the blow myself. Gripping the rail, I lean out over that horrible drop, my vision doubling, tripling.

The Prince skids to the edge of the bridge. They're lower now than when they began, only three stories above the pit and the mist. He's lost his sword—it lies some feet off. Ivor hastens to fetch it. Now he prowls toward the Prince, who lies winded. Why does he not get up? Does he not see the danger advancing?

Ivor raises the sword, brings it hacking down. At the last second, Castien rolls. The blade rings against stone, and the Prince springs to his feet, lunges at Ivor, wraps his arms around his middle. There's a moment of struggle there on the brink. Then . . . then . . .

My eyes widen with horror, with disbelief.

The Prince falls.

This time, there is no nimble turn, no graceful landing. There is no slowing of time, no moment to grasp and hold onto. One instant he's there, looking up, hair streaming about his face. I have enough time to think he will twist in the air, perform some impossible feat, catch hold of the two lower bridges. But he passes through them, one after the other.

The mist swallows him. A flare of red light burns where he entered.

The crowd goes deadly silent. Somewhere far away, Lord Kiirion's voice counts down the time from ten. That's what he'd said, wasn't it? A count of ten and no more before Ivor's victory is declared. But what does it matter? Surely there can be no returning from such a fall into such a place.

He's gone.

He's gone.

I'll never see him again. Not to accuse him, not to beg him, not to rage or plead or hate him. Not even to love him.

He's gone. Fallen into horror. Carrying my heart with him.

"*Five . . . four . . .*" Kiirion's voice intones from above, "*three . . .*"

Suddenly, one of the vast coils ripples out from of the mist. Slimy, hideous, covered in enormous suckers underneath, it lashes up, almost all the way to the lowest of the bridges, like a sea serpent rising from the waves. On its unfurling ridge, a figure runs in great leaps and bounds, balancing with impossible grace. One long stride after another, and at the very crest of the coil's swell, just before it drops back into the pit, he leaps. His body stretches out, one arm extended.

"*One!*" Lord Kiirion cries just as Castien catches hold of the lowest bridge and, with a ripple of muscle, hauls himself up.

The crowd explodes, frenzied with relish. Lords and Ladies alike leap from their seats and hang over the balconies, screaming and shouting and tearing out their own hair in unchecked admiration of the feat they just witnessed.

I cannot join them. My throat is closed tight. I grip the rail and think this must be happening to someone else. It's a story, perhaps—some tale of a faraway handsome prince, a hero, a legend. I'm reading it in the pages of a book, passing the time with idle thrills while I myself remain safely curled up at home. My reason simply cannot accept that this is real. That I'm here. That I'm watching this take place.

The Prince sprints along the bridge now, his gaze upturned to Ivor, who stands five bridges up, looking down with an expression of absolute shock. Then he lets out a roar and starts to run as well, leaping down from one bridge to the next. The Prince stops, turns, head craning to follow his enemy's movements. With a graceful pivot, he changes direction, springs to the next bridge, and meets Ivor just as he descends.

The blow he lands across Ivor's face sends the fae lord sprawling. The sword spins from his grasp, flashing as it clatters. For a moment, it looks as though it will go right over the edge of the bridge, but by the grace of the gods it remains there, teetering on the brink.

Ivor pulls himself up, lunges. Takes Castien around the middle and backs him up as though to hurl him back into the mist from which he just escaped. By some twist or trickery I cannot follow, the Prince slips free of his hold. He strikes Ivor in the side. The massive fae lord staggers, falls to his knees.

Castien grips him by the hair atop his head then slams his face into the stone. When he draws his head back up again, Ivor's face is a mass of blue blood.

"Make it stop."

I whirl about, wrenching my gaze from the battle to see Estrilde kneel before Lodírhal. Her face is ferocious though her voice is pleading. "Make an end to it, Uncle. I beg of you."

Lodírhal sits forward in his cushioned seat. One shaking hand grips the rail before him as he peers out on the scene below. His clouded eyes are brighter than before.

"Only you can call it off," Estrilde persists. "You are king! Spare your champion, who has only ever served you with the true loyalty of a son. When has he ever disappointed you, failed you, betrayed you as Castien has done?" She leans in closer, breathing her poisonous words in his ear: "Ivor would not have let your wife die."

Lodírhal blinks. But he says nothing, makes no move.

"Make it stop!" Estrilde cries, her voice strangled, guttural. Even her glamours are slipping now in her agitation. "Make it stop, or I swear I'll—" She raises a hand as though to strike the old man. I take a single step, a protest on my lips, uncertain what I will do.

Lodírhal, however, does not need my help. One hand comes up, catches Estrilde by the wrist. His grip is stronger, firmer than I would have believed possible. Estrilde is equally startled. She gapes at him as he turns his haggard face to her.

"Let the gods' will be revealed," he says.

Another horrible gasp from the crowd. I whirl only to see that Ivor has got the sword. He stands with it raised to shoulder height, the hilt gripped in both hands. The Prince stands before him, breathing heavily, bleeding from his nose, his lip. Ivor draws near, one step at a time.

I can do nothing. In that moment, I can't even breathe. The Prince is spent, exhausted. He doesn't look as though he has any strength left in him. But that light is still in his eye—that burning, savage glow.

With a roar, Ivor charges. The Prince springs, catching the edge of the sword across his ribcage, a long, bloody gash. But at the last, he drops low, kicks out with one leg, catching Ivor hard in the knee. Ivor grunts, pitches. His arms wheel, the blade flashing.

Then, with a single thin cry, he falls. Tumbles. Reaching for handholds, missing by inches. He twists around, his eyes staring wildly up into the crowd. I feel as though they find me. As though they burn directly into my soul. Then the mist consumes him in a flash of light and churning darkness.

Lord Kiirion begins his countdown. No one stirs. No one breathes. No one voices a word. Any moment, Ivor might do the impossible. We've seen it done once already, haven't we? He might yet emerge from the depths, borne on the very wings of the gods and fate, returning to crush his opponent.

The Prince stands on the edge, staring down, while I stand at the rail, staring at him. Willing, hoping, praying. Dreading.

"Three . . . two . . ." Lord Kiirion says. Just as he cries, *"One!"* Castien turns. Looks straight up at me. His face breaks in a triumphant smile.

The noise of the crowd is like thunder from the high heavens, threatening to shatter the very foundation stones of this arena and send us all crashing down into that pit. Flowers, garlands, banners, jewels rain down upon Castien from every side. The hated Prince, the forsaken heir, now beloved by all who look upon him. Their champion, their future king.

But he has eyes only for me. Across that distance he gazes, the light of love shining in his face. For a moment I can forget what he has done. For a moment I feel nothing but joy that he lives, that he breathes, that he exists still in this same world with me.

Abruptly his face contorts. One hand presses to his side. He staggers. Lifting his eyes to me once more, his brow puckers in something between surprise and . . . pain.

The next moment, he collapses. Right there in the middle of the bridge. From some faraway place, I hear my own voice screaming out his name.

40

THE CROWD IN THE PASSAGE OUTSIDE THE QUEEN'S suite is ten times the size it was before. It seems as though everyone in Aurelis has come to offer congratulations or services or simply to catch a glimpse of the king's new heir. Or at the very least his corpse.

Castien was carried off the bridge by members of the Aurelis guard. From the viewing box, I couldn't tell if he was alive or dead. I still don't know. What happened? Had Ivor done something to him? Hurled a last bolt of magic before plummeting to his doom? Had he dealt the Prince a mortal wound in the thick of the battle, and I'd somehow not seen it? Or was that cut across his ribcage worse than I realized?

These questions and more pound in my head as I push,

elbow, duck, sidle, and otherwise force my way through the crowd to the front chamber. The doors are open; it's even more densely packed inside. Lords and Ladies, servants and Obligates are packed into every possible square inch of space, crowding shoulder-to-shoulder.

There are tears on my face. I scarcely notice them, but they trail hot and fast down my cheeks, dropping onto the front of my gown. "Please," I beg. "Please, let me through. Please, please." No one pays any attention. No one notices or cares. What does one demanding human maid matter in the face of all these grand events?

Finally, in a last bid of desperation, pinned between an elf-woman in a violet gown and a fat gnome who positively reeks of onions, I close my eyes and whisper: *"Lianthorne."*

Immediately, there's a ripple of movement through the crowd. The next moment, my heart stops as I hear a familiar voice shouting: "Get out! Get out of my room, you gods-blighted, damnable oglers! If I spy even one of your objectionable faces within twenty feet of me in the next five seconds, I'll start setting Noswraiths loose, so help me! Now, will you kindly make way for my *wife?"*

A collective gasp, not unlike those I heard in the arena. I'm not sure how, but every eye in that room suddenly pivots, fixing on me. All those fae gazes, disbelieving, disapproving. Disgusted and dismayed.

A hand drops on my shoulder. Startled, I turn. Look up. Up into the serenely beautiful face of Ilusine. She does not look back but instead sweeps her golden eyes across all those gathered round. "You heard your master," she says, her voice clear and hard. "Make way for the Princess of Vespre."

To my utmost surprise, the fae back away, bowing their heads, bending at the waist, sinking into deep curtsies. Ilusine propels me forward, guiding me through the throng all the way to the bedchamber door. There she releases me. I glance up, uncertain if I should thank her. The Soliran princess's expression is closed. She simply inclines her head before turning and sweeping away, vanishing along with the rest of the dismissed crowd as they file out of the queen's suite.

A last few stray fae and a couple of human servants sidle past me, murmuring politely as they escape. Then I am alone. Facing the doorway of the queen's flower-strewn bedchamber and the figure seated upon her great, canopied bed.

Castien is half-naked, a bandage wrapped around his ribcage. He's not bothered to replace any glamours, and looks unusually tired, sweaty, bruised, and battered. But that triumph has not faded from his eye.

"Darling!" he cries at the sight of me and holds out his arm. "I wondered when you'd get here. Come, give your victorious husband a little peck on the lips, will you?"

I stare at him, immobile. My gaze travels slowly up and down his body, taking him in. There's something different. Something I can't explain. Something more than the mere lack of glamour. "What happened?" I asked, still not budging from my place in the doorway. "You . . . you fainted, and I . . ."

"Oh, that." The Prince smiles drolly. His hair is still tied back, but that stray lock escapes and falls across his forehead. He tosses it back only for it to immediately fall again. "It would seem when Lord Ivor met his sorry end, the curse he'd placed upon me broke as well."

"The . . . curse?" I echo dully. Then I blink and shake my head. "You mean . . . you mean it was *Ivor* who . . . ?" I cannot bring myself to finish.

The Prince lets his arm fall and sits back a little more comfortably on the bed. He sighs, his breath ragged, his skin unusually pale. "I've suspected for a long time but never had any proof. Yes—it was Ivor who bargained with the crones and placed that curse upon my human blood. He saw an opportunity to drive a deeper wedge between me and my father, creating a void at Lodírhal's side. A void he was more than ready to fill. It worked like a charm too, I'll give the snake that much!" He tips his head to one side, smiling at me yet again. "Never thought I'd live to see the day—but it is my great honor to be able to present a decidedly uncursed husband for your pleasure, Darling." He raises an eyebrow. "And I do intend to make myself pleasing. Of that you may be certain."

I can neither move nor speak. His curse. *His* curse. It's broken. The curse worked by the crones and inflicted on him, rendering his life painful and treacherous by turns. He's free now. Free and whole and . . . and . . .

A surge of loathing swells in my heart. "Why did you do it?"

He frowns, lines creasing his brow. Despite his weakness, he pushes to his feet and starts toward me. Hastily, I duck back out into the now-empty front room. Marching to the lounger I grip the back of it, leaning heavily.

"Darling." The Prince's voice is gentle behind me. "Darling, what's the matter? Was it so horrible as all that, watching the rite? I'm sorry for that little tumble I took—I didn't want you to see that. I didn't want you to be afraid. I hoped you would know that nothing in all the worlds—not even ridiculous tentacled demons from the *quinsatra* abyss—could keep me from you."

Suddenly he's behind me, gripping my shoulders. Trying to turn me to him. "Please, Darling, look at me. Let me see that lovely face of yours. Let me know that you're all right, that you're here. That you're mine."

At his urging I spin about, lift my gaze to his. But I cannot see him. I cannot see the Prince, my Prince, my Castien. This man . . . he's a stranger.

"You must free him." My voice is cold, hard.

"What?" The Prince's frown deepens. "You mean Doctor Gale? I gave you the bloodgem. It should be a simple matter to exchange with Estrilde now—"

I shake my head. "Not Danny. Oscar. You must lift the curse you placed on him."

The Prince's face goes very still. He blinks once. Then abruptly he lets go of me, backs away several paces. "Ivor told you."

I nod.

He spits a bitter curse. "How did he find out?"

"Does it matter?"

After a moment, the Prince shrugs. "I suppose not."

"And it is true."

His jaw ticks. But he nods.

Tears spill through my lashes, stream down my cheeks. "Why? Why did you do it?" I stop, my throat closing on a sob. When I'm sure I've mastered myself, I continue, "He was only a boy. He was fifteen—without a mother, a father, a sister—no one to look after him."

"Yes. But his potential was tremendous." The Prince looks me in the eye, gazing deep. Willing me to understand him. "And his pain was profound. I knew it was only a matter of time before he took up his pen, and then . . ."

I shake my head. "You don't know that. You don't know what he may have been, what he may have written. You took it from him, his gift, his strength. You took away his hope."

"I merely suppressed the potential for terrible disaster. It's my responsibility. To protect Eledria from the monsters men like him create."

"Men like him? What about me?" I press my fists to my chest. "*I'm* the one who did it. *I'm* the one who broke your precious Pledge, brought a Noswraith into being, and killed your mother. *I'm* the one who's guilty. Not Oscar. He was innocent. He's always been innocent. He never harmed you or yours. He never harmed anyone! Yet you were crueler to him than you've ever been to me. You gave me back my power, urged me to use it, urged me to be strong. But you crippled him! Broke him and left him as good as dead!"

"I didn't have a choice." He hangs his head, his voice low, rough. "I visited him every so often. Just to see if it was yet safe to let the curse go. Each time, I was only more convinced I'd done right. That boy's soul is steeped in darkness. If he is ever set free, that darkness will seek to find liberty somewhere. He will put it onto paper, send it forth into the world, and let the combined magic of weaker minds bring it bursting to life. Make no mistake—I've seen it happen. Time and again. I've watched a newly-spawned Noswraith lay waste to scores of innocents in a single stroke. I cannot stand by and let it happen, knowing I could have prevented it."

"So you'd condemn my brother to this miserable half-life existence?" I shake my head, sidling away from him, backing up further and further. "You don't even know him, yet you judge him so harshly!"

"I know him better than you do. Because I see him truly."

You're not seeing rightly.

"I see the darkness in him and the unwillingness to let it go. He sits in it, brews in it. It's seeped into every fiber of his being."

"You're wrong," I snarl. "You're wrong! You don't know anything about him! He's a beautiful soul, sensitive and caring and so terribly alone! He wouldn't hurt a fly. And if I was there with him now, the darkness would soon leave him. You're the one who's made him like this. Your curses and your Obligations. You're just like all the rest of your kind—cruel and heartless, manipulative."

I could not have hurt him more if I'd struck him across the face. The Prince reels back, eyes wide. "Is this how you see me, Darling? Have I not shown you my true heart? Have I not proven myself willing to lay down everything for your sake? My city, my people. My very life."

"None of it matters." My voice is high, desperate, my heart pounding painfully in my throat. "What do I care what you'll give up for me if my brother—my dearest, my heart—remains suffering in torment? And by your hand."

The Prince takes several steps toward me, holding out his arms as though to catch and crush me in them. I draw back. "Don't touch me!"

He looks horrified. "Darling—"

"And don't call me that. I cannot bear it. I cannot bear you, the sight of you. That you would do what you have done. That you would kiss me, hold me. That you would take me. Knowing all the while if I found out the truth it would destroy me." I'm weeping uncontrollably now. I can hardly see him through the blur of tears. "I loved you." My voice cracks.

"Loved?" he repeats. "And what are your feelings for me now?"

His face is so heartbreaking, it nearly moves me to pity, to regret. I steel myself against it, draw my shoulders back. "What do you think I feel for the man who has tortured the one I love most in the world?"

He is silent. For a long, terrible moment. Then, very quietly: "Go on. Say it. Let me hear it."

"I loathe you." The words whisper from my lips like poisonous fumes. "I despise you. I . . . I *hate* you. For what you have done."

He turns away. His back, his shoulders are like a wall between us. I stare at him, silently willing him to turn around, willing him to look me in the eyes. Willing my own voice to somehow find the right words to say, the courage to speak and tell him I didn't mean it. That no matter what, no matter my pain, I could never truly hate him. Never.

But I am not fae. I am human—so I can lie. And lie so thoroughly, even I begin to believe it. So the Prince does not turn. And I do not speak. And we stand there in that terrible atmosphere of hatred and hurt, unable to escape. Unable to find one another.

At last, he says softly: "Your Obligation is ended."

"What?"

He lifts his head but still does not turn, does not face me. "When Ivor lost the battle, all his possessions came to me. Including his Obligates. I'd intended to break your Obligation as a . . . as a wedding present, shall we say. Instead I shall make it my parting gift."

All the air seems to have fled my lungs. I can only grip the back of the lounger, squeezing hard as my body sways.

Finally the Prince turns, gazes down at me. To my horror, there are tears swimming in his eyes. "I've come to a realization, Darling. I've said it to you more times than I care to count—but until this moment, I've avoided saying it to myself: you cannot save one who does not wish to be saved."

His words wash over me, ice cold. I shiver but make no answer.

"I thought I could save you," he continues. "I thought I could somehow prove to you your own worth. I thought I could show you with my life, my death, my love that you matter more than you've ever let yourself believe. That you are not your brother's keeper or whatever small, sad, pathetic thing your father, your mother, every damned voice in your head has convinced you that you are. I thought I could be enough.

"But you don't want me to save you. You would rather hold yourself captive so that you need not leave that brother of yours behind in his darkness.

"I cannot save you. So I must do what I've begged you to do all this time—*let go.*"

My lips part. "What are you saying?"

"I'm saying you are free. Free to return to your brother. Once you're gone, I will see the gate between this world and yours broken. You will forget your life here in Eledria. It will be nothing more than a faint memory of a dream."

"And you?"

"I won't forget. Not a single moment." His lips curve in a terrible, agonized smile. "Not so long as I live."

He turns then and marches to the window. Summit Night is giving way at last. A flush of dawn stains the edge of the far horizon beyond the rooftops, towers, and walls of Aurelis. By that glow, he looks so stern, so lordly. The rightful master of this great domain. A terrible fae, a treacherous lord, a manipulative schemer, curse-caster, and betrayer.

The man I love.

"What about Oscar?" I say softly. "Will you lift his curse?" The Prince growls. It's a ferocious sound and should send me fleeing. But I stand my ground. "You cannot leave him as he is. I beg of you, please—"

"Stop!" He holds up a hand. "You know I can't bear it. You know you have but to say my name, and I will do anything for you, though my soul be damned for it." He turns then, his eyes bright, dangerous. "But know this: if I lift the curse, your brother is no longer safe. The minute, the very minute he puts pen to page and creates something strong enough to take life . . . I will come for him. I will cut the head from his shoulders, and you will watch it roll."

Gone is the prince I knew. Before me stands an otherworldly being I could never imagine kissing, loving, caressing. I tremble deep inside but meet his gaze boldly. "It will never come to that. As long as I am with him, I can keep him from the dark."

His teeth flash. "You think very highly of yourself."

"I know him. I know my brother. I believe in him." I drop my gaze, lower my voice: "Break the curse."

Something snaps in the air between us. Some frisson, some tension there and then gone. Though I cannot say for sure, I suspect that across veils of reality, somewhere in a world far from here, Oscar has just drawn his first deep breath in many years.

I bow my head. Wipe tears from my cheek. "Thank you."

"Don't thank me," the Prince snarls. "This is the last time I let you make me your accomplice." He turns back to the window. "Now go. Before I change my mind."

Suddenly the pull is there. That connection between us, that need, that longing to stay. I want to go to him, to wrap my arms around him. To kiss him and kiss him until the hard, cold, dangerous monster gives way once more to the beautiful, tender lover.

Summoning all my strength, I turn away, go to the door. Touch the latch. Pause. So many words crowd on my tongue. Words for the children. Words for Lir. Questions about the library, the *gubdagogs*, Mixael, Andreas, Khas, and Umog Grush. Even Anj and his zealots. And Vervain. Poor Vervain locked away in her tower, locked away with her own madness and nightmares. My heart cries out for each and every one of them. These people for whom I've come to care so deeply.

I close my eyes and see the dusty broken-down grimoires of the library. The slim little volume of *Dulmier Fen*. The many monsters I've labored so long to contain, to control, to . . . to understand. I don't want to leave them either. I don't want to abandon my work. Everything in me urges me to stay. To be the person I've grown to be while in the Prince's service. Somehow I cannot help feeling she is—or was—my best self.

Instead I look back over my shoulder. He stands with his back to me now, gazing out the window. His back is straight, his shoulders set and hard. The forbidding prince, the deadly fae. My husband. Now a stranger to me.

"Be well, Prince," I whisper.

He growls softly: "Goodbye, Darling."

Then I pass from that room into the passage beyond and shut the door behind me.

THE PRINCE

I STAND AT THE WINDOW GAZING DOWN ON THE WALKWAY just visible below. It winds through the gardens of Aurelis, empty now as the betrothal revelers have dispersed, their thirst for entertainment quenched on Ivor's death and my hollow victory. They'll be back in time, gawking and eager as ever. When my father dies. When I'm made to endure the indignities of coronation. Friends and enemies alike, each nipping at my heels, eager for whatever piece of me they can get. And I will perform the part to which I was born, the game which never ends. Their king. Their master. Their plaything.

At long last movement catches my eye. The garden is no longer empty, not completely. Two figures step into view. One clad in footman's livery, limping and in pain. The other small, upright.

A graceful figure in a flowing green gown. A gown which, not too long ago, lay in a pile beside my desk.

I watch her go. Watch her make her way through the gardens, down to the Between Gate. Away from this world. Away from me. Forever.

Part of me—some vain, foolish, feeble part—still hopes. Still wishes, still dreams. That she'll look back and see me standing here in the window. That she'll gather those skirts and take off running, fly back to my open arms. That I'll have the chance to beg her forgiveness and hear her whisper there is nothing to forgive. That she understands. That she loves me too much to let this be our end.

But I always knew how it would end.

Whatever she feels for me—it's not enough.

She takes a bend in the path. Vanishes from my sight. Not yet gone from this world, and yet . . . it feels so final. My last glimpse of her. Like the final setting of the sun.

I grit my teeth and suck in a breath. Pain. I knew it was coming. I didn't know it would be so soon, so swift. So sharp. Sweat breaks out across my brow, and though I do not want to, I hold out one hand, force myself to look at it, to truly look at it.

I watch the golden glow of ageless fae glory dim. Grayness sets in, spreads.

"So," I whisper. "It's begun already."

INTERNATIONAL BESTSELLING AUTHOR

SYLVIA MERCEDES

ENTHRALLED

PRINCE OF THE DOOMED CITY:

BOOK 5

Clara must finally confront
her demons once and for all . . .
but will she be in time to save
the Doomed City and
everyone she loves?

ABOUT THE AUTHOR

SYLVIA MERCEDES makes her home in the idyllic North Carolina countryside with her handsome husband, numerous small children, and the feline duo affectionately known as the Fluffy Brothers. When she's not writing she's . . . okay, let's be honest. When she's not writing, she's running around after her kids, cleaning up glitter, trying to plan healthy-ish meals, and wondering where she left her phone. In between, she reads a steady diet of fantasy novels.

But mostly she's writing.

After a short career in Traditional Publishing (under a different name), Sylvia decided to take the plunge into the Indie Publishing World and is enjoying every minute of it. She's the author of the acclaimed Venatrix Chronicles, as well as The Scarred Mage of Roseward trilogy, and the romantic fantasy series, Of Candlelight and Shadows.

Printed in Poland
by Amazon Fulfillment
Poland Sp. z o.o., Wrocław

35471767R00314